Nightmare Lullaby

Praise for Nightmare Lullaby

Nightmare Lullaby is a wonderful balance between the perfect fantasy book to snuggle up with and the mystery that keeps you on the edge of your seat. It weaves human emotions together with gripping characters and a constantly-moving plot. I highly recommend it!

I just finished, and wiped away the tears. To add to my earlier praise:

A beautiful tale, vivid and rich with color. It drew me in and held me tight, all through to the finish. You and your Meliroc plucked at my heartstrings and played a magnificent symphony. Pure artistry! I can't recommend Nightmare Lullaby enough.

Nightmare Lullaby

*For Jennifer —
in friendship —
Nan Monroe*

Nan Monroe

Gilded Dragonfly Books

Atlanta

Copyright © 2016 Nan Monroe

All rights reserved.

This book or parts thereof may not be reproduced in any form without permission in writing from the publisher, Gilded Dragonfly Books. The scanning, uploading and distribution of this book via the Internet or via any other means without permission of the publisher is illegal and punishable by law. Please purchase only authorized electronic editions, and do not participate in or encourage electronic piracy of copyrighted materials. Your support of the author's rights is appreciated. The publisher does not have any control over and does not assume any responsibility for author or third-party websites or their content.

All characters and events in this book are fictitious. Any resemblance to persons living or dead is strictly coincidental.

ISBN: 978-1-943095-21-6

Cover Design:	Gina Dyer/GDB
Photography:	Gina Dyer
	Depositphoto
Interior Design:	Melba Moon
Editor:	Yasmin Bakhtiar

Dedication

To my wonderful husband, Matt. The love story is always about you.

Contents

1. Pierpon brings home a stranger who is stranger than most 9
2. Meliroc goes through an interview and answers a call 20
3. The Exploits and Adventures of Valeraine the Victorious, Volume One: The Ivory Giant and the Dreams of Darkness........................... 35
4. Meliroc finds a use for Cedelair.. 50
5. Cedelair follows a trail, and Meliroc chooses risk....................... 57
6. Cedelair breaks his routine.. 70
7. Meliroc seeks an unfamiliar song 80
8. The sorcerers dole out comfort 93
9. Meliroc hears the voice of Sorrow.. 109
10. Cedelair sees for himself... 118
11. Meliroc ponders the mystery of love 127
12. Cedelair looks in on a nightmare 136
13. Meliroc encounters an old friend, and Pierpon stands firm 145
14. Cedelair looks up from the ruins... 154
15. Meliroc learns the cost of transformation 170
16. The Exploits and Adventures of Valeraine the Victorious, Part One, Continued: The Monster in Its Lair.. 180
17. Cedelair prays and plants 188
18. Meliroc steps over the line 197
19. Cedelair faces desperate measures... 208
20. Meliroc confronts the enemy 215
21. Cedelair looks into the past, and Meliroc seeks a way out 223
22. Last... 233

The Nightmare Lullaby

Prologue

The last sane man in the town of Boldithe trudged up the rickety steps of the bell tower, with a short future in mind. The top of the tower, four stories above the square's pavement, would suit his purpose.

He had thought of composing a note to explain what had befallen Boldithe. He might stuff it into the stone hands of the stone sentinel that towered over a broken fountain. When the trade wagons arrived some merchant might find it and gain at least a glimmer of the reason the town stood empty now. But his hand shook too wildly to write. Even if he could make decent letters, he could not form sensible phrases. He was just sane enough to know what was happening.

Reaching the top, he glanced down at the streets and envisioned them as they had been such a little time before, full of people going about their business, working, trading, talking. He could recall the signs he'd failed to spot when it would have mattered – a hand's nervous fidget, a voice's sharpness, an eye's distracted look. Tiny marks of a disorder had taken root and grown into screams, blows, torn hair and bleeding faces.

They had all wandered off to die on their own. Only he remained. In a day or so his hand would start to shake. A few days later he would dribble at the mouth and claw at his face, while everything that met his eye blackened into a vision of fear and disgust. Even now he saw the cobblestones dark with blood and the statue's face twisted into a murderous leer. Soon that hellish, soul-shaking shriek would never leave his ears.

Unless he stopped it.

He lurched forward against the autumn gusts. He looked once more at the empty street below. Holding his breath, he jumped. His mind had time for one last thought.

She did it.

1. Pierpon brings home a stranger who is stranger than most

The bells' music cascaded down the cliff-side, rushing over the valley and the town square below. A silent crowd stood still in its spell. A light snow had been falling since late that morning, but nobody minded or even moved to brush off the chill white dust. None of the listeners had ever heard bells like these before or felt the almost marvelous tranquility their music inspired, a sense of perfect contentment within that moment. What could any grief matter as long as this music played?

The music came from a bulky wagon perched on the ridge, dimly visible through a silver haze. The practical townsfolk wondered how it had gotten there. The more fanciful listeners imagined a pair of wings tucked underneath it. With its unearthly tones, almost anything might be said of it. Perhaps the Lifelord's own hand had set it there. More than one listener could hear His breath in these notes.

Yet soon enough the music swept away all thought of anything but itself. No one in that crowd wished to be anywhere else.

***

Pain seared through Pierpon, turning his breath into daggers of ice in his chest. His eyelids froze shut. In his mind's eye he saw the winter-devil of so many nightmares, its gaping mouth sending forth a cloud of bitter breath to sting him. Then a balm swept over him. A hand, he realized after a moment, warm as a hearth-fire, lifted him free of the smothering cold.

Nearby a drunkard swung from a bell-pull, creating a head-pounding clamor.

Water dripped from Pierpon's eyes. Through the blur he could discern the outlines of a massive woman in a long black cloak. As his vision cleared he found green eyes staring down with cat-like curiosity. A tremble started in his toes. In his exile he'd grown used to the idea that only magicians, with their supernatural sight, could see him. This creature was either a sorcerer or something other than human. Perhaps both.

Clad in the simple style of a traveler, she wore black boots and trousers and a high-collared indigo tunic under the cloak. But it took him two good blinks and a rub at his eyes to make out anything like a face, near-invisible as it seemed against the snow. Her skin and her long, tangled hair were white – not pale, but the absolute white of an ivory statue given life by a demigod.

She had a clear brow, a sharp, slender nose, upswept cheekbones, a delicate mouth, pointed chin, and slightly pointed ears, a little like his own. Her elfin face seemed out of tune with her gigantic stature. From his vantage point of four inches, ordinary humans looked enormous, but he took the measure of the folded legs along with the length from her waist to her head. She was an authentic giant, at least eight feet tall. Such towering brutes lumbered through slumberers' nightmares, swinging their clubs and threatening to roast any flesh-bearing thing within reach. He rolled in her palm, glancing about for an escape path.

She did not look hungry. A muted glow in her eyes suggested distraction. Her head tilted toward that ringing row nearby.

She set him down upon her leg and scooped up a handful of snow. As she breathed upon it it dissolved into water. With her free hand she helped him to sit and brought the water to him. He sniffed at it. "It'll warm my insides, it will," he remarked with a pat of his ribs. "Much gratitude, ma'am." He lapped up the water from her palm, and by the time he'd drunk it dry, the last remnants of the killing cold had left him.

With a self-conscious twinge he attempted to smooth the wrinkles from his damp gray smock and breeches. He bowed from his waist. "Master Pierpon of Jicket-Castle, at your service, madam."

The giant put a finger to her smiling lips and shook her head. He read her gesture easily enough. *Pray keep quiet for now.* He followed her gaze to a ledge a little above them, where sat a wagon with a shining silver roof. The wagon's sides quivered whenever the racket swelled. Something inside it was making this noise.

The faces of a listening crowd in the valley beneath echoed the giant's rapturous look, though perhaps less intense. Among them he spied a familiar lace-trimmed straw bonnet and under it honey-gold ringlets, a dimpled face, and a bell-skirted gown of bright coral taffeta, standing out amidst the dark woolen coats and scarves and caps like a pink rosebud sprouting from a patch of brown leaves. Like the others, Valeraine stood stock still, attention riveted to the racket-making wagon. What did she and the rest hear in it that he could not? Distracted by the clamor, she did not miss him and would never dream he'd managed to slip out of her basket hours ago.

The row faded to silence. Pierpon's rescuer gazed at him with friendly eyes. A soft voice sounded in his ear. "Pier-pon."

He blinked. The voice came from the giant, but her lips did not move.

"Indeed!" he crowed. "Of Jicket-Castle, home of the jicketies."

The corners of her mouth trembled upward, yet still did not form the words: "You hear me?"

"Of course. We jicketies have excellent hearing, we do."

"Jickety," she echoed, her voice apparently coming from a pulsing light in her eyes. "Jickety... I have never heard of such a thing."

"Most folk haven't."

"I know all about strange beings," she told him. "I should know you."

Pierpon smacked his tongue around a bitter taste. "By 'strange' you mean 'not human', you do." He sniffed. "Since they're the ones who write down the stories, they're 'normal' and we're not. How exactly are you an authority on 'strange' beings, big white creature no more human than I?"

"Encyclopedias. Indices. The one I'm reading now is most inclusive, but I don't recall coming across a Jickety. And you hear me! Nobody ever hears me except..." She rubbed at the bridge of her nose. "What is a jickety, exactly? A sort of sorcerer who can make himself tiny?"

"Jicketies are the lords of nightmares, dwellers in the darkest cellars of the dreaming mind," he proclaimed. "Have you never seen a black shadow leap into your path at the top of the stairs? Or felt a pair of unseen hands fling you over a precipice?"

Her mouth hovered between a smile and a frown. "You do that?"

"Only in dreams and only to those who deserve it. So, so, giant of snow, what manner of thing are you?"

She smiled sadly, a furrow in her brow. "I haven't been indexed, either."

"Good for us! We've escaped their definitions, we have." He grinned at her. "What's your name?"

"Meliroc."

"Meliroc?" he echoed with an encouraging wink. "Fitting name, that. You're big, like the roc of the east. Do you suppose you're kin?"

The light in her eyes danced. "I like to imagine we are. I tell myself I was born from a roc's egg, with the most beautiful pair of silver-spotted wings. My jealous siblings hurled me out of the nest, and I lost my wings on the way down." She mimed a deep sigh. "If you're found only in dreams, how is it you're here?"

He drew himself up with a defiant scowl, arching his shoulders. "Trapped by treachery. I'll tell you all if you tell me first. What brings you here?"

"That." She pointed toward the noisy bell-wagon. "Wondrous, is it not?"

"The mountain didn't tumble down, there's the wonder," he scoffed.

"It wouldn't have. The snow was still." Meliroc rested her fingertips upon its surface. "The breeze itself stopped to listen. That's the music's power."

"Hmph! That din?" He twitched his bristly black mustache.

"I heard it call to me just as I was waking and I had to follow it." She shook her head, the glow of delight in her eyes shrinking into a serious glint. "That's what I wish were true. In prosaic terms, I'm looking for a Master. . ." Her lips squinched. "Cedelair."

"The sorcerer, Cedelair?" Pierpon cried, a jolt in his heart.

"Yes." She drew in a breath with a smack of distaste. "The sorcerer, Cedelair." A fog puddled in her eyes. "Are you acquainted with him?"

"Know him? Ha, ha!" He did a jig-step, snapping his fingers. "Why, mam'selle Meliroc Snow-Giant, I lodge with him! I can take you straight to him, I can. But what, if I may ask, do you want with him?"

"I can only speak of it to Master Cedelair himself."

"Somebody sent you to him, did they?"

"No." Her mouth twitched into a grim frown. "My must led me here."

He ground his teeth slowly, working out the confusion in his mind. In his time with Cedelair and Valeraine he had picked up a few rudimentary facts about magic as the humans practiced it. This creature might be moving under a "geas", a magical compulsion. He noticed for the first time a faint, almost imperceptible shiver in her fingers.

"What is he like?" she asked.

"Somewhere in mid-life. Thin and bony. Tall, though you beat him by two feet, you do. Frowns most of the time. Not ill-natured, though, is Master Cedelair. He'll treat you fair." He scratched at an itch on the tip of his ear. "It's his apprentice you've got to be on the watch for. Valeraine. She's to blame, she is, that I'm here."

"He has an apprentice?" She tilted her head. "That's different."

"How so?"

"None of the rest... Never you mind. Does he have a specialty? A particular area of magic he's most skilled in?"

"He makes potions, he does. Sells 'em to the folk around town."

"Then it might be worse, I suppose." Her fingers closed around a handful of snow and squeezed until water streamed through. "I hate sorcerers."

"Coming from you, that's odd. You are a sorcerer."

Meliroc stiffened. "Do not call me that detestable word."

"You like 'conjurer' better? Magician? Wizard?"

"None of them suit me."

"Now, my amiable snow-giant, I don't like a quarrel, I don't, but how did you save me when you found me?"

"I warmed you."

"How?"

"I have a sort of coal inside me, just here." She placed a hand over her heart. "I can make warmth from it."

"A coal inside your heart?" he returned with a bewildered squint. "With that you turned the snow into hot water?"

"Yes."

He clicked his tongue. "Sounds like sorcery to me."

"It is not." She arched her shoulders, bridling. "It's merely how I'm built."

"All sorcerers are built for magic, are they not?"

She glared at him, mouth drawn tight. "Sorcerers meddle in the order of things because they can. People matter no more to them than specks of dust on the wind. You're to be pitied if you live among them."

"Why, then, bother with Master Cedelair?"

"Because I must."

A tear trapped in place by steely determination gleamed like a tiny diamond at the corner of her eye. His heart smarted under a sudden weight. After a minute's reflection he could put a name to the sensation. He winced. This sympathy for another creature, like the searing cold, was clearly a side-effect of this coat of flesh and bone. Let Valeraine be only a little scared at his absence, and he'd soon cast it aside and fly homeward on the wind. In the meantime, someone needed his help.

"They won't use you ill," he told Meliroc. "I won't let 'em." He struck a martial stance, hand on hip, fist brandished. "Let them try to hurt you and I'll make them sorry." He beamed up at her as a flicker of hope broke through the shadow in her eyes. "We're to be friends, you and I."

"Friends." Her strange mind-voice came out as a contemplative murmur. "A good word."

***

Meliroc had a wheelbarrow which she explained held all her goods, including a tent under which she sheltered. She pushed it before her as she trudged down the hill towards Cedelair's cottage. Perched on her shoulder, Pierpon directed her steps.

"You said you would speak of yourself," she reminded him with an eager sidelong smile. "You must help me fill that empty spot in the compendium where a jickety should be."

"Ha, ha!" he cried, rocking on his perch. "Attend, my friend, to the exploits of the cleverest jickety who ever turned shadow into monster!" He launched into a recitation of nightmares he'd molded to wake the consciences of countless erring humans. She didn't have to know that he'd lifted these exploits from friends' stories and the

Sagas of his people. Failed on the first try – far too short and uninspiring a tale.

Gluttons he'd trapped in famine, forcing them to watch as children starved. Vain ladies he'd given dogs' or sheeps' heads. Misers found all they touched crumbled to dust. Then there were the simpler scares in which he'd transformed into toads and snakes and spiders and other creatures that made hapless humans shiver. To himself he blessed his acquaintances' grinning boasts. He was putting them to worthy use, to cheer up a friend whose every step nearer the sorcerer's cottage grew heavier, yet whose eyes brightened steadily as he piled story onto story.

He came at last to his meeting with disaster in the form of a dainty golden-haired maiden named Valeraine, his first try, though he wasn't about to tell Meliroc so. Why had he been sent to terrify the little vixen? He still didn't know. He'd sifted with care through her dreaming mind and found it at peace with the world. Yet he'd had orders, and he'd slipped into her dream with no doubt of success. No one ever talked about failure, after all.

"She wouldn't be scared!" he protested. "Night after night I tried, I did. I turned into a constricting serpent, and when I had her all wrapped in my coils she tried to pet me! Then I became a huge spider, and while I was binding her like a fly she admired my weaving! Falling off cliffs, getting locked in dark rooms – nothing worked on her. And when I couldn't make the scare after seven nights they kicked me out of the castle. Until I frighten her I can't go home. But gone are my powers."

Meliroc nodded slowly, an unreadable thought at work behind her eyes.

"Today I tried something simpler. She always carries me into town in a basket, under a blanket. Just before we reached town I slipped away, I did, hoping she'll be frightened if she looks for me and can't find me. But I planned poorly." He swung his arms. "I'm not used to this case of flesh and blood. It can freeze."

"But you've been gone from her a long while, have you not?" Meliroc returned, with a considering look. "The longer you're gone, the more likely she is to worry. Fear may be creeping upon her slowly while she wonders what can be keeping you."

Pierpon snickered. "Good snow-giant, you could be a jickety, you could."

"So if she's frightened you get to go home?"

"Yes!" He gripped her sleeve as he kicked his legs.

"I'll be glad for you. But sorry to lose you so soon."

"And I you, as well, mam'selle Meliroc." His eyes ran up and down the length of her profile, noting the melancholy cast of her smile. A forlorn thing she looked, plodding towards something she dreaded. "Where do you come from?" he asked her.

She pursed her mouth as if the question required thought. "Most recently? The town with the bath-house with the scarlet curtains and jasmine water. Before that there was the library with the stained-glass windows of scholars in magenta robes and cowls. Before that there was the tavern with the sweet mustard. Normally I don't like mustard, but this was lovely."

"You misunderstand. I asked, I did, where do you come from?"

"And I'm telling you. I can never remember the names of the towns where I stop. So I fix my mind on something special about each one of them."

"Where do you come from?" he pressed, with a twinge of impatience. "Where were you born? Raised?"

She shrugged. "Don't know."

The lackadaisical tone without trace of worry or regret roused a pang in him. "What do you mean?"

"I don't remember what you would call 'growing up', though I suppose I must have. We all do, don't we? We are born, we grow, we live, we die. But I simply am." She tilted her head with the reflective look he already found familiar. "I watch. I read. I learn."

Still she spoke with no note of complaint. Had she pitied herself he might have pitied her less. As it was, the thought ventured across his mind that perhaps he shouldn't go home until he had thought of some way to help this creature. She had done him good service, after all.

This wretched cage gave rise to such mad thoughts.

***

Dusk had deepened to indigo dark by the time Pierpon arrived at Cedelair's cottage with Meliroc and her wheelbarrow. A ring of moonlight leant a silvery shimmer to the brown log facade and even the black thatched roof.

"Valeraine's doing," he mentioned. "She thinks she's quite the hand with magic because she can simulate moonlight. She uses a spindle to weave the circle."

Her eyes half-closed as in a daydream, Meliroc stepped into the moonlight pool. With a tremulous smile she folded her arms over her chest. "Beautiful," her mind-voice whispered.

"It's practical, too, it is," he explained. "Know you the gold-caps, good reader of indices?"

"Imps with long white beards and pointed yellow hats," she replied, scowling faintly. "They like to creep into cottages and turn everything upside down, and spoil the milk and bread."

Pierpon nodded as an approving tutor might. "They're especially fond of sorcerers' cottages. The magic draws 'em. But moonlight holds 'em off."

Meliroc shuddered. "Tiny things make me nervous."

"Tiny things like me?"

"You are different," she assured him, brushing his brow with her thumb. "You hear me."

"Seems a bit peculiar, a great being like you afraid of imps and hobs."

She arched her neck as her grimace gave way to a cool smile. "Me you can always see coming."

With a single hearty chortle he let the matter drop. "Wait here, snow-giant, while I go in and get them ready for you," he advised, clambering down her arm and hopping nimbly to the ground. As he glanced over his shoulder he saw her draw herself up stiff and proud. Then she tightened her mouth to smooth all expression from her face.

Grasshopper-like he danced across the yard. Then he scurried up the side of the door and wrapped himself around the knob. The door popped open, and he dropped soundlessly to the floor, nudging the door closed behind him. Tiny though he was, he did not lack strength.

The scent of roasting chicken drew his gaze to the fire, where two plump brown birds sizzled on a spit. Underneath squatted a fat black iron pot containing a liquid which, if the froth of murky purple bubbles on its surface was any indication, Cedelair intended for some magical use. The crag-faced gent kept one eye on the potion and the other on the timepiece in his left palm.

At the table sat the obviously not panic-stricken Valeraine, staring up at an egg that hovered in the air above her, mouthing an incantation in one of the secret magic languages. Pierpon wondered exactly how many minutes she had held this egg aloft. A good many he guessed by the furrow of her brow. Soon enough she would set it down to spare herself further headache. The jickety knew just how to greet her.

Slipping up behind her chair, he shinnied up the chair-leg. He lifted himself from the leg to the seat, then to the back, then up the left side, taking care not to brush against her skirt or the puff of her sleeve. Reaching the top, he sidled toward her ear. The egg now spun just above her face.

"Drat you!" he shouted.

She drew a startled breath as the cord of concentration snapped. The egg plunged to land – and crack upon her dainty upturned nose.

She should have flown into a fury. Instead, the vixen leaped up from the chair with a laugh. "My jickety's come home!" she cried as she drew a dry cloth from the cupboard and wiped her face.

"Did you doubt he would?" Cedelair asked in a weary voice, dipping his long-handled spoon into the froth. His eyebrows knitted as if he'd half hoped his peculiar houseguest would stay away for good.

"Of course not." Her face now clean, Valeraine sauntered toward the spit. "But it can't have been very comfortable for him in that snow. You could have chosen a more practical season to run away, Master Pierpon."

Fuming, Pierpon hopped down to the table with a snarl. "You could have chosen a better time not to be scared!" He stamped his foot and swung his clenched fists, expecting his insides to explode with rage and then wondering why they didn't.

Oh, yes, Meliroc.

Valeraine chuckled. "Don't sulk, Master Pierpon. We waited supper just for you."

He matched the two puny chickens on their spit against the size of the visitor outside and shook his head. "That won't be enough, I'm afraid."

"It's always been plenty before."

"Not now." He rocked back on his heels. "You were wrong not to be worried about me, you were. I got myself buried in a snow-drift. I would have frozen to death, but I warmed back to life in the hand of a giant."

Valeraine rose up on her toes with a grin of excitement. "A giant, you say?"

Impatience flickered at the corners of Cedelair's sour mouth. "What sort of giant?"

"The sort who waits outside to have a word with you, Master Cedelair," returned Pierpon, with a nod toward the door. "Won't you make her welcome? We owe her, we do, at least a bite of supper and a warm by the fire."

"Her?" cried Valeraine, her beam brightening twofold.

"Eight feet of her," Pierpon answered.

Cedelair pushed himself up from his chair with a grunt. Then he started for the door, grumbling under his breath. Valeraine skipped at his heels. Pierpon crept up last of all, darting down the table leg, his gaze straining upward to the sorcerers' faces.

Cedelair pulled the door open and stared into the moonlight pool. There stood Meliroc, a glimmering white tower, eyes ablaze with an expression that Pierpon could not decipher. Valeraine's mouth dropped open. Cedelair shaded his eyes with his hand as if he thought that what he saw might be a trick of the light.

"Master Cedelair?"

The sorcerer blinked. He cast a quick glance from Meliroc to Valeraine and back again, perhaps wondering whether his apprentice might have thrown her voice. "That is my name," he replied, arching his shoulders. "This is Valeraine, my apprentice." He gestured behind him. "What do you want?"

"I have come to labor for you."

Cedelair scratched his ear. "Your pardon?"

"My name is Meliroc," said the voice emanating from the looming apparition, "and I am your servant."

2. Meliroc goes through an interview and answers a call

From my travel and my readings I know of the veixals.

They are the dark-seers who haunt those sinners the law cannot touch. They walk invisible and silent, but the guilty can feel their shadows. One brush of a veixal's finger to the back of the neck will blight all hope of comfort. The erring soul must wander from town to town, proclaiming his crime like a madman in the streets while horrified townspeople pelt him with stones. He cannot even put an end to himself. He lives on in misery, trembling in cold or heat. No one can outrun a veixal.

As I stood before each new master to pronounce myself his to use as he pleased, I sensed a veixal's shadow hovering over me. I felt its touch in the shiver that would never leave my hands. Some ice-thing chased me, yet I could not remember my crime.

I'd come to a lovely town nestled in a silvery valley that would shine emerald bright in the springtime. Crainante. I knew my must would drive the name from my head the moment I left it. But now I fixed it firmly in my mind, along with the name of the sorcerer to whom I'd been guided. *Cedelair.*

I called up the last of the melodies the glorious carillon had played for me (only me, my fancy sang) that afternoon. The vital, feeling part of me raced after the song. With what remained I studied the man.

In any crowd I could spot the sorcerers, seeing through their surface differences to the sameness at their core. I glimpsed it in this man's pinched mouth and the brittle arch of his neck. The pixy-man had painted him perfectly. Gangly, with a wrinkled, sharp-featured face, chilly dark eyes, and long, thinning gray hair pulled into a horsetail. His iron gray long-coat with its strangling collar suggested a rigid spirit. Yet I noticed a dusting of earth on its hem and soil-clods clinging to the boots below it – and to the right of the cottage, a thriving garden plot, a patch of spring green against winter's white. This sorcerer used his talents to defy the seasons, to grow plants for his elixirs.

My previous masters had all but dragged me over their thresholds. This one favored me with a scowl. "Who sent you?" he snapped in a gruff, gravely baritone that might have once been rich.

"No one," I thought at him. "My must led me here."

"Your 'must'?" His inhospitable eyes raked me from top to bottom.

His apprentice, a slight girl with a doll-like face and bright golden ringlets, pushed past his elbow and hopped over the doorsill. Her azure eyes took my measure with no apparent scorn or alarm. She curtseyed before me with an affable smile. "Mistress Meliroc. Won't you come inside?"

I examined the door frame – higher than most, thankfully, but still I was forced to duck as I followed the girl into the cottage. Her master came in behind us.

Tilting my head just so, I walked into the main room, then sank comfortably to my knees for a good look around. A polished hardwood floor spread before me, decorated with a shaggy white hearth-rug. Near the fire squatted a rough wooden stool, where Jickety Pierpon perched with folded arms and watchful eyes. Sky-blue papering wilted on the walls. Four high-backed wicker chairs guarded different points in the room, their bright gold cushions embroidered with red marigolds. Off to the left, a neatly crocheted powder-blue cloth covered an ebony table. A tall clock issued deep, steady ticks. A well-stacked bookshelf leaned beside an open cabinet fixed to the wall. In that cabinet rows of tiny phials stood in a proper color spectrum.

Mulberry froth bubbled on the rim of a pot on the hearth. I wondered at this elixir's function and pictured Master Cedelair commanding me to taste it. *Drink this, so I can see if you go into convulsions.* But I might have fared worse. He could have been another transmogrifier. Imagine hours on end of being turned into different things, like a broom to sweep soot or a bowl to hold steaming hot soup or a hammer to pound against a nail, and staying conscious while you're used. Nail. Hammer. Pain. Shaking.

As I locked my fingers together and forced the memory down, Valeraine approached me with a wooden tray topped with a mug of water and a roasted chicken breast. "We were about to eat." She held the tray out to me. "Have a bit of supper."

My stomach back-flipped at the smell of hot food. I couldn't quite calculate how long it had been since I'd enjoyed a meal fresh from the fire. *We were about to eat.* They hadn't known I was coming. This girl, this sorcerer, offered me food she'd meant for herself.

I knew well what a sorcerer's hospitality was worth.

"I cannot take this," I told Valeraine with a shake of my head.

"Please, eat," she urged. "You're our guest. Bad things always happen to hosts who don't offer their guests something to eat. You wouldn't condemn me to such a fate, surely." She nodded from me to the tray and back again.

Helpless to ignore my whirling stomach, I took up the chicken and tore into it. Valeraine, meanwhile, set a thick white cushion at my heels. When I sank down upon it, she brought one of the chairs to sit opposite me.

"Let us understand each other," Valeraine began once I'd picked the bones clean. "You say you've come to be our servant?"

"That is right." I unfastened my cloak and let it fall to the floor behind me.

"We don't need a servant," pronounced Cedelair, standing aloof beside the table. "We cannot afford to keep you."

"I need no wages."

"You see the size of my cottage." He gestured toward the room's open space. "Do you think it likely that we'd have a place to put you?"

"I need no chamber. My tent outside will shelter me and all my goods."

Valeraine flinched. "Won't you be cold?"

"No, mistress." I breathed deep to check my heart-fire and found it steadily burning. "I do not feel the winter."

"She has a coal in her heart, she has," put in Master Pierpon. "That's how she saved me."

Cedelair's mouth twitched. "Lodging aside, you will need to eat," he said to me. "I daresay you are a heavy feeder."

"I assure you, Master Cedelair, I am worth my meat and drink."

"Ah!" Valeraine snapped her fingers. "There's the point we should pursue. What are your skills, Mistress Meliroc?"

I met this question with a startled cough. My other masters had never bothered with it. They'd had their own ideas about how to make use of me. If these two sorcerers had no similar notions I wasn't about to give them any. "I can chop and carry firewood. Shovel snow. Tote heavy loads. The sorts of things you might expect of someone my size."

Valeraine shot her master a look I could easily read. *We could use someone like that.*

"I have other abilities." I sent a quick smile to Master Pierpon. "Your friend there tells you I have a coal inside my heart, which has plenty of uses besides saving little men from snow-drifts. With your leave, I will demonstrate. Might I have an empty cup?"

Valeraine's full skirt swished into the nook that served as a kitchen. Cedelair did not even twitch as she passed him, but kept his searing cold stare fixed on me. I matched his look, poring over the crags of his face. My skin prickled at a wrongness about him stirring very near the surface. A little more attention and I might pinpoint it. But Valeraine returned with a tin cup, and my thoughts turned back to proving myself useful.

I rose with a right-ward bend in my neck. Opening the door, I dipped the cup into the mound of snow just over the doorsill and packed it full before I carried it back inside between my hands, concentrating, stoking my heart-fire.

"Observe." I held the cup under Valeraine's nose. Cedelair moved a few steps closer to better his view.

With a long breath I summoned the heat to my hands. As it shot through my fingers into the cup, the snow began to sink and drip. Soon I had reduced it to a pool of steaming water. With another push of heat it bubbled in a boil.

Valeraine beamed. "Oh, I say!"

"Consider the practical applications," I pointed out. "You have a potion brewing there in your pot. It takes some while to bring it to boil, does it not?"

Cedelair nodded in admission, though his frown did not soften a jot. Again I sensed that secret I would spy if I looked at his face from just the proper angle. "If I set my hand on the rim, I could make it boil within a minute."

Cedelair drew near me, arms stiff, jaw clenched. "What else can you do?" he demanded.

"I can read and write. I could handle your correspondence."

He covered his mouth as he turned a laugh into a cough. "I don't 'correspond.'"

"Don't you, sir?" Valeraine put in. "You sent the *Gazette* in Nisslaire a notice for an apprentice. That's what brought me here." She cast an approving nod my way. "I think she will do very well."

As I looked from her to Cedelair, my breath cooled in my throat. Behind the crags and wrinkles, I saw another face – young, sharp and angular, bright and keen of eye. "You are not old!" my mind cried out before I could rein it in.

Cedelair's face barely changed. He spoke from deep in his throat. "You may stay here tonight, Mistress Meliroc. Tomorrow we will decide what is to be done with you."

So ended my interview. I felt a shudder at my back, frightened for the first time of being sent on my way. I might have to fall on my face before this icicle of a man and tell him, *If you don't let me work for you, I will die.*

As if that would matter to him.

***

What does it mean to be good?

I'd read of goodness in books, and often I imagined it in the faces and manners of people in the towns I passed through. Apparently no one could be truly good in isolation. Good people smiled at each other, aided each other, depended on each other. Good people loved and were loved.

I'd found the pixy-man almost frozen in the snow-drift. I didn't like pixies. Why hadn't I left him and walked on? That music – that was it. The music had found some secret thing in my heart and drawn it out of hiding. When I remembered Jickety Pierpon coming to his senses in my hand a thought blossomed in my mind for the first time.

I might be good.

I had to find out more about him. Why, for instance, wasn't he burning with fury at the failure of his plan, as I would have been in his place? Instead, he whistled, chipper as the well-known lark, as he watched me raise my tent.

"There was never a very strong chance," he told me. "She knew I had to come back to her eventually."

"All the same, she might have been a little worried." I frowned at the yellow lamplight in the window, showing me where they were.

"It's not her fault, it's not," Pierpon explained. "For her I'm something like the invisible playmate that children have. As far as she knows, only she and Cedelair can see me. I won't chance showing myself to the people in town."

"I see you."

"But you, too, are magical. A sorcerer, even if you deny it." The little man clicked his tongue. "Truth to tell, I forget I'm mortal sometimes. I'd have been more careful in the snow, otherwise."

At this I nodded. It made a sort of sense, in view of the number of strange beings who did walk invisible. Veixals.

"Don't worry." Pierpon winked at me. "I'll get the better of her yet. In the meantime, snow-giant, we'll be capital chums."

Chums. Almost as good a word as "friends". A warm wind began to circle my heart-coal.

With my tent secure and my bundles unpacked, I stretched my gray wool blanket over the snow and sank down to read. I reached for the thickest of the three books I carried with me, the strange-beings compendium, and tried to consider how Pierpon's kind had been left out of it. Instead I caught myself wondering exactly what end I would meet if Cedelair turned me away. My gaze kept gliding up to that lighted window.

"You'd love to hear what they're saying now, wouldn't you?" chuckled Pierpon with a jerk of his head toward the tantalizing casement. "I can listen for you, I can."

"Please don't. Just talk to me and keep my mind from it."

Hopping onto my blanket, he tilted his head up at me with an interested spark in his eye. "All right, then. What shall we talk about?"

"What's the thing you love most in all the world?"

"Tears. Human tears. Now, now, don't look like that," he chortled when I gaped in horror. "Tears have value, they do. When a man wakes from a nightmare and weeps into his pillow he's learned something, and he'll put his wrongs to right. Humankind would be lost without us, mam'selle Meliroc."

I tried to weigh this explanation, but it ran up against the wall in my mind that sealed off things I could never remember – people's names, places' names, my "childhood". I winced at a knocking in my head. "I never remember my dreams," I told Pierpon.

He knitted his wiry eyebrows. "Oh?"

"But they must be horrible, because when I wake I find my face soaked with tears and my muscles sore as if I'd been shaking all night. I must have done something abominable once, and when I dream it comes back to me, but when I wake it's always gone again. How can I learn from that?"

A tiny hand touched mine. "That's not how we work. And I can't imagine, I can't, you being guilty of a terrible crime."

"You scarcely know me."

"I know you saved me. I know you have kind, warm hands."

I stared at those work-weathered hands, with their tremble that had become second nature to me. "They shiver."

"That's because you feel so much, even more than you realize." He let out a whispery whistle. "So what's the thing you love most in all the world?"

The memory of the carillon's songs rang through me, quickening my blood-flow as only my favorite thing could. "Music!"

Pierpon clutched his sides with a laughing grin. "You're serious, you are?'"

My small friend's indifference to music was a grave flaw. I resolved to take him in hand and teach him better. "How much do you know about music, Master Pierpon?"

"Valeraine the Vixen has a little wooden pipe. When she blows into it, it makes a noise she calls 'music'."

A penny-flute, one of the many instruments I'd tried to teach myself to play. All had shattered to splinters under my fingers. "Had you never heard music before you came here?"

His black curls quivered as he shook his head. "We don't bother with it back home, we don't," he declared, almost a boast.

Was there a time when I hadn't known what music was? As my mind fled that dark and dead-silent past, my heart-fire trembled under a press of sympathy for Pierpon. "When you hear Mistress Valeraine play, how does it make you feel?"

"Tired."

How much work I had ahead of me! I thought of another thing I loved, which he would surely appreciate. "You know what else is wonderful?" I leaned toward my friend with a hungry grin. "Monsters."

He cocked his head, intrigued. "You don't say!"

"Oh, indeed! Why do you think I like to read about them? So that I can see them skulking across the walls of my tent and tell myself stories about them."

"Ooh! Tell me one!" He hopped onto my leg, tucking his knees in his arms.

Since I'd had this very thing in mind, I nodded and conjured an image of a fearsome entry in my compendium. Loronur – a swamp-dwelling goblin with skin as tough as tree bark and webbed hands that snatched at the ankles of unlucky trespassers. "There was a loronur," I began, "who lived at the bottom of a fetid swamp, a creature who reeked of rot. One day he saw the shadow of a long-legged crane above the water and thought, This will make a fine supper. So he put his head above the surface and heard the crane making a strange whistling sound through her beak. Each time she whistled a lark on the limb of a nearby tree sang back to her. And as the loronur listened something came into his heart that he didn't quite know what to do with. He forgot he was hungry. He thought only of the music."

"Poor fellow." Pierpon chuckled. "He'll starve."

"The sounds wakened his every sense. They reached the part of him where he felt most strongly and put it into order. He sank back down to his home and set about looking for a way to make those sounds himself."

Penny-flute – snap! Violin – snap! Mandolin – snap! *Why not give it up, dear Roc? You were not formed to make music.* That cold whisper of a voice. The Bitter Chord, I called her, out of tune.

Pierpon tugged at my sleeve. "So, did he find it, did he?"

"He is still looking. He has failed many times, but he can't stop trying."

The little man let out a chortle. "You made the swamp-demon the hero!"

"Of course. My monsters are always the heroes."

A tune slipped shyly down the breeze, so soft at first that I couldn't quite make out the instrument. It folded light, cool fingers about my heart, then rang into me as it grew louder, a cool wash to soothe the spirit... Ringing. The sound I heard was bells. The tune was coming from the carillon.

Pierpon arched an eyebrow. "What's amiss, snow-giant?"

I couldn't answer him. The song was closing my mind to all thoughts but itself. It pulled me to my feet. I drew my cloak around my shoulders, my thoughts pounding with one insistent drum-beat drive. *Get closer to that sound. Find the music where it lives.*

Pierpon tugged at the hem of my cloak. "Mam'selle Meliroc! What's the matter?"

I strode forward, the music guiding my steps. A flicker of thought crept past the rush of song. Pierpon sounded confused. I would owe him an explanation later, once I understood what was happening.

***

Of all musical instruments, only the carillon conceals its player, making it easy to imagine that it plays itself. Now I sensed a magical mind within it. Hadn't I learned to shun magic, to loathe its practitioners? Why did I relish this spell when I should have been fighting it?

The trees, bushes, and rocks I passed on my uphill march flickered in the corners of my eyes like smoke-trails from a fire. Only the music was tangible. The figure of the carillon blazed silver in the distance. Fingers of light stretched out to draw me toward it. Once I reached it I caught my wheezing breath and dropped to my knees before it. Its gleam subsided into a quiet shimmer.

"What's-this-what's-this-what's-this?"

The sharp whistling voice jolted me. A creature half the size of Master Pierpon hovered in the air beside my ear, jerking its head at me. Long gray hair spilled down its back and sides, nearly covering the dusty gray rags that draped it. The oval thing atop the rags could not really be called a face, for it boasted only a wide, lipless mouth and a pushed-in nose. Where were its eyes?

"What's-this-what's-this?" it squeaked, pinching my chin.

Distaste squirmed in my stomach. Pierpon might have gotten around my prejudice, but he hadn't overthrown it.

"Tell us who you-are-you-are-you-are!"

I thought my name, hopeful that it might hear me.

Nightmare Lullaby

The tiny creature gave an irritated trill. "Are you simple-simple-simple?" it jabbered, shaking its fist at my nose. "Say who you are! What you are!"

"Whishk?"

The black curtain in the window fell aside, revealing a hawk-shaped golden mask. Its glint shot ahead of the opening to strike me full in the face. Through the blare I traced the outlines of a man's figure shrouded head to foot in white.

"What causeth this agitation, my whishk?" A resonant baritone voice folded about me like a downy quilt.

"That!" Again the gray will-o'-the-wisp shook its fist at me. "Make it go away! It's too big-big-big!"

"Be not uncivil, good whishk." A touch of admonishing hardness crept into the voice, yet still it rang rich and wonderful. "Draw thou nearer, stranger." The man's white-gloved arm slipped through the window to beckon to me.

"Send it away!" The imp bobbed up and down in mid-air, puffing in indignation. "It's no good. It can't even speak!"

The mask tilted rightwards. "Is this true, maiden pale?"

I placed a hand to my lips, then sadly nodded.

"And doth that justify thy rudeness, whishk? Be still, if thou canst not call on thy good manners." The mask's glint softened upon me. I felt a smile in it. "Wilt thou stand? I would see thy full measure."

I climbed to my feet. My shadow stretched out to the carillon-wagon, swallowing the masked man.

"Ah!" The voice sounded more pleased than disturbed. "A tree thou art, made all of alabaster moonbeams. Didst my song reach thy ears, moon-tree?"

I nodded yes, kneeling once again. I didn't want to loom over this man. "Moon-tree" – a beautiful name! How he spoke it! I grinned, a delighted tremble in my toes.

"Too big-big!" fumed the dusty imp. "Send it away-away!"

"Heed not the words of my whishk, fair moon-tree," the man said. "I am Feuval. Dwell I in this box, with my musical bells." He stretched out his hand, then rested his fingertips against my cheek. "My music have I given to many villages, yet no listener hath ever spoken back to me." A note of sorrow rang in the marvelous voice.

I glared down at my quivering hands. *Shrink from this man. Distrust him.* I tried to picture myself bolting back down the hillside to the safety of my tent, but the image slid through my fingers.

"At each place I do visit, I send forth a summoning, a song that can only be heard by a friend. For so long none hath heeded it. Yet tonight it hath brought thee." He drew his hand away and rested it on the window-ledge. "I wish that I might learn thy name!"

A cool gust bore down on my heart-fire. This man obviously had magic. A sorcerer would hear my mind-voice. "Meliroc," I thought at him.

"Why knit'st thy brows so?" he asked. "Fear thou me?"

I summoned every shred of energy to force my mind-voice past that gleaming mask. "Meliroc! Meliroc!"

"Thou'rt distressing thyself." The wonderful voice rang gentle. "Be at peace. I ken thy heart. I called it hither." He tilted his head toward me. "Dost thou play a musical instrument?"

I shook my head.

"But thou hast wished thou might?"

I nodded.

"Then my apprentice shalt thou be," Feuval pronounced. "I shall teach thee to give life to the stirring inside thee which led thee here."

How? my mind screamed.

"'Tis a pity thou art mute," he said, fumbling for something under the window, "but I shall give – thee – aha!" He drew himself upright again, a strange object in his hands, eight wooden planks fixed to a thick black board. "This shall be thy voice."

He raised a mallet and struck the left-most plank, and out came a chime, a star's gleam. The mallet danced lightly down the other planks, raising a succession of notes that shone in a constellation. This was an instrument! The planks were rooted on bells, a miniature carillon.

Gripping it by its sides, he reached through the window and held it out to me. "Take it."

I wanted to wrest the instrument from his hands and see what constellations I could shape, but memories held me still. So many broken instruments and the Bitter Chord's mocking laughter. *You were not formed to make music.*

"Take it," the masked man repeated more firmly.

My stomach swirling, I claimed the instrument, then the mallet. My fingers folded around the polished wood.

"Now, play the scale."

Don't break, don't break, don't break... I lifted the feather-weight mallet and dropped it cautiously on the top plank. A bright twinkle answered, my own star.

The instrument held solid. In its ring I heard it accept me. A tremor surging through me, I sent my mallet skipping down the planks as I'd seen him do. Each note rang sweeter than the last. The light-strings from the great carillon wound more tightly about me, and I imagined them as the threads of a chrysalis, promising to transform me into – what? Surely something better than I was.

"Take it with thee," he instructed, "and draw from it a song of thine own making. A melody of a merry heart. On the morrow's eve I will summon thee and hear what mettle is in thee." He snapped his fingers, then jerked his thumb to his left. "Go thy way, moon-tree. Begin thy work."

I got to my feet and started away. I wasn't sure of the way back, but I had left deep tracks in the snow, a happy consequence of being eight feet tall. The moon lit my path. As I walked I explored my new instrument and fixed each note in my memory, not as a star-gleam but as a ray aglow with its own vivid hue. Cornflower, heliotrope, marigold, coral, canary, jade, verdigris, leaf.

A song of a merry heart. Running the scale up and down, down and up, I questioned whether I had ever felt merrier in my life. While the rainbow notes bedazzled me I couldn't think of the problems my new situation might bring. I could even endure laboring for a transmogrifier again with the joy of these bells in my ear.

A sneeze made me jump. For a queasy second I thought Feuval's eyeless imp had followed me. Then a tug at my cloak drew my attention downward, to a tiny man with tight black curls and pointed ears clinging to the folds near its hem.

"Master Pierpon? Have you been there all this while?"

"Naturally I have," squeaked the little man as he clambered up to my shoulder. "Could I have let you wander off on your own, all ensorcelled? I wouldn't call that the action of a friend, I wouldn't."

"You were worried about me?"

"Of course! You should have seen yourself. You could have marched right off the side of that cliff."

A warm wind fanned the embers of my heart-fire into a dance. No one had ever worried about me before. I was sure of that.

"You should do that with Mistress Valeraine," I advised. "Imitate what you saw me do. She'll think you in the grip of some black magic."

Pierpon tightened his lips at this plan but did not answer me. Some other idea winked in his eyes, a thought he wasn't ready to speak. I sent the heat from my heart-fire shooting up to my shoulder to warm him as I carried him home.

I kept testing my instrument, rearranging the notes, envisioning their patterns as web-strings of colored light. When we reached my tent, Pierpon was still squinching up his face, busy with that same thought. As I knelt on my blankets, resting my instrument and mallet at my knees, I began to worry about him, and to hope my delight in my new music was not somehow distressing him.

"You shouldn't go back to that wagon," he muttered, leaping from my shoulder to the blankets. "You shouldn't go back to that man."

"Why not?"

"He's dangerous, he is. Worse than a hundred Cedelairs."

"He couldn't hear my mind-voice. He isn't a sorcerer."

He squared his shoulders. "You think only sorcerers are a threat, do you? Ah, snow-giant, you're much too clever to be so foolish."

I lifted my mallet and played three notes with lightly sweeping strokes. The notes sustained a half-beat longer. Now that I had each rainbow light fixed in my mind, I could experiment with rhythms. Pierpon, poor tone-deaf rascal, couldn't understand. "Master Feuval wouldn't hurt me," I protested. "He would only give me what I want."

"And what is that?"

"My own music. I'm that loronur I told you about, looking for a voice to sing with."

"Ask Vixen Valeraine to teach you how to make noise. She'll help you, she will."

"That wouldn't do," I told him. "Normal instruments always break when I try to play them. But this... I've never heard music quite like it before. It makes me hope for things I've hardly dared think about. Things I'll find the right words for if I keep playing."

I swallowed a breath as I stared down at the hand that held the mallet. My fingers were steady and calm. It came to me that they

32

hadn't shaken since they'd closed around that handle. My opposite hand still shivered. I tried an experiment and dropped the mallet soundly upon a key. In my mind's eye the verdigris light hovered in the air. For as long as it lingered the shiver in my hand stilled.

I needed this music. How could I make Pierpon see?

I locked gazes with him. "Listen."

I called up from my memory a tune I'd found nestling near a brook on my last long walk to a new servitude. I imagined it in the carillon's glad chimes and felt a wondrous sense of beginning come upon me. Shaping my mind-voice into that sound, I sang it for Pierpon.

"What do you think of that?" I asked when I was done.

He cleared his throat, a confusion of sparks in his eyes. "Quite nice."

"What? Not 'noise'?"

"Not exactly," he admitted, a quick look down at his feet.

Progress! "Now, if you had something like that inside you, wouldn't you want it to be heard? And if you met someone who could help you, wouldn't you ask for that help, even if it were dangerous?"

Pierpon scratched the back of his neck. "I suppose I would. But I don't trust Master Gold-mask, I don't. I don't trust anybody whose eyes I can't see. Then there's that horrible little thing with no eyes at all. Ugh!"

"I didn't like him either. All the same, I must go back."

"Well, if I can't talk you out of it, the best of things must be made. Whenever you go to visit Gold-mask, please take me with you, please do."

"What if you go home?"

"Never mind that for now. Promise you'll take me with you."

I tousled his hair with my thumb. Such a wonderful thing, to be worried about! "I promise."

"He's left you a bit of sense, good to see." He jerked his head toward the cottage with its two lighted windows. "I'd best go inside before the vixen faults you for keeping me up too late. Good night, snow-giant. It won't be so bad here, it won't with you around."

"Likewise, Master Pierpon."

I watched him skip across the moon-white lawn. Then I looked back down at my instrument, caressing the keys with my fingertips. I fancied the strands of silvery light from its parent still weaving and winding close about me, a breath of spirit. This little bell-board was magic. My very own magic, perhaps strong enough to shield me from my masters.

    I took up my mallet and began my work in earnest. Soon enough I would have to give myself over to dreams too dark to remember, but not yet.

3. The Exploits and Adventures of Valeraine the Victorious, Volume One: The Ivory Giant and the Dreams of Darkness

Valeraine the Vexed slammed shut her mighty oaken writing desk. Now was not the time to write letters. Her parents could wait. They would mistake any missive for an ignoble complaint about her closed-minded master and would seek to wheedle her into returning home. As if she needed rescuing from Crainante! City folk could never comprehend the magic to be found in the country.

She loved her situation. She could peer from her window at a stretch of meadow rimmed by majestic oaks and pines, so much grander and more powerful than Nisslaire's boxy crammed-together cottages with their "lawns" of green-painted pebbles. Then there were Crainante's thatched-roof shops and bounteous markets, so much cleaner than the ragged little fruit stalls and butcher's carts that cluttered Nisslaire's streets. And the people! Every day as she traversed Crainante's well-swept cobbled paths, she met with friendly folk who smiled and spoke when they passed her and greeted each other with trust and good will. She even liked Master Cedelair most of the time.

So he could be cranky on occasion. What else could she expect, given his tragic past? He had taught her much about the proper ways to channel the energy that flowed through her. She was learning to employ the Tongues of Power given to her to equip her for an extraordinary fate. She'd come here able to levitate an egg for barely a second. Now she could hold one in the air for almost ten minutes.

But Valeraine the Vainglorious was meant for grander things than egg levitation. If her master refused to see this she would, well, persist.

Brave Bennelise and the Cursed Mountains beckoned from her bed. Beside it, her wooden penny-flute whistled to her. Both would surely speed her journey into slumber. Yet how could she content herself with reading of Brave Bennelise's victory over the bloody-toothed Giant of Cormboise, when a giant now lurked outside her very window? The towering ivory woman with the heart of coal-fire meant adventure at hand. How could Set-in-his-ways Cedelair want to be rid of her?

"We cannot keep her," he had pronounced, his jaw set in stone. "I will not have some ghastly hulking golem from who-knows-where haunting my home."

All politeness, she'd pointed out, "Sir, we may not have much of a choice. She's obviously under a geas. Let's just give her a few tasks to do. Where's the harm?"

"There may be quite a bit of harm. We can't be sure of her real purpose here."

"We could find out quickly enough."

Master Cedelair had locked withering eyes upon her. "How?"

"The Seventh Tongue." Her words had shrunk to near-silence under his gaze.

She'd felt the snap of his ire. If she wanted to see his face redden, she had only to mention the Seventh Tongue. "A last resort," he'd insisted, his voice sharp and deep.

"Sir, we wouldn't have been given the Seventh Tongue if we weren't meant to use it on occasion."

"Not now."

"But the point remains, she's under a geas. What better way to be rid of her than to remove it?"

"That can take time."

"Time well spent, I think, the chance to do a good turn." Valeraine's chest had swelled with the spirit of Brave Bennelise, her mentor in print. "Sir, would you let me try? She can be my servant. You wouldn't have to bother with her at all."

He'd chortled under his breath. "Do you imagine looking after a giant will be as simple as looking after a lost puppy?"

"Far from it, sir. But I'll learn all the more."

Cedelair had flexed his jaw as if gnawing on some idea. "You'll have your answer tomorrow. Now, off to bed with you." He'd turned his back to her, unwilling to hear another word on the matter.

He was not truly an old man. A night's hard thought on the question of the giant could rouse a dormant spark of adventure in him. So Valeraine hoped, as with a cool breath she pored over the pages of her book and saw and felt with her mentor, Brave Bennelise. That great hero pushed through a relentless blizzard where ice demons lurked in the drifts. They crept toward her, their crystal daggers raised.

A shadow crept into the corner of Valeraine's sight. Pierpon the Petulant, the fairy come from the world of nightmares to be her companion, skittered across the top of the bureau to his doll-case bed. He brushed the melting snow from his sleeves and favored her with his usual chin-tucked pout. "Evening, vixen," he muttered, climbing into the box.

She closed the book gently on her finger. "How is Meliroc settling in?"

"Oh, she'll do just fine, she will, with me to help her," answered the nightmare fairy. "You are going to let her stay, aren't you?"

"I've asked Master Cedelair to let me have charge of her," she proclaimed. "I could use your help with her. You seem taken with her."

"She saved me, she did," he reminded her. "And it's good to have someone about the place who's a bit more like me."

Valeraine choked on a laugh. "Like you?"

"Another 'strange being' as she calls us. Don't make the mistake of thinking we are nothing alike just because we look nothing alike. She understands my calling. She was even giving me advice on how to frighten you."

"Well, then, from your observation, what sort of creature is she?"

Pierpon rose up on his knees and leaned over the box's edge. "Lonely."

"Lonely." Valeraine turned her mind's eye on the monster's face. Sadness lurked behind the bright barbs of resentment in the eyes. Melancholy Meliroc.

"I thought I was lonely," pursued the nightmare fairy, "stuck here with you, away from my people. But at least I know where my people are. I'm not sure she even has a people. I wonder if she's ever had one true friend. So if you keep her, the best thing you can do is be a friend to her."

"I'd like to befriend her," Valeraine admitted, "but I'm not sure how." Meliroc's eyes flashed again in her memory, burning through her with an expression she could not mistake. Hate. So much hate. A wild thing chafing at her chains, a serpent whose fangs had been drawn – such was the giant. But Valeraine, who preferred snakes to kittens, found her irresistible.

"It won't be easy, it won't," admitted Pierpon. "She's got a grudge against sorcerers. But if anybody can get around that grudge, you can, Vixen Valeraine. She loves noise, that kind you make with your pipe. Play it for her, and that might go a ways, it might."

Valeraine laid her book aside and turned her thoughts to her penny-flute, fingering the stops and imagining the bright trill of tunes. Everyone knew music could tame the most fearsome beast. All the same, she would let Pierpon think she couldn't have hit upon the idea without him. "You're being helpful, Master Pierpon."

"It's her I'm thinking of," he scoffed. "Someone so lonely may seek friendship in wrong places, she may. Annoying as you are, vixen, I know you'd do her no hurt."

She gave him one of her wide, warm smiles that always annoyed him. "It doesn't matter who you were thinking of. It's sound and useful advice."

Taking a focusing breath, she raised the flute to her lips, the same flute with which Rysselide the Redoubtable had charmed the crocodile demons on the banks of the Moringa River and with which Zeritte of the Lightning Hands had blown the signal for the rebels to storm the castle of Jouvelon the Poison-King. It had come into Valeraine the Venturesome's hands by marvelous chance. She opened her thoughts to a bittersweet tune, "The Dove's Lost Love". She sent the first stream of air through the pipe and set her fingers dancing as the note rose. Pierpon sank into his doll case, pleased with the success of his persuasions.

She laid the flute aside and settled into bed, pulling the quilt up to her chin. "The Dove's Lost Love" echoed in the air to lull her to sleep.

She woke, shaking, a scream in the back of her throat.

Sweat drenched her brow and hands. Her heart slammed against her chest. The lace collar of her night-dress threatened to strangle her.

Nightmare Lullaby

She yanked at it and a button popped loose. Blinking, she cast a frantic glance around the room to assure herself that everything she saw was real and familiar. The moonlight-flooded window. The mahogany bureau. The writing desk and chair. The posts of her bed and the rumpled blue quilt. Pierpon, snoring in his box, enjoying his usual dreamless sleep.

She was safe now. She pulled her spine tight, lest her teeth rattle most unheroically and fought to recall the dream that had convulsed her. She could remember only a single shriek – an unearthly cry of pain beyond healing.

***

She struggled to think of the day ahead, with its familiar routine. Which people might she see as she strolled up and down Crainante's side-paths with her basket full of potions? Might Acelin, the butcher's apprentice, stick his handsome brown-haired head through the door of his master's shop and nod to her when she smiled at him? With this thought bright in her mind, Valeraine the Voluptuous donned one of her favorite dresses, an ice-blue muslin with a flowing white lace sash and a pleasantly lifting bodice that showed just enough bosom. Pierpon snickered from his box. "You'll freeze in that gown, you will."

"Thank you for your concern," she returned with a wink, "but winter colors are hideous."

He sniffed. "A sorcerer shouldn't care so much about clothes."

"Because I'm Master Cedelair's apprentice, I should share his dress sense? Where's that written, I'd like to know?" Pinning her lace-trimmed straw bonnet in place, she peered into the mirror and decided she looked nice, indeed.

Yet a difference had crept into her eyes. She had to stare so hard into the glass to find it, that for an instant she could glimpse a long line of Valeraines standing behind her reflection, all with the same peculiarity – a tiny light, spinning like a whirlpool, throwing off frightened sparks. It would surely go away once the shiver in her stomach tapered off and the cares of the day absorbed her. She pinched her cheeks to raise a comely blush, then turned from the mirror and strode into the main room. Pierpon skipped after the swishing hem of her skirt.

Cedelair the Censorious had already set bread and butter on the table and was standing beside his chair with his accustomed stony look. From day to day he looked the same, in his shapeless dark gray coat and brown trousers and smudged, battered boots. He carried his tragic past in the very dust of his clothes. His apprentice ached in sympathy each time she gazed at him.

"Good morning, Valeraine," he greeted with a curt nod toward the door. "Be so good as to call our visitor in."

So Meliroc was a "visitor". Sighing under her breath, Valeraine stepped onto the front stoop and shouted her name.

The flaps of the tent flew open and the monster pushed her way out, then rose to her full looming height and approached the doorsill with the grace of a tall masted ship. "Hey ha hee and a happy morning, snow-giant!" Pierpon called out with a wave. "Come and have breakfast. Quite an eyeful, ain't she, vixen?"

Valeraine answered with a distant nod as she gaped. Was ever a being so frightful, yet so fair? – skin white as a ghost yet smooth as pearl, features sharp as a dagger yet fine as chiseled glass, eyes bright as a sunlit emerald yet wild with the danger of a serpent in coil? She wore a shimmering tunic of gold-trimmed ruby, with a skirt that brushed the top of her knee, and smart black trousers. Her black leather buskins were polished to a glinting shine. A black lace ribbon drew her silk-smooth white hair away from her face. The ebony cloak draped over her proud shoulders. She was dignity incarnate.

She is bound, Valeraine reminded herself to ward off a jealous twinge. *She might just as well be wearing iron manacles.* She stepped aside from the doorway with a gesture for Meliroc to enter. The giant ducked inside, arms taut at her sides, her attention on Cedelair, who held her fate in his hands.

"Mistress Meliroc, I have an answer for you," he announced in a grim, forbidding croak. "I neither need nor want a servant, but certain things you've said convince me it might not be safe to send you away. My apprentice has asked me if she might keep you. Would you object to being her servant?"

Meliroc did not turn her head, but Valeraine could spot a flicker of confusion behind her eye. "No, sir."

"Then her servant you shall be," Cedelair declared. "She is responsible for you. I am nothing to do with you, and you are nothing to do with me. Do you understand?"

"You use plain language, sir," Meliroc replied.

"And do you agree?"

Meliroc cast a brief glance toward Valeraine, her features serene yet her green serpent eyes still hot with hatred. "My must sent me to you," she said to Cedelair. "But since Mistress Valeraine is your apprentice, in serving her I serve you. I do not disobey." She bowed her head toward her new mistress. "What must I do?"

Must. Valeraine was already half sick of the word. "Just now, Mistress Meliroc—"

"Meliroc, if you please, ma'am. You are mistress here, not I."

The young sorcerer ground her teeth. "Very well, then, Meliroc," she corrected herself, "you must take breakfast with us."

***

Be a friend to her, Pierpon had said. Any hero who wanted to live very long always heeded the advice of tiny companions. Yet how to begin? A walk into town seemed sensible, so she asked Meliroc to accompany her on her errand. The monster responded with a nod and a most unservile look.

Clutching her basket and tucking her chin, Valeraine marched forward. The pitiless wind drove hard against her face and seared past the shields of lace and pale blue muslin. "Bears have the right idea about winter," she grumbled. "Sleep through it."

Meliroc, holding pace beside her, glanced down. "You are cold?"

Valeraine nodded with a fierce shudder.

Meliroc lifted her left arm, unfurling her ebony cloak. "Walk under here. You will be warmer."

Valeraine took the measure of the space with an unheroic gulp. The giant could easily smother her in that cloak – well, perhaps not, bound as she was, but she might wish she could, which was nearly as bad. Yet a breath of warmth against the young sorcerer's face proved too sweet to resist. Stiffening her spine, she ventured into the folds. As Meliroc dropped her arm to cover her, delicious heat spread down Valeraine's arms to her frozen fingers, down her legs to her frigid toes.

She grinned up at Meliroc. "Thank you."

"I serve you," said the giant, stepping forward, drawing her mistress with her.

So they walked on, safe from the winter's bite. Yet warm though she was, Valeraine's shoulders still quaked from the memory of last night's unholy sleep-scream.

Silence trailed behind them as they strode into the square, as if a hush-spell billowed from the sweeping folds of Meliroc's cloak. Vendors with their carts of vegetables and fruits and hothouse flowers, calling musically to passers-by, caught sight of Meliroc, and their songs died in their throats. Customers, merchants and artisans alike poured out of the shops to stare. Some of them raised their index fingers to trace a "protection" against evil over their hearts.

Valeraine the Vivacious smiled at them so broadly that her mouth ached. She stepped clear of the cloak's warm security and held up her basket. "Medicines!" she crowed. "Me - di - cines! For toothache, headache, stomach ache! For stiff and burning joints! Potions to clear vision, potions to steady the nerves! Me-di-cines!"

A few people blinked, but no one moved or spoke.

"Medicines!" she called again, striding down the street, the white apparition's shadow stretching after her. "From the hand of the sorcerer Cedelair, who can cure any ailment! Cures for toothache, headache, stomach-ache!" Still no one came near.

"Let them have a few minutes to stare, ma'am," Meliroc thought-spoke, her face as impassive as ever. "They'll start talking again soon."

Valeraine took heart, knowing Meliroc would hardly spout false hope to make her feel better. The giant must have met with such thick silences many times before. "Medicines! Me-di-cines!" the sorcerer cried on in a heroic brio. When she had marched up and down four blocks, the crowd unfroze at last, and the townsfolk began to nudge each other and whisper.

Milotte, the gem-seller with the habitual cough, shuffled off the side-path toward Valeraine, holding up a hand. The sorcerer slipped her hand into the basket and brought forth a bright heliotrope phial, and placed it in her customer's palm with a sympathetic squeeze. By the time Valeraine put her payment away, the thin, sniffling woman had already dashed to the opposite side-path. Four other customers followed, each one keeping his eyes low and speaking as little as possible.

"Well met, young Valeraine," spoke a friendly voice at her elbow. She turned to find glassworks artisan Master Odilon, clad in his usual canary-colored coat and olive-green wool scarf. Beside him, plump little Mennieve in her black-trimmed navy gingham greeted her with a cozy smile.

"I'll take a toothache cure," the bookseller announced, fumbling in her sash-purse for the fee. "I'm sure I'll need it before long, the way I gobble chocolates." As she handed over the coin, she peered up at Meliroc. "Good morning to you, madam," she greeted with a cheerful curtsey. "I'm Mennieve. I sell books. You're fond of reading, aren't you? I can always tell. Who might you be?"

Meliroc the Mute cast a wistful smile down at the bookseller, clearly longing to return the greeting. Valeraine rested a hand on her arm. "My friend can't speak," she explained to Mennieve. "Her name is Meliroc. She's staying with us a while."

"Please tell her I like to read," Meliroc urged her in a tense thought-voice.

"And she likes to read," added Valeraine.

"Ah!" Mennieve smacked her lips, a twinkle in her eye. "You must come visit my shop sometime, lady Meliroc."

"Just where did you find her, young Valeraine?" asked Odilon, his smile a little cooler than Mennieve's.

"My parents and I were on holiday at Lippe," the sorcerer ventured. "Our carriage got stuck in a mud-bank, and Meliroc pulled us out."

Odilon tugged at his chin. "I've been to Lippe. Never saw anybody like her there."

"There isn't 'anybody like me'," Meliroc put in with a diffident glance at her shoes.

Odilon gave her a quizzical look as he handed Valeraine two crowns for a headache curative. Inching toward the glassworks, he gazed over his shoulder, as if trying to remember something. Mennieve, meanwhile, touched the giant's hand before turning and bustling away. Meliroc's mouth sank into a thoughtful frown.

More customers lined up to buy elixirs, their nervous smiles as bright as their coins. Meliroc gave each of them a studious look, a habit unlikely to put them more at ease with her. "They are all frightened." When the quiet thought-voice crept on tiptoe into Valeraine's ear, just under her chat with a customer, she stiffened and locked her smile in place.

"Not of me," the giant explained. "Something is in their eyes."

Valeraine sharpened her gaze on the eyes of the customer before her, Thandif of the square jaw and gray mutton-chop whiskers. She noted the strain in his smile and the touch of a whimper in his normally gruff voice, as if a fearful memory dug its claws into him. A tremble settled in her spine as she noticed a tiny white light whirling in the dark of his eye, the same light she'd glimpsed in the mirror that morning.

Half-turning to Meliroc as more customers approached, she ordered her thoughts into words, to speak to Meliroc as the giant spoke to her. "You say they all have that look in their eyes?"

"All the ones I have seen, yes."

"Even Mennieve?"

"Hers was the worst."

Valeraine stretched her mouth into a customer-greeting grin. Seven of them had gathered in a half-circle around her. Peering into their faces, she found the same whirling light in every eye, spelling out nightmare like a red-blazoned banner.

She had yet to choose a specialty, but the workings of the *Seventh Magic Tongue*, the *Tongue of the Mind*, came most easily to her. A quick word or phrase in that *Tongue* opened a path between her consciousness and others' for her to see as they saw, feel as they felt. Cedelair hated this practice. It was too dangerous, he declared, to be employed to solve common problems. Yet the problem she faced now was hardly "common." She had to know just what lay behind that whirling light.

She broadened her gaze to absorb all seven faces and called the needed phrase into her mind. She tensed her lips and formed the words discreetly, to take a single short step into their heads.

Screams battered her, searing into her mind – so much pain – it would burst from her head, pour from her ears and her eyes – agony – so much–

She reeled, the cobbles fogging beneath her. Meliroc clasped her shoulders to hold her steady.

"Mistress Valeraine, are you all right?" Vociette of the pale red hair brushed Valeraine's elbow. The sorcerer smiled and nodded, even as she shook. Heroes don't shake! she snapped at herself, tightening her muscles.

Valeraine blinked as she took in Vociette's concerned face. A different *Seventh Tongue* phrase filled her head. *A' zhiera' shiech* – to the back of your mind. She sent the scream to the distant reaches of Vociette's consciousness and watched the whirling light dim in the weaver's violet eyes. She laid the same gentle spell on each customer.

As each spark of horror receded, a tingle of pride brushed up her back. For such work as this she had been given the *Tongues of Power*. She was healer, comforter, vital part of this clean, well-swept town.

Yet she could not turn the spell on herself. The scream roared through her memory in all its terror. No human could make such a sound.

It faded from her thoughts only when a ringing melody flowed down from that mysterious wagon on the hill to cover the square in song.

***

The bells' music had eased the pain in Valeraine's head. Now, in the silence of the homeward walk, she felt it coming back. A dark suspicion was taking root inside her, to twist and tear like a thorny vine. She reached into her sash and drew out her penny-flute. She brushed her fingertips fondly over the stops, then pursed her lips and began to play.

"Though Gone, You are Near," a ballad in a minor key, rocked her heart in its arms, then lingered sweetly after the last note. Her eyes half-closed, she shifted into a new mood and raced into a jig called "Hail the Harvest". A strange tingle fired her nerves. Had she ever played so well before, with such a clear, sure tone? Somewhere in back of the merry trill she could hear Rysselide's and Zeritte's spirits applauding.

As the jig ended a different tune slipped into her mind. She had never heard it before and could not guess how she was hearing it now. Yet somehow she knew it, this melodious cry of longing. With a shiver of joy she poured the tune into the flute, her fingers finding the proper stops without fail. She closed her eyes, the better to feel it. Its bittersweet spirit hovered about her heart as the final note dwindled into silence.

When her eyes slowly opened, she found Meliroc gazing down at her with almost blinding concentration. Now she understood where the new melody had come from. Meliroc had sent it into her. She searched the giant's eyes in vain for that coiled-serpent hate. *Play for her.* She grinned at the thought of Pierpon and his blessed advice.

"Who taught you to play like that?" Meliroc's thought-voice was tentative, as if she feared the question might offend.

Yet it thrilled Valeraine. "My home city Nisslaire is full of music," she said. "Every neighborhood block has its own music teacher. All the children on that block take lessons from her. We come home from school and start practicing at the same time and raise the Death-wight's own racket."

A smile darted across Meliroc's face.

"My parents, well, bless them, they wouldn't deny me much, but they did not like the idea of my taking up an instrument and adding to the cacophony. I had to keep at them for months before they realized I wasn't going to stop asking. They finally let me go to Mistress Tiurelle. When I went into her sanctum, she had a violin, a clarinet, a miniature harpsichord, a cornet, and a penny-flute all laid out on a long table. She played a chorus on each of them, then she asked me which one I wanted to learn. I chose the penny-flute, because it sounded the most like bird-song."

Meliroc nodded with a contemplative look. Still Valeraine saw no trace of those sparks of hate. Had she driven the evil spirit from the ivory giant's heart with the aid of Rysselide the Redoubtable's marvelous penny-flute? The yearning tune lingered in the sorcerer's memory. She had never managed to make her way to that sweet and mysterious place where new songs were born, yet Meliroc had. *Is it right that I should envy you, you prisoner?*

"Are you ever homesick?" Meliroc asked suddenly.

"It took me three months here just to stop crying," the sorcerer admitted.

The hate-glint flickered behind Meliroc's eyes. "I have never known a sorcerer to cry."

"I don't know how Master Cedelair put up with me. I got used to this place, got to like it. But sometimes I still miss that din of a dozen instruments practicing at once."

Meliroc quickened her pace. Her jaw clenched, as if she were rebuking herself for unbending even a jot.

What has happened to you, poor, sad creature, to make you so hard? Valeraine fixed her mind on a single crucial question and held it fast, until at last they reached the cottage, and Pierpon poked his head above the cloth with a friendly grin at Meliroc. Her gaze softening, the giant scooped the tiny man up in her palm and set him on her shoulder.

"Where did your 'must' come from, Meliroc?" the hero-sorcerer asked in a cautious voice. "Who set it on you?"

"I don't know what you mean by 'set it on'," the giant replied, her brow furrowing as at a headache. "It came to me, that's all."

Valeraine swallowed annoyance. Geases did not simply "come" to someone. "Who was your first master?"

"I don't know his name." Meliroc drew her mouth tight. "I never remember their names."

"Can you tell me how he treated you?"

The giant nodded, hate blazing in her eyes. "He had a special talent for entering people's minds, for riding in their skins," she said in a dead-calm thought-voice. "He was bedridden. He would put himself in my head and move me about, relishing my size and strength. He would force me to climb up and down hillsides and swim across ponds so he could feel the wind on my face, the water on my skin. He kept me at it until I was so weary I limped back, and then he would make me do kitchen work."

"That's dreadful," Valeraine whispered.

"He nearly broke me once," Meliroc went on. "He had some quarrel with a merchant I never understood rightly. He sent me to the man's house and made me beat him. He forced my arms to swing, my fists to strike. He wasn't satisfied until the man lost his senses. But his son saw everything, and when my master called me back to him, he knew the young man would follow. So he closed his fingers about my mind and pulled till the strings loosened. I knew just enough to understand what he'd done."

Sickened, Valeraine spat bitterness from her mouth. Pierpon shook with outrage, fists clenched.

"The young man came in to accuse me, and my master laughed and pointed at me where I was lying on the floor, dribbling at the mouth. 'Look at her, lad! She can't even sit upright!' The young man stared at me awhile, then walked away, at a loss for what to do. My master reached inside my mind and gave me back my wits, and while I was reeling and sick, he gave me a flippant little smile and said, 'Dishes, Meliroc.'"

Valeraine's stomach convulsed. "Abominable."

The giant arched her neck, a tremble at the corner of her lip. "He was the first, but by no means the worst. Whom shall I tell you about next? The hypnotist? The levitator? Or the transmogrifier? He'll give you a good laugh."

Valeraine gritted her teeth. "Do you see me laughing, Meliroc?"

"Perhaps you do not wear your laughter on your sleeve."

Crimson-faced, Valeraine the Volcanic wheeled away from Meliroc, threw open the cottage door and slammed it behind her. She stormed past Cedelair, who was too hard at work with his grinding pestle to heed her.

She hurled her chamber door shut with the same thunderous slam, then she paced around her bed, her stomach winding in knots. How-dare-she-how-dare-she-how-dare-she! her mind shouted at each creaking step. Bleached fiend! Had either of them asked for her grudging service? How dare she see Valeraine of Nisslaire, healer and comforter, wielder of the marvelous penny-flute, as a villain! With seething breaths Valeraine swiped the air with her fist. *I'm trying to help you, monster!*

A question broke through her ire like a gentle tap on the shoulder. How was Meliroc to know this?

Valeraine, who had been loved and indulged most of her life, forced herself to step into the giant's place, her will bound to another's, her heart screaming in rage and aching for want of a scrap of help or comfort. Meliroc clearly had dozens of stories in the same vein. What reason had she to expect better treatment here?

The heat drained from Valeraine's face. A show of temper would not alter how Meliroc saw her. She needed a tangible expression of good will, a gift. What would the silent giant want? The memory of her sad little smile at Mennieve gave Valeraine the answer.

She pulled open her night-stand drawer to take up a pencil and a book full of blank pages. She had intended to use it as a diary, but her work had kept her too busy to write in it. She tucked the little book and pencil under her arm and left the room.

Cedelair, still grinding the stems of his plants, again failed to glance up as she passed him on her way to the front door. "Troubles with your giant?" he mumbled, barely audible.

"Nothing I can't handle, sir," she replied and swept out the door.

Meliroc sat with her elbow propped upon her knee, smiling at Pierpon, who perched on her upper arm with an eager, listening grin. "– to fetch the Fire-Lily of Long Love from the old king's garden," she was saying. "The king always kept his cross-bow at the read, and an empty space on his wall reserved for the goblin's head."

Valeraine stood stunned. With her attention on Pierpon, the monster looked quite gentle, almost harmless! The few words

Valeraine caught of the story sparked her curiosity. She wanted to learn who the goblin and the old king were. But as soon as Meliroc heard her step she stifled her thought-voice and rose to her feet, lifting Pierpon to her shoulder while she favored her mistress with the usual hate-spiced glare.

"I have something for you," said Valeraine, holding the book and pencil towards her. "It's a writing book. For when we go into town. If you want to say something to someone, you can write it in here. It isn't much, but at least you'll be able to communicate, and it might help the townsfolk get used to you."

Meliroc closed her fingers around the book with a half-bewildered blink.

"Do you really believe all sorcerers are alike?" Valeraine asked her.

"You can't help it," Meliroc explained. "You haven't enough experience with not getting your way."

"Well, we're not. Some of us seek noble deeds to perform, like Brave Bennelise. You've read the Bennelise books?"

"No."

"I'll lend them to you. Anybody who likes kings and goblins should appreciate them. What I mean to say, Meliroc, is that I have no wish to exploit you. Far from it. I want to help you. Rid you of your geas. Set you free to follow your own bent."

With an arch of her shoulders, Meliroc drew a few steps toward Valeraine, throwing her shadow upon her mistress as if to remind her how much taller and stronger she was. "You might not like my bent."

"I'll take that risk," proclaimed Valeraine the Venturesome, squaring her shoulders likewise. "But I can only help you if you let me. You'll have to trust me, Meliroc. Can you do that?"

The giant's mouth twitched into a half-broken smile. "If I must."

"And stop saying 'must'!"

Meliroc nodded.

4. Meliroc finds a use for Cedelair

Left to my own devices, I sat near the mouth of my tent, my fingers squeezed tight around the writing book. The pencil lay beside me on the ground. I didn't dare lift it, lest I snap it in two, then crush it to pieces between my palms. Valeraine! That porcelain doll with her lark-singing flute, tempting me to thoughts of friendship! I hurled the book against the rear of the tent and gripped the snow under my hands and sent waves of heat to melt it, 'til steam escaped my fingers. I wished my eyes might blast that little book to cinders where it lay.

But I would need it. With it I could write my name for Feuval. I needed him to know it, as much as I loved the nickname he had given me. Curse Valeraine and her treacherously useful gift. I knew what she was about. Neither she nor any other master would actually consider freeing me from my must. The gift of a servant who could never say them nay was far too precious. But she wanted me to take that small, fatal step and trust her. Once I did that, in would go the knife.

She was indoors now, busy at her own lessons. I would not be needed for some hours, she said, so I could amuse myself how I liked. If I could steady my spinning head, I might finish my task for Feuval, so I pushed the thought of Valeraine to the rear-most reaches of my mind, took up my mallet, and hammered out a sequence of notes. The old quiver in my hands stilled the minute the chimes' ring leaped into the air.

I took in the view from my canvas doorway – the brown log cottage, the scruffy snow-dappled rose bushes flanking the doorsill, the muddy pale gray tracked yard, and the garden plants that seemed to shine with emerald fire, their tender stems shivering in the breeze. My gaze rested there. Music could begin in the smallest things, like a dot of sunlight on the tip of a leaf. I took my chimes and mallet under my arm and walked toward the garden.

The small black side door opened. Out strode the iron-spined Master Cedelair, a burlap sack slung over his shoulder and a small brown packet in his hand. He turned on me the cold, tight-lipped frown he might give a trespasser who had crushed his plants under foot. As I locked gazes with him I raised my chin and made my face a stone mask. His stare pored over me, like chilly fingers prodding me up and down, examining. Much of a sorcerer's danger lay in the gaze. I flinched at a memory and blinked.

Cedelair headed down the white stone walk-way that divided his garden in half without a backward glance at me. I watched him, a curious tickle at my neck. In another minute I might have a hint of how he managed to keep a garden growing in winter's icy dead.

Kneeling, he pulled up a patch of goverwort, taking care to leave the roots in tact. Flecks of moist earth dropped from them as they dangled. He twitched his lips as he watched the flecks fall into the soil-bed. He opened his sack and slipped the plants inside. Nothing unusual in this, except for his gentle touch and soft look. Yet I sensed something wonderful about to happen. I drew a few short, discreet steps closer to the garden's edge.

Cedelair emptied the brown packet onto the loose soil before him. He slid his fingers into it, his lips forming words. A spark flashed in his eyes, the first burst of lightning in a brewing storm. His neck rippled, straining under that tight collar. His lips moved faster – a whisper, and then a low, soft rhythmic chant in one of the "magic tongues" with which sorcerers cast their spells. I drew closer still, stepping onto the walkway, staring at the wrinkled hands that rested upon the soil.

He threw his head back as his chant became a call. His voice rang with a dreadful glee that shook my spine. The corners of his mouth trembled up, tense with hope, until at last he fell silent. A wild, joyous glow overspread his face. Under his fingers I could clearly see tiny sprouts of green.

He rose to his feet, slapping the loose dirt from his coat and trousers. He wrinkled his nose as he glimpsed me.

"Kindly leave my garden," he said, his voice flat and empty.

I drew a step back. "Have you always been able to do that?" I asked him.

His face did not change. "Have the courtesy not to come into my garden without my permission."

I backed off the walkway and strode to my tent, head high. I'd seen enough. I knew how Cedelair kept his garden thriving. Now he could keep it to himself, the nasty not-old thing. I had my own work to do. I plopped down and set my bell-board in my lap.

A song of a merry heart. What did it mean to be merry? To have something beautiful send your heart into a dance? Like fresh green plant-buds sprouting to life under your fingers? My memory's eye settling on Cedelair's ecstatic face, I dropped the mallet on a single key. The note seized my heart, and I held my breath tight as I listened for the next.

As another note followed, and another, and another, his delight became my own.

***

"That's why it sounded like chimes."

Valeraine stood at my elbow. I couldn't guess how long she had been there. Safe in my imagined chrysalis of light, I had heard, seen, and felt nothing but my new tune.

"When you sent your song to me, I thought the notes sounded a little like a glockenspiel," my mistress went on. "Now I see why. What a cunning instrument!"

"Thank you." I wished I'd heard her coming in time to hide my bell-board.

"I hate to take you away from it, Meliroc, but I need your help with dinner." She cocked her head toward me, a glint of conspiracy in her eye. "It's time we showed Master Cedelair how useful you can be." She led me toward the cottage with a springy stride. "You've made an impression on him, you know."

"I know," I returned, for she hadn't said what sort of impression.

"He told me you were 'busy making a frightful racket'. That's how I knew he liked your tune. The more he likes something, the harder he tries to pretend he doesn't."

Inside we found Cedelair perched on his stool beside the fire, where three smaller pots hung in the stead of yesterday's massive cauldron. He gave me a warning glare, as if he feared I might presume to boil his potions. In answer, I flexed my jaw at him, assuring him with my eyes that I had no intention of setting a fingernail on his sacred pots, and I followed Valeraine into the kitchen, where Pierpon sat cross-legged on the counter-top.

My part was to show that with the aid of my heart-fire I could cut meal preparation time in half. Valeraine had already shredded carrots and drizzled plum sauce over the brisket we'd picked up at the butcher's shop in town. All I needed to do was add my warmth to the stove's heat, to speed the meat's cooking. It demanded little concentration, so Pierpon pressed me for an ending to my story of the "Goblin of the Crimson Cave". Though I wasn't eager to share one of my monster stories in the sorcerers' hearing, I hadn't the heart to deny him.

Valeraine, who had slipped outside with spindle in hand to ring the cottage with magic moonlight, returned with a chuckle on her lips. "You're sure to like the Bennelise books. You can take the first one with you after dinner."

I nodded to her, a chill in my stomach. Valeraine seemed determined to gain my trust with things. I should have nothing to do with them. But I wanted to read that book.

By the time the goblin triumphed over a suspicious king and won the Fire-Lily of Long Love for his sweetheart, the meat was ready for serving. Cedelair left his stool to watch Valeraine slice it into three portions. "The largest slice for your servant, Valeraine," he remarked with a sharp smile. "Though even that may not suffice." He sniffed and added, not quite under his breath, "See if Mistress Overgrown doesn't eat our larder bare within the week."

Valeraine set the three portions at the center of the table and nodded to me. "Take your pick, Meliroc."

I peered closely at the slices. Once I found the smallest, I claimed it with a frosty glance at Cedelair. He gave a tiny harrumph as he dropped into his chair.

With half an eye on him, I cut my slice into the daintiest bites I could manage and nibbled my way through my meal, dabbing my mouth with my napkin at each swallow. Pierpon, crouched before Valeraine's plate, sputtered into his hands, then stuffed his mouth to its fullest capacity, to declare himself the heaviest feeder at the table. I threw him a wink, the embers of my heart-fire stirring. But if Cedelair got our joke, he didn't appear to appreciate it.

He returned to his stool while Valeraine and I cleared the table. He kept a disapproving eye on me as he stirred his pots. An impulse burned in me to hurl a cup at his head.

With all the dishes at last put away, Valeraine cast a satisfied grin at the clock. "You see, sir? We've finished in half the usual time, all thanks to Meliroc."

The elder sorcerer grimaced. "Of course. The marvelous coal in her heart. She can roast a brisket with her fingertip while she bores us all with silly fables."

I grinned at a tickle in my throat. "What is it about me that offends you, sir?" I kept my mind-voice cool, though amusement crept in. "Is it my size? Or my complexion? Or do my eyes remind you of some girl who broke your heart?"

He drew a sharp breath through his teeth. "I'll tell you, Mistress Meliroc," he said, rising from his stool. "You show up in our yard without a word of warning and expect us to make a place for you. In common circles we call that rude. But because you have a geas hanging around your neck, we must pity you and make you welcome, whether we wish to or not. You cannot expect me to be happy about that."

Valeraine rested a hand on my arm. "That's not fair, sir."

"That," returned Cedelair, pointing a bony finger at me, "is not fair."

The young man behind the old mask flashed into view, his eyes sharp with the sting of pain from an injury that had nothing to do with me. Ignoring a tug of curiosity, I bowed and retreated through the front door.

As I passed through Valeraine's ribbon of magic moonlight, I smiled briefly at the shimmer it cast upon the snow and wondered what sort of place I had come to, where my expectations were upended one after another. I took up my instrument and held it steady in the crook of my arm, playing triplets as I wandered along the edge of the moonlight pool. I ventured to imagine striding down a town square side-path, delighting passers-by with spirited melodies, hearing coins drop at my feet. The music in my mind rang out so deliciously loud that I failed to hear the front door open and close.

"You forgot this," squeaked a voice below.

A downward glance showed me a maroon leather book hovering four inches above the ground. I knelt and picked it up to find Pierpon standing under it with upraised arms.

"Valeraine asked me to bring it out to you," the jickety explained. "Said I'd be more of a comfort to you than she would."

I nodded. Sensible of my new mistress. I read the gold-lettered binding – *Brave Bennelise and the Soldiers of the Black Duke*. Tucking the book under my arm, I lifted Pierpon to my shoulder. He seemed to like it there.

I drew a long breath, loosening my knotted heart. "I never imagined sorcerers' magic could be beautiful. I've only ever seen it do hurt. But here a girl can shed light from a spindle and a man can make plants grow under his fingers."

The pixy-man let out a whistle. "It makes you wonder, it does, what else they can do, eh?" He tilted his head with a winking smile. "Set you free, perhaps?"

I pulled my nerves tight. Moved as I might be by certain of their spells, I wasn't ready to admit that possibility. "If I were Valeraine, and I were looking for a good deed to perform, I'd find some way to send you home. Humankind would be lost without the jicketies, after all. You should be back at your post."

"There are plenty back home, there are, to do my work. As for me, I could learn a bit by lingering here to see how Valeraine frees you. Even Cedelair might help."

"Cedelair despises me."

"He doesn't think much of me either, he doesn't. But in the end, his itch to learn will prove too much. Tell me, snow-giant, where's the first place you'd go if you were free?"

If I dared imagine that I might shake myself to pieces. I found a whimsical reply in the expectant sparkle in Pierpon's eye. "Jicket-Castle, of course."

The little fellow chortled. "Your foot wouldn't fit through the door, it wouldn't!"

"Then I would sit outside and admire it."

"There's no path for a human to Jicket-Castle."

"I'm a strange being, remember?" I pointed out with a lofty arch of my neck. "Perhaps I'm a demi-goddess in disguise, and all paths are open to me. It is my sacred mission to go to the Home of the Jicketies and gift your people with music."

He pursed his lips, his head sagging a little to the side. "I wish it were," he mumbled. "I wish you could come home with me."

I brushed his nose with the tip of my thumb. "I could, in a way. You could carry out my mission. When you're back amongst your friends, whistle this tune for them, a bit of me that will fit through the door."

With a light, tripping touch I played my new melody for him. By the time I'd finished the fourth measure, my tone-deaf friend was bobbing his head in rhythm with the sprightly tune.

"Where did you find that?" he asked, his smile half incredulous.

"In Master Cedelair's garden."

Whatever the sorcerer might say or do, he couldn't take back the song he'd given me.

5. Cedelair follows a trail, and Meliroc chooses risk

Cedelair shook his head with a sigh as he picked up the book lying open, face-down on Valeraine's chair. He had lost count of the number of times he had told his apprentice not to leave books this way, but she never could remember.

He glanced at the title on the spine and frowned. *The Magical Art of the Geas.* He'd noticed her poring over this volume, her frown deepening steadily until at last she had pleaded a sick-headache and slumped off to her room. He'd warned her. Magicians' books offered minute instructions on how to lay a geas in place but never bothered to mention how to get rid of one.

After he slid the book back into its place on the shelf, he took down one for himself, *Sacrifice Magic among Belfaire's Hill Folk*, bound appropriately in blood-colored leather. He settled down on his stool, letting his back and shoulders slack. With half-closed eyes he wondered how it might feel to drift off into sleep.

In five years he had not slept. A satisfying wall of wakefulness stood between him and visions which would carry him back to that moment of horror and pain, of wrinkles chiseling into his skin and the brittle smirk on his enemy's face. Sometimes he girded that wall with the most gruesome tales he could find. The spine-chilling blood sacrifice customs of Belfair's hill folk were especially useful. But this night something new kept mixing in with the grim words – chimes that gleamed like sun on a clear stream, playing a cheerful tune.

Valeraine had told him of the efforts she'd made to befriend Meliroc, most notably the songs she'd played on their walk home which had moved the giant to share a melody of her own invention. They'd felt like friends in that moment, a current of song flowing one to the other. "We ought to be friends," she'd concluded, "and I'm sure we would be if her former masters didn't stand in the way."

Cedelair had met this plaint with a disinterested grunt. He had to keep a careful eye on the outsized ogre, but he would think no more of her than he could help.

Yet there it was again, weaving its way through a blood-dripping paragraph – that funny little tune, drawing a smile to his lips. Something of himself seemed to move in that song. Yet it had come from her. He slammed the book shut and set it down at the foot of his stool. He sprang to his feet and started for the door.

Drawing his long gray coat about his shoulders, he strode over the front step and into the light-pool. He caught sight of Meliroc treading across the lawn, her bell-machine and mallet tucked under one arm and the writing-book Valeraine had given her clutched in her opposite hand. She strode with a purpose, headed somewhere. Answering a call.

"Best go after her," he whispered. Following the tracks she had made, he marched beyond the reach of the moonlight spell. As he stepped into darkness he mouthed two words of the *Second Tongue, the Tongue of Light*. A pale blue flame sprang up from his palm to light his way.

Something in this sojourn might shed some light on how he and Valeraine might rid themselves of the intruder.

***

The carillon had first called me to it with a bittersweet song, yearning in its ring. Tonight's summoning song rang with the gladness of one greeting a long-absent friend. The light-threads stretched out from my vision of the wagon to draw me close, an embrace such as I'd felt only in daydreams. Soon I found myself running toward it.

Yet the song died as I sank to my knees before the wagon. The light-threads loosed their loving hold. Silence dropped stone-heavy upon my ears. I stared at the curtain and waited for a golden mask to appear. But the curtain hung dead still. Perhaps it fell to me to break this smothering quiet.

Nightmare Lullaby

With a cool breath I began my new song of a merry heart. The wooden walls shimmered once more. The light-threads slipped forward to twine about me in time with the rising tune.

A flurry of notes flew out of the carillon. Startled by a bolt of delight, I tightened my hold on my mallet as it hovered over the next key. The carillon held its breath, waiting for me to go on. In my mind I replayed its notes, and with another joyful rush I understood. They would give texture to my simple melody. I let the mallet fall. Two chimes from the carillon answered me. Encouraged, I played on, listening to the carillon's answers, its notes merging with mine. In my mind's eye golden walls rose around me and a vaulted azure ceiling arched above, a temple for my merry-hearted hymn to fill.

When the song ended I rested my mallet upon the snow, my head teetering dizzily. The glow of the carillon's walls dimmed but did not vanish.

"Thou hast pleased me even beyond my hope."

My eyes met the bright gold mask. Feuval leaned over the rim of the window, and his eyeless imp hovered above his left shoulder.

"I set thee a challenge and thou hast overleaped it." The satisfied hum in his voice whipped my heart-fire to a frenzy. "Since thou speak'st not, fair moon-tree, thine eyes perhaps can tell me how such a song of joy was found."

My name is Meliroc, I scrawled into my writing-book, *but I love "moon-tree"*.

"MEE-li-roc?" he tried out when I showed him the page. I shook my head with a smile. "Me-LI-roc?" he guessed, and again I signaled that he had it wrong. "MEL-i-roc?" I nodded, my breath growing short. My name had never sounded so beautiful.

I wrote down in as few words as possible the story of Cedelair in his garden. Then I handed him the book and waited as he read it.

"Ah! This would explain. This Master Cedelair is thy friend, then?"

I shook my head, while my heart sank into my boots. Were I to spend any substantial time with him, Feuval would have to know about my must. How would he see me? Still the same proud "moon-tree" or a pathetic slave?

"Thine eyes show me distress," said Feuval. "Has this Cedelair harmed thee?"

With burning face I wrote as plain a description of my must as I could. No, Cedelair had not hurt me, yet. But I was still his servant, even though he might claim I belonged to his apprentice Valeraine.

Feuval nodded and grunted over my words. As he returned the book he stretched out his hand in a beckoning gesture. Inching forward on my knees (I still disliked the thought of looming above him), I folded my fingers around his. "This is why thou didst hear my call," he said. "Thou art my kin."

The imp spun in mid-air with an indignant whistle. "No-no-no!" it chattered. "Ugly big-big is not like you, sir!"

"She hath suffered as I have, and ugly she is not," Feuval snapped. "Hide thyself, whishk."

The imp sank beneath the window and out of sight.

Feuval returned his attention to me. I felt the brush of compassion in the gleam of his mask. "Thou'rt trapped," he noted, "and thou look'st to music to set thee free. Hath I the right of it?"

It can't take my must away, I scrawled. *But it gives me a room to hide in.* I held the open book out for him to read.

"I have felt like thee, fair moon-tree." His voice grew bitter. "I, too, am trapped."

I winced at a sting. *How?* I wrote out in large letters.

"Hast thou seen me outside the confines of this wagon?" he pointed out, slapping his palm against the side. "Nor shalt thou ever," he continued when I shook my head, "unless a miracle doth release me."

"Careful, snow-giant," came a tiny whisper behind my ear.

"There was no youth in the world more foolish than I, and for that folly I paid dearly," Feuval explained. "I believed I was the true heir to the bards of yore. I had only one aim, to make music such as none had ever heard before and none would surpass thereafter. I found this carillon in the deep of the woods, alone and silent. I looked into the wagon and found no one inside, only the bells waiting to be awakened. I sensed magic. Think'st thou I should have fled?"

I couldn't answer, by pencil or by gesture.

"I did not. I stepped inside. I touched a bell, and as it shook the wagon closed me in. I knelt at these bells and played for hours, never tiring or hungering. Then I began to sense something amiss. I should have hungered. I tried to leave. But the wagon would not open."

"Sounds like one of your monster-tales," the little whisperer remarked.

"From that day to this I have not left this wagon. When I played the carillon it became my master. I must play, whether I will or no. So, seest thou," Feuval concluded, his voice once again a warm caress, "I know thy grief."

The carillon's light pulsed in answer to his words, a living, listening, fearful thing holding the man fast in a prison of song. *My music have I given to many villages, yet no listener hath ever spoken back to me.* How long had it been since he'd heard a human voice, or any sound at all, save the gibbering of the tiny dust-demon and the ring of the bells that caged him? Had the very thing in which I'd always sought refuge become torture to him? When love of music died in agony, what remained?

Tears pooled in my eyes as his tale sank in. Habitually I held tears in, but now I bade them fall. They were the least this man deserved.

"Thou weep'st for me?" His voice sounded its gentlest yet. "Ah, sweet moon-tree, weep thou not."

I have a friend who says tears are valuable, I scribbled. *A sign of a lesson learned.*

"What lesson hast thou learned?"

That I have wasted far too much time feeling sorry for myself.

He brushed his thumb across my cheek. "I would have thee weep no more. Rejoice, rather, in the comfort thou hast brought me in such a little time."

A puff of wind stirred my heart-fire. I remembered Pierpon in my hand, the heat from my fingers pouring into his nearly frozen body, and my jolt as he'd come back to his senses. I gained an inkling why I'd grown fond of the pixy-man, despite my usual aversion. Pierpon was the first creature who was better for having known me.

Please tell me how I can help you, I printed.

He patted my cheek. "Thou hast already begun. If thou wouldst comfort me still more, bring me a song to make the hardest heart weep."

I frowned. Why should Feuval, trapped in the unhappiest situation I could imagine, want a song of sorrow? I wrote out the question as my mind formed it.

"Thou'rt young yet," he pointed out, "or thou wouldst know that such songs can heal. Perhaps seeking one out will help thee learn. Go thou, Meliroc, my moon-tree. The carillon will summon thee when thou art prepared." He pressed the book into my hand and drew back from the window. As I bowed my head, the heavy curtain dropped between us.

Pulling myself to my feet, I turned from the carillon and started for home. Once I'd walked a safe distance Pierpon hopped from my cloak-hood to my shoulder. The carillon-prisoner's gold mask lingered in my mind's eye, and beside it the little round head of the eyeless imp. Whishk. My mind locked on this word. The compendia of strange beings had not omitted it. I sharpened my eye on the little brute's image, to match it with a drawing in an index. W for Whishk.

Whishk: a phantom no bigger than a human thumb. Faceless but for a wide, usually grinning mouth, it is almost always found in its customary habitat, the graveyard. Whishks keep the graves in order and will suck the life from anyone who threatens to rob them. This protectiveness has earned the whishk the name "Attendant of the Dead".

Attendant of the Dead... yet the whishk was away from its graveyard... attending to the carillon... with its master, shrouded in white and masked with gold. The mask still hovered before my vision with the soft glow of sympathy it had exuded when Feuval had told me, "Thou art my kin." The satin-gloved fingers took it by its rim and pulled it down, revealing not a face, not even a skull, but a fall of ashes.

The full weight of his story hurled me off balance. "Snow-giant!" Pierpon shrilled, gripping my sleeve as I stumbled. My arms and hands flailed out. My book and pencil and instrument toppled. I dug my feet hard into the snow and locked my knees to fight my way back to steadiness. I reached up to brace Pierpon with the cup of my palm.

"What on earth is wrong?" the jickety cried, his eyes bulging from their sockets.

"Feuval's not alive." My voice sounded leaden. "His whishk is a grave-spirit."

Pierpon blubbered his lips. "Master Gold-mask is dead?"

"Not alive," I corrected him.

"My dear snow-giant, if you're not alive you're dead, you are."

I shook my head. "My masters have spoken of things between. Neither alive nor dead. He can't leave his wagon." The idea seized me with a cold, skeletal grip. I imagined a crust of chalky gray rot on the cheek those white satin fingers had touched. "If he were alive, that wouldn't be possible. He would have to eat. He'd have to relieve himself."

"Of course," Pierpon snickered. "Should be obvious what he is."

The idea sharpened, taking on an even darker color. "The carillon did something to him. He was alive when he went into the wagon, when he started to play."

"You think the carillon killed him?"

I cast a shuddering glance down at the instrument at my feet. "I think it changed him. Made him into something that would never have to leave it. Not a spirit, not even a revenant, but something that's never been indexed." Again I pictured the mask's soft glow of sympathy. "Like me."

Pierpon cocked his head to the side. "Well, then, it's something you won't want to meddle with. You can leave that thing he gave you to rot, you can, and come along home and think no more about him."

My stomach wrenched at the sight of the bell-board Feuval had taken from the carillon. It had the same resonant ring. The carillon had transformed Feuval from a living man into an undefined thing. What might this portion of it be doing already to me? I imagined the rot eating its way over my face, until it too crumbled in an ashy heap.

I knelt to retrieve my writing book and pencil. My hand brushed against the mallet. It rolled sideways against a key and a soft chime emerged, like a sigh.

"Leave it!" Pierpon snapped.

Leave it, I echoed to myself. *You'll be safe then.*

Its keys already glistened with damp. I fancied it vanishing under a fall of snow. My breath scalding my throat, I knelt beside it. "Let's go!" Pierpon shrilled in my ear. Yet I heard him no more than I might a whistle in a storm.

I ran my fingers over the planks and fancied the chrysalis-light washing over my hands. I felt it sweeping through me, caressing my spirit with airy fingers, whispering a promise to share its mystery – the something I'd read of in books, and seen in the smiles and nods and warm glances between friends and sweethearts on village side-paths. The something that binds people to each other or to a certain spot or even to an object. The something that makes them good. Of course it wasn't safe. Such a thing never could be. If Feuval had felt it, little wonder he'd stayed and played, and lost himself.

I could help him love music again.

Pierpon squeaked a warning in my ear. "If you take up that thing again, I'll be your friend no more."

I took him in my palm and brought him face to face with me. "You said Feuval's story sounded like one of my monster tales," I reminded him. "If you were to find the Goblin of the Crimson Cave all alone and comfortless, would you deny him your help?"

"Yes!" he shouted, clenching his fists.

"I don't believe you. Look whose hand you're sitting in."

"That's not the same at all," he grumbled with a pout. "I know your goodness. What do you know about that man, except that he's 'not alive' and has a silky voice and calls you 'moon-tree'? I can call you 'moon-tree' if it means so much to you."

"I like when you call me 'snow-giant'," I told him. "All right, then, perhaps it's not quite the same. But when I wept for him, Pierpon, I felt something move inside me, as if I were growing wider within. Like I felt when I saved you."

"He isn't worth your care. I feel in my bones, I do, he'll harm you in the end."

"Perhaps. But I feel something in my bones, too. This is work I'm meant for. Whatever he may be, I can't turn my back on him."

"No, I don't suppose you can," he grunted. "That's to your credit, not his."

"Then you'll still be my friend?"

"Yes, mam'selle Meliroc. That's my folly."

Grinning at him, I set him back on my shoulder and took my bell-board and mallet under my arm once more.

***

"Mistress Meliroc."

Cedelair stepped into the moonlight pool from the shadows of the trees. He frowned as usual, yet I noted a peculiar trace of softness in his eyes. Pierpon stood up on my shoulder. Cedelair acknowledged him with a crinkle at the corner of his lip.

"Will you take a cup of hot tea with me?" the sorcerer asked.

Nightmare Lullaby

My heart-fire threatened to fold into itself. My master had figured out at last that he could use me to test his potions. I replied in my calmest mind-voice, "If I must."

"This is an invitation, Mistress Meliroc, not a command," Cedelair clarified. He twitched his eyebrows at Pierpon. "You, sir, are free to go to bed."

"You don't command me, you don't," Pierpon snapped, squaring his shoulders.

"I will take tea with you, sir, if Master Pierpon joins us," I offered. I did want to hear what Cedelair had to say, and I would feel more secure in his company if Pierpon were near. If he tried again to dismiss the jickety, I'd know he meant no good.

Cedelair scratched behind his left ear. "Sounds fair enough. Pray come inside, both of you." He beckoned over his shoulder as he passed through the door.

As I followed I saw him hook his bronze kettle above the fire. "I just now decided I wanted some," he remarked. "It will take a few moments to heat, unless you'd like to make yourself useful, ma'am."

I dug into my heart-coal, stoked the fire, and called it up to my hands. Once my fingers' steady touch had the water boiling, I passed the kettle to Cedelair, who had gloved his hands with hearth-mittens. "Aren't you afraid you'll be burned?" he asked.

"No, sir. I don't burn."

"Hmm. This waxes interesting." He clicked his tongue. "Do you mean to say that if your cloak caught fire and the fire spread, it wouldn't even singe you?"

"I've never thought to try that, sir."

Pierpon chuckled while Cedelair poured out the tea with no change in his expression. I sharpened my gaze to catch if he should slip something unwelcome into one of the cups. When nothing went into them but tea and sugar, two lumps each, I relaxed a little. I took my cup from his hands and carried it to the shaggy white cushion Valeraine had set out for me. As I sank down I set Pierpon on the cushion's corner. I tilted my cup toward him, and he rose on tiptoe and slipped his head over the rim to drink.

"What did you wish to discuss with me, sir?" I asked the sorcerer.

"What age are you?" he asked in return.

"The age I am, sir."

"Don't you know how old you are?"

"Not exactly."

"Ask her how many summers she remembers," Pierpon suggested.

"I am most grateful for your assistance, Master Jickety." Cedelair's voice could have sliced through glass.

"I remember three summers," I proclaimed, with a haughty tilt of my head.

Cedelair let out a scoffing grunt. "You're telling me you're three years old?"

"I can't say for certain, sir, but that's all I remember."

"And of these three years, how many have you spent wandering at the will of your 'must'?"

I did a quick calculation. "Eleven months and sixteen days."

"Ah!" He nodded, pleased at this precise reply. "How many masters?"

"Six." I ran my memory over only the time I'd spent wandering. I did not count the Bitter Chord, and would not speak of her unless I was forced.

"Then we are your seventh," mumbled Cedelair. "How fortuitous. How long did you grace your other masters with your presence?"

"Never under a month, sir, forgive my unwelcome news."

He gave a hemming cough. "Could you describe them to me?"

I shook my head. "I can't remember their faces."

"Of course," he muttered into his cup. "I suspect, Mistress Meliroc, that you're as much a mystery to yourself as to us."

"To Mistress Valeraine, you mean, sir," I returned.

"Your pardon?"

"I'm as much a mystery to myself as to Mistress Valeraine, not to you, sir. Remember, I am nothing to do with you, as you are nothing to do with me."

Pierpon covered his mouth to hide a smirk. "Quite right," returned Cedelair, unruffled. "You do well to remind me. All the same, since this is my household and you are a part of it, whether I like it or not, I reserve the right to the odd moment of curiosity about you. It's not every day, after all, that one meets a fireproof giant."

"Of course, sir. I'll answer you as well as I can."

He rose from his stool and moved toward me, examining my face with an almost fierce stare. "If I showed you a face, might you remember if you'd seen it before?"

I rubbed at my eyes. "Showed me a face?"

"If I were to call a face to mind," he explained, "and pass the memory on to you, do you think you might recognize it?"

"Are you looking for someone, sir?"

"I'm merely curious if you've chanced to cross paths with an old acquaintance of mine." A spark flashed in his eyes like the flick of a blade. *An acquaintance he hates.*

Pierpon stood rigid, glowering at Cedelair. "You mean to use magic on her?"

"Not without her permission," Cedelair replied. "It's not my way to intrude where I'm not wanted." I would have appreciated this sentiment more if I hadn't read the unspoken addition in his eye, *unlike certain large ivory-skinned people I could name.*

"It will last less than a minute," he assured me. "And indeed, it's no more than you did this afternoon, when you sent a song into my apprentice's head. Yes, I know about that," he added when he saw me start. "This will hurt you no more than you hurt Valeraine, and it will be a great favor to me."

It would do me no hurt, my thoughts echoed, but the loss of a little bit more of the hate on which I depended. He and his dainty blonde cohort had already chipped away at it. Now I saw its echo in that blade-edged look in Cedelair's eyes.

"Show me the face," I bade him, "and I'll tell you if I recognize it."

His lips curled in a ghost of a smile for only an instant before his dark eyes absorbed every jot of expression. He whispered a single word, and a woman's face burst into my view, young, with a certain flatness of feature. One might forget this face less than an hour after seeing it but for its vivid sea-blue eyes. As these eyes held my attention my skin shivered, for here lay the sign of the sorcerer, the glint of careless cruelty. Her lips were set in a light, easy smile, as if she were looking at a butterfly impaled on a rose's thorn.

I closed my eyes and shook my head. "I've never seen her," I told Cedelair.

"Could she have been one of your masters?"

"All my masters have been men." Except the Bitter Chord, I remembered with a familiar cringe.

With a rumbling cough, the sorcerer lowered his head. "It was no very high chance," he murmured. "All the same, Mistress Meliroc, I am obliged to you." The hint of softness in his eyes grew more distinct. "You may bear watching, after all."

I tilted my cup again to share tea with Pierpon while I pored over Cedelair's brittle features with an insistent tug of curiosity. I tried the same question I'd asked that afternoon. "The spell you work in the garden – when did you first discover you could do that?"

Cedelair cleared his throat behind his hand. "Why do you want to know?"

"I'm only wondering how sorcerers discover their magic. My other masters weren't the question-answering kind."

"And you think I am?"

"Well, you've already asked me more questions than they ever did."

Again he coughed. "I had a favorite tree," he explained, with a brief glance toward the window. "I'd climb it and rest in its branches and imagine it was a magical traveling tree that could carry me away to distant lands. The winter I was seven years old, it went to sleep, and when spring came again it didn't wake up." He gnawed lightly on his lip, a wistful mist in his eyes as if he were looking with longing on that lad of seven years.

"My father said there was no help for it. It would have to be cut down.So I decided to sleep in its shade one last night. All I wanted was for my tree to be whole again. Then I heard something singing to me, a voice coming from my own mind but in a language I'd never heard before. I laid my head beside the roots and whispered those words into the ground. In that instant I understood them. By morning my tree had sprouted new leaves."

My heart-fire skipped. "You saved it."

"Yes. It keeps watch over the house."

I suddenly knew the tree he meant, the magnificent spreading oak that threw its shade over the track to his door. In my fancy my song of a merry heart rang out in all its joy. I envisioned the scrawny brown-haired lad whispering life back into a tree's dead roots and saw the very short step from him to the man who buried his hands in the soil and called buds to sprout from seeds.

Nightmare Lullaby

A bolt of ice shot up my spine. I drained my cup dry and stretched to my feet, tilting my head. "I bid you good night, Master Cedelair. Thank you for the tea." After a friendly wink at Pierpon I made for the door with all speed. I launched myself over the threshold and dashed for my tent, grinding my teeth 'til I fancied they smoked.

I stretched myself on my pallet and clutched my coverlet, hurling Cedelair out of my mind. The last face I pictured before sleep swept me under was masked in gold. A song that can make the hardest heart weep...

6. Cedelair breaks his routine

As he prepared for his first venture into town since Valeraine had come to him, Cedelair refused to anticipate how the townsfolk might look at him.

When Valeraine came into the parlor, with Pierpon skipping behind her skirts, the sorcerer's imagination slipped free of its cage. He pictured himself through her eyes, a "freshly laundered man" with his long hair slicked back, his cheeks and chin cleared of stubble, and his brown boots polished to a blinding shine. He'd donned his spare long-coat, royal blue with silver buttons, and a maroon silk neckerchief. He'd traded his rumpled brown trousers for a sharp-cut black pair. No one dressed with such attention just to putter about in his garden.

Her bewildered stare lost clarity for an instant before she said, "You're going into town, sir?"

He nodded. "I need something from the bookshop. I'd like some words with you, as well, so if you please, leave the jickety behind."

"What?" Pierpon snapped with a belligerent scowl. "Why should I stay here? It's not as if I'm interested, it's not, in all your magic talk."

"Mistress Meliroc must stay here, as well," Cedelair added to Valeraine. As he'd expected, Pierpon's look brightened at once. The poor little man so adored that giant.

"Yes, sir," Valeraine agreed, still staring.

They walked side by side toward town. Valeraine tugged at her ice-blue shawl, grumbling that they should have brought Meliroc, after all, while Cedelair told her of a wagon that shone in the dark, and a man with a golden mask and a deep, soft voice, and bells that rang like crystal. It all sounded like an episode from one of Valeraine's overblown adventure books. Thankfully his apprentice knew how rarely he read fiction and would never suspect him of inventing fictions of his own.

He'd learned the literal truth of the phrase "makes my skin crawl" when Meliroc had appeared in his yard. He kept remembering stories of golems, clay statues brought to unnatural life that would do a master's will until some havoc in what passed for their brains prompted them to smash everything in sight. *My name is Meliroc, and I am your servant* – very much what a golem might say. But could golems weep or pity a thing most would shun? *Perhaps I have been mistaken about her.* The thought settled lightly in the back of his mind.

Valeraine heard him out with a pensive expression then said, "We have to put a stop to it. Tell her plainly she must never see the man in the wagon again."

He would have thought to handle the matter in this sensible way, but for the unwelcome curiosity seducing him. "I'm not sure we should. A song that can make the hardest heart weep! Think of the power in such a thing."

"I am thinking of it," she said, "given into the hands of that undead being. Who knows what he'll use it for?"

"If he has it, we will have it," countered Cedelair. "It might prove useful in any number of ways. We can stop it if we need to. Let's see how she goes on."

Valeraine smiled as she caught his idea. "There is this," she mentioned. "Twice when I've been in town I've heard those bells. It's very strange, but while they're playing and even for a moment after they've stopped you feel better about things."

Cedelair nodded, recalling how he'd felt when the carillon had played along with Meliroc last night. "They cool the overheated places inside you," he suggested.

"That's it!" she cried, snapping of her fingers. "Surely a thing like that can't be altogether evil. You're right, sir. We watch her. But her safety comes first. You've made her my responsibility, and I don't take it lightly."

With a flush of pride in her Cedelair returned her smile. "Of course not."

They trudged forward, mulling over their separate thoughts until Valeraine touched his arm to draw his eyes to hers. "Sir, how much do you know about nightmares?" she blurted out.

"Very little, apart from what your friend the jickety tells us," he answered.

"Have you ever known a magician or a magical creature to have the power to turn dreams into nightmares?"

"No."

"Or to afflict an entire town, to give them nightmares at the same time?"

"No, but that's not to say such a thing is impossible. Why?"

She gnawed hard at her lip. "For two nights now I've woken up with shakes and sweats, the way people wake from a nightmare. I can't remember what I've dreamed except for one thing – an unearthly scream, full of all the griefs in the world."

Cedelair coughed away a snicker. Her last words could have come straight from one of her books. "What makes you think everyone else has a share in it?"

"Look in my eyes, sir. Look hard," she bade him, leaning toward him.

He sharpened his stare, sifting through the sparks and shadows in Valeraine's eyes. There it was, a tiny spinning blare that ran counter to all he knew about his fearless apprentice. The terror of it spread over his own skin.

Valeraine blinked. "Yesterday I noticed the people in town all have that same light, as if we'd all been hearing the same scream." She glanced down at her shuffling feet, as if she had done a thing he'd disapprove of.

"You wouldn't by chance have stronger evidence, would you, Valeraine?" he asked, one eyebrow raised.

"What sort of evidence, sir?"

"*The Seventh Tongue.*"

"Yes." She turned back to him, her gaze sharp with defiance. "I had to know. It turns out I was right. I heard screams, all the same scream. You may disagree, sir, but I think I did right."

"I'm not vexed with you this time, Raine," he assured her, with a tentative pat on her shoulder. "It was best to find out."

"Then you think we could be under a curse?"

"That I have to doubt. Who could have laid it?"

She flinched, her brow furrowing. He could guess how she was thinking out the question. Magic could not creep out of the air unsummoned. As far as she knew, she and her master were the only ones in the vicinity capable of wielding it – except –

"Your giant," he said for her.

She shook her head. "I doubt she's the type. She did save Pierpon, after all, when she had nothing to gain by it."

"You said you've been hearing this scream for two nights now? In that time, what is new in your life?"

"I don't believe she has anything to do with it," she insisted.

"It may not be her fault. It could be part of that 'must' of hers. It's time we learned more about our outsized acquaintance." He softened his look. "In the meantime, I'll give you something to ward off sleep."

He swallowed a black taste in his throat as they moved into the square. Valeraine had told him in eager detail of the stir Meliroc had caused there. It seemed his appearance was nearly as shocking. The townsfolk gaped, nudged each other, tugged at each other's arms. A flight of whispers dogged his steps. *Old Cedelair! The recluse comes! What could have drawn him out of his hole? Something to do with that hulking ghost from yesterday, most like.*

Valeraine quivered with anger. "'Old Cedelair,'" she snarled under her breath. "They know right well you're not old. How dare they!"

He rested a calming hand on her arm, warming a little at her indignation on his behalf. They had their reasons, all of them. His mind ran back to the days when he'd dashed down these side-paths, giddy from the music of all the wonderful new languages in his head. There – he'd called out in the *First Tongue* to smooth the cracks from a window in the counting-house. There – he'd sung under his breath in the *Fourth Tongue* to heal the bruised peaches in the greengrocer's stall. There – he'd whispered the *Third Tongue* to call a cherry tart from the baker's tray into his hands. That had been naughty, true, but less than a second later he'd sent two roines from his pocket into the baker's coin jar. Every day, every step, he'd looked for chances to show off his powers. He'd thought his neighbors might be grateful, or at least amused.

"When he is grown, Crainante will have its own full-fledged sorcerer," his parents had boasted. Years later, Crainante still hadn't decided how it felt about that.

Before the bookshop door, he took leave of Valeraine. "Tell Mennieve *a' zhiera' sheich*," she whispered just before she squeezed his hand then strode down the street, launching into her ware-cry. "Me-di-cines!"

***

Fimbre's Books, the sign still read seven years after Master Fimbre's death. Cedelair wondered why he had bothered to hope that Mennieve had changed it at last. In her mind this was still, and would always be, her late husband's bookshop.

At the sight of the white stone house towering over the little red brick shop, Cedelair felt a heavy hand pass over his spirit. The *Echo House*, he'd called it in those days when he and Mennieve's son Rybert had romped through its halls, shouting to see who could raise the loudest echo. Now its shutters were locked, its door boarded up. He glanced at the withered ivy vine clinging to the trellis and thought briefly of shooting life into it with a chant in the *Fourth Tongue*. No. A waste magical energy. That which kept Mennieve from changing her bookshop's name also prevented her from selling or renting that house.

He opened the shop door and called out to its owner. The plump little woman, wearing her familiar blue gingham gown and white Hollandish cap that barely covered a frowsy bun of gray-blonde hair, darted around the shelf she was stacking and clasped him by both hands. "Cedelair, dear lad!" she cried. "Now my day's truly joyful."

He enfolded the bookseller in a friendly embrace, smiling sadly to hear her call him "dear lad" as she had in former days. "Come back into the parlor," she urged with a pull at his arm. "I'll boil us up some tea. It's high time we had a proper chin-wag. Though I suppose you've come in looking for something quite specific."

"I have," he admitted, "though I won't say no to a chin-wag." He gave her a grin to match her own.

He let her tug him gently past the rows of stacked shelves into a tiny room with a wooden cot, two oak chairs, a rickety table, a black iron stove, a kettle, and a cabinet that housed a set of blue china – the room where she'd lived ever since Fimbre's Books had ceased to be Fimbre's Books in all but name. As she brewed their tea he listened with an attentive face while she told him news of his old acquaintances.

"I've never had the chance to tell you just how wise you were in your choice of apprentice," she remarked once the round of information was done. "What a sweet, clever young lady Valeraine is! I trust she does well at her lessons."

"Quite well." Knowing Mennieve disliked brief answers, he added an account of Valeraine's recent mastery of a challenging spell. "But she's young yet," he concluded, "and a bit inclined to go off scatter-shot."

"You did your share of scatter-shooting not so long ago, young man," Mennieve pointed out. "I hope you're not too hard with her."

"I try not to be. But most girls her age adopt stray kittens, not stray giants."

"Ah, yes," said the bookseller with a knowing tap of the chin. "I wondered how you might be getting on with the stunning colossus at your cottage."

"Stunning?" He considered the word before nodding in admission. "The sight of her would stun most people, true."

"I liked the look of her," Mennieve pronounced. "It's surely hard for her, being so different from everyone. So be kind to her, too, won't you, dear lad?"

He reached out to squeeze her hand. "For your sake, dear lady, I will."

"For my sake, nothing!" his old friend scoffed. "Do it because it's in keeping with your own good nature."

Cedelair shifted in his chair. Winking from her eyes was the same spinning light that marred the gaze of his apprentice. It rubbed against a burning sore at his heart.

"You look as if your tea disagreed with you," Mennieve remarked. "You love tea, so that can't be it. Did some frightfully unpleasant mission bring you here?"

He rose to his feet, turning his thoughts back to his original purpose. "Why does anyone come to a bookshop?"

"Ah!" She clapped her hands together as she sprang up from her seat. "You're starting a new area of study! And here I thought you'd left no magical stone unturned. Unless of course you're dipping into fiction."

"Certainly not," he returned. He was already following her down the circuitous path through the stacks toward "his" shelf, stocked with all manner of books on sorcery from histories to how-to's. He swallowed a sigh as he considered how long she must have hoped he might stick his head in the door to ask if any new books had come in.

He had his reasons, good reasons, for staying away from town. Now he looked inside himself and found a black sludge, a sickly selfishness.

She patted the side of the shelf. "What might you be looking for?"

"Something on song-magic. Song-spells, songs of power, that sort of thing."

"Is that what young Valeraine's going in for? I approve."

"Not Valeraine," he corrected, thinking in the same breath that song-magic might indeed suit his apprentice. "I believe the 'stunning colossus' may be dabbling in it. Do you have such a book?"

Mennieve nodded, casting her gaze down the top row. "Here!" She pulled out a thick book with forest-green binding and passed it to him. The blazon on the front read *Musical Enchantments*. "That covers quite a lot. History as well as descriptions of spells."

"Precisely what I need. How much do you want for it?"

She patted his arm. "Cedelair, dear lad, I won't ask so much as half a roine for it if you promise you'll come to visit me again within the week. Bring the fair giantess with you and I'll let you have another book gratis, any you'd like."

"You'll lose money," he teased.

"I'll make it back on the latest Sir Arturo of Gedalia."

He winked at her. She chuckled and squeezed his arm. "I'll come back within the week," he assured her, "and I'll bring a potion for you that will give you rest without sleep."

Her eyes narrowed in a puzzled squint. "Why?"

"To keep the nightmares away."

"Rest without sleep?" She laughed. "Is that even possible?"

"It's impossible as magic always is," he pointed out. "For you I'd make miracles." He placed a hearty kiss on his old friend's cheek, then whispered low in her ear, "*A' zhiera' shiech.*" A prickle of aversion tightened his nerve-ends at the sound of the *Seventh Tongue*.

He glanced into her eyes to find the terrified blare had diminished. Reminding himself to thank his apprentice, he hugged

Mennieve in farewell and left the shop, his book tucked under his arm.

He started down the side-path with home already in view, thinking hard about what that mark in Valeraine's and Mennieve's eyes could mean. On the edge of his vision he saw people staring, leaning closer together as if he frightened them.

A chime tumbled down from the nearby hills. He turned toward it as if by compulsion. On a cliff-side just within view he saw the shape of the carillon wagon.

More notes slipped after the first, forming a bittersweet pattern. The song wound about his ears, a wishful plea, an attempt at hope. His heart shuddered as he recognized a minor-chorded version of the merry song Meliroc had played the night before. It swept over him, soft and warm as a spring shower, touching those strands in his heart he'd thought mired in foulness. A mist welled behind his eyes.

The ringing stopped. For an instant his heart held still, before he let loose a breath, flexed his shoulders, and started on his way once more, drumming his fingers against the book that would hopefully give him a clue what sort of power this carillon possessed. Questions knocked against each other in his head. At the center of every one stood that white marble golem.

***

Valeraine caught his coat sleeve and fell into step beside him. She cast a glance down at the snow-dusted pavement, which her master took as a sign that she had something vital to say but couldn't quite find words. He decided to help by sharing his news first. "I saw that mark of fear in Mennieve's eyes. That phrase you suggested seemed to help."

Still eyeing the side-path, the girl coughed. "You know Odilon's daughter Loliette?"

He nodded, recalling a tiny girl with chestnut locks and hazel eyes. She would be ten years old now.

"Today I went to buy some new phials at Odilon's side-shop. Loliette was sitting behind the counter, so still I didn't notice her at first. When she saw me she started to rock in her seat and mutter things like, 'She did it. All her fault. She's to blame.'"

"And naturally you had to learn what she meant," Cedelair remarked with a dry scowl.

"I had to try seeing past the scream, to the nightmare she forgot." Valeraine's cheeks pinkened, but still she met her master's glare. "I can show you what I found."

She breathed a phrase, quick as a snake's strike. By the time he realized what she'd done black clouds had blotted her from view. The faint outline of a vaguely female face flashed through the murk, flying straight toward him. The eyes, the one clear feature, blazed white with an expression of fathomless rage that made him quake. The hollow mouth opened to let out a monstrous shriek. In that instant, grief unlike any he'd known tore deep into his soul.

Then he was looking into Valeraine's face. "That's the cry I've been hearing," she informed him. "I told Loliette *a' zhiera' shiech*, and it calmed her a bit, but somehow I don't think that little spell will be so effective much longer."

"I see." Cedelair swallowed, a sting in his throat. "Do you still think some sort of magical curse is involved?"

"I'm almost certain, sir."

With a shudder he started a mental list of all the reasons why what she spoke of could only be some freakish coincidence. Yet however hard he tried to push it down, one idea kept bobbing to the surface of his thoughts. If Crainante were under a curse, he, Crainante's sorcerer, had a duty to save it.

Valeraine folded her arms and tucked her hands into the folds of her shawl. They plodded homeward in silence.

The sound of chimes reached them as they climbed over the hillock to the cottage. Meliroc knelt near the mouth of her tent, the bell-board at her knees, and Pierpon squatted beside her. After a moment's listening, Cedelair perceived they were playing a game. Meliroc would play a sequence of eight notes, arranged differently each time, and Pierpon, seizing the mallet with both hands, would play it back to her. She mixed up the rhythms to challenge him further, but each time he repeated the sequence, both notes and rhythms exact.

A gleeful light flashed in her eyes each time Pierpon succeeded. "Well done!" her mind-voice shouted. "I'll make a music lover of you yet!"

Cedelair swallowed a breath. Even last night when she'd drunk tea with him in the parlor, faint trails of dried tears on her cheeks, he'd failed to see her clearly – the fierce emerald eyes, the fey-delicate features, the fall of alabaster hair. Perhaps the radiant delight in her had cleared the clouds from his eyes. "Stunning colossus," he muttered under his breath, praying an instant later that Valeraine hadn't heard.

The moment Meliroc glanced upward to see the sorcerers, her happiness dimmed. She rested the mallet upon the planks, rose to her feet, and willow-walked toward them, her head slightly bowed.

"There is something I must tell you," she said.

7. Meliroc seeks an unfamiliar song

How I did not want to do it! I would rather have been gutted by a thousand tiny fish-hooks and have my head staved in with an andiron than contemplate it. But Feuval needed me. This strange new sense of being needed made me giddy and desperate. I could not shrink from any course that might aid him. I must – no, "must" wasn't the word. I *would* ask the sorcerers for help.

"I have work to do in my garden," Cedelair informed me, "but if you would accompany me there, you can tell me whatever you like." His beckon to me, his interested look, made him appear almost alien, as if Cedelair had vanished in town and a doppelganger had come home in his place.

He bade me wait while he changed into his work clothes, the closest he'd yet come to giving me a direct command. Very quickly the Cedelair I knew returned, with flinty frown and soil-brushed gray coat and pack slung over his shoulder. "Come," he said, with a wisp of a glance at me.

I followed him across the stone walkway, taking care to tread in his steps. When he stopped he half-turned toward me. "When I've finished my work, I will hear you."

He dropped to his knees, and with all due caution I followed his example. I watched him slide his fingers into the soil and draw the plants out by the roots with that same affectionate care I'd witnessed before. A father might look on his children as he gazed at these plants. Perhaps he saw them thus, since he nourished them with his own life-force. Did he apologize to them when he ground them up for potions?

A leaf brushed against my arm. For a moment I fancied a plant was trying to get my attention, and I turned toward it, smiling. The tall-stemmed emerald beauty bobbed in the breeze as if in greeting. My fingers itched to touch it. Cedelair would object, but he was deep in his ritual, barely aware of me. I rested my fingertips against the cap of leaves and envisioned a heart within it, and the flow of deep verdant blood.

With a twitch of his shoulders Cedelair turned, and I snatched my hand away from the plant. "That one is *imfaphia amorat*," he said, his look indecipherable. "The main ingredient in love philters. I've never used it, but it's handsome to look at."

From the corner of my eye I saw *imfaphia amorat* bow to me once more, a stately lord inviting me to dance. My heart-fire flickered at the sunlit gleam of its leaves.

"Well, Mistress Meliroc, what have you to say to me?" A note of curiosity tempered the usual chill of his voice.

My throat tightened to the strangling point. "Two nights ago I heard a song no one else could hear," I began. From there I unfolded my strange story, watching his face for signs of disbelief or ridicule. He heard every word without the slightest change in expression, save for a barely discernible flicker of eye.

"You need a song that would make the hardest heart weep, am I right?" At my nod, he went on, "As I understand it, you have quite a bit of experience with hard hearts."

I hadn't considered my memories of my old masters might help me in my task. Steeling myself with a breath, I thought of the worst of the lot, the fat little transmogrifier, always smiling, humming, bobbing happily when he walked, the most cheerful person I'd yet known. He'd brightened with special glee when commanding me to change shape. Be a shovel, Meliroc, to dig the dirt. Be a wheelbarrow, Meliroc, to carry a load of stones. Be a hearth-mat, Meliroc, for me to wipe my boots. I seethed through my clenched teeth.

I couldn't remember his face, but I could imagine it, round, ruddy-cheeked, with tiny blue eyes. What could make that merry face cloud with sorrow? I struggled to imagine his features creasing in grief, but they only beamed more mockingly. I envisioned a white hand squeezing his neck, fingernails digging into his flabby skin, and then his lips flapping, his eyes rolling backward. My heart-fire skipped eagerly at the fantasy, but it wasn't what I needed.

Cedelair's smile twitched. "I don't think I want to know what you were thinking about just then," he remarked, a hint of a chuckle in his voice.

"I can't think what would make them weep," I admitted.

"Did none of them have a family? A wife or a child?"

"No. I think the mind-rider may have been a widower. He kept a painting of a woman on his wall, but I never saw him look at it."

"What about friends? Apprentices?"

"No apprentices. No real friends either, that I could see."

He coughed. "Your 'must' has apparently sent you to a certain type of master. I'm not sure I care to consider what your presence here may say about me." He pulled at his chin. "I don't doubt you've known pain. But pain and sorrow are not the same. Try this. Think of something you love."

My bell-board sprang into my thoughts, the mallet dancing down the keys, the notes swirling and glimmering about me. "Music. My instrument."

"Good. What else?"

"Reading."

"What else?"

I cast a wide gaze around the garden. "Colors," I told him. "Green especially. If a Lifelord exists, that color is his signature."

Oddness blinked in his eye. I tried to recognize it, but it slipped out of reach, leaving me with a sense that I'd made some impression on him. "Is there anything else?" he prompted. "Some little something you take pleasure in?"

"Baths. A good hot bath with perfumed water."

His throat rippled as if he swallowed a laugh. "Think of all these things, Mistress Meliroc. Think hard. Let yourself feel your delight in them."

I half-closed my eyes and willed my fancy to do the work he bade. I set myself in a bath-tub full of hot water, steam rising from its surface, lavender scent teasing my nose while the music of my bell-board wove around me, my chrysalis glowing green – and visions played in my mind, shaped from books I'd read, full of places worth seeing and people worth knowing. A drunken smile tickled my lips.

"Now everything's gone," Cedelair announced. "The smell of the water, the sound of the chimes, all gone. Your senses are drowned in darkness."

I sank into the water. The bottom of the tub vanished, sending me plunging down, down. The silent blackness tightened about my neck.

"You will never rise from the dark," he went on, his voice icy, pitiless. "All that you have loved is lost to you. You'll never know it again."

His words fell like bricks on my chest, pushing me still further down.

Cool fingers brushed my brow. I cautiously opened my eyes to the sky, the white-yellow sun, Cedelair's craggy face. "You felt something heavy upon your heart, didn't you?" he said. "A weight that leaves a hollow behind?"

"Yes."

"That, my dear Mistress Meliroc, is the very tip of sorrow."

I gasped as my chest convulsed. He set his hand on the back of my neck to steady me. "It's all well and good to try to imagine yourself in this Master Feuval's shoes, to empathize with him, but you cannot understand sorrow until you've felt it yourself. For a real taste of it, one might go to the Lac d'Esprit-Triste."

The name danced off his tongue, and I caught it. "Sorrow spirit lake?"

He nodded, a winking flash behind that ever-present hardness of eye. I'd been wrong to think he had only one facial expression to his name, perhaps two on a fair day. "It's a local legend. Something we whisper about when we huddle by the hearth on stormy nights."

"Then there's no such place?"

"I don't say there is, and again, I don't say there isn't. I've heard about it all my life. We say it can be found in a clearing in the deepest valley of these hills. Sorrow herself lives at the bottom of that lake, and all passers-by can hear her keening."

I strove to see it in my mind's eye, a still, clear pond, the moon casting a poignant glow on its surface in sympathy with the haunt below. "How far is it – how far do they say it is from here?"

"A little under a day's walk," he replied. "Back at school we youngsters were always boasting we'd make the journey to find it. Then we'd meet someone who claimed he'd seen it, all shaking and wild-eyed and babbling about the voice he'd heard. He'd calm down a little, but thereafter he'd wander the side-paths with a look to break the heart. Anytime we saw someone with a look like that, we'd make a prayer-sign and say, 'He's been to Esprit-Triste.'"

A cold breath brushed my neck. A little under a day's walk to a place no one – no sane one – was sure even existed? I might lose two days or more wandering in no clear direction, only to return to my tent with nothing that might help Feuval. Yet my vision of the pond, even the ring of its very name, made me think a song waited there.

"I'll have to set off at first light," I mentioned, driving iron into my spine.

Cedelair shook his head. "Steady now, Mistress Meliroc. The place is a legend."

"But you think it exists, or you'd never have mentioned it. And if it does, my song could be there."

Shadows deepened in his eyes. For a troubling instant he looked almost gentle. "You'd stride right into a storm's path, wouldn't you, if it meant getting a song."

"If it meant getting that song," I amended.

"What answer would you have when Sorrow starts to speak to you? When her voice drives into your mind and heart? What music would you hear? Is the man in the wagon worth it?"

I felt a hand at my throat, but I held his gaze.

"There is one thing that might protect you. Those who went mad always ventured there alone. If someone accompanied you, you might withstand it."

I raised my hand to cover a grin. Thought-strings that had dangled in confusion suddenly knit themselves together. His mention of the Lac d'Esprit-Triste had been a calculated prompt. He wanted to go. He needed me. Oh, for a proper voice to laugh with!

"None of those maddened ones was a sorcerer," he added. "I may be just the protector you need."

"As you might feel safer with me along," I pointed out. "Perhaps Pierpon and Mistress Valeraine ought to come along, too. Safety in numbers." The thought of making the journey alone with Cedelair wilted my smile.

"Not bad thinking," he assented with a brief nod. "You're quite sure you want to risk this?"

I answered with a firm, steady nod, and the winking light flashed again in his eye. I shivered, curious. What attraction could the Lac d'Esprit-Triste have for him? Helping me was surely the least of his motives. I was on the verge of asking him outright when I heard him mutter, "Fortunate fellow, this Master Feuval."

"Fortunate how?"

"To have a friend in you."

I arched my neck and gave him a cool smile. "I can scarcely contain my wonder, Master Cedelair. It sounds as though you've come to think better of me."

"You have some merits I didn't expect." With a soft grunt he rose to his feet, slapping the dust from his long-coat. "Now that we've arrived at a plan, I have business inside. If you will, Mistress Meliroc." He gestured for me to rise and follow him. He was not going to leave me behind in his garden.

I did as he bade, shadowing him down the walkway and up to the back door. "You may come in if you like," he suggested as he opened the door.

"No, thank you, sir," I replied, drawing a step back. The close, cramped cottage held no allure for me. I wanted to walk upright under the winter sky. Without another word or gesture he stepped inside and closed the door.

A tremor started at the base of my spine, suspiciously like delight. I could not think what reason I had for such a feeling when an uphill march toward an uncertain destination lay ahead of me. I strode, swinging my arms, trying to think.

That Cedelair's good opinion might please me, that I might care for even half a minute what a sorcerer thought of me, simply did not bear consideration.

***

"I need your help."

Valeraine stood before Pierpon with head bowed, hands clasped at her waist, mouth wilted in a crushed-lily frown. He'd thought to be brusque with her for pulling him away from Meliroc, but unwonted compassion checked his annoyance. The vixen was so used to being sure about everything, or at least pretending she was, but now he sensed uncertainty bearing down upon her.

"I need you to help me remember something," she told him, a tremor at the corner of her lip.

"How could I do that? I've got no power, I don't, thanks to you."

She leaned toward him. "The *Seventh Tongue* can work both ways. I can invite you into my mind, to find out what I've forgotten. Then, once you know it, I can see it inside your thoughts."

"Assuming I agree," he grumbled.

"You'll want to see this. It's a nightmare."

He jolted. "Has some other jickety been after you? That's not fair, it's not!"

"I don't think it's a jickety's work. You might be able to tell me what is behind it. Nobody knows more about nightmares than you, after all."

Pierpon scratched at a curious itch at the back of his neck. What had made his valorous vixen shake? His blood heated. This could prove key to his victory, his home-going, and she was handing it to him!

"How does it work?" he asked her, stretching his spine.

"Very simple." She leaned closer, eyes wide. "Look steadily into my eyes. Concentrate on what you see there."

After a nod Pierpon locked his gaze with Valeraine's. She had remarkably pretty eyes, he had to admit, a lustrous azure. Had she not been a sorcerer dozens of beaux might have trailed in her wake.

In a low voice she murmured a phrase he could not understand. Cool invisible fingers folded about his mind and drew him with gentle swiftness into the shadows of the eyes before him. Those shadows swirled close about him like the walls of a tunnel, a pale glow in the distance.

The glow shot forward, swallowing him.

He – she – was tucked in bed, her flanncloth nightshirt scratching at her neck. With a heavy blink she took note of her surroundings. Her bed hovered five feet above the ground, and the outdoor scents of snow and bark made her nose itch. A wall of smoke blocked the moon and stars. She shivered at what sounded at first like a rumble of thunder, but after an instant grew into a cyclone's roar.

Then came a scream that shook the sky. Every sorrow great and small, miseries present and past and future, combined in that sound. Its anguish lacerated her.

A whirring skitter tapped the edge of her half-paralyzed consciousness. As it grew louder the bed began to spin. A tiny figure climbed over the edge of the mattress, man-shaped but only two inches high, clad in a red smock and trousers and a bright yellow conical hat. His white beard reached his knees.

Gold-cap. Her mind formed the word, but she could not move her lips to speak. The wizened manikin sneered at her with a hissing cackle. He waved his arm, and at once a horde of the things swarmed over the edge of the bed. Onto her they climbed, pinching, jabbing, swatting, winding themselves into her hair and pulling with all their might. "Moon-weaver, moon-weaver!" they gibbered. "We've got you, we've got you!"

"We'll pay you out for your meddling!" squeaked one.

"We'll pay you out for your pride!" piped another.

"What shall we do, oh, what shall we do with you?" the horde chorused.

The wrinkled fellow who'd led the charge hopped through the crowd and perched on the crown of her head. At his motion the other gold-caps fell silent. He stretched himself up and lolled out in a squeak fat with importance, "For the moon-weaver's crimes against our brotherhood, I sentence her to die alive!"

"Die alive!" the throng sang out in unison.

The bed tilted, and Valeraine slid feet first from the mattress. The gold-caps held her fast in mid-air, while the leader, still perched atop her head, snapped his fingers and ignited a candle glow to clear the smoke. The walls of a stable surrounded her.

The gold-cap leader tumbled from her head to her shoulder. "Here's how it will be," he told her. "First, we're going to slice your throat. Then we'll skin you. After that we'll flay you clean and eat your flesh raw. Then we'll sport with your bones."

"I'll be past caring at that point." How she found her voice she could not think.

The gold-cap leader howled in derision. "No, you won't," he cried, "because you'll have to watch!" He leaped from her shoulder to hover in the air. "Comrades," he commanded, "remove her soul!"

Their needle-fingers tore her out of her flesh like a strip of cloth. A small detachment flew with her to the stable loft, where a nail protruded from a plank. There they hung her, and there she dangled like an old coat, while a few feet away the other gold-caps stabbed and pulled at her paralyzed body.

"Throw her down!" the leader called, and they cast her body to the floor. She felt the force of the fall. On her hook she wriggled in pain. The eyes of her body stared up at the ceiling, wide but vacant.

From his smock the leader drew a knife three times his size. Swish! In a flicker the body's throat was cut. Blood gushed from the wound, and the head sagged to the side, hair falling over the senseless face. Above, the soul Valeraine writhed from the blade's sting.

She was dead now. Beyond pain.

The instant they began to strip the skin she found herself mistaken. Every scrape and peel reached her as harrowing agony. She twisted and screamed on her hook, desperate to free herself and fly – where? She could not return to a pile of bones. She could only raise a dismal moan as the gold-caps played nine-pins with her leg bones and beat wild rhythms on her rib cage. "Take care you don't break anything!" their leader called out. She wondered why it mattered.

"All right, that's enough," he declared at last. "Gather the bones!"

The creatures did his bidding with a whirr of protest.

"Arrange them properly!"

In the center of the carpet of skin they assembled the bones into a crude skeleton-shaped heap. Over this they draped the loose skin like a quilt. She shuddered at the sight of this rag-doll Valeraine while the gold-caps whistled and danced in a circle around it.

"Now!" the leader cried, drawing a switch from his smock and striking the heap of skin and bones.

She felt a racking jolt as the heap sprang upright, the bones rejoined, the skin sealed over them. It stood on its feet and turned its head, yet the eyes stared ahead at nothing, no spark of thought behind their glassy blankness. The gold-caps jeered in sing-song, tugging at the hem of her night-smock.

"Those who cross us never thrive!

She's skin and bone! She's dead alive!"

The thing trudged forward. In the stumbling gait and the empty stare, the soul on her hook found more dread than in *all the strokes of the daggers. She let out a cry that rocked the stable walls.*

Pierpon doubled forward as the dream released him. Valeraine closed her eyes. His thoughts were his own again. Yet still the sting of the knives lingered, sickening him. His head shook with that dreadful scream. Tales from his childhood stirred in his memory. An old enemy of his people, a fiend with a vile scream. What was it called?

Valeraine forced herself to meet Pierpon's stare. She breathed another smoky phrase then stiffened as if receiving a blow. Her lips shivered as if she were on the verge of tears. "I always knew they hated me," she mumbled, a quaver in her voice. "I couldn't have guessed how much."

With an awkward tug at his heart, he rested his hand on hers.

She choked. "Is it a spell?"

"Yes," he answered, fighting down a grimace.

"You're certain?"

He nodded. "This is not a jickety's work, it's not. Any of our nightmares would have let you go before you felt that sort of pain. For us, fear's only a means to an end, and we never cause pain. Yet something was in your dream with you, a wicked thing that likes suffering. We need to find out, we do, where that scream comes from." He clenched his fists till his fingernails bit his palms. "Dreams are sacred," he growled, a wolf awakened. "Anyone who would meddle in dreams like this should be whipped and hanged and chopped into bits!"

Her neck rippled as she swallowed. "Even if it's our lovely giant?"

His blood simmered, ready to boil, but he kept his voice soft. "Meliroc? A thing like this would never enter her mind. She's decent, she is."

Valeraine regarded him with a firm stare. "How much do you really know about her?" she asked him. "How is it you're so attached to her?"

"She saved my life."

"I know that, but"–

"She held me here, she did, in her palm." He traced the groove at the center of his hand. "Once she'd warmed me back to my senses, she turned a fistful of snow into a pool of hot water for me to drink. She smiled as she watched me, happy to see how I'd recovered. She has kindness in her very fingers, Valeraine. Maybe I don't know very much about her, but I know she's good."

His shivering calmed. His story had taken him back to that meeting, to the soothing warm water in the snow-white palm and that concerned, curious smile on the face above him. His conviction deepened, a firm and girding force. He loved Meliroc, and he would defend her with all his strength against unjust accusations.

Yet his anger with Valeraine dwindled. Considering what she'd suffered, he couldn't blame her too much for her unclear thinking. She wasn't such a bad lot, his vixen. She didn't deserve what this something-or-other was putting her through.

He rested a hand on her arm. "We'll find out who's doing this," he assured her. "You'll see for yourself, you will, that it isn't Meliroc."

***

I would not go inside until I was called for. I immersed myself in Valeraine's hero book. The fearless protagonist lived a life unencumbered, of will rather than must. I could not choose but dream myself into the armor of the woman with a sword at her hip and a quiver of arrows and crossbow at her back who took on monsters of all shapes, sizes, and appetites and won the worshipful gratitude of innumerable people in countless towns. Brave Bennelise of the Thousand Friends.

I had read past its halfway point when Pierpon fetched me inside. "So Cedelair says he'll help you," he remarked as I carried him to the door. "He and Valeraine were talking about it. We're going to visit some lake spree something."

"Esprit-Triste," I corrected him. "Lac d'Esprit-Triste. The home of Sorrow herself."

The pixy-man wrinkled his nose. "Sounds delightful."

"Mysterious, rather," I corrected. "So mysterious that no one's absolutely sure it exists. If we can find it and meet the Spirit head-on we'll come back with a tale that will have people singing our names down the generations."

"Now you sound like Vixen Valeraine, you do," he remarked with a chuckle.

"So what if I do, I do?" I threw the door open and strode inside. Even with my neck cricked I imagined I stepped with Brave Bennelise's martial swagger.

Nightmare Lullaby

Cedelair and Valeraine conversed in one of their secret tongues. As soon as they saw Pierpon and me they slipped into plain-talk without dropping a beat of their discussion. "– lose no time getting this medicine to as many as we can," Valeraine was saying. "This is urgent, sir. Ah! Meliroc, come here. Please boil this potion for us." She gestured to a fat black pot hanging over the fire. Despite the please and the mild voice, her eyes were full of command.

Drawing my heart-fire up from my chest, I gripped the rim of the pot, taking half a glance down at the green-black sludge inside.

"It's an anti-sleep draught," she explained, "for friends of ours who are having nightmares."

Nightmares. Like the dreams I never remembered, that I woke from with raw throat and red eyes and tear-soaked face.

"Do you remember when you said all the people in town were frightened? Something in their eyes?"

A strange, ghost-ridden light... I nodded, again seeing my favorite of the people I'd met in town, the little woman with the checkered dark blue dress and round, kindly face. Mennieve. What could frighten that good lady so? I squinted at a pang at my temple. My mind was struggling to snatch something free of the murk in my memory, something about that light.

"It comes from dreams we've all been having," she explained. "You can see it in my eyes, I know. Pierpon doesn't have it because he doesn't dream, and Master Cedelair doesn't have it because he doesn't sleep."

I glanced from Valeraine to Cedelair and noted the heavy shadows in his eyes, the sign of weariness. I felt vaguely sorry for him.

Valeraine's face brightened with a new idea. "You said you saw that fear worst in Mennieve's eyes, right? So you could tell if some are afflicted worse than others."

"I believe I could," I assented, with that twinge in my head.

"There's our answer," proclaimed the young sorcerer. "First thing tomorrow morning, sir, Meliroc comes with us into town. She can point out who is suffering worst. We give the medicine to those who need it most."

"I thought we were going to the Lake Spree-something," Pierpon put in, with a look that suggested he was far from unhappy with the change of plans.

"This must come first," Valeraine insisted. "It's more important. You see, don't you, Meliroc?" She clutched my elbow. "Help us with this, and as soon as we're finished we'll set off for the Lac d'Esprit-Triste. My moon-spindle will light our way." For an instant I envisioned her in an armored breastplate, with a sword at her hip.

Brave Bennelise of the Thousand Friends, loved because she had saved so many. "I will help you gladly," I told Valeraine. "My errand can wait."

"That would suit," admitted Cedelair, with a measured nod. "We stop at the bookshop first, since we know it goes especially hard with Mennieve." He cast a slight smile my way. "She's quite curious about you, Mistress Meliroc. She asked specifically for me to bring you by for a visit."

Again I remembered the round, gentle face, the warm voice, the touch. Lady Meliroc, she'd called me. I did want to see her again, in her house full of books. I wanted to see Cedelair give her a potion I'd boiled for him to put out the horrible ghost-light.

A shivery tingle swept through me while I watched the froth in the pot begin to bubble. Me-di-cines! This was what they did, Cedelair with his garden and his cauldrons, Valeraine with her basketful of little bottles. They mixed healing for their neighbors. They mended the rips and frays in the health of their town. Never had my other masters done such things. I considered Cedelair's idea that my must was guiding me toward a certain type. If this was so, why had it led me here, to him and Valeraine?

I laid the question aside and helped them ladle the potion into phials. This tingle, this sensation of sharing in work to be proud of, was settling into my skin. I would enjoy it as long as I could.

8. The sorcerers dole out comfort

To fire sturdiness into his back and pride into his shoulders as he marched toward town, Cedelair drew on the comfort of a sense of duty done, solid and stone-strong. However the townsfolk regarded him, he was bringing them relief. He would not let himself think "for a little while." He still clung for dear life to his "freakish coincidence" theory, even though Pierpon had backed Valeraine. The thought of malign magic aimed against his town brought only one face to mind. Such a forgettable face, with such venom lurking beyond it! His nerves would fray if he dwelled on that memory.

Tearlac could never return. He'd seen to that.

He pulled the bell at the door of Fimbre's Books and heard q"uick footsteps beyond it. The door flew open, and Mennieve stood before him, smiling, weary strain in her eyes. She had not even tried to sleep.

Her eyes widened as she looked from Cedelair to Valeraine to Meliroc. "Oh!" she gasped with a quiver of glee. "Come in, friends, come in!" She squeezed Cedelair's hand, then Valeraine's, and then bobbed a beaming curtsey before Meliroc.

"I have the kettle ready and waiting," she told them, stepping back from the doorway. "Do join me in a cup of coffee." She watched with a curious eye as first Cedelair, then Valeraine passed through the door, and then Meliroc, taking quick measure of the doorway's dimensions, ducked in after them. The bookseller's gaze drank in her towering guest, her mouth gaping in a fascinated grin.

Meliroc walked stoop-shouldered after Mennieve, smiling in awe at the abundance of books. "Have you read all these?" she asked. A second later her smile stiffened as she remembered that Mennieve couldn't hear her.

"Our friend asks if you've read all these books," Cedelair told Mennieve.

Mennieve stopped and turned with a blink. "Pardon?"

"She is mute," he explained, "but she can speak with her mind so that we sorcerers can hear her. If she doesn't object, I can tell you what she says."

As Mennieve gave another delighted gasp, Meliroc tilted her head at Cedelair. "How will she know you're not putting words in my head?"

He relayed in the dry tone of the thought-voice, "How will she know you're not putting words in my head?'"

Mennieve grinned. "It's quite simple, lady Meliroc," she replied. "That didn't sound at all like Cedelair."

With a chuckle of a smile, Meliroc nodded to Cedelair – her permission for him to speak for her.

"As to your question," Mennieve said, "I read as many of them as I can, but I could never read them all in a lifetime. Just as well, for I never have to fear running out of things to read." She ushered the three into her tiny parlor and watched keenly as Meliroc knelt on the floor.

"So you have your elixir for me?" the bookseller said as she handed Cedelair his cup. "How am I to take it?"

"Two drops at night. This bottle should last you a week." He drew a phial from his coat pocket and set it on the nearby counter.

"A week!" Mennieve handed a teacup to Valeraine. "I could take it for that long?"

"I've taken it for longer," Cedelair admitted, "though I wouldn't recommend that. It's best to use caution with such things." He frowned, his heart going into a slow, steady sink. When the week was done and Mennieve slept again, would that monstrous scream be lying in wait? No! A coincidence, whatever Pierpon said, whatever Valeraine thought.

Mennieve again turned her smile full of wonder on Meliroc. She passed a cup into her hands, and then with a cautious finger brushed her chin. "How did you guess I like to read?" Meliroc asked.

"It's my business to spot readers," Mennieve explained after Cedelair spoke the question. "I can even make a good guess at the sort of books they like. Let me see..." She took Meliroc's chin in her hand. "You like histories, don't you? Encyclopedias, too. You like to gather facts. And yet there's such fancy about you."

"Lately I've discovered a liking for adventure books as well," Meliroc mentioned, with a glance toward Valeraine.

"Oh ho," Mennieve hummed. "Mistress Valeraine's influence, I see. Still, an adventure book or two won't do you any harm. The more sorts of books one likes, the better, I think."

Valeraine shot Cedelair a "so there" look, rose from her seat, and backed toward the door with a farewell curtsey to Mennieve. "Odilon's daughter needs one of these," she explained, patting the side of her basket. "I want to get to his shop as soon as he opens." The doorbell jangled as she swept out of the store.

Mennieve's smile grew wistful. "She has a bright spirit," she mumbled. Turning to Cedelair, she let out a long, low sigh. "It worries me..."

He tried to smile. "What, that I'm not nice enough to Valeraine?"

"Of course not. Under all your quills you're a good-hearted porcupine. I can speak frankly before you, can't I, dear lad?"

"I'd be sad if you didn't," he assured her.

"You should know," she told him with a tense sigh. "Your visit yesterday stirred some talk. Some people – not many, mind you, but some – are saying it's a sign we have some dark spell sitting on our necks. I told them you just wanted to buy a book, but who listens to me these days?"

He rested a hand on her arm. He fancied the scent of dark workings stinging his nose, like fruit burning to foulness in the sun. "Do you feel I should investigate, Mennieve? Do you sense bad magic when you sleep?"

"It has crossed my mind," Mennieve admitted.

With churning stomach Cedelair sharpened half an eye on Meliroc. As much as he loathed the Seventh Tongue, he needed to see past that face, if only for an instant. Let Mennieve speak just a little more about her troubles... His lips formed words so cautiously that his old friend might not notice.

"You know I'm no stranger to nightmares," she said, "but they've always been much the same. About Fimbre, about Rybert."

A tiny part of himself split off from the rest to slip through the window that divided his consciousness from Meliroc's, to see and feel with her. She took in the names Mennieve spoke and wondered with a press of sympathy who they were.

"But this is something else." Mennieve's voice sank into a solemn low. "I can't remember it. I feel its horror, but I might feel better if I could only remember."

Like my own dreams, Meliroc was thinking with a stabbing ache. Some dark thing always chasing, never catching. She doesn't deserve that.

"Instead all I recall is that awful shriek," said. "It drives a shiver into my bones whenever I think of it. But it doesn't make sense!" She gripped Cedelair's hand. "Bad magic? Who would do this? Why?"

There is no why with a sorcerer, thought Meliroc, anger burning in her blood. They play their games at the expense of others whose feelings mean nothing to them. Her blazing eyes suddenly locked with Cedelair's. With a quick breath he retreated from her thoughts.

"I can't believe that anyone would do such a thing deliberately," Mennieve affirmed. "I can only put it down to some terrible quirk of fate."

The words dropped a weight on his chest. The very thing he most wanted to believe rang hollow and false in his ears. "We'll help. We'll do all we can."

Mennieve patted his cheek. "I know you will, dear lad." Her smile came back. "Rest without sleep. That should be interesting! But you must let me pay you."

"You need not -"

"Nonsense! I owe you a book. I told you, any one you like." She entered the store with a brisk step, glancing over her shoulder to be sure Cedelair was following her.

"I don't have time to choose a book," he said. "We're very busy today. We need to distribute our medicines."

She bobbed her head. "Then let me choose one for you. Perhaps something your guest will enjoy! Yes, I know the very one." She strode purposefully through the maze of shelves, Cedelair at her heels, until she homed her gaze on one binding among the many, an indigo blue. "Ah!" With a smack of satisfaction she drew the book from the shelf – *Love Poetry of Ancient Farienne*. "She'll like those. Trust me."

Without further word on the matter, she darted back to the little parlor, humming under her breath. Cedelair tucked the book under his arm and followed.

Meliroc had unstrapped her bell-board and mallet from her back, and was now checking the tone of each chime. The sorcerer listened with half-open mouth, wondering at the resonant notes that plain-looking contraption could raise. *Kho-laeth.* He'd discovered the word while poring over his new book last night. He fancied the white giant fading into transparency as she played the scale's last note. With a tightening at his heart he told himself he really ought to warn her. Yet he wanted to hear her play.

"How cunning!" Mennieve cried, beaming down at the instrument. "Cedelair mentioned you were a musician."

Meliroc favored the bookseller with a steady gaze. Her eyes, so fierce with hate only a minute ago, now radiated compassion. "I have a song you should hear. Something for you to hum to yourself when you start to think of that horrible shriek."

Cedelair smiled as he spoke her words. He could guess what was coming. His mind began to play the song she'd shared with the carillon-man even before she struck the first note. By the time the tune was finished, its merriment glowed in Mennieve's eyes. In that instant she looked as young as Valeraine. She leaned forward to place a hearty kiss on Meliroc's cheek.

"I'll sing that tune to myself every day," she proclaimed. "I'll whistle it to everyone who comes calling and tell them all about the lovely being who taught it to me."

Meliroc's gaze suddenly clouded. A second later she returned Mennieve's kiss.

"We'd best go, Mistress Meliroc," Cedelair muttered, glancing at the floor.

The giant packed away her instrument and rose to her feet. With a regretful sigh Mennieve led them to the door, then stepped with them over the doorsill and onto the side-path. The square had fully awakened, the sun gleaming down on the frosty cobbled streets, the curtains drawn from the shop windows, the black tarpaulins pulled from the stalls to reveal apples and winter cherries and scarlet-dyed paper flowers, and buyers and sellers milling and muttering. Cedelair saw them notice him, and nudge and whisper to each other as they had yesterday, though they stared with eyes a little wider, cheeks a little paler. Of course. Meliroc was with him.

Mennieve squeezed her strange guest's hand. "Please come again soon, lady Meliroc," she urged warmly, "and bring your music. Best of luck in your work, dear lad." After a chuck at Cedelair's shoulder, she bobbed and bustled back into her store.

Cedelair breathed through a tight throat, frowning at the cobbles under his feet. "That was a good thing you did just now, playing your song for Mennieve. A good and generous thing." His eyes rose slowly to Meliroc's face.

But he found no softness there, only cold-burning indignation. "Have you anything to ask me, sir?"

"No."

"You seemed to want to know something," she countered. "Ask me now, then, out in the open. You needn't go sniffing about in my mind. I've nothing to hide."

At this he had to snicker. "Truly, Mistress Meliroc, that must be the most amusing thing I've heard in years. You have everything to hide. You are the most hidden being I've ever seen or read or dreamed of. You're even hidden from yourself."

He felt her snap – her jaw lock, her spine stretch, her body turn itself into a broken-off shout. The hate-light flashed dimly behind a cloud of sadness in her eyes. "What did you expect to find when you looked inside me?"

Whether you might have had a hand in giving people nightmares. She was the most likely suspect, assuming he accepted Valeraine's theory. Yet he'd seen nothing in her but grief for Mennieve and rage at whatever would harm her. She had comforted the bookseller the only way she could.

He needed to answer her, and could find only a crooked half-truth. "I wanted to know what you thought about this nightmare trouble."

"What did you imagine I would think?"

"I wasn't sure. That's why I looked. How you reacted would show me what sort of heart you have. Yours, it seems, is aptly large."

"Anyone with a scrap of decency would care about that woman's suffering," she said. "You can learn about me as an ordinary man would, even if I am 'hidden'. You don't need to resort to sorcery."

"Is a bit of mind-sniffing among the worst indignities you've had to endure?"

"Far from it, sir. But I was beginning to expect better of you."

The glint in her eyes, not hate but somehow worse, forced him to look away. The people on the opposite side-path gawked as they ambled past him. They must think him half mad, to argue so with a creature who couldn't speak. They couldn't know how eloquent she was in that voice only a few could hear.

"We need to get on with our work," he mumbled. "We need to find Valeraine."

***

The glassworks loomed over the square, a bulky brick ogre belching thick gray smoke. Five side-shops stood in its shadow. The one preferred by Valorous Valeraine stood at the northern-most corner, a small brownstone hut with wide windows for showing off glassware. Gem-like rods dangled from a string over the eastern window, so that light from the rising sun would carpet the floor with a glimmering rainbow. When Valeraine stood at the rainbow's center, she could absorb its magic and feel her limbs swell with strength.

Odilon had been journeyman to Xuot Nimbletouch, Cedelair's glass-master father, and had been friendly with Cedelair in the old days. For her he always had a smile and a friendly word. Yet today he had only a chilly glance down his long, thin nose. "It's you again, is it, young Valeraine? Already used up yesterday's bottles?"

Valeraine, approaching the counter, glanced into the shadows of the back wall in search of little Loliette. She found her perched on a stool in the corner, hunched and still in her wrinkled sienna dress, her lips red and raw from gnawing. If ever innocent sufferer needed a hero's assistance, it was this child.

"I haven't come to buy, Master Odilon," the young sorcerer explained in the mild, soothing voice this situation called for. "I've brought this." She drew out one of the phials of wakefulness potion. "It wards off sleep, but with a difference. Your body gets the rest it needs. For Loliette, if she pleases." She set the phial on the counter with an expectant glance at the child.

"Hm." He beckoned to Loliette. "Lolly, dear, look here." As she ambled from her stool, he held the sea-green bottle before her unblinking eyes. Valeraine winced to see those eyes' natural color all but obliterated by that whirling light. A demon stood at the center of that light, waiting for a hero's sword to strike it down.

"*A' zhiera' sheich,*" Valeraine whispered. The nightmare light flickered, yet spun on.

Loliette's throat convulsed in a guttural growl. "All her fault."

Valeraine leaned cautiously toward the little girl. "It gives you respite," she told her. "Two drops at night, and the scary things won't come near you."

Loliette bared her teeth. "She – she – she..." Crimson heat rushed to her face. "She did it!"

Jagged half-bitten fingernails raked Valeraine's face, leaving a lacerating sting. She stumbled as her head reeled with shock and pain. "I do apologize, young Valeraine, but you'd best leave now," Odilon declared, throwing a protective arm over his daughter's shoulders.

Fighting to gain her breath again, she teetered to the door and stumbled over the threshold onto the side-path. When she touched her cheek, blood dampened her fingers. Her spirit doubled over in hurt confusion. She searched her memory for some helpful example from her mentor, Brave Bennelise, but in vain. What could any hero do in the face of a blow from a child?

It took less than a minute for the people on the side-paths to notice her. Their stares pelted her. Their gasps and muttering slapped her ears. She pointed her chin toward the sky and marched forward, all business, her face cast in iron. No one must glimpse past this mask – not these folk she had come to aid, not Master Cedelair, and certainly not the resentful giant.

Her master bolted toward her and clasped her shoulders. "What happened?" he asked in a panicked whisper.

"I can't say," she told him under her breath. "Not now."

Warmth swept over her as Mighty Meliroc, the geas-bound, drew near. Valeraine inched away from her. Better to feel the cold winter wind than the cold satisfaction in a pair of green eyes. "Me-di-cines!" she bellowed with all her strength, offering relief from headache, belly-ache, double-vision, and over-sensitive teeth. She would speak of the sleep cure only to the people Meliroc indicated.

"That one in the wine-colored gown." The mind-voice came low and soft. Valeraine ventured a quick upward glance from the corner of her eye and saw the giant nod toward Andranette. The spindly vegetable-seller was limping across the street with a scowl. Valeraine dipped her hand into the basket and closed her fingers around the elixir that would soothe inflamed knee joints.

"Cure for my knee, if you please, young mistress," Andranette requested with a twitching frown. "Gracing us with your wise presence again, I see, Master Cedelair."

Valeraine flinched at the woman's rude tone, but her master only nodded.

"Get into a fight, young mistress?" the brusque woman inquired as she handed over her coin.

Drawing out a bottle of the anti-sleep draught, Valeraine shrugged. Andranette and many others would hear her shameful story soon enough, but not from her lips. She leaned toward Andranette and lowered her voice to a whisper. "This is a new medicine." She pressed the phial into the vegetable-seller's palm. "To prevent nightmares."

Andranette sniffed. "Who said I was having nightmares?" she snapped, a bit too loudly for Valeraine's comfort.

"Nearly everyone has nightmares once in a while," the young sorcerer returned, straining at calm. "Two drops will do the trick. Keep it til you need it."

Snatching up both phials, Andranette pivoted on her heel and stomped away. "The ones who need the most help may be the least civil," Meliroc observed.

At last Valeraine met her eyes and found tension in them, as if her mind were straining after something. "Thank you for helping us, Meliroc," she murmured.

"I serve you." Meliroc cast another nod down the side-path. "That one. The one sniffing into his handkerchief."

Valeraine set her mouth in a sympathetic smile as she prepared to meet with another special customer. Orqual the candle-maker did not ask about the scratches on her face, but he stared so fixedly at them that her stomach squeezed in disquiet. With half-closed eyes she called up Brave Bennelise's stern face and drank in her strengthening mantra. *Healer and comforter. I will not yield.*

So the morning's routine set in. "That little round fellow with the tuft of white hair at the top of his head." Coviet the bone-setter took the sleep cure with a mumbled thank-you and paused long enough to shake Cedelair's hand. "That one, with the scarlet waistcoat and the silver cravat." Sundiffe the counting-man nodded as he claimed his curative, his gaze darting right and left and down. "That one, with the freckles and the bonnet with the gold ribbon." Vociette the weaver smiled through a teary mist and stammered out her thanks. "That one, with the thick gray coat with the big yellow buttons." Embe the journeyman potter scowled and spat on the ground.

To each one Valeraine whispered her benediction. *"A' zhiera' sheich."* The whirling nightmare light did not abate as distinctly as it had yesterday. The scream was growing too loud to fit in the back of their minds.

"Medicines! Me-di-cines!" The mimicry fired a dart of ice into Valeraine's back. Acelin the butcher's apprentice strode toward her, his handsome features dripping with acid scorn. "Come get your venom-in-a-bottle!" the boy sneered in a hateful falsetto. "What are you selling today, little poison-snake?"

Valeraine's face burned. Poison-snake. From her predestined sweetheart.

Cedelair the Stern drew a half-step toward Acelin. "Leave us," he commanded, "and do not let us see your face again until you're ready to apologize."

In the very same instant as "apologize," Meliroc said, "That one."

Valeraine tightened her trembling fingers around a bottle of anti-sleep draught. "I have something for you. To keep the bad dreams away."

"Hmph! The only bad dream is you," Acelin snapped.

"I said leave us, young man!" thundered Cedelair.

"It's not his fault," Valeraine insisted, as much to herself as to her master. She was fated to love this lad, and she would help him whether or not he wished it. She held the bottle toward him. "Take this. Two drops at night. Your body will rest, but your mind won't dream."

Acelin snatched the phial and held it up with a sniff of appraisal. Valeraine rubbed at a mist in her eyes. The boy's glare told her all too clearly what she was to him – a thing of horror. Unless he could be brought to trust her, he wouldn't take the medicine. Forcing herself to meet his bitterness headlong, she called into her mind the Seventh Tongue phrase she needed. *"E' shorsha' vardai."* I am your friend. The first syllable slipped through her barely moving lips.

"What are you doing?" He jerked his head in outrage. "Hoodoo me, will you?" He dashed the phial to the pavement and ground the shards under his heel, spreading the elixir over the stones in a sick-green stain. "That's what I think of you and your poison!"

Before she could snatch a shocked breath he closed the gap between them and landed a slap in the very spot Loliette had marked. She reeled backward into Cedelair's arms, tears welling from the throb in her cheekbone, but she seized the image of Brave Bennelise and drew herself upright, her whole body clenched. Heroes knew how to answer blows. She might be powerless to retaliate against little Loliette, but Acelin would not find her hands so tied. Curses swarmed like hornets in her pounding head. Make him scratch at itches that would never soothe. Make him hear disembodied voices crying at him from all sides. Make him glimpse a hideous reflection in every mirror he passed. Yes, that would be a fitting riposte. The words of the curse boiled in her throat.

The first word was nearly out when a white lightning-bolt darted between her and her foe. Choking, she saw Meliroc the Miraculous seize the boy by the powder-blue neckerchief, haul him off his feet, give him a single firm shake, and hurl him ten feet down the side-path.

Valeraine glanced about to find every eye in the square turned toward them, every face blanched with shock.

Cedelair advanced on Acelin, who lay sprawled on the pavement. "Mistress Meliroc looks after us now," he announced with a nod toward the giant.

Acelin scrambled to his feet and took off at a run, not slowing down until he had hurled himself over the doorsill of the butcher's shop and shut the door behind him with a ringing slam. Valeraine blinked. Her eyes were drying. Her memory called up Acelin's face as she'd first seen it, the sparkling eyes, the smooth, sleek features – all hiding a black-souled bully. Her old infatuation lay lifeless as lead. Had she really almost cast a curse on him, to her own shame and her master's? She could still feel those bitter words on her tongue.

She squeezed Meliroc's hand with a fervent, shaking "Thank you."

The white lips curled in a faint smile. "I serve you."

Valeraine the Victorious arched her neck and called out, "Me-di-cines!" once more. Cedelair took her arm, and Meliroc resumed her watchful stance behind them.

But no one approached them for the rest of the morning.

***

When their work was done, they bent their steps toward the hiding-place of the Lac d'Esprit-Triste and the mystery that had fascinated Cedelair throughout his childhood. He gazed at the silver-white hills with the tingling hunger of those youthful days. Once he found the lake, no more would people whisper its name with a shiver of dread.

Sorrow might sing away that black sludge clinging to his heart.

Yet a gnawing worry tempered his eagerness. Valeraine unfolded her story as soon as they had gone a safe distance from town. Odilon's daughter had scratched her face. The child had glared at her with such terror that in that moment she had felt herself a monster. "When word spreads, they'll think the worst of me," she concluded, with a discomfited frown. "Add to that the business with Acelin. They'll talk and talk and talk, and every word will make them more afraid of us."

Cedelair could only scowl and nod, for she was right. The Acelin incident would be hashed over for weeks to come. Too many people would forget that Acelin had provoked Meliroc by striking Valeraine, and remember only that Acelin was small and Meliroc big. In quarrels between little men and giants, who sided with the giants?

"I know we're not here to be loved," Valeraine shrugged. "But I don't see how we can help them if they trust us so little."

He winced at a memory of twelve-year-old Valeraine just arrived in Crainante telling her new master of her ambitions. She would find a town to serve, and the people there would regard her as a friend. New mothers would call upon her to shield their infants from the dark imps that might make them ill. At funerals she would speak the spell that prevented demons from waylaying the spirit on its journey to the Land of Light. She would cure blighted crops, purify foul wells, sing songs of power to bless each harvest. She would involve herself in birth and death and everything in between. Everyone would trust her. The Sociable Sorcerer. His own old hopes and dreams on her naive lips.

"You're not here to be loved," he'd rebuked her. "Nobody loves a sorcerer." Was she learning the lesson at last? He felt no satisfaction, only a queasy chill.

At the foot of the hills they stopped, and Valeraine unpacked a lunch of cheese and apples and spread a taupe wool blanket over the snowy ground. Pierpon tumbled from his hiding place in Meliroc's cloak-hood to snatch up a wedge of cheese and gobble it down. Valeraine chuckled, as usual, to see the tiny man eat so voraciously. But Meliroc did not swallow a morsel. She moved to the blanket's far corner, unstrapped her bell-board and mallet and sank to her knees. Setting the instrument upon her lap, she played with a light, soft touch. The tone of the notes matched her crestfallen frown.

Hoisting another cheese wedge onto his back, Pierpon skipped over to her and plopped down beside her. He fixed a sympathetic gaze on the mallet's abstracted dance over the keys. Clearly he could tell, as Cedelair could, that some trouble preyed on Meliroc's mind, and she was playing it out on her bell-board.

Valeraine had unpacked an ointment from the medicine-basket and was quietly applying it to the scratches on her face. After patting her shoulder, Cedelair stretched himself to his feet and approached Meliroc. She glanced at him but did not pause in her playing. "I like your friend," she told him with a melancholy smile.

"Mennieve is a dear woman," he agreed, sinking down to sit opposite her.

"She's an old friend, isn't she? A friend of your childhood?" At his nod, she continued, "You're to be envied, growing up under the wings of someone like that."

"Is anything the matter, Mistress Meliroc?" He leaned toward her. "I hope you're not upset about that business with the butcher's boy. Believe me, you've no cause to feel ashamed or even embarrassed."

She shook her head. "This look I see in your people's eyes. Everyone has it but you two. It reminds me of something, only I don't know what." She set the mallet down and sank her fingers into the snow. "I'm used to not remembering certain things, but this I keep feeling that I ought to remember. That it's important."

His stomach clenched. "Important how? Why?"

"If I could remember, I'd know." She took up the mallet once more and played another haphazard string of notes, their tone sharpening with her frustration.

"What exactly can you remember?"

"Books I read," she answered without hesitation. "Songs I hear. Places I've been – hills and trees and streets and buildings."

"But not people?"

"There's where it gets confusing, sir. I remember every word my old masters ever said to me but not their faces. As for other people, when I'm passing through towns on my way to a new master I can lock each face I notice in my memory, but it's different in the towns where I stop. There's something indistinct about the people there, as if I'm looking at them through a mist." She broke off, dropping the mallet. Eyes half-closed, she rubbed at her temple.

Pierpon sidled closer to her, then gripped her cloak and vaulted himself upward. Cedelair watched, curious, as the manikin made a skittering leap from the cloak's hood to the rim of her black hair ribbon and stretched himself on his belly and pushed forward so that his arms dangled over her brow. With a flex of his fingers he proceeded to massage her forehead, kneading the skin just above her eyebrows. Meliroc grinned, open-mouthed, at his attentions. The young-old sorcerer smiled at a stirring of liking for the jickety.

Considering her words, he felt an unwelcome pull at his heart. Most forgetting spells simply wiped the memory clean, leaving the bespelled with a blank-slate consciousness. But someone had laid this spell with calculating, cruel precision. Meliroc's memory had been blocked at specific points, to prevent her from discovering some crucial thing. Cold, bitter cold. He could feel, not simply know, that a terrible wrong had been done her.

"I've tried to remember before," she told him. "Rather like trying to overhear a conversation that concerns me. But it's different this time. Perhaps because I'm different somehow." She took up her mallet again and sent it drifting over the keys. Pierpon climbed down to her shoulder, patting her neck.

"Would you let me try to help you?"

Her mallet froze. "What?"

"Help you recover some of your memories." He coughed hard. "You could tell me about some of the things you do remember, and I would look inside your mind to see if I could catch a glimpse of something hidden. I don't like such spells as a general rule, but in this instance it could be worth a try. It may show us how to put an end to your 'must'."

"You're serious?" Wonder trembled in her thought-voice. "You really would rid me of it?"

"How else could I make you go away?"

She met this remark with a laughing smile. The mallet bounced upon a key, and the note rang out in joy. A playful thought tripped into Cedelair's mind. *Must I caution you against meddling with my giant?* With a sidelong glance he bade Valeraine be still.

Meliroc gazed down at her bell-board, eyes burning with a battle between hope and fear. She played a three-note sequence. A spark leaped each time the mallet hit its mark.

"Sir! Did you hear? Did you see?" she cried, quivering with surprise.

"You're quite good with those bells," was all he could say.

She shook her head. "Those notes aren't in the scale! My instrument shouldn't be able to sound them. But I could hear them in my head. It gave me the notes I heard in my head! For a minute I saw it shine silver, like the carillon-wagon."

A hand of ice gripped Cedelair's heart. *Kho-laeth. Tell her. Warn her.*

"If it glows like the big bell-wagon," Pierpon spoke up, "don't forget the man inside that wagon isn't in the best of shape. I'd hate it, I would, if you ended like that, my good snow-giant."

"I know – I know – I have to be careful, careful, careful," she returned, her thought-voice breathless with excitement. "But this – with this I can play any song I like! Anything in my head! Now I'm sure to find the song Feuval needs." She leaped to her feet and began to pace, cupping her hand behind Pierpon. Cedelair watched her with a lurch in his stomach. She might say she had to be careful, but the blaze of ecstasy on her face burned away all signs of caution.

"Master Jickety wants nothing from you but friendship, Mistress Meliroc," he pointed out. "His is the best advice to heed."

She answered with a distracted little nod. Cedelair suspected she had barely heard him. Her pace became a dance. She spun slowly, a dreamy tilt in her head, while Pierpon tightened his grip on her sleeve.

"Magic, magic, he sent me magic," her thought-voice chanted in broken sing-song. "He knew, he must have known I'd need it." Her bedazzled smile brightened as she tossed her head side to side. She danced like a child in an excited frenzy. "If I spin fast enough, I'll turn into a hurricane!"

"Do-o-on't!" Pierpon cried, blubbering his lips.

She stopped in her spin and pulled the little man down from her shoulder to clasp him in an embrace, kissing the curly crown of his head. As soon as she released him he clambered back to his perch with a grunt, brushing at the wrinkles of his sleeves, while she looked to Cedelair. "Your plan is worth a try, sir." She stiffened at a catch in her thought-voice. "I will trust you." She stepped toward him, her hand outstretched in an offer to shake on their bargain.

He rose to his feet and slapped the snow from his long-coat, then took her hand. "I'm gratified, Mistress Meliroc, but curious. Why should you choose to trust me now?"

The blinding glare on her face softened into a dreamier glow. She clasped his shoulders. For an instant he feared she would hug him as she had Pierpon.

"Because I've just started believing in miracles," she said.

9. Meliroc hears the voice of Sorrow

I didn't know myself.

I couldn't think what madness had transmogrified me into someone who would give a sorcerer permission to rifle through her thoughts. But no sorcerer I'd known before would have asked permission. Cedelair seemed to think no one should touch my mind without my consent. He seemed genuinely sorry he had made that mistake. The thought of this turned my spine to icy water.

He terrified me.

The others I had loathed but never feared. After only a day with them I could see their tortures coming. But I had no way of knowing what Cedelair might say or do next. That he'd been inclined to send me on my way should have been all the warning I needed that he wouldn't follow the usual rules. He hadn't wanted me, yet he'd let me stay. For my sake? What hope had I of predicting the words or deeds of a sorcerer who thought like that? All I could think to do was stop expecting Cedelair (and Valeraine, for that matter) to behave like a sorcerer, or what I'd assumed a sorcerer to be. Then I mightn't feel as if my every step fell upon shifting sand.

Was it so bad a thing not to know myself? I might like this stranger-self, this being born of the musical chrysalis, far better than the hopeless sore of resentment who had scowled at me from mirrors for so long. Perhaps if I wanted to get to know her all I needed was to play my bell-board and let loose all the songs in my head.

Pierpon, lucky fellow, enjoyed the ride in my lowered cloak-hood, while Cedelair, Valeraine, and I scrambled up and down hillsides in search of our possibly imaginary lake. We climbed with our waists rope-bound and our hands linked, I in front (since my marches between servitudes had given me more experience than either of them at traversing hillsides in winter), Cedelair just behind me, and Valeraine bringing up the rear, blanket fastened around her shoulders and basket strapped securely to her back. I sent the warmth from my heart-fire in a stream through the hand joined with Cedelair's, that it might flow through him to his apprentice. I served them, I reminded myself, more from habit than from my usual conviction that what I was doing meant nothing to me.

All the stories Cedelair had heard throughout his youth told him the lake was no more than a day's journey from Crainante. Having nothing better to go on, we climbed up, and down, and up, then down again, searching every valley. To make good use of the time, I did as my master had suggested and told him about the last village where I'd stayed, the home of my last master, perhaps seventy miles from Crainante, to the east I supposed. My sense of direction and distance always blurred when my must pulled me toward this place or that, but Cedelair heard my guesses with a thoughtful nod.

He bade me describe the place in the most meticulous detail I could manage. Images rose before me – the soapstone statue of a man in military garb (not so different from the one here in Crainante, for every town had its own stone soldier), and a boy in floppy knee-breeches bouncing a ball off the stone man's legs, and a girl with bright red curls and a basket of scarlet roses, calling out in a soaring soprano that she had blooms to sell, blooms to sell, and a stocky young man with a cheerful grin purchasing a single bloom and handing it to the chestnut-haired maiden on his arm, then suddenly turning bashful as she beamed at him. I let my mind-voice flow freely, finding a touch of story in every description.

All the while I spoke I heard Cedelair mumbling under his breath in a strange lingo with a lot of v's and hard c's and sh's. I felt a gentle tug at the back of my head, my master drawing the strands of my memory into himself. What he thought of it all I could not imagine. His reactions were as unpredictable as his actions. I had no idea how all this tugging at my memories could make any impact on that black void. Yet it pleased me to talk to him this way, and to know, regardless of the reason, he was interested. All of us, in the depth of our hearts, want to be heard. The more I talked, the wider I grinned, heady with joy.

Yet he terrified me.

***

Not only did we scarcely know where we were going, but none of us could guess how we would know when we found it. We came across frozen ponds and brooks and frosty brush-forests that gleamed in the sun, all very lovely in their wintry way, but not what we sought. As I sealed these shimmering trees and streams in my memory, songs bubbled in my head, and I felt the weight of my bell-board at my back. But these songs were likewise not what I looked for, so I banked them down and bade them wait for a later hour.

Dusk had deepened to dark, and Valeraine had drawn out her spindle to flood our path with moonlight, when we reached the banks of Sorrow's home. All the lakes and streams we'd seen thus far had been at least partly frozen, but not the tiniest patch of ice marred the still surface of this water.

We found nothing else remarkable at our first glance, and I detected a curl of disappointment on Cedelair's lip. It scarcely deserved the name "lake", being more of a murky and mud-swirled tarn. Yet as we drew closer a dark blight snuffed out the tune dancing in my head. At the next step nearer my heart began to sink under a sudden weight. A gray fog hovered as if it had floated up from the water. In it I – imagined? – the sallow face of a woman, torrents of tears washing her sunken cheeks.

Pierpon hopped to my shoulder. "Now we've seen it. Let's go home."

I would gladly have complied, had my feet not been rooted to the spot. I felt myself shrinking, sinking into that shroud-black pool. Panic gripped me, smothering my heart-fire. I could not glance down at my masters, or even turn to look at Pierpon. The face in the fog would not let go of my gaze.

An unseen hand was shaping my own likeness. Green eyes slashed through my head like a wildcat's claw, pushing me down into the murk while they gloated above. I tried to tell myself I wasn't really moving at all, that Sorrow was working an illusion. But I cringed at the water's icy sting.

"You are nothing more than what I say you are."

The Bitter Chord threw everything out of harmony. Her face I would have remembered had she ever allowed me to see it. Her words emanated from that vision of me in my own mind-voice.

"Think nothing beyond what I tell you. Feel nothing, because you have no soul."

My likeness's eyes fired wrathful barbs to tear apart my insides.

"The Lifelord has no share in you. Cry to him with all your might and main, and he will never hear you."

A scream welled in my throat, hot and angry. I had no voice fit to hear. Must not, must never scream!

The vision's white mouth stretched wide. A shadow darkened the brow, shrouding the green eyes, obscuring all the features until only two tiny points of light remained. As a fresh wave of cold sank its needles into me the light-dots paled to yellow. The shadow took on the aspect of a deep ochre cowl. The Bitter Chord herself now hovered over me with all her venom.

"You've never been free," she whispered. "You never will be."

I hungered to tell her that she would never see me again, that she might haunt my past but could no longer torture my present or claim share in my future. But still my mind-voice lacked strength to be heard. Tears burned in my eyes. I fought to turn away. If I could free myself from those horrible yellow lights I might just manage to speak, and even in the pulsing pain find the beginning of a song.

"Song? What song could you find? What do people sing about? Kindred, friends, sweethearts. Warmth in a mother's smile, joy in a friend's handshake, bliss in a sweetheart's kiss. What has any of that to do with you? Why should anyone love you?"

Her question cut to the heart of me and split it open. I let loose a flood of tears. The Bitter Chord's image swam above me like the moon. Carillon bells pealed to thrust the query home. *Why – should – any – one – love – you?*

"Meliroc." Someone called my name in a tone of misery like my own. While I sank, silent and stone-frozen, my tiny friend had managed to find his voice.

"Meliroc!" Louder this time, almost a scream. A plea for help.

I breathed in, feeling for my heart-coal. It lay heavy and cold in my chest, and I fought to strike a spark of fire into it. If I could I might crack the ice that held me trapped, and reach for him. I sealed his call in my mind's ear, then replayed it.

At last one spark buried itself deep, sending a shock of heat through me. When two tiny hands pressed against my neck, the ice about my mouth cracked. My mind-voice managed a feeble squeak. "Pierpon."

"Meliroc – I know that's you." His voice lost some of its panic. "But I can't see you. It's like I'm in a pond and the water's all black."

"I am there with you." I dug into my coal, stoking the fire with all the strength I had left, that its heat might reach the killing frost around him. The murk above me started to shimmer. I looked for Pierpon and found a translucent shade hovering over my shoulder. Clenching against a bolt of pain, I wrenched my arm free of the ice and folded my fingers about this Pierpon-cloud.

A net folded around my mind. Thoughts hung from it like stones. *They threw me out. My friends are gone who knows where. They might be right beside me but I can't see them, can't hear them, can't get through the wall to where they are.*

The stones pressed upon my chest, threatening to sink me out of being. But I seized my heart-fire, shaping it into burning hands that would throw them off. I would free Pierpon to rise to the surface.

The stones burst apart. Their dust thickened into a long black cord which wrapped itself around my heart. *Can't see them, can't hear them.* The words mingled with the bitter peal of the carillon: *Why should anyone love you?* The two sorrows twined fast about each other. I could glimpse, just past the hateful image of the Bitter Chord, a white-washed stone palace with silver spires and a vermilion door – Jicket-Castle, where the pixy-man longed to be. I felt him fighting, and a brush of hope stirred us both. In his eyes I was in trouble. He was trying to save me.

Clutching at the thread of new strength, I called out to Cedelair and Valeraine. Their shadows hovered in the clouds over the castle, their faces twisted with grief. I spread my fingers, willing them to clutch my hand, preparing to draw their sorrows into the helix Pierpon and I had made.

A thin, wrinkled hand gripped my first two fingers. A face rushed at me, oval and young, with dimpled cheeks, a clear brow, warm russet locks that curled neatly about the nape of a cream-white neck, and light brown eyes, just now misty with tears. The dim shadow of the handsome face reflected in those eyes shriveled into a bony figure with sagging skin, a more grotesque vision of Cedelair's affliction.

Then came a quavering voice: "I would have gladly seen you grow old alongside me. We'd have wrinkled together. But this is too much for me." The too-kind squeeze of a hand, and a cool peck on the cheek. Farewell. Then the sound of something breaking.

A tendril of fire leaped up from my heart-coal to lash me. My words to Valeraine rang coldly in my ear: You sorcerers don't have enough experience with not getting your way. I felt their unfairness in the face of my master's despair.

In the Bitter Chord's stead I now saw a perfect sphere ringed with white flame. Three phantoms surged through the murk towards that light. Our sorrows swirled together, tightening.

A hand closed about my wrist. A shriek knifed the water like a lightning-flash as a boot came down hard upon my heart. A new icy blast swirled around my heart-coal. Through the black above me savage faces grinned and leered, horrible gibbering crawling tiny things, their voices chirping so fast that I could catch only two words, shrill with unholy triumph. *Dead-alive.*

My bones rattled with pain. Pygmy blades flashed through the dark. Thoughts plodded across my pounding head in a voice drained from crying – Valeraine's voice. *If I sleep, it comes. I thought if I remembered it I might be stronger, but it doesn't matter. Nothing I do can stop it from coming unless I stay awake forever.*

I imagined myself limp and drained, eyes raw from weeping, battered by the nightmare I could never remember. I was used to such sensations. But this cry came from someone whose contentment all Pierpon's dark visions had failed to shake. I shot a current of sympathy toward Valeraine, to wrap itself around her grief and draw it into the cord. The white-fire orb hovered brighter, nearer. Straining, I caught the fourth string we needed to reach it. The others were working, too, the energy of their efforts pulsing through me. The orb's beams brightened and reached down to pull us from the pool.

I knew with cold clarity that as I was feeling their sorrows, they were enduring mine. They had all seen the Bitter Chord, had heard her dissonant whisper. I felt the press of their pity even now. But we had to fight and feel as one, to make the cord strong. *The Rope of Four Sorrows.* As the orb's light brushed against it, it began to sway and bend in a serpentine dance.

In that dance I felt the first stirring of music.

The cord spun faster as minor notes became chords and chords knit themselves into measures. I heard triumph in this ever wilder undulation, a frenzied delight in feeling. The melody rang through me so loudly, so brightly, that I needed no effort to send it to the others. They heard it with me. It belonged, after all, to the four of us.

Senses restored, I knelt on the banks of the Lac d'Esprit-Triste, shaking and breathless. Pierpon sighed upon my shoulder, caressing my neck, and Cedelair and Valeraine clasped my hands. We all shared the same dizzy grin. Soon enough we would break apart and blush in embarrassment. But in this wonderful, shuddery instant, we were dear to each other.

Interlude

Ordinarily Mennieve was quite content to sit beside the window with an open book in her lap, but this day a restlessness stirred in her hands and feet. The tune Lady Meliroc had played kept humming in the back of her mind, whispering of the pleasures of sunshine and breeze, even winter cold. A leisurely stroll through the square would suit her humor. After gently setting her book aside she donned a maroon shawl and a brown wool cap and strode out onto the sidepath, straight into a harangue.

"We should stop this thing before it starts!" thundered Holbart, the roots of his yellow beard burning an angry crimson.

Intrigued, Mennieve slipped to the rear of the group clustered around the blacksmith. She jostled Andranette's elbow and mumbled apology, while the bony woman shot her a glower.

"We should pull this creature up short," Holbart went on. "Make her tell us her business here. And if she won't answer us straight we show her the way out of town, see? With a whip and a good stick!" He drove his fist into his open palm.

"Might take some doing," Orqual pointed out. "She's bigger than any of us."

"But there's only one of her," countered the young potter Embe. "We'd stand a good chance if we combined our efforts."

"We throw ropes over her," declared Holbart, his eyes bright with the hope of violence. "Let her know whose town this is."

Mennieve scowled at the stray mutters of agreement. She could have easily guessed that Holbart would take a dislike to Cedelair's elegant colossus after a single look. Six feet seven inches tall and stockily built, the blacksmith took great pride in being Crainante's largest citizen. He would never stand for being out-bigged. But the unfortunate incident involving the butcher's apprentice had brought him willing listeners.

She opened her mouth to speak, but little Coviet proved too quick for her. "It's not as if she's done anything wrong."

"Nothing wrong?" cried Andranette. "Poor Acelin! Nothing wrong?"

"The lad's not hurt," the banker Sundiffe pointed out. "Nobody's been hurt."

"Yet," snapped glassworker Subert. "But what happens the next time this thing of Cedelair's takes a notion to bowl somebody down the street?"

"Anything that big has got to be dangerous," agreed Embe.

Mennieve forced a single laugh. "Most giants in stories stand twenty to forty feet high. She's quite dainty by those standards."

"Acelin provoked her," put in Orqual. "Why not just give her a wide berth?"

"So that's your plan, chandler? Let the big bitch have the run of our town, and we all too scared to look her in the eye?" cried furniture-maker Grazon.

"We don't know that she means us harm," Sundiffe spoke up. "Most likely she's here to protect the sorcerers."

"We leave them alone, she'll leave us alone," agreed Coviet. "How hard would that be?"

"So it comes back to Cedelair," growled Holbart. "Him and his blonde imp. They're the ones running things now, eh?" A fresh chorus of bitter grumbles met this suggestion.

Heat rushed to Mennieve's face. "Cedelair has always been our friend," she snapped. "As long as you're imagining things, Holbart, try fancying how it would have gone with us five years ago, if he hadn't been here to defend us."

"He's been shut up in his home ever since then," Andranette put in. "Like as not he's changed in more ways than his face. Who among us really knows him now?"

"I know him," Mennieve pronounced, her shoulders squared. "Better than any of you. To suggest he's scheming against us is beyond insane."

"Then what does he need Mistress Big for?" Holbart flung back. "Why would he need 'protection'?"

Enraged, Mennieve wheeled away from Holbart and his cronies. Before she could bolt down the side-path, a hand gripped her arm. She hissed like a boiling kettle, then jerked her head to find Odilon gazing at her with concern.

"How can you listen to that nonsense?" she snapped. "He's your friend, too."

Odilon's lips twitched, as if at a guilty thought. "That's why I've got to listen," he whispered, leaning toward her. "There may indeed be trouble on the rise."

"What sort of trouble?"

"I'm not sure exactly. I heard some gossip when the trade wagons came to the glassworks last week. I didn't think much about it at the time, but now I'm not so sure." He lowered his voice to a whisper. "Boldithe – about seventy or eighty miles away – you know it?"

Mennieve shook her head.

"Not much to it. Half the size of Crainante. When the wagons stopped there, they found it empty."

"Empty, as in–?"

"As in, 'nobody there'. No sign of people anywhere, except one. A man lying on the pavement, dead, all but bones. One of the traders recognized his cloak. He was Boldithe's sorcerer."

"Ah," returned Mennieve, nodding slowly. "Strange, but surely it has nothing to do with Cedelair."

"Well, I never said it did, did I? I only said it might. That's why his friends need to keep a careful eye out. Me, I don't believe for a second that giant comes from Lippe."

Mennieve trembled in fury, just as a golden note swept down from the hills.

10. Cedelair sees for himself

Breathless and foot-sore, Cedelair and his party reached the house at mid-morning. He knew that his apprentice would need at least one long day to recuperate as he saw her stumble over the doorsill with a drowsy giggle. Pierpon tumbled down from Meliroc's shoulder, half-asleep, as soon as she passed through the door. She caught him in her hands and gave him to Valeraine, who carried him to her chamber. The little man was snoring to shatter the windows even before she closed the door. Cedelair tried to think of his garden, the one thing that could always fire his nerves, but he could picture only a faded green haze. He sank into his hearth-side chair, stretched his legs, dangled his arms, and let his head flop to the side.

Meliroc, who had worked hardest of all, looked the most awake. She knelt beside him, regarding him with an intense, slightly confused stare. "I don't know what to say, sir." A hint of the new song's tears crept into her mind-voice.

He straightened his neck. "What do you feel?"

"I think it's – gratitude. No one in my life has helped me as you did."

"What do you imagine I've done for you?"

"You gave me my song. Again."

"Again?"

"I found my last one when I watched you work in your garden."

Cedelair let out a cracked sigh. So that was why he'd recognized himself in that joyful tune.

"This new one is as much yours as it is mine," she explained. "And Pierpon's and Mistress Valeraine's. We found it together when we pulled each other free." Her smile spread wide in a moment of silent laughter. "I think I like you, sir. And I like the feeling. That's what I'm grateful for."

Cedelair's breath hardened to an icicle in his throat. Meliroc did not disguise her feelings. If she said she liked him, she meant it. Yet the last thing he wanted was to like her in turn. She insisted on making the matter difficult for him, the wretched looming imposition, reaching out to wrest him from Sorrow's grasp, brightening his old friend's face with a song. "You should get some rest," he told her.

She shook her head. "I'd rather practice. I need to work out precisely how I want this song to sound."

He drew himself upright in his chair. "Your instrument is indeed wonderful, Mistress Meliroc," he remarked, taking *Musical Enchantments* from the table where it rested, "and your command of it quite remarkable." He leafed through the pages in search of the entry he wanted. "But there's something you should be aware of."

"My bell-board is dangerous," she volunteered in a mind-voice quite fearless.

"What makes you think so?"

"I feel it. I'm always thinking about it. And I don't forget where it came from."

"Yet you are not afraid of it?"

"Not when I weigh what it might take against what it can give."

"What it might take. Ah, but there's the point." He handed the book to her, pointing out the relevant entry with a tap of his fingertip. "Read that for me, please."

"*Kho-laeth*," she said in the plain tone of a scholar reciting a lesson. "A musical instrument with the power to subsume the musician who plays it. Believed to have been shaped and enchanted by fey who wished to enslave mortals with musical talent, the kho-laeth endows the musician with a strange form of immortality, a half-life, with his soul bound forever to the instrument." He saw no change in her face as she read, save for a barely perceptible darkening of eye.

"Sound familiar?" he asked with a pointed look.

She nodded. "The carillon is a kho-laeth, and it swallowed up Feuval, probably long ago." She mind-spoke in the same scholar's voice, but her mouth wilted a little.

"Your instrument is starting to take on some of its parent's power," he returned with a pointed nod. "There's no record of what a graft of a kho-laeth might do."

"I see. An unknown commodity. All the more dangerous."

He leaned toward her, puzzled. "And still you're not the least bit afraid."

"It's done more good than harm so far. I'd need more than the words of an old book to make me give it up."

He drummed his fingertips on the arm of his chair. He did see her point. He had only to remember Mennieve's face as the tune of joy rang out. "If we avoided doing anything that might be dangerous we'd never learn anything new. I want to make you aware of the risks, that's all."

"That's most kind of you, sir," she returned. "Perhaps I"– Her thought-voice winked out as her gaze flew to the door. He sensed her drawing herself tight, listening.

He planted his feet on the floor. "Mistress Meliroc?" She blinked, her whole attention centered on something beyond that door. "Mistress Meliroc?" he repeated in a low, cautious voice. "Can you hear me?"

She blinked again. "Yes." Her thought-voice seemed to come from a distance. "Feuval wants me. But you should come. You should hear when I play our song for him."

***

Cedelair trudged uphill into the bright blue with Meliroc alongside him, bell-board and mallet tucked under her arm. Her cloak billowed towards him, throwing gusts of warmth against his back and shoulders. Twice she had tried to envelop him in that marvelous cloak, but he had stepped aside, avoiding her nearness. At least the bite of winter felt natural and familiar.

Even in the glow of mid-morning the carillon-wagon shone with the pale silver shimmer of moonlight. Meliroc relaxed her shoulders as its summoning spell released her. Sinking to her knees, she looked from the bell-wagon to him, her face bright with the excitement of a child sharing a secret.

The carillon-wagon's glow winked out. "Now I wake him," Meliroc told Cedelair, raising her mallet. The instant the first note rang out, the planks of the bell-board began to gleam.

The giant paused a moment, tensing with wonder, then launched into the Song of Four Sorrows. Even as Cedelair drove steel into his spine, his eyes began to swim. A song to make the hardest heart weep. He felt its power as he listened. The tune could break open the hard heart to let light in. It could redeem, as surely as any of those bad dreams the jickety wove for sinners, and far more beautifully. As tears slid down his face, faces loved and lost drifted across his mind's view. The black sludge in his heart began to slough away.

The carillon did not join in this time. The small bell-board was doing all its parent's work and more, singing out the notes in all the poignant richness with which the musician heard them. Instead of absorbing Meliroc, this graft seemed to be absorbed into Meliroc, moving at her will, the voice of her soul.

The final note hovered in the air like a whisper of good-bye. Meliroc inched closer to Cedelair, her taut stare fixed on the curtain that hung over the wagon's paneless window. "When he shows himself," she said, "will you speak for me, as you did when we visited your friend?"

He coughed hard. This fresh sign of trust moved him more than he liked. "Certainly I will." The curtain swept aside, and the gold mask appeared, casting a light of its own to fall upon first Meliroc, then Cedelair.

"What business hast thou here?" he demanded, a searing sharpness in his deep melodic voice.

"My name is Cedelair." Cedelair rested a tentative hand on Meliroc's arm. "Mistress Meliroc lodges with me."

"I called not to thee," returned Feuval.

"Mistress Meliroc asked me to come, to speak for her. I can hear when her mind speaks."

"Thou'rt the Cedelair who doth hold my moon-tree prisoner?"

"No," came Meliroc's quick reply. "My must holds me prisoner, not Master Cedelair." A laugh crept into her mind-voice. "Truth be told, he's a prisoner, too. I can't leave him, and he can't get rid of me."

Smiling despite himself, Cedelair repeated what Meliroc had said, though he doubted the carillon-man would accept him as her voice as easily as Mennieve had.

"As to his being here, it's as he says. I asked him to come," the giant continued when Feuval did not reply. "He helped me find the song you needed, and I thought it right he should hear when I played it for you."

Feuval made a strange sound as Cedelair relayed these words. "A generous sentiment, fair moon-tree. How helped he?"

"That's a thrilling story," she replied, arching her neck. "To get your song, we had to venture to the home of Sorrow itself, a tiny pond nestled in a valley quite near here." Her thought-voice took on an eager storytelling brio, which Cedelair strove to capture when he echoed her. "The townsfolk call it the Lac d'Esprit-Triste, and all who have gone near it alone have lost their minds in grief. I knew that I could find the song there, and when Master Cedelair saw I was determined to go, he offered to go with me, along with his apprentice Valeraine and our friend Pierpon. We thought that together we could take what we needed from Sorrow and still keep our wits.

"Sorrow is a wicked thing, and as the saying goes, she loves nothing better than company. She would gladly have dragged our minds and hearts down into the bitter murk of her waters. She hovered in a silver fog and took the shape of the things that grieved us most. Down we sank, each alone, under our weight, until we remembered that we weren't alone. We reached out to touch each other, joined our sorrows together, and pulled each other free." She cast Cedelair a brief, bright smile. "So you see, without him I'd have been quite lost."

As soon as the relayed message left his lips, Cedelair shook his head. "She gives me far too much credit," he told Feuval. "All our sorrows might have joined, but only she could have made a melody of them."

"Did you like the song, sir?" she asked. "Is it what you were hoping for?"

Feuval stretched forth a hand. "Oh, my dear," he breathed, "draw thou nearer."

As Meliroc rose to her feet, strode toward the window, and knelt once more, Cedelair felt the frost sharpen to ice at his spine. The carillon-man caressed her cheek and wove his fingers into the thick of her hair. The sorcerer turned his face to hide a grimace of distaste. Perhaps Meliroc felt affection in this touch, and couldn't, or wouldn't, see the web being spun around her. Or perhaps his own closed mind was working against him, showing him danger where there was none.

He glanced again at the wagon and found Feuval holding Meliroc's chin in his hands, his masked face hovering close to hers as if he would kiss her. "Shall I tell thee what thou'rt doing for me?" crooned the carillon-man, his voice so soft and low that Cedelair almost couldn't hear him. "Thou art returning to me what I have lost."

Nightmare Lullaby

"Can a song do that?" Meliroc asked him, her eyes shining with an almost painful hope. Cedelair did not translate.

"What be it that mak'st a being alive?" Feuval pursued. "Joy and tears. Thou'rt bringing me life, moon-tree. I am nearly whole again."

Cedelair felt his heart pulled tight, a knot at the center of a cord. He could feel himself in Feuval's place, trapped in non-life, hoping to knit himself a new soul from the songs the giant brought him.

"I hath sent thee to find melodies," the carillon-man went on, "and both times thou hast exceeded my hopes. There is but one thing missing." He drew his hands away at last, and her head sank. "Bring me a song that reveals the truth of love, and I shall be free once more."

She stood and backed away from the wagon, coming to a stop beside Cedelair. "Master Feuval," she said, her gaze still fixed on the gold mask in the window, "have you heard the term 'kho-laeth'?"

Cedelair smiled as he echoed her question. So this ghost-fellow's voice and hands had not stolen away all her wits. "Never," the carillon-man replied.

"It's a musical instrument that absorbs the musician who plays it," she explained. "Begging your pardon, it sounds very like what the carillon has done to you."

"Thou'st no need to beg my pardon," Feuval returned, a bemused chuckle in his voice. "'Kho-laeth.' So it hath a name!"

She nodded. "My instrument is part of yours. Might it be doing the same thing to me?" Cedelair translated with care, voicing the doubt that was not quite fear.

"Thou believ'st my gift would harm thee, moon-tree?"

Cedelair feared Meliroc might wilt at this, but her thought-voice remained steady. "I know you meant no harm when you gave it to me. No gift could have pleased me more. There's always risk when you want something badly, but if I could, I'd like to know what I'm risking." Again he smiled as he repeated the words, with an odd little swell in his heart.

The gold mask sank. "I will take it back from thee, if thou fear'st it. Not for my very soul would I see thee come to harm."

Meliroc shook her head. "I won't return it," she said, "until I have found your love song." She bowed her head in farewell. "And now, with your leave, I will begin my work and listen for your summons."

Cedelair relayed her words, and then, stiffening, spoke for himself. "Understand this, Master Carillon-man. Your 'moon-tree' is not without friends." He turned his back on the wagon without waiting for a reply. He strode forward, while the giant kept pace beside him, keeping him warm. He wondered if she noticed that the carillon-man had not answered her question.

She balanced her instrument in the crook of her arm. The mallet drifted down the planks in a new strain of "thinking music". A swirl of light hovered around the board, a sign of the growing magic, but the light on Meliroc's face, a mix of awe and tenderness, concerned him more. The Sorrow Song winked through these notes like a star behind a cloud. Her mouth curved in a wistful smile. He thought he heard her speak, her thought-voice a trace of a whisper. "If I lost myself to it, would I be so very unhappy?"

A pang struck his heart.

Neither spoke again until they reached the cottage. Meliroc stifled a yawn. Her head teetered lazily. Fatigue was at last starting to muffle the music in her mind.

"Get a bit of rest," he suggested with a nod toward her tent.

"I need to work," she returned, a weary slur in her thought-voice.

"Your work can wait. Get some rest." He set his jaw. "I order it."

She gave him another laughing smile. "You're a harsh taskmaster, sir." She drew a step away from him, shaking her head. "What a fix I'm in now! What have I to say about love?"

***

Valeraine still kept to her room, resting but not sleeping, enjoying the relief of the potion. Through the crack in the door Cedelair could hear the rattling hum of Pierpon's snores. Just as well that one slept and one rested, tucked away in the room they shared. He needed stillness for the spell he was about to perform. Flames licked at the kettle hanging from its rack. In another minute the water inside it would be ready. He needed only a still surface and a thin vapor of steam.

Meliroc could have helped him. But she was the last person he wished to know what he was doing.

With steadying breath he closed his eyes to ready his mind for the work. Working a charm of concentration, he called forth the memories he'd drawn from the giant that afternoon. Faces flickered before him like the candle-glow on the pages of a book. He saw these strangers as she saw them and felt the tingle of her curiosity as she observed them moving through their routines, the tug of longing at her heart as they called out greetings and shook hands – longing to be a part of these things she watched from a distance. *She wants love. That's why she yearns toward the carillon-man. It isn't only the music.*

The parade of people grew more distinct before his mind's eye. Two stood out, a very old pair with withered faces and bent shoulders browsing around a gem-vendor's stall. The man spotted a bracelet with azure stones. Twitching his head, he addressed the vendor, while the woman watched with an uncertain frown. A coin changed hands, and the old man slipped the trinket around his lady's wrist. Her eyes, blue as the gems, widened with joy.

Cedelair fixed his gaze firmly on the old lady's pop-eyed expression. This should be what he needed. He judged the water ready now. He opened his eyes, taking care to keep the face sharp in his mind as he claimed a porcelain teacup from its hook in the kitchen. He poured the water into it and watched as the ripples stilled. A vapor rose from the surface to warm his nose. When it cleared away the woman was staring up at him. Mumbling over the water, he shifted into the Sixth Tongue, the magic language that supposedly could "reveal what was concealed," to call for the power to see beyond the memory-block to the truth.

For half an instant the face vanished. He thought he must have bent too low over the cup and stirred the water with his breath, and he bit back a stream of curses. Then the face glimmered into view once more. He could tell it had changed. He remembered the sign that Valeraine had shown him and centered his searching stare on the woman's eyes. Something fearful lurked behind the childlike joy.

The nightmare mark.

So Meliroc was trying to remember she had seen that mark before in the last town where she'd stayed. Someone didn't want her to remember it. He recalled horrible yellow eyes blaring from beneath a shadowy cowl and a whisper as bitter as any blow. *Why should anyone love you?* Cedelair could see why someone might love Meliroc – what? No, he couldn't.

"One face doesn't serve as proof," he remarked with a weary sigh, resigning himself to searching other faces the same way, even though a headache was already settling in for a long stay. He poured over the faces one at a time, replenishing the water from his kettle. His headache mounted, and with it his heartsickness.

The nightmare mark lurked in every eye. This town had suffered as Crainante was suffering now. No longer could he find the most threadbare excuse to deny that some magical plague was at work, spread by an unwilling, unwitting carrier. Meliroc.

She brings the nightmares. But how?

11. Meliroc ponders the mystery of love

A vigorous chore can steady an unsettled mind. Even if Cedelair and Valeraine hadn't needed fresh firewood I would have volunteered to split logs for them, for I woke in a humor to swing axe against wood. I struck at my troubles with each blow I landed. Feuval needed another song from me, about a feeling I knew almost nothing about. *Split!* Had I told Cedelair I liked him? Had I actually meant it? *Split!* I was so tired of not remembering things! *Split!*

"You need to slow down a bit, mam'selle Meliroc." Pierpon stood upright in my cloak-hood, clinging to the back of my neck. "You'll exhaust yourself, you will, before you're half done."

Right again, pixy-man. I banked down my heart-fire to let the wintry air cool my chest, and I adjusted my grip on the axe-handle and raised it over my head, my gaze fixed on the log on the block below. Where could I look for a love song? *Split!*

"Imagining yourself chopping up Cedelair?" Pierpon snickered.

"No," I snapped. "I like Cedelair." *Split!* "Now that I begin to know him." *Split!*

Pierpon snapped his fingers. "Well, I'm glad, I am. Now that you like Cedelair, maybe thinking about those others won't hurt you anymore."

Startled, I shifted my aim in mid-blow, and the log toppled off the block as the axe nicked its side. Since coming home from Sorrow's lake I hadn't thought about my old masters even in passing, and I hadn't even realized it. I checked my heart for the hate I had so long depended on. I couldn't find it. I didn't want to.

I set the log back in place, then pictured the wood breaking apart. *Split!* I winked at Pierpon as I carried the firewood to the pile beside the door. "Don't throw me off."

"It's true, isn't it?"

"Of course it's true. That's why it threw me off. You're a vast deal wiser than you should be."

"Have you forgotten a jickety's work?" he returned, with a wink of his own. "When we enter dreamers' minds, we get a glimpse of all they know. Oh, we learn wisdom fast, we do, at Jicket-Castle."

Jicket-Castle, of the shining white walls and silver spires. I considered Pierpon, wrenched from the world he knew, forced into what he called a "fleshy cage". I'd seen him in his sorrow, racing for the door of the castle but never reaching it.

Laying down the axe, I sank to the ground. He hopped into the cup of my palm. "You could frighten Valeraine quite easily, you know," I told him.

"Oh?" Pierpon cocked his head, a playful glint in his eye. "How, say you?"

"She uses her moonlight-spindle to keep the gold-caps away from the house," I pointed out, "and now we know gold-caps are the one thing she fears. She must be very careful to keep that spindle in a certain place."

Pierpon nodded. "I've seen her put it away, I have. Never thought there was any fear in it." He twitched his whiskers, thinking.

"What if you were to hide it? When she can't find it, she'll be beyond frantic. That night you'd sleep in your own bed in Jicket-Castle."

He whistled through his teeth. "You're ruthless, mam'selle Meliroc," he remarked, more admiring than condemning.

"You'll never get home if you're squeamish."

"It's a good plan, it is." His head drooped a little. "But I'm not sure I could do it after last night. It seems – cruel."

"I know." I could imagine all too clearly Valeraine's eyes turning blind-white with horror. "It would only last a wink of a second," I assured him and myself. "You could put the spindle back just as you were leaving. I'd comfort her. I like her, too. But one instant of fear and you're free, as you should be."

"I may have better means of getting free. If I can help put a stop to this tampering with dreams, my people won't care that I couldn't scare Valeraine. They'll call me home, they will, to a hero's welcome." Again he twitched his mustache, as if working out a problem. "I should be free, eh? Why so?"

"You helped me when I had a headache."

"Such a small thing."

"Such small things are the work of great souls."

He patted my hand. "Nobody's ever said such things of me. The way you talk, I could even believe it. But I'm not the one who can take a bundle of griefs and turn it into a melody so beautiful nobody can resist it. You're the one, you are, who should be free." He stretched himself across my wrist. "Who is that woman, snow-giant? The one with the hood and the yellow eyes?"

The Bitter Chord. At even the fleeting thought the pain could grip me. Her eyes swooped down on me, raining blows on my head till the very roots of my hair ached. My heart-fire shrank to a flickering wisp.

What Pierpon saw in my face I could only guess. "Forgive me!" he cried, shrill with alarm. "I didn't mean it! Please, I don't care to know! None of my business, it is!"

I snatched at a frosty breath. The Lac d'Esprit-Triste might have swallowed me had his hands not gripped the back of my neck. "It's all right. I don't mind telling you. She was what you might call my guardian before my must started leading me. She sheltered me, taught me to read and to mind-speak, sewed these clothes for me." I tugged at the sleeves of my burgundy tunic. "But that whispering voice of hers always made me shiver, so cold it was."

Pierpon nodded slowly, a glint of an ache in his eyes.

"She'd hurt me with her look. She could do that. She was a fierce sorcerer. Light from her eyes would dart out from the shadow of her hood and shoot pain into me. She wouldn't stop until I writhed and screamed." My teeth began to chatter. "That scream – I hated it– horrible – voice"–

As another shock of cold choked my thought-voice to silence, the jickety tightened his clasp on my wrist. My heart-fire pulsed. "I never knew why she did it," I managed to say. "Maybe she despised me for being so big. It felt as if she was trying to shrink me. But I tricked her. Every time she sent me pain, I imagined myself feeding on it and growing taller, until my hair could brush the stars.

"But you were bigger than her. Couldn't you have gotten away?"

The question rubbed a raw point, but I held my voice steady. "To go where?" I said. "To do what? She made me afraid of myself and what the world would make of me. At least she gave me books to read."

"How did you get free at last?"

"She disappeared." Thick darkness closed over my memory, a door hammered shut. "One day she just wasn't there anymore. Then I felt my must for the first time, pulling me. I left that place, convinced that nowhere I could possibly end up would be as bad." I recalled with a twinge the hope with which I'd set out that day, that the strange pull might lead me to places that would welcome me after all. "I should have understood the Bitter Chord has likenesses everywhere."

"Bitter Chord?"

"My name for her."

Pierpon nuzzled my wrist. "She has no likeness here, snow-giant."

My heart-fire vaulted high. "No," I told him, "she doesn't."

I caught him up, pressed him against my neck, and kissed the top of his head. He grinned at me in answer. A happy ache pulsed through me. This little man had made a point of looking after me ever since he had brought me here. He worried about me! Better still, he made me feel as if I were fit to be worried about, as if I were good. My old oppressor was wrong. Someone did love me, and I loved him in turn.

I held him a while longer, then I pulled myself up to my feet and back to my chore. As I worked I told him about my last trip to the carillon-wagon with Cedelair at my side. "So now the old haunt wants a song about the truth of love, he does?" he remarked. "That's a tricky one. Where will you look for it?"

"I'm not sure yet," I admitted. "But when I find it, you'll be in it."

***

Waiting for lunch, Pierpon and I played our game with my bell-board. To make it fair, I restricted my conscious thought to the notes rightly in the scale. But each time Pierpon copied my sequences, strains of an azure melody wove around the back of my mind. His know-all glance, his saucy squeak of a voice, the strength in his tiny hands, everything I loved in him flowed through those strains. My heartbeat quickened as they strengthened and ripened into song.

Nightmare Lullaby

Pierpon studied my face. "You've found something," he guessed. "Would you play it for me?" From the eager flash in his eye I could tell I'd accomplished at least one good thing. He was no longer indifferent to music.

With a nod, I opened my mind to let the new song fill it. When I began to play I watched and listened as magic came back into the instrument. The chrysalis folded about me, quickening my every nerve. Only when the last note settled into place did my breathing calm and my spirits tumble down from their height.

This sweet song was part of what I needed, but not the whole.

"I know, I do, why I never thought much of music before," Pierpon spoke up. "I had to hear it the way you play it."

I pressed him to my neck again as I locked his words in my memory. My eyes fell on the parlor window, where one of the curtains stirred. I glimpsed a craggy face beyond it and stiffened. Why should Cedelair watch us?

Lunch followed quickly. Over cheese-and-carrot soup I gave Valeraine my version of the last trek to the carillon-wagon. I kept half an eye on my master, who frowned over his bowl as if beset with indigestion. Now that I'd begun to like him, did he like me less than ever? Rubbing at my temple, I excused myself from the table and ducked out the side door.

The garden rose up before me, its green hues shining. I started down the walkway, casting a careful glance at each patch of plants I passed, wondering what they healed. I listed the ailments I'd heard Valeraine loll out, all problems of the body, none (save the elixir that offered respite from nightmares) of the mind or soul. But surely Cedelair could conjure these plants to do what he liked. The idea drifted idly across my mind that somewhere in all this green might lie the cure for a broken heart.

I froze in my tracks, taking a notion like a blow. Would I never be able to complete my song until I'd had my heart broken? I'd started the book Mennieve had given me. The romantic verses of ancient Farienne wove through my imagination like whispers of tunes. In all those poems love danced hand in hand with grief.

A sidelong gaze fell upon the gentleman-plant, which waved to me with a courtly beckon. *Imfaphia amorat*, the plant used to make love potions. A mad idea set me trembling. Absolutely never. I might not quite know myself, but I was not so far removed from what I'd always been that I would seriously contemplate–

"Mistress Meliroc."

I jolted as I turned to face my master. He looked at me as if he had forgotten some question he wished to ask me. "You have taken to my garden, I see," he remarked with a hint of a smile.

"I imagine anyone would who got a good look at it," I told him, forcing cheerfulness into my thought-voice. "I wonder how many words we have for different shades of green. Emerald, aqua, forest, celadon, citrine, chartreuse... I'll count them sometime." The familiar sack was slung over his shoulder. He had come out to work. "Am I in your way, sir? I can leave"–

"No." He caught my wrist. "Stay."

The veins in his neck pulsed, as if a hand gripped his throat. That unasked question was hurting him. I gave him a coaxing nod. "Have you something to tell me?"

His jaw hardened. "Mistress Meliroc, do you remember your dreams?"

"Why do you ask?" I returned, clenching to calm the words in my mind.

"Because the key to your *geas* may lie there," he explained. "You don't, do you? Remember your dreams." He arched an eyebrow. "Should you like to remember them?"

Remember my dreams? Understand what I was being punished for? To have that black deed clear before my view... The knowledge could kill me... or save me... "Yes. I don't want to be hidden from myself."

His throat rippled again. "I may be able to help you. But I would need to enter your mind while you sleep. Do you want me to do this?"

"If it meant you could find a way to set me free, sir."

"That's it, then," he returned with a nod. "Tonight."

"Tonight," I agreed.

With that matter settled, I thought he might relax. But a pained glint still burned in his eyes, some disquieting thought yet unspoken. I wondered what he might have found in those memories he'd drawn from me. Nothing that would free me, obviously.

Free. Freedom. Feuval. None of us were free, and each of our freedoms depended on somebody else. Feuval's lay in my hands. I had half of it already. I stood so close! There it was again, the mad thought, jostling other thoughts out of shape. *Imfaphia amorat* winked at me from across the walkway.

Cedelair stared at me with a drawn-tight smile. "You're thinking of Master Feuval, I expect," he guessed.

"Partly," I admitted, still with half an eye on the love-potion plant.

"It's quite a riddle he's set for you," he remarked in an off-hand tone. "Hundreds of thousands of songs have been written about love, yet none of them are good enough for him? He must have quite a bit of faith in you, to think you could do better."

"It wouldn't be better," I explained. "It would be mine, my gift to him, and that's what he needs, I think." With all my strength I fired ice into my spine. "Master Cedelair, I need you to break my heart."

"What?" Cedelair nearly choked on the word.

"I need my heart broken. It's the only way I'll find this last song. Would you – please – make a love potion for me? A taste of *imfaphia amorat*?"

He squinted in disbelief. "You want me to feed you a potion?"

"You feed potions to your friends all the time. Your elixirs solve their problems. Surely what I ask isn't so different."

"It's very different. I told you before, I've never used *imfaphia amorat*."

"Then this would be your chance to try it out."

A pained glint blared in his eyes. "You really do think we're all alike, don't you?"

"Not anymore, sir," I insisted. "The others tested their powers on me without caring if they hurt me. But in this you'd be helping me."

"How do you imagine *imfaphia amorat* could help you?"

"Unrequited love. That's one of the keys to a broken heart, isn't it?"

Cedelair shook his head with a bitter scowl. "I won't do it, Mistress Meliroc. Let that break your heart."

I turned away from the finality in his eyes. I felt a grinding in my belly, a determination to get that potion one way or another. My other masters would have fed it to me in an eye-blink. But now, curse my luck, I had to reason with a good man.

Cedelair laid a gentle hand on my elbow. "I know how a broken heart feels," he told me, "and I wouldn't wish it on anyone, even... I certainly wouldn't wish it on you."

"But you remember what Feuval said," I pointed out. "These songs are what life is made of. Hardly anyone makes it through life without getting their heart broken. If it's to happen to me, I'd rather it be when some good might come of it."

His flinty gaze softened a fraction, and I knew I'd won a point. "A foolhardy thing," he muttered, flexing his jaw.

"Not so foolhardy," I countered. "It would be the safest way. You could control it. Make its effect finite. My heart would be broken only for a little while."

He paced forward, muttering at every step, heading straight, though he might not realize it, for the *imfaphia amorat*. "I do not like this," he repeated. "Not one bit." Yet I could feel him mulling over the chance to try a new spell that could bring the wildest force of heart and mind under harness. A good man he might be, but he was still a sorcerer.

"You've no idea what you're getting in for, madam," he said. "If I did this, I would have to give your love an object." His pacing slowed. "Whom would you love?"

My head drooped a little. "Someone who wouldn't requite me." That was all I knew.

He gave a dry snicker. "You haven't thought this through at all, have you, overgrown child that you are. You think if you showed an interest in one of those young sparks in town, he wouldn't try to make the most of it?" His eyes flashed, then narrowed, as if a new idea had struck. "Only one thing will persuade me to do this. The potion must make you love *me*."

Startled, I fought to drive fresh strength into my spine, while the sober quarter of my mind called out, *Give in. He has beaten you.* I might be willing to like a sorcerer, but I was ill prepared to love one. I must have grimaced, for Cedelair smiled, evidently thinking he had won.

Only this short step lay between me and the song that would give Feuval back his life.

"Very well, Master Cedelair," I returned in my steadiest thought-voice. "Please prepare a potion that will make me fall in love with you."

***

I carried the little bottle under stars so fiercely bright that the snow-covered ground and the frost-touched trees shimmered like diamond dust. I held my breath a few moments. I was in no great hurry. Cedelair needed some time to explain the situation to Valeraine, who was bound to object. I was to remain outdoors until called.

I thought I should have explained the situation, since the idea had been mine, but he'd made his request with such a worried look that I couldn't deny him. The cool quiet of the outside air would do me good as I faced this tiny rose-pink glass demon I held in my palm. "Without fear there is no courage," I quoted Brave Bennelise, then clenched my teeth and plucked out the stopper.

A sick-sweet perfume burst out. With my tongue trying to retreat down my throat, I clamped a hand over my nose and brought the bottle to my lips. I closed my eyes and tipped it. The elixir tasted like watered honey. As it slipped down my throat I held very still, emptied my mind, and waited.

Nothing.

No surge of unrecognizable feeling, no sudden swelling heart or galloping pulse. I felt no different by even a jot. The courtly *imfaphia amorat* had proved a cheat.

Disappointment dropped its weight. I ground my teeth against it. I would make another plan. I hadn't failed Feuval yet, and I wouldn't now. In the meantime, I could practice the first part of the song. I hurried to my tent and plopped down on my blankets. As I drew my bell-board onto my knees, I let my mind's eye rest on the shadow-veiled garden. How many words for the color green?

Celadon, citrine, chartreuse... Cedelair.

Green man. My green man.

His name sank into my heart and turned it inside out.

12. Cedelair looks in on a nightmare

Cedelair had read that most men would rather face a stampeding elephant herd than an angry woman. Looking into his apprentice's rage-swollen face, he believed it.

"You must be having a game with me, sir," Valeraine snapped. "You didn't do what you said." She charged across the room, the floor rattling under her stomp. "Knowing what she's been through, you wouldn't have done such a despicable thing!"

"She asked me to do it." He frowned at the smallness of his voice.

"You should have said no!" the young lioness roared. "What was in your mind, sir?" Before he could muster a reply, she railed on, "One minute you tell me she's my responsibility, and the next you're trying out love potions on her! Lifelord save us both if it actually works! Maybe you bungled it. We can hope."

Cedelair nodded, almost smiling. The girl might calm if she could know how much he shared this hope. As it was, he could only stand still and take her tirade as no less than he deserved. What had he been thinking? He owed Valeraine and himself an answer. "I feared she might be falling in love with that carillon-man. I thought she'd be safer loving me than him."

"Why should you care? You said you wanted nothing to do with her."

"I still want nothing to do with her," he insisted.

"Humbug! You're in love with her yourself. You're jealous of the carillon-man, and rather than try to win her honestly you've put her under a love spell."

To hide his shock, Cedelair drew his mouth into a line. "Would you mind repeating that? I'm quite certain I misheard you."

"You love Meliroc yourself!" she shouted, stamping her foot.

"You're daydreaming. I do not love your giant and never will."

"Oh, I know you don't think you do, sir, but you do. I would sympathize if you hadn't done such a shameful thing." She shook at a fresh surge of anger. "I promised Meliroc she wouldn't be exploited, and you've made a liar of me!"

Cedelair breathed in a low sigh as understanding dawned. He rested a hand on his apprentice's shoulder, and though she stiffened she did not draw away. "None of this is your doing," he assured her. "I know I was wrong to give her the potion, but whatever happens, she won't blame you."

"But she's my responsibility," Valeraine reminded him again, her voice softer but still sharp. "You might at least have said something to me first."

"I don't think you could have talked her out of it."

"I would have tried, I would," a high, shrill voice spoke up. Cedelair glanced toward the corner to find Pierpon standing against the wall, scowling in the shadows.

Cedelair met Valeraine's eyes, pointed a thumb at the jickety, and jerked his head toward the door. Valeraine smiled at the little man. "Pierpon, dear fellow, would you mind going outside and keeping Meliroc company for a while?"

As the jickety headed for the door he frowned at Cedelair over his shoulder. "If you've made my Meliroc unhappy, master, I'll find a way, I will, to make you unhappy." He jumped up to catch the doorknob, twisted it, and leaped over the doorsill.

Cedelair closed the door after him, puzzling at another odd twinge of liking for him. With a painful breath he turned back to Valeraine. "There is worse, I fear. A matter that needs our attention at once."

"The nightmares," she guessed, unbending a little. "Have you found out something, sir?"

"Regrettably, yes." In a low, somber voice he told her what he'd seen when he'd examined the giant's memories. Only when he fell silent did she shake her head.

"It doesn't follow that Meliroc's guilty," she said, more calmly than he'd expected.

"She is key to it. Think, Raine. That's what she's been trying to remember – she's seen that mark before. Someone doesn't want her to remember. Why do you suppose *that woman* would block it?" He spoke of that woman instinctively, the memory of the hooded specter strong in his mind.

Valeraine wrinkled her nose. "You think '*that woman*' whoever she is, is using Meliroc as a carrier? Spreading the spell as she follows her *geas*?"

"The woman we saw at Esprit-Triste wouldn't shrink from such a thing."

She shuddered. "Oh Lifelord, poor Meliroc. Sir, we have to help her."

"We will. But we won't know how, until we've found her out." He gave her a hard, resolute look. "Tonight we're going to look inside her dreams. She's given permission."

"Was this before or after you gave her that love philter?"

"She wants to know the truth," he said, fighting to keep the swell of irritation from his voice.

"Then you'd better be prepared to tell her," she countered. "I take it you haven't said a word about what you found in her memories."

"There's little point in upsetting her yet. We need the full truth. By tomorrow we should have something we can use."

Valeraine arched an eyebrow. "You keep saying 'we'. I take it you want me to take part in this dream-invasion?"

"This is a *Seventh Tongue* matter. I admit you may be more adept there than I am. Besides, as you've pointed out, she is your responsibility."

He'd hoped to see her eye brighten at his trust in her. Instead she responded with a crestfallen nod. "Shouldn't we call her in now?" she asked, with a quick glance at the door. "It seems harsh to make her wait outside so long."

He nodded, struggling against an uneasy chill at his back. One glance into Meliroc's eyes would tell him if the potion had struck home. He needed to know. He didn't want to know.

With a grunt he pulled on his coat and strode out into the yard. Cheerful chimes greeted him, strings of eight notes repeated. Meliroc was sporting with Pierpon again. Smiling in hope at this sign his elixir might have failed, he quickened his pace.

"Mistress Meliroc," he called, "you may come inside if you like."

Nightmare Lullaby

A distinctly unmusical thunk followed, a mallet dropped without much care for where it fell. He heard her fingers pulling hastily at the strings that held the flap shut. An instant later it fell open, and her head appeared in the canvas doorway, with Pierpon clinging to her shoulder like a tom-kitten. Stepping back, Cedelair watched her emerge until at last she unfolded to her full height. He doubted he would ever grow used to standing under the eyes of such a tall being. But he forced himself to look up to meet those eyes, and found them shining with the philter's spell. *Imfaphia amorat* triumphant.

She spoke no word as she walked beside him to the cottage, a book cradled in the crook of her arm and Pierpon rocking on her shoulder. But he felt her gaze, her shy little smile, the warmth that rolled over him like a swelling tide. *Green man – my green man – I'd hold you – kiss you until the light comes into your eyes–* The thoughts poured into him on the current. Once she played the song she wanted so badly, the effect would fade. He'd taken care to fix an ending point. He hoped she would lose no time.

For the hours that followed, the four sat silent in the parlor, each of them full of thoughts too heavy to confide. Valeraine pored over *The Magical Art of the Geas*, hoping to stumble onto a clue she'd missed the first time through. Cedelair thumbed through *Musical Enchantments*, struggling to fix his attention on the page and stop his eye from drifting toward Meliroc. The giant's gaze kept throwing warmth at him. She, too, had a book open in her lap, the volume of love poems Mennieve had bestowed. Pierpon, seated on her arm, gazed down at the pages. She would read a page, then smile at Cedelair, read another page, then smile again. He felt her yearning to say something that might interest or delight him, yet she kept silent, fearful of sounding foolish. She thought it best just to lend him her warmth.

Lifelord save me from what I've done.

When she closed the book at last, Pierpon hopped down from her arm. She turned her eyes again to Cedelair, a quizzical tilt in her head. "Sir." Her thought-voice brushed against him like a tentative touch on the shoulder. "Would you please tell me something about yourself?"

His breath grew short. "What do you want to know?"

"Something real." He saw her shudder and gnaw at her lip. "Tell me about something you enjoyed doing when you were a boy."

Strange, chilly thoughts broke into his mind. *Crime chasing me... veixal... I'll know... he'll know...*

Locking his mind on thoughts he knew were his, he cast his memory back over the days before trouble had left its first mark. A bubbling stream, the water swirling over his toes, friends bellowing with glee as they splashed themselves up to their calves...

"My friends and I used to go wading in Doriot Brook," he said. "Four of us – Feot, Rybert, Roselise, and I. As soon as the weather turned warm, we'd pull off our boots and stockings and run barefoot down the hill to that stream. Roselise was the smallest of us, but somehow she always managed to reach it first." He tried for a moment to remember when he'd last spoken Roselise's name. "For hours we'd splash and shout and skip over the river-stones. We'd do our share of sliding, and we'd end up with bruised knees, but that was part of the fun."

"Naturally," agreed Meliroc, beaming as she drank in his story.

"The sun would pour down through the trees and make the ripples shine. We'd chase the glints of light, calling them evil fairies and trying to step on them."

"Oh, dear." Meliroc shook with a laughing grin.

"Then we'd sit down on the bank and tell wild tales about all the places we'd travel and the adventures we would have." He saw Valeraine lean forward in her chair. "Perhaps even then we knew we were only dreaming."

"What became of them?"

He stiffened, gripping the arms of his chair as one waiting to have a splinter drawn out. "Rybert was Mennieve's son," he began. "Pneumonia took him during a hard winter. We were eleven." He clenched his teeth at the old sting.

Meliroc's eyes misted. *Green man, I wish I could carry your grief for you.* Her feelings wove their way into his.

"Feot left for the city when he was sixteen. We wrote to each other for a while, but life has a way of filling up your days."

She nodded, understanding. "And the girl? Roselise?"

Roselise, small, quick to laugh. Everything Meliroc wasn't. "She broke my heart."

The giant's head sank. "I'm very sorry, sir."

He gave her a sad but assuring smile. "It's all right. It's the way life works, you know. Happy memories walk hand in hand with sad ones."

"I'd like to see that brook," she mentioned, with a trace of a smile. "Would you show it to me?"

The hand at his heart squeezed lightly, a gentle nudge. "When you are free of your geas, we will visit Doriot Brook."

She nodded, tacitly accepting this answer while her mouth wilted into a solemn moue. Fear flashed in her eyes. "How will it work, exactly? Going inside my dream?"

To business, he sighed to himself as he rose from his chair and approached his potion cabinet. "You'll need this." He plucked a dusty heliotrope bottle from the top row. "A sleep draught. Very powerful." When he tossed it to her, she caught it in her left hand. "When you're ready to sleep, drink it, then settle down here." He gestured toward the open space on the floor.

Taking the space's measure, she shook her head. "I doubt I'd sleep at all, scrunched up there."

"Drink that potion and you'll sleep anywhere, at any time. Once you're asleep, I'll do the rest."

"It won't hurt?"

"Not one bit." He attempted an encouraging smile. "Nothing at all to be afraid of."

"Nothing," she echoed, "except what you will think of me – Sir, could we wait? Until the love-spell wears off? Then it won't matter so much..." She broke off with a furious shudder. "No. Best to have it over with."

"Is this absolutely necessary?" Pierpon spoke up, patting Meliroc's hand.

"You want Mistress Meliroc set free, don't you?" Cedelair returned.

"Of course, but"–

"He's right." Forcing a smile, Meliroc tousled the jickety's hair with the tip of her index finger. "Some things need looking at full on, ugly as they may be. Get some rest of your own, my friend. I will be all right."

Cedelair could hear the jickety grinding his teeth as he stomped toward Valeraine's open chamber door. He shot another dagger-glower at the elder sorcerer before he vanished into the room. But Cedelair scarcely noticed. Meliroc's mournful stare held him fast.

Inching toward the open space, she downed the potion and flopped onto her side, head bent and legs folded. "I am ready."

***

Colors all around.

Families of reds, greens, blues, yellows, shades of every description swirled and dipped and winked at one another in no logical pattern that Cedelair could see. Ghost-white fingers dipped into the chaotic rainbow to weave wild, blinding tints the waking world did not know. Cedelair's head hurt to behold them, while Meliroc's spun with joy. As she mixed each cast it sang to her in pure, clear notes, until a melody rose from the profusion.

A face bent down, the same snowy shade as the fingers. The lips kissed the surface of the colors, and the tongue lapped them up. The eerie liquid slid down Meliroc's throat, strong with a flavor like no familiar food or drink. As it settled on her chest, she threw her head back and spread her fingers wide. Streams of colored light exploded from her mouth, her fingertips, and the ends of her hair. Weight left her. She hovered in the midst of the rainbow. Her bones were dissolving, her flesh and skin melting into the light. She was becoming the colors. The melody soared, the song of Meliroc's bodiless spirit.

A whip with a flint-spark at the tip flashed through the colors. A wave of pain struck her, rendering her solid once more, pinned against a cold stone wall. The colors spilled out, leaving no trace behind. A figure draped in a hooded ochre robe rose before her, barely half as tall as herself but full of threat. Two fierce, cold yellow lights blazed out from the shadow of the hood.

"Think yourself rid of me, do you?" At each syllable a barb sank into her skin. Pain ripped through her skull. She pressed hard against the wall, as if she hoped to pass through it and escape.

"All you are, I taught you to be. I taught you to read." A force shot forth from the points of light, slamming into her shoulders and neck. "I taught you to use your mind to speak." Another blow, lower, against her breast-bone. She bit her cheek, and the flat taste of blood filled her mouth. "I taught you what music is." A third blow, straight into her stomach, knocked the breath from her. She collapsed to her knees. "I am in every breath you draw and every thought you think. You can't escape me."

The points of light wrapped a barbed cord around her throat. As it tore into her neck, her sobs sharpened into screams. She fought hard to hold them inside. No voice. No voice. But her body quaked with them. She wished she might faint, slide out of consciousness and end the agony, but her senses were only sharpening.

Her mouth wrenched open. A scream erupted from it.

Every sorrow, every pang, every blow ripped through that scream – not merely the pains she'd suffered, but oceans of suffering she had never known. She writhed, eyes growing red with maddening misery. Her limbs convulsed. Her bones were lengthening, changing strength and texture. Her arms spread to vault her upward. She began to spin, her head thrown side to side. Still she screamed, a hideous, inhuman cry. Cedelair recognized it as the scream Valeraine had shared with him.

She spun faster until her features and form were lost in a blur. A gale roared beneath her outstretched arms, swallowing her feet, legs, and waist. Two heavy feathered cords sprouted from her back. These wings arrested her spin at last. At one more shock of anguish, her mind shattered into dust. Meliroc was gone.

In her place hovered a thing of horror such as Cedelair had never beheld even in his darkest dreams. He could not put a name to it. Rather like a fury, part bird, be-winged and feathered from the chest up, but with a womanish face, its features contorted in quenchless rage, its mouth open to reveal razor-like teeth. Its gray hair twisted and tangled, and its eyes glowed a furious rose. Below the chest, a white cyclone raged, holding her aloft more surely than the wings.

The figure in the cape and hood shrank out of sight.

The thing launched itself into a night's sky unbrightened by stars or moon, its horrible open mouth emitting a blackness that would stain any soul it touched. A sweet freckled face rose before Cedelair. The eyes met his, and the delicate pursed mouth twisted into a cruel grin. An ugly laugh stabbed at his ears, worse than the monster's screams.

That monster flew and cried without thought. It knew nothing but pain. Its only relief was to loose that pain into the world, to fire it into everything that heard it scream. Everything asleep.

Cedelair gasped. With a jolt he wrenched himself back into his own mind, into the dim candle-light of the parlor. Valeraine glanced at him with a tremulous smile, the horror in her eyes matching his own. Thus he knew she had come back with him.

Meliroc lay on her side, shaking, her knees tucked against her middle, her face twisted with the agony of the dream. Her mouth stretched wide in a scream, but no sound came forth. Tears poured down her cheeks. He ventured a look into her wide-open eyes and found there the furious whirlwind that held the fiend aloft, a monstrous echo of the nightmare mark in the eyes of the victims.

One thought sank into his mind with the pitiless weight of an avalanche. *This thing must die.*

***

He felt Valeraine's questioning stare as he rose to his feet. He could not look at her now. She could not know what he meant to do until too late for her to stop him.

He opened the silverware chest and took up the sharpest knife. Tucking it behind his back, he moved past his apprentice with cautious step. Again her eyes followed him, but still she did not speak.

He knelt beside the sleeping thing. One quick slash across the throat would suffice. She would not even wake. No, it, *it* would not wake. That "Meliroc," that strange interloper with her mind-voice and her music, was merely a glamour that kept the fiend concealed. He fingered the knife-handle, watching the white fury-wind spin in the thing's eyes, seeking in it some thread of the familiar green. He found none. Yet he knew that when the fiend woke, the glamour would reappear, the shadow that could so easily convince him it was a real person with thoughts and feelings.

He raised the blade, training his eye on that point in the neck where blood flowed fastest. At the same moment the thing convulsed with a low, cracked breath. The head twitched. The eyelids fluttered. The knife dropped from his hand as she – not it – looked at him with tear-shining eyes.

She threw her arms about him and clasped him close.

13. Meliroc encounters an old friend, and Pierpon stands firm

Through the teary blur I felt more than saw Cedelair beside me. I held him for dear life, my head whirling in a riot, my chest aching with even the tiniest breath, my muscles burning as if I'd been embroiled in a hard fight. He turned brittle in my clasp but did not push me away. When I dropped my arms I heard him breathe a relieved sigh, and I opened my eyes cautiously, trying to conjure so dreadful a vision of what I would see in his face that the reality would prove a comfort by comparison.

No. Nothing could have prepared me for his look. Revulsion blared from his eyes and quivered in his scowling mouth. His glower hammered at my heart, harder by far than the Bitter Chord's blows. I forced myself to lock my gaze with his and to ask what needed asking. "What did you see?"

He clenched his jaw. "I cannot tell you."

"Why?"

"I will tell you in good time."

"That's not an answer, sir."

"Leave it. There's your answer."

My mouth dropped open in a perfect O. Had my master just commanded me? Leave it? How could I leave it? Only what he'd seen in my dream could make him look at me this way. And now he would not tell me?

He'd tricked me. So like a sorcerer. *Sir, you promised.* My mind-voice formed the words, but when it tried to send them a pang racked my head. My master had ordered me to leave it. I could not disobey.

How dare you, sir! Again my mind-voice longed to shout, and the pang shook me doubly hard. Past the fog of pain I saw Cedelair's pitiless face. I could not even cry out to protest his unfairness. Damn him!

I turned to Valeraine and found her staring down at her hands in her lap. "Mistress Valeraine? Do you know what he saw?"

She drew in a wincing breath. Of course she knew. He'd probably shown her. *Can you tell me?* I tried to speak the question, and once more my head pounded. So I could not get around my master's command by addressing myself to his apprentice.

I turned a scalding glare on Cedelair. Knowing no look of mine would shake him only angered me more. My heart-fire churned in a way I knew well, sending its heat through every clenched nerve. My fingers burned with lust to break something, to tear something to pieces. Yet that tremor of soft warmth, that yearning towards him, moved through my veins. If I couldn't tear or break, I would caress his cheek and bathe his brow in kisses.

"Leave us awhile, please, Meliroc," Valeraine whispered in a meant-to-be-soothing voice, with a nod toward the door. "I need to talk with Master Cedelair. We will call for you soon."

Her tone rattled my raging nerves. "Call for me? Soon? How shall I come back in? Squeeze under the rear door?"

"Meliroc, please-"

"'Please'? You should learn from your master, good Mistress Valeraine. No one says 'please' to me." I strode for the door. "I will gladly go outside, because I can't bear your faces a minute longer." My gaze drifted to Cedelair, giving the lie to my words.

I let a door slam be my final word and smiled a little as I imagined it splintering from its hinges. Leave it, indeed. Damn them both.

I drove my boots hard into the snow. With my hands still itching to break, I decided that taking up my instrument would not be the best of ideas. Instead, I forged through the moonlight pool into the dark, not caring where I was going, wanting only to be away, and wondering just how far I could walk before the leash pulled me back.

I breathed in, summoning strength to my legs and feet. A blanket of black cloud had smothered the stars I'd been admiring a little time before. The darkness around me seemed a living thing, despairing, lost. It needed company. *Darkness, take me in. Let no one find me.*

Where I would find myself when dawn came, I could not care. But it would be as far from Cedelair as these remaining hours of night would carry me.

***

"Pierpon? Please wake, Pierpon."

Pierpon blinked at the candle's glare, his foggy just-awakened senses taking note of Valeraine's troubled face. "What are you about, vixen?" he grumbled.

"We need your help," she told him.

His pulse raced. Only once had either of the sorcerers asked for his help – when Valeraine had called him into her nightmare. He threw off his covers and sprang from his box. Scrambling down the edge of the bureau, he ignored Valeraine's gestured offer to carry him. For a moment he blubbered his lips at the touch of the cold hardwood floor under his feet, but he steeled himself and scampered after her into the parlor. Cedelair sat in his high-backed chair, wearing a somber scowl.

"Pierpon." Valeraine reached out toward him with a cautious look, as if she were about to thrust her hand into a beehive.

He pulled a frown. "Yes, what is it, now you've pulled me out of bed?"

"Please touch my hand and look into my eyes."

"Why?"

"I need to show you something."

"I remember that dream of yours, vixen, down to the last bloody detail."

"This isn't from my dream." Her look grew plaintive. "We've caught a glimpse of the thing causing the nightmares, but we need your help to identify it."

He coughed hard as his mouth went dry. The spires of Jicket-Castle gleamed silver bright in his mind. "Well, then, let's have a look, let's."

She took his hand between her fingers. Her whisper in the alien tongue fastened his gaze on the dark of her eye. A fog swept her face away, and he felt more than saw that strange force in her eye approaching him. His stomach froze. The fog dissipated as a figure pushed through it, coming closer, closer, until it hovered overhead, beating a freezing wind down upon him.

He had never seen this being before or anything like it. All the same, he knew it. The wide dark wings, the twisted face, the mouth that belched black smoke with its scream – all familiar, as if he'd met them every night in dark dreams of his own. The word his memory had been fumbling for now came to him, cold and terrible.

"*Leyshak.*" He gulped, gagging as his stomach seized in revulsion. "Where did you see that?"

Valeraine exchanged a quick frown with Cedelair before turning back to Pierpon. "In another dream. You say this thing is called a *leyshak*? What exactly is it?"

Pierpon fought to stiffen his jaw as the grotesque face leered in his memory. "How could somebody dream of a *leyshak*? No one even knows about them!"

"Master Jickety, kindly explain yourself," Cedelair intoned in a low, rasping voice.

"We're the lords of dreams," Pierpon said. "We used your dreams to make you all forget. This was well before my time, sir. I only know the old stories. How the worst of nightmares grew minds and souls and became *leyshak*. How they could send whole cities mad. How we drove them away and saw to it no human ever remembered them. They're gone! We got rid of them, we did!"

"Obviously you didn't," grunted Cedelair, his mouth drawn tight in a snarl. "One of them must have slipped your nets, because it's loose and flying around Crainante."

"It can't be." The protest shriveled on his tongue, while the details of Valeraine's nightmare rushed at him in all their fury, setting his stomach swirling with the urge to vomit. Some living thing had been in that dream with her, relishing her pain. The *leyshak* fed on pain. "It doesn't make sense. No human could know what they look like."

"Pierpon," said Valeraine, "this image didn't come from the dream of a human."

"What, then? Did you capture a gold-cap? Even he wouldn't know what a *leyshak* looks like."

Cedelair and Valeraine exchanged a frown. What Pierpon read in their eyes dropped a stone on his heart. His mind bolted away from an unendurable thought.

"Jicketies don't exist for us humans except in dreams," the girl noted to her master. "Yet here is Pierpon, hurled out of his natural sphere, corporeal."

"Your fault, you might add," grumbled Pierpon.

"Suppose the same thing happened to the *leyshak*," Valeraine went on, ignoring him. "Somehow it was banished into our realm, and it had to take on some solid form."

"That's not quite what happened." Cedelair's eyes gleamed with an idea. "It was caught. Someone captured it and pulled it into the waking world."

Valeraine's eyes brightened, too. "Someone with power."

"Power enough to force it to take a certain corporeal shape."

"Something big. Many would relish wielding such strength over a big thing."

"A giant."

"No!" Pierpon screamed as if they'd run him through. "Not my Meliroc, no!"

Valeraine gave him a melting look. "You know whose dream we were about to look into when you went off to bed, Pierpon," she told him in a soft, kind voice. "And if what you say is true, the only being who could dream of a *leyshak* is a *leyshak*."

Pierpon gasped as the unendurable thought gripped his chest. "How dare you," he snapped. "Meliroc is not a *leyshak*. She is good. I know her better than you do."

The sorcerers spoke to each other, with nary a glance at him. "That's another thing. Whoever caught this creature – the yellow-eyed woman, let's say – cast a spell she couldn't control," Cedelair expressed his theory.

"Give the dream-thing a solid form in the waking world, and there's no telling what she might develop into," agreed Valeraine.

"So now we have two beings in one, Meliroc with a soul of her own and the destroyer in the dream. That fits with what we saw."

"She was dreaming of color and song, in keeping with her waking nature, and then"--

"That woman turned up, hurt her, goaded her --"

"– Roused the *leyshak* --"

"– And Meliroc was burned away."

"Shut up!" Pierpon's shout rattled the ceiling. "She's not some insect under glass! She's Meliroc! She's decent! She's my friend!"

Valeraine cast an abashed glance at him. "She's also a *leyshak*."

"Curse you!" he roared, brandishing his fist. "Why did you have to meddle with her dream anyway? Not to help her, that's plain."

"We needed to know what she is, Pierpon," she explained. "She turned into a hideous thing with a terrible cry, the same cry you heard in my nightmare."

Fired by a swell of rage, he dashed for the door, intent on finding Meliroc and warning her what these magicians thought of her. He leaped up to fold himself around the doorknob.

"It's not easy for us to swallow either, Master Jickety," Cedelair called after him.

"Is it not?" Pierpon scoffed. "You seem to be having a grand time, trading your theories. But let me tell you this. I love her whatever she may be. Try to harm her, and small as I am, I will stand between you and her."

He twisted the knob, then sprang through the open door, closing it with a heavy backward shove.

He bolted through the moonlight ring toward the shadow of Meliroc's tent. Though the night was nearly as pitch-black as a windowless room, he could make out the open flap. Ignoring the bite of the snow under his feet, he tiptoed through it. No sign of her lay within, no lump under blankets, no dim glimmer of a white head. When he banged his toe against her bell-board and the thing let out a muffled clang of protest, he knew she couldn't be far. Hopping, grinding his teeth, he made his way outside again, peering right and left, in search of her. Even in this dark she would glow.

Yet he found only shadows all around.

"Meliroc!" he called out, cringing at the sting of the falling snow. "Snow-giant!"

Still no sign. The sorcerers must have said something to wound her, and she had wandered off to nurse her injuries alone. She had to come back. Her geas notwithstanding, she would not abandon her instrument. Shaking the snow from his hair, he crawled back into the tent, then nestled against her pile of thick blankets. Imagining he could feel her warmth in their folds, he sank into them. As he drew them about him until they swallowed him, he indulged in a vision of home, but not as he'd known it. Meliroc was there, kneeling at the center of a ring of his comrades, listening to their boastful tales and laughing in a voice as bright as the bells she played. With a sigh he drifted into slumber.

He woke to an itchy nose and a thickness of breath. With a cough he elbowed his way up from the bundle of blankets. He blinked at the light that swept in through the opening. Dawn already? He didn't think he'd slept so long, or so deeply. Meliroc still had not returned. The light fell upon her bell-board, and he smiled at the thought of the next game they'd play. He crawled to the mouth of the tent and poked his head outside.

Where the cottage should be, he found a wall of fire.

***

Foot-sore and out of breath, I sank down. A light snowfall melted on my hands.

I couldn't guess how far I'd walked. I suspected I'd been trudging in circles. I still felt the closeness of surrounding trees. Silence held me fast, a tangible thing with strangling hands. It couldn't hold sway forever. Music had to follow on its heels, the first chirp of a bird as morning came. Could the song that followed silence be the song Feuval needed? With hard-fought breath I pulled my shoulders back. I still had a task to perform.

I yanked myself upright. As I started forward, I imagined my bell-board in the crook of my arm and my mallet in my opposite hand. I let my longing for my instrument guide my steps. My ties to the place, stronger even than my must, were drawing me. A pixy-man with a porcupine mustache was sleeping in a doll case, his dreams untouched by the trouble in the parlor. I wanted to be near when he woke. I quickened my pace, stretching out my hands to feel my way around the trees.

Clearing my mind of all but my bell-board and Pierpon, I willed my must to snap its reins and pull me back to my temporary home. Once there I would decide what to do about Cedelair. A tremor swept up from my toes, and my nerves cooled in relief. I knew where to go. I pushed myself faster.

On I walked, feeling the tightness of my string. How odd to take pleasure in it, to know I'd drawn upon it of my own will! I blinked against a light-headed rush, not quite sure if the eerie yellow-white glow up ahead were reality or a dream of a phantom city where towers were lit even at deepest night. My nose wrinkled at the scent of smoke. After another two steps, my breath thickened with it. A bolt of fear jostled me out of my dizziness. I charged toward the light, my every sense now blade-sharp.

Through the last line of trees I could see Cedelair's cottage wreathed in flame. Pierpon huddled near the door of my tent, rocking back and forth as he sent anguished wails up to the sky. That I didn't see Cedelair or Valeraine could only mean they were trapped within those burning walls.

I centered my every feeling on my heart-fire. *Shrink*. It dwindled and died with a tiny gasp of smoke. I needed cold. I visualized the blue-white of an iced-over window pane and willed that color into my heart. My fingers grew numb. My limbs stung as needle-shards of ice swam in my blood. Satisfied that I was colder than even the winter around me, I hurled myself at the place where the door should be.

The sorcerers huddled together, crouched low on the floor, whispering in one of their secret lingoes. Flames had devoured walls, shelves, cabinets, chairs, clock, yet an unseen magical hand held them off from Cedelair and Valeraine. They might shield themselves with a spell, but they couldn't snuff out the fire and break free.

I stretched my arms and swooped down upon them, hoisting them off the floor, one under each arm. He stiffened, while she gripped my waist. I leaped through the fiery wall, keeping my frost-cloak folded close about them, and dropped face down upon the snow outside.

With a grunt Cedelair rolled out of my grasp and drew himself to his knees. Valeraine's shaking arms wrapped more tightly about my waist. As my teeth rattled, I willed the cold away and called my heart-fire back into being, my eyes closed tight. I heard a thunderous crumbling, the cottage falling in upon itself.

Blinking, I scooped up Pierpon and set him on my shoulder, and he threw his arms about my neck. I folded an arm about Valeraine as my own heart plunged into my shoes. Cedelair knelt apart, staring empty-eyed at the ashy ruins of his house. My gaze drifted toward the great oak he had saved. At least it still stood strong. Bitter comfort, indeed.

Valeraine hiccoughed, then peered up at me with wet, red eyes. "We were practicing meditation spells," she sniffed.

She was small as a child in my arms. It felt right, somehow, to comfort her as I'd seen mothers soothe their weeping youngsters, holding her close to my breast and stroking her hair.

"My idea," she went on. "Sometimes meditation can answer hard questions, if we sink deep enough." She glanced down, like one who had said the wrong thing. "It worked well. I was in some place of perfect quiet, where I couldn't even feel myself breathe. I thought I heard something fall, but it seemed to come from the other side of a dream. By the time the smell of smoke broke in on us, it was too late." She convulsed, locking her fingers around the folds of my tunic. "We shielded ourselves as best we could. If we'd stopped speaking the spell for one second, the roof would have come down on us. We couldn't have kept it up much longer."

I nodded. Her voice sounded raspy and hollow from speaking a long while. "Anything could have started it," she choked. "A splinter tumbling out of the hearth, or even a word one of us might have mumbled in our trance, anything, and we'll never know." She squeezed my waist. "You saved us."

I glanced from the pile of blackened rubble to the golden head resting against my chest, to the slender man in the stiff frock coat with his grim, tearless face, to the garden just a few feet away, still green and thriving. Relief ran through me like a balmy wash. I had gotten them out. The question of whether my must would have demanded I save them didn't matter in the slightest. I'd gotten them out because I'd wanted to.

Cedelair rose to his feet and approached me. I felt the chill of his distaste, a milder version of the earlier loathing. Yet something in his eyes defied my efforts to name it.

"You're real, aren't you?" he grunted, a question too strange for a reply.

14. Cedelair looks up from the ruins

A gray haze shrouding his senses, Cedelair breathed a phrase in the *Fourth Tongue* and slid his fingers into the soil. He cupped his hand about the tangle of roots and gently drew the fene'vaith plant from the earth with its source of life intact. He wondered idly why he bothered, when over the next few days it and all the plants from his garden would be ground into powder for potions. A more practical person would yank it up as quickly as possible. But snapping a root went against Cedelair's nature, and his nature was nearly all he had left.

He heard Meliroc's canvas roof collapse and forced his mind to turn from the vision that racked it – tendrils of fire curling around the walls that had sheltered him all his life – and toward more practical matters. He and his household needed somewhere to stay. He had sent Valeraine to toll the great bell in the square and give the news of what had happened, and Pierpon, surprisingly, had chosen to go with her, tucked in her skirt-pocket, rather than stick close to his adored Meliroc. By the time Cedelair was finished in his garden, all Crainante would know how he had lost his home, and he would know just what friends he still had. Mennieve, of course, would do all she could for him, but her bookshop hadn't room enough to shelter him and Valeraine, or space outside for Meliroc to pitch her tent. Splitting up was not to be considered.

A light, warm wind draped around his neck like a scarf. He rose to his feet, slapping the soil from his knees.

"Can I help?" Meliroc asked him.

He turned to face her and saw behind her the big wheel-barrow loaded but for the plants. Yet she had evidently ducked inside her tent just before striking it, to make herself presentable. Only her ebony cloak bore the marks of last night's disaster in a few singed frays around its edges. Clad in her black trousers and dove gray satin tunic, her hair billowing white down her shoulders and back, she resembled a frost queen of ancient legend, beautiful but too forbidding to inspire affection. What absurd notions girls could entertain!

"You've done quite enough, I should think," he replied, forcing a smile lest she misunderstand him. "I ask your pardon. What I did last night was beneath me." Thank the Lifelord she would never know he'd nearly done her a far worse wrong than forbidding her to ask questions.

"I know it was, sir." She tucked her chin a little. "Were we to keep to our better natures all the time, it would be nothing short of a miracle."

"You don't hate me anymore, I see."

"Not at the moment," she returned, tilting her head. "I might say the same to you."

He bit back a dry laugh, thinking how easily he could repeat her own words. Not at the moment.

"I ran away last night," she said. "If I'd been closer at hand, I could have prevented this." She gestured toward the ashes of the house. "I didn't guard you as I should have."

Again a laugh rose to his throat, and this time he let it out. "I drove you off. Truth to tell, I'd expected you'd run away."

"That is some relief," she returned, an echo of his laugh in her eyes. "I couldn't bear your thinking I hated you so much that I'd stand by and let your house burn, and only pulled you out at the last minute because my must forced me to."

He shook his head. "That's not like you, Mistress Meliroc."

"What am I like, then?"

He looked hard into the ghostly face before him and thought of the memories he'd drawn from her, now locked in his mind to stay. "You're someone who fights every day to hold onto the part that chooses," he said, "the part where music lives. Someone who would rather love than hate."

She stepped forward to close the gap between them, then clasped his hand, ignoring the flecks of soil. "Thank you for that." Her mind-voice spoke in an intense whisper. "I will remember it whenever I feel frightened of myself."

He looked down, then around him at his garden, his chore still only two-thirds done. Her mouth wilted into a solemn frown. "This task must give you pain. Are you certain I can't help? I've watched how you bring the roots up. I think I could do it."

"And spoil your nice clothes? I wouldn't hear of it." He looked her up and down, noting the way her peculiar dress style, the boots and trousers and the skirted tunics, accentuated the lithe length of her frame. "Do you ever wear gowns?"

Mirth-sparks blinked shyly in her eyes. "Modish gowns? With outspread skirts? Try picturing me in such a garment." She cupped her palm around the corner of her lip. "Here she comes, ladies and gentlemen – the Walking Tent!"

A single guffaw escaped before he could cough it away. She had no business making him laugh at such a time. His shifting gaze came to rest on the bell-board. "There is something you can do for me. Play the 'Song of Sorrow'."

"I would have thought you'd had your fill of sorrow."

"Trust me, Mistress Meliroc. That song is just what I need to hear."

With a little shrug she unhooked her bell-board and mallet. She caught the board in the crook of her arm while he moved further into the garden. Heaving a shaky breath, he sank to his knees and slipped his fingers into the soil as the first notes sounded, sweet, clear, and heartbreaking. Meliroc's voice.

How had he persuaded himself she was a mere illusion, the fair form of a foul thing?

He let the tune take hold of his heart and settle there, wearing away the last of the black sludge that had numbed his feelings for so long. Tears slid down his stony face. He welcomed them.

***

Valeraine met Cedelair and Meliroc at the door of Fimbre's Books. Her shawl lost to the fire, she was swallowed in one of Meliroc's tunics, a black-trimmed burgundy that ill matched the seafoam muslin gown underneath. She waved a floppy sleeve in greeting. Beside her stood a stocky young man in bottle green livery, with a blunt, square face and carrot-red hair. Cedelair might have managed to recall his name, if he hadn't been distracted by the sight of the shutters of the big house behind the shop, thrown open to admit the light.

Nightmare Lullaby

"Go in, sir." Valeraine tilted her head toward the bookshop door. "Mennieve has hot tea waiting for you. She'll tell you everything you need to know. Meliroc, we could use your strong limbs just now, if you please."

Pushing her wheelbarrow before her, Meliroc trudged after Valeraine and the strange young man. Cedelair saw them disappear behind the shop. Then she heard the door of the big house, so long boarded, creak open and slam shut.

He called to Mennieve from the shop doorway and hurried down the corridor of shelves. His friend bolted out to meet him and draw him into a hug. "Cedelair, my lad," she cooed, patting his back. "My poor, poor lad." With a gentle clasp of his hand she drew him into the parlor, where, as Valeraine had said, a cup of hot tea awaited him. "You still have friends aplenty, never doubt that," she assured him. "Trust us old folks."

"I trust nobody more than you, Mennieve," he returned. "Valeraine said you would tell me everything. Why are the shutters of the big house open? Why did Meliroc and Valeraine go in there with some redheaded fellow I can't quite remember?"

Mennieve squeezed his elbow. "Because you're going to stay there. Remember how you used to love to stay overnight at the Echo House? Of course everything's frightfully dusty, so I got some young people in to tidy up. The young man you saw is Bonfert. He's Sundiffe's head under-servant."

"Sundiffe?" Cedelair recalled the counting-man had been good friends with his parents. He'd come to dinner often, and Cedelair had always been told to keep to his room during his visits. Cedelair had always found him prickly and standoffish.

"I told you, trust the old folks," said Mennieve. "We remember Xuot and Alysotte, and we remember you. We remember what you did five years ago."

"I didn't do any — "

"Shush, my lad. You were a hero then, no mistake. And even so, more than one of us owes you for that potion you gave us." She gave his arm another friendly squeeze. "I've asked Bonfert to take you shopping after we've had a chance to chat. Anything you need to make you comfortable while you sort out what to do next."

Cedelair kissed Mennieve's brow. His mind was running through the Echo House with the wonderful winding banister, the perfect steepness for young boys to slide down, and the hallways with plenty of room for those boys to romp, and the closets and corners perfect for hide and seek. Whenever his parents had made him angry he had threatened to run away to the Echo House.

"I never dreamed you'd open that house again," he murmured.

"Why not? It's the perfect place for you, with plenty of room for you and your apprentice and your good colossus. Besides, as long as I don't have to go into it, it's no trouble for me, is it?"

"All the same, I'll never be able to thank you enough."

She patted his cheek. "Nonsense, Cedelair. This is my atonement."

"What in the Lifelord's name for?"

"For letting you stay shut away in your house and never doing anything about it. I could have come to you, dear lad. You could have used a friend, and I stayed away." She kissed his cheek. "And I think Rybert would be glad to have you living in his house for a while."

Tears spilled down as he leaned on Mennieve's blue gingham shoulder, not the first he'd shed this day and not, he feared, the last. When he felt too tired to cry more, Mennieve gave his cheek another kiss and gently drew back from him. "Your tea's gone cold," she noted. "I'll get you a fresh cup."

She bustled to the stove, humming low under her breath, a tune he knew well, Meliroc's joyful song. Meliroc this, Meliroc that. Would he be forever thinking of that name? "Mennieve, do you think you can be in love without knowing it?"

"Odd question," Mennieve returned with a wry whisper of a chuckle, passing the teacup into his hands. "Could I be in love without knowing it? I gravely doubt it. Could you? It's a possibility."

"Why? What's the difference between us?"

"You're a man, my dear," she explained with a pat on the back of his hand. "Men don't know half of what's in their hearts. A feeling has to leap up and take them by the throat for them to know it's there."

"That's nonsense."

"I had to tell Fimbre he loved me. He didn't know it until he heard me say it. But why do you ask?"

"Valeraine thinks I'm in love."

"Well, lad, I hope she's right. It's high time you were in love again."

"An object like me?" he scoffed. "I'd look more ridiculous than usual paying court to some respectable lady."

"That 'respectable lady' would be quite lucky. You're a fine young man, Cedelair." The stress she laid upon *young* did not escape him. "You have it in you to make a good woman very happy indeed."

A warm hand folded around his heart to soothe the ache of grief. He wrapped his arms about Mennieve and kissed her cheek.

***

Cedelair studied Bonfert, taking in his air of hyper-competence, his iron straight posture, and his formal, clipped speech, not aloof but not dripping with pretended grief or instant friendship. In short, the sort of man Cedelair preferred to deal with just now.

"I am to help you find any provisions you might need," Bonfert proclaimed. "Clothing, food, and tools for your work. Master Sundiffe says he will cover all expense."

Cedelair started a mental list as he and his household set off with Bonfert down the side-path. Cauldrons, pestle, grinding bowl, cutting board, knife...

His stomach clenched at the sight of the throng drifting after them. Meliroc moved to guard him, stretching out a protective arm. A few of them called the Lifelord's blessing down on him in his hour of need. Most simply stared, intrigued to see how he would handle himself in this crisis. In an old, practiced way he ironed all traces of expression from his face, determined to keep his grief to himself. Some moments he could almost hold his head upright without effort. At other times he feared he would snap in two.

He moved through the next hour in a daze as the efficient Bonfert led him and his household to the clothiers and handed over coin for two sets of trousers and shirts and a royal blue long-coat for Cedelair and an ice-blue knit winter shawl and three gowns for Valeraine. Cauldrons, cutting-board, and grinding pestle were swiftly acquired afterward, along with a basket, a wooden penny-flute, and a spindle with which Valeraine might weave moonlight. Bonfert divided his time between making sensible deals with merchants and chatting amiably with Valeraine, who had discovered he shared her taste for adventure books. More than once he drew her back from the brink of tears with a mention of the exploits of Black Elbrit and his bold right hand, Dorysse. I like him, Cedelair decided.

The elder sorcerer himself walked in the lead as the little group strode toward Master Odilon's side-shop. Odilon must have sighted their approach from his window, for he flung the door open and called out a hearty greeting. "My dear man, what a dreadfully unhappy business! Do come in. Your friends, as well." He nodded to them as they entered one by one.

Meliroc knelt beside the string of multi-colored rods hung over the window, her gaze drinking in each shade. Cedelair thought he could hear her mind-voice whispering their names, a chime tinkling at each one. *Aramanthine, celeste, jacinthe, heliotrope, vermilion...* She met his look with a smile. "Colors have notes," she told him. "They sing."

He cast a quick glance down at his toes then turned his full attention on Odilon. "Take all the phials you like," the glassworker was saying, leading Valeraine toward the counter with a hand on her shoulder. "It's the least I owe you for the potion you gave my Loliette. She's much better now, see?" He gestured toward the moon-faced child in the wrinkled dress, perched on the stool behind the counter.

"Lolly, my love," her father coaxed, "is there something you'd like to say to Mistress Valeraine?"

The little girl gnawed at her lip. "I'm sorry, Mistress Valeraine," she mumbled.

"I'm sorry, as well," Odilon said. "Whatever you need, my good Cedelair, say the word."

"Thank you," Cedelair returned with a quick nod. His attention drifted back to Meliroc, who still gazed down the line of sunlit rods.

Loliette gave a woeful sniffle. "Who is that?" she whispered, shoulders hunched.

"That's Meliroc," Valeraine answered, seeing the direction of Loliette's frightened glance. "She's our friend. She saved us from the fire last night."

"Did she, indeed!" Odilon beamed at Meliroc. "Well done, large lovely!"

Loliette scrunched up her quivering face. "I hate her," she grumbled.

Wrenched from her reverie, Meliroc turned toward Loliette, who shut her eyes with a fearful squeak. "Loliette!" the girl's father snapped. "Apologize at once!"

"I won't!" wailed Loliette, jumping from her stool and darting toward Odilon. "She's big and frightful and I hate her!" She buried her face in the folds of his canary coat. "Please, Papa, make her go away."

Meliroc stood and approached father and daughter with a coaxing smile. "He has not the power to make me go away, little one," she said. "But you do."

Loliette raised her head with a dazed blink. Seeing the giant above her, she quivered and hid her face once more.

"She says you have the power to send her away, young Mistress Loliette," Cedelair translated.

"You needn't be afraid of me. All monsters have the same weakness. It's very easy to defeat us, once you know it. Shall I tell you?" Cedelair repeated her words in their soothing balm-like tone. Again the child looked up, favoring Meliroc with a longer glance, a spark of curiosity in her eyes.

"Cedelair, do you mind telling me what this friend of yours is about?" Odilon snapped, a protective hand upon Loliette's shoulder.

"I'm not quite sure," Cedelair replied, "but she means no harm. Come, Mistress Loliette. Will you hear the secret?"

Loliette nodded in answer.

"We cannot endure ridicule!" Meliroc made her thought-voice an eager whisper. "If you whimper and cry, that only encourages us, but oh, how we tremble at the very thought of being laughed at!"

A chuckle darted across Odilon's face as Cedelair-as-Meliroc spoke. "She's right, you know, Lolly," he said.

The little girl drew her shoulders straight. She peered furtively at Meliroc.

"So you see, if you want to defeat me you have only to mock me. Sneer at me, like this." Meliroc screwed her face into an ugly grimace.

Odilon cast an encouraging wink at his daughter. "Go on," he urged. "You can do it."

The little girl bared her teeth and flared her nostrils in fierce imitation. Meliroc flinched as if the child's glower had slapped her.

"Now call me a silly name," she said. "Say, 'Smelly Meliroc'."

Cedelair fought hard to keep the laughter from his voice when he spoke for her. Valeraine let out a giggle. "Oh, this is good," Bonfert mumbled under his breath.

Odilon nudged Loliette's shoulder. "Go on. Make fun of her. 'Smelly Meliroc'."

The little girl fired a defiant sneer into the giant's face. "Smelly Meliroc!"

Meliroc winced and shook. "Oh, that stings! It burns!"

Odilon grinned. "There, you see? It works."

The child took a single step toward her adversary. "Smelly Meliroc!" she cried. She stuck out her tongue, stamping her feet.

"Oh, oh, oh!" Meliroc reeled backward as if from a blow, then threw an arm over her eyes, as if to shield herself from the sight of Loliette's mocking face.

The little one puffed in triumph. Shaking her finger, she began to skip in a circle around her weakened foe. "Smelly Meliroc! Smelly Meliroc!" she called out in sing-song.

Meliroc doubled over as if she'd been punched hard in the belly. Pressing hands to ears to block out the wounding taunt, she stumbled toward the door.

Odilon let out a hearty laugh. "See, Lolly? You're driving her away!"

Loliette homed in for the kill. "Smelly Meliroc, smelly, smelly Meliroc!" she chanted, chasing after the giant with upraised fist. "Into the well with smelly, smelly Meliroc!"

With a jolt, Meliroc threw the door open.

"Hail, Loliette, the giant-slayer!" Odilon crowed as she disappeared over the doorsill.

Loliette tossed her head with a proud grin. "See there?" she boasted, slapping her hands together. "She's not so much!" She hugged her father as she passed him on her way back to her perch.

"Now that you know your power," Cedelair told Loliette, "you should use it wisely. Not everything that looks like a monster is a monster. Mistress Meliroc is our friend. Yours, too, as you'll understand one day."

"She has a funny voice," Loliette remarked off-hand.

Cedelair forced a chuckle. "I know. She sounds like me." But he knew, with a tingle of trepidation, that wasn't what she'd meant. Might he have another pupil in a few years time? Mercifully Loliette didn't dispute him, but simply relaxed on her stool, the fearful, distracted glare in her eyes diminished almost to nothingness.

He wondered why this show Meliroc had put on for a little girl should impress him more than her life-saving heroics of a few hours before.

***

Dust-covers now stripped from the furniture and ornaments, the Echo House looked exactly as it had when Cedelair was growing up. Memories surrounded him on every side, lurking in the cream-white walls and the spread-rugs with their pink and blue floral designs and the chairs and divans with their lace doilies and peacock-blue satin cushions. "I don't see why we can't have a place as big as the Echo House," six-year-old Cedelair had whined to his father. "Aren't we rich enough?"

"This was my father's house," Xuot Nimbletouch had explained. "I wouldn't move from it for all the world's gold."

Cedelair's stomach gnawed and churned. He longed with shuddering desperation for the brown oaken walls, the crudely stitched hearth-rug, the plain wicker chairs.

Bonfert led him to his room, complete with a fireplace he would find useful for boiling his potions. He set about his work as soon as was politely possible, grateful for the familiar steady chop of the knife and grind of the pestle. If he closed his eyes tight and imagined hard enough, he might convince himself he was home again, and the fire and everything that had followed were the terrors of a dream. Except the business with Meliroc at the glass shop. That he wanted to keep.

He worked without stopping, with only the bare minimum of thinking, until a tug of curiosity to know how Valeraine was settling in drove him toward her chamber. "Thank the Lifelord you're here, sir," she said as she opened the door to him. "Perhaps you can get some sense into him." She stepped back from the doorway and ushered him in, then gestured toward Pierpon, sitting cross-legged atop the dresser, a scowl souring his face. Cedelair could tell the little man's anger had been brewing since the fire.

"Master Cedelair," he sniffed, "I am sorry about your house, but I haven't changed my mind. I will not, I will not help you hurt her."

"I don't blame you." Cedelair drew a step toward the dresser. "But don't you want to help her?"

"Of course!"

"Help us, and you'll help her," Cedelair went on. "You'd know far better than we would if there's a way to put a stop to the damage a *leyshak* does, without killing her."

"I don't believe she's a *leyshak*!"

Valeraine shook her head in apparent disbelief in the jickety's stubborn obtuseness. "What possible reason could we have to lie, Pierpon?"

The manikin stared down at the grain-wood beneath him. His eyes could have burned holes into it. Cedelair gave him the sort of tentative smile he might give a terrier growling in rage. "Do you imagine she wants this horror inside her?" he asked in his gentlest voice. "Don't you see how much better it would be for her, if we could send it packing? Help us, Pierpon."

Pierpon's shoulders gave way a little. "She doesn't know," he mumbled. "Her heart would break, it would, if she knew."

A pang struck Cedelair. He'd gotten through to Pierpon because they both wanted the same thing, to save Meliroc from that evil in her sleep. She shouldn't exist. Foul magic had fashioned her. Yet she was here and real. Her eyes glistened with love when she looked at him. He hadn't bothered to predict how that love-light might make him feel.

Pierpon cleared his throat. "There's only one way to get rid of a *leyshak*."

Valeraine grinned, delighted at the success of her master's persuasion. "How?"

"You've got to get to it in dreams," he explained. "Make it show itself as itself, then strike it down. But it was easy for us. We weren't the ones being terrified. If I were my normal self, I could smite this *leyshak*, I could. But I can't go inside your dreams, and I can't have a dream of my own." He set his jaw. "One of you will have to do it, and I don't know how."

Cedelair frowned at another heavy sting. Again he must invade Meliroc's dreams in search of a way to destroy her. No! To save her. Somehow, he would save her.

"Thank you," he told Pierpon.

The jickety scoffed. "I am thinking of her."

Cedelair scratched the back of his neck, uncomfortably conscious of Valeraine's eyes upon him. "As am I."

***

For dinner, Cedelair, Valeraine, and Meliroc shared cold meat, bread, and coffee with Mennieve in her bookshop parlor. Valeraine secreted bits of the meat and bread into a napkin to carry back to Pierpon, who was still determined that no human but Cedelair and Valeraine would set eyes on him.

Cedelair offered Meliroc his arm. "Would you come with me, please, Mistress Meliroc? I need your assistance with some potions."

"Yes, sir." She gave Mennieve a lingering farewell look, the last to leave the bookshop and to pass into the Echo House.

Valeraine strode down the corridor to her chamber, while Cedelair led Meliroc toward his own quarters and asked her what she thought of their new lodgings.

"I hate the way we came to them," she told him, "but I can't help liking them. There's room for me to walk upright and to spare. I can look at the ceiling, see?" She tilted her head back. The ceiling stood a good two feet above. "Master Bonfert even set up a bed for me. A bed! Do you know I've never slept in one before?" Her mind-voice reached an excited pitch, but she quickly rebuked herself. *Shameful to enjoy this place, with what he's lost.*

"This was my favorite place when I was a boy," he mentioned, to assure her. He ushered her into his chamber, where three pots hung over the hearth yet no fire burned. He'd tried to light the logs, but even the sight of a flicker on a match had nauseated him. He couldn't think how he had managed to light the lamp on the night-stand.

"I take it you need me to bring these to boil."

"And help me bottle them. Do you mind?"

"I serve you." She spoke the words almost cheerfully, and again he cringed at that love-struck twinkle in her eye.

"All the same, it's better to be asked, don't you think?" He cleared his throat. "I give you permission to ask me any questions you please."

The twinkle brightened into a steady glow. "My questions will keep for now," she told him, resting her hand on the rim of the uppermost cauldron and tightening her mouth in concentration. In less than five minutes she had all three potions boiling, and as he chopped and ground the plants for the next batch, she dipped the phials into the brimming pots.

"You don't know much about me, do you, Meliroc?"

Just as the question left his lips, he felt a clutch at his heart, another sensation that came from her. He had called her by name without the formalizing "Mistress", and she had seized on it.

"I know a bit," she replied with a tentative smile.

"If someone were to ask you, 'What is Master Cedelair like?' what could you say?"

"He's a man who saves trees and grows plants to heal people," she offered. "He may keep to himself, but he'll always lend a hand in times of trouble."

He let out a gloomy chuckle. "You must have wondered why I keep to myself."

"I always thought it was to do with your – accident." Her thought-voice sounded painfully careful, a tiptoe over fine glass.

"Yes, my 'accident' is part of it, but it started before then." He pulled at the rip inside him, hardening his face as the pain grew. "I was fifteen. My parents had decided to visit some relations in Fandaire, a pack of bores, I thought. I chose not to go with them. I liked staying here on my own. But on the day they were supposed to return, I waited, but they didn't come." He stared down at his shaking hands. "Do you know how loud silence can be, Meliroc?"

Her hand moved toward his, fingers outspread. "I think so, sir."

"Word finally came. Their carriage had overturned. Killed them." He envisioned the messenger's shadow in the doorway and heard a creaking, emotionless voice telling him he was orphaned. A knife dug into the rip.

She gripped his hand. He felt her mind groping for words and finding none.

"I lived here on my own after that," he told her. "One of the bores might have taken me in, but none of them fancied having a young sorcerer under their roof."

He shivered at the chill that brushed over her heart. "Abominable."

"I wouldn't have wanted to go, in any case. I wanted to stay in my parents' house." He drew himself tight. "If there's one thing lads of fifteen are truly good at, it's feeling sorry for themselves, and I was setting up to be the champion of self-pity. I avoided all my friends. I almost hated them because their parents still lived. I made a terrible mistake."

"One you could still mend."

"Perhaps. Sometimes I forget it hasn't been so very long since they were here. I forget I'm not old." He half-turned toward her. "Do you despise me now?"

"Of course not. You made a mistake, yes, but only because you loved them so. Love like that is not to be despised."

He met her eyes with an attempt at a smile. "You say very funny things for a three-year-old."

"I watch. I read. I learn. Though I think I've learned more in the past few days than in all the year before." She leaned toward him. "What were they like?"

"You'd have liked them," he told her. "My father was squat and round and half bald. He liked to smoke his pipe and prop up his feet before the hearth and quote verses from the Life Book. I got my looks from my mother, tall and dark and thin. She loved to sing. I remember her sitting by my bed when I was sick, stroking my brow and singing lullabies. Her voice could make the worst sickness bearable."

"Do you remember the songs she sang?"

"Every note."

"Could you sing one for me?"

The rip smarted afresh, even as warmth from her touch wove within it, to mend it. He envisioned his mother's face, with kind mist-gray eyes and quiet smile. He arched his shoulders and sang.

"The gleams of the stars kiss your brow,
The beams of the moon touch your face.
They love you, oh, they love you,
As I love you,
My child of grace.

The butterflies set out to meet you
As you set foot in their lands.
They fly about your fingers,
Never fearing
Your gentle hands.

Their rainbow wings surround you,
Rejoicing to have found you,
Till at last the dawn brings you back to me."

Just after he fell silent, he could hear his own voice as Meliroc heard it, and quivered as she did with bittersweet joy. He had never thought he sang so well.

"Could you use it?" he asked her. "For the carillon-man's song, I mean."

"Definitely."

"You may go work on it, if you like. I'm nearly finished here." He hoped the rush of heat to his face did not show in a blush. "The sooner you compose your song, the sooner that potion will be out of your system."

"I don't want it out of my system."

"What?"

"I wish it would last and last and last."

He fought to make sense of the rush of feelings that came from her, the tremulous hope, the dizzy exaltation, the sharp ache, the chill of despair, all wound together in a beating knot. He had never felt like this, not when Roselise had stirred his heart, not even when she had kissed him good-bye.

"I don't understand," he told her.

"I can scarcely understand it myself." She loosened the grip of her fingers to a caress. "Last night you looked at me as if I were the worst thing that ever lived. It ran through me like a sword, that look. I can feel it even now when I remember it."

"Then don't remember it."

"That's just it," she countered, shaking her head. "I want to remember it. It hurt me, yet I wouldn't lose it. I don't want to be empty anymore. To be full you have to love, and love hard. You have to let yourself be hurt." He felt a new stirring in her, the tinkle of chimes. "My song. It's waiting for me."

"Off you go, then." He nodded toward the door.

She leaned down to place a cool kiss upon his cheek, and then, breathing in to tighten her nerves for the task ahead, she started for the door. "This is a night for butterflies." She slipped out, drawing the door closed quietly behind her.

He stared at that door for a long time, the tingle of that light little kiss seeping into him. He fought to call up the image of the winged whirlwind fiend, and reached for the disgust he'd felt when he had first seen it. But the fiend would not appear. Instead he saw the glimmer of emerald eyes, the sheen of long white hair. The knots of his nerves snapped loose. A feeling leaped up to take him by the throat.

Curse you, little Raine, for being right.

15. Meliroc learns the cost of transformation

My mistress was absent from her chamber, called away by Cedelair. When I peeped through the door, Pierpon stretched out his arms from his new box. I came to him, took him up and set him on my shoulder.

"You've found the song!" he cried in a joyful hush. "I see it in your eyes, I do!"

"Come with me and be the first to hear it."

***

It was indeed a night for butterflies, a night to dream of ungainly ground-bound things springing into flight. The wings of my song fanned my heart-fire. By the time I reached my chamber and took my bell-board on my knees and my mallet in hand, the melody was straining for the sky. I held my breath, closed my eyes and began.

The threads of my chrysalis drew tight about me, pulling apart my shell of skin and bone to let loose a being of pure music. I reveled in my change and in the emotions that surged through note and measure, as any fledgling might rejoice to take wing. Wind rushed through me, the searing gales of winter and the perfumed breaths of spring swirling together into one glorious breeze. Rain, thunder, lightning, and the glow of sun on a cloudless day moved in me as one. Joy and sorrow, high and low. Life itself.

Love.

The melody ended. I reeled, exhausted as flesh and bone closed over me once more.

Cedelair should have been there. He would surely have noticed the melody he'd sung for me beating at the heart of my new tune. He would have taken comfort in what he'd helped bring to light, and perhaps he wouldn't have minded if I brushed my lips against his... Hadn't he told me that once I'd found this song the love potion's effect would dissipate? My blood shouldn't still warm at the thought of him.

At a light tug at my shoulder-sleeve, I opened my eyes. Pierpon gaped at me, shuddering. "You liked it, didn't you?" I asked him, almost astonished that my still-whirling mind could manage words. "Please tell me you liked it."

"Mam'selle Meliroc," he whispered, "you're glowing."

I looked down at my hands. The light of my chrysalis had settled over my skin like a glove of shimmering mist. I grinned, but my small friend shook his head. "Don't go to that wagon again," he urged, tightening his hold on my tunic. "Something is happening to you, snow-giant. I don't like it, I don't. Stay away before it's too late."

My neck tingled when I tried to tell myself I felt no different. I held my hand before my face. I swept my hand through the air. The light trailed after my gesture, sparks bursting in the candle's glow.

"You didn't say you liked my song," I reminded Pierpon.

"I can't say I liked it, exactly," he answered. "Too mild a word. But I won't be the same now I've heard it."

I beamed at him, pleased at this praise. "I don't even know if it's what Feuval needs," I told him. "He hasn't---"

Called me yet, I would have finished, but my next breath brought my summons, more joyously urgent than ever, weaving through the cracks of the closed window. "I must go this once more," I told Pierpon. "This song will be the end of it." I drew my cloak about my shoulders and fastened the clasp.

"Or the end of you," he grunted as he climbed into my cloak-hood.

I leaped to my feet and rushed after the summons, down the halls and out into the night. In my fancy's ear my own melody mingled with the carillon's notes. I no longer had a shred of doubt of its power. It would unlock a cage, free a soul to fly upon the wind. Could music have a finer aim than that?

I took no note of the change in the distance I walked. Only when I came to a stop before the wagon did I notice the stiffness in my legs and knees. I sank down with some relief, feeling my muscles un-knot.

Before the dead-dark wagon I checked myself to see if I was still shining. I was.

Calling to mind every story I'd ever read about magic flight, tales of abused orphans taming winged horses or finding carpets with sorcery in their weave, I let the new tune pour out of me a second time. The wagon's walls burst into unwonted brilliance in answer to my offering, like a smile of benediction. It was delighted with me.

The curtain drew back, and I squinted as always at the spark of gold that shot from the raptor mask. I could sense the deep-drinking stare behind it. My heart wound tighter than I'd thought it could go.

"That song must have cost thee much," said Feuval, a hint of a tremor in his voice. "Thou'rt valiant, moon-tree, to lay such a tune before me."

I drew out writing book and pencil and scrawled with trembling fingers *Is it what you needed? Are you free?*

"I am whole," he said, stroking my hand as he passed the book back to me. "Where didst thou find such a song to turn the soul upside-down?"

How I wished I had Cedelair beside me to speak my words! As it was, I could only jot down a short explanation of how I'd pleaded for a potion that would break my heart, how Cedelair had obliged me very reluctantly, how I'd loved and hated him at once, and how he'd shared with me a lullaby his mother had taught him. The words seemed disjointed, inadequate. I frowned as I watched him read them.

"This man, it would seem, hath pointed thee toward every song thou hast brought me," he remarked in a hem-haw tone.

I nodded. *Those we love give us what we need,* I wrote.

"Then thou lovest him yet?"

My head still teetering in the haze of the song, I pictured Cedelair's face, just as it had looked when he'd sung for me. Again my heart-fire leaped with a thrill of longing. *I don't know*, I scribbled, my fingers suddenly stiff.

"What knowest thou?" he returned, his voice a nudge. "What knowest thou most strongly in thy heart?"

Again I lifted my hand before my eyes, enjoying the strange fluorescence. *I know my song, I wrote. I know it has power to break the heart and mend it again. And I know it came from me.* I remembered Pierpon's tweaking words when I'd declared my hatred of sorcerers. They'd irked me then, but now they rang with promise. *I am a sorcerer.*

"Thou art," he agreed, "and thou wilt be."

But have I done you good? It's all for nothing if you can't walk free.

He brushed his silken hand against my cheek. "And what dost thou imagine would become of my poor carillon, if I abandoned it?" he asked, his voice dripping with pity as for a living thing. The walls shivered in response.

You are a person, I wrote. *It is only some bells in a box. You should matter more.*

He gave a scoffing snort as he read, and he pushed my book back into my hands a little roughly. "Some bells in a box? Think'st thou so?"

What life it has comes from you. Can you not I see it walk free? Can't with my own eyes?

"Dear moon-tree." He sighed. "This carillon liveth as I do. It hath given life to me these many years. I cannot now abandon it without a thought."

My nerves tensed. *Then why have you asked me for songs?*

Again he patted my hand as the writing-book passed between us. "To see if thou wert indeed the one we sought," he explained. "'Tis true I now have the means to fly free, but for one thing. Someone must step into my place." He reached out to seize my shoulders. "Only thou canst free me, thou being of music, when thou join'st thy art, thy gifts, thy soul with the carillon."

My mouth hung open. My ears had been working a minute ago, I was sure, but now I could not credit what I heard.

"I could only leave once we found the carillon's true match." He tightened his hold on me. "Long have we searched and hoped and waited for thee!"

Blinking through a fog, I tried to make sense of what he said. He had led me to believe that in bringing him the last song I would liberate him from a life that wasn't life. Yet the song, all the songs, had only been tricks to bind me in his stead. My friend with the wonderful embracing voice was a deceiver, a scoundrel.

"Dear, beautiful moon-tree," he crooned, "frown not so." He ran his thumb across the creases in my brow.

It wasn't true, it wasn't... yet I quaked in revulsion while my heart-fire raged. With a spring I broke free of him and wrenched myself upright to tower over the wagon. Feuval jolted, and my furious heart rejoiced to see I frightened him.

The bell-board lay shining at my feet. Its light pulsed, and the brighter glow of the wagon flashed in answer, talking about me in a language I knew not. I raised my foot to kick the kho-laeth graft into splinters, but a second later I got a better idea. I bent down to seize it by its ends and lifted it high above my head, baring my teeth in a snarl. I glowered down at the masked man and saw his hunched shoulders tremble.

With all my strength I dashed the instrument down, missing the window by only a whisker. The man let out a muffled groan as it shattered.

Pure agony shot through my back and it spread through my every atom. I cried out before I could stop myself, that same ear-splitting cry that had shaken my mind to near madness when the Bitter Chord had forced it from me. I doubled over, collapsing to my knees beside the broken bell-board. The pain hammered me. The horror of the scream hovered knife-cold in the air. Not quite knowing what I did, I took the pieces in my arms as I might an injured child.

The light on my clothes and skin spilled onto the instrument. A faint, uncertain glimmer spread down the splintered keys. The contraption convulsed, and in the same moment something pulled my spine tight. The breaks were knitting themselves back together, the splinters smoothing, reaching, and joining. Light-strands circled it and me, binding us together. As the wood mended, my pain subsided, and relief flooded me as if I had saved my own life.

The bell-board gleamed with new health. I kissed it, holding it fast to my breast as I clambered back to my feet. "Seest thou," hissed Feuval, "it is too late. The carillon is part of thee now."

I held in a groan with all my might. I would not foul the air with my voice again. Still keeping one arm close about my instrument, I knelt to retrieve my book and pencil. I then stretched myself upright again. One thought held steady amidst the chaos in my brain – I would never again kneel before that window.

My quaking fingers could barely grasp the pencil. It took me three tries to write out *Do I have no choice?*

Nightmare Lullaby

"Choice?" he scoffed. "What choice desirest thou? Thy anger is most foolish, moon-tree. No more wilt thou be bound to serve men who use thee cruelly. No longer wilt thou endure scorn and fear because thou'rt molded out of the common way. Best of all, thou wilt make music! The tunes thou hast shaped with that mere scraping are naught compared to the melodies thou wilt create with the carillon at thy disposal!"

His words tickled and teased my ears, yet I held myself rigid as steel and scrawled my next message with a heavy hand. *Didn't you hear my song? Did you even understand the truth you asked me to find? Without pain and fear and grief, without freedom, there can be no music.*

As I wrote I spoke with my mind-voice, conscious of Pierpon in his hiding place. Oh, the told-you-so's I had coming to me!

Feuval made a soft hemming sound as he read my retort. "I have not explained myself as I should," he admitted. "This carillon hath a purpose, to heal and to comfort. All who hear its songs feel its blessings. We go where we sense great need, and we hath sensed the greatest need of all in thee. Thou'rt broken, poor moon-tree. The carillon would give thee back thyself. And once it hath mended thee thou shalt mend others! Thou wilt hold its power in thy hands."

The wagon's glow pulsed, confirming its prisoner's words. Bitterness filled my mouth. The words disgusted me all the more because I heard a soft strain of sense in them. *To heal and comfort... to be mended... hold its power in my hands...*

He was answering my question, though perhaps he didn't realize it. There was a choice, or he would not take such trouble to persuade me. He reached for my wrist, but I dodged his touch and thrust my arm behind my back.

"Turn not from thy chance to mend," he pleaded, his voice a melting beckon. "What hast thou out in the rough, hard world?"

My mind scrambled after something solid I could claim. Pierpon, but he would soon leave me. Cedelair, but he would never love me. Valeraine, but I would lose her, too, if my must could not be broken. What was it Cedelair had said when he was trying to teach me about *sorrow*? Tell me the things you love... The beginning of a tune in my head, warm bath-water, the wonder of words in books...

I have me, I wrote and spoke. *My body and my soul. They aren't yours to take, yours or that thing you serve. If I am broken, I will mend myself! Now I ask you again, what choice do I have?*

His shoulders sagged. A tiny gray head peered over the window-sill, its wide mouth twisted in an ugly grin. When it snickered Feuval aimed a swat at it. "Oh big-big, poor big-big," the whishk crooned in mock-sympathy. "Your own fault!"

"Thou hast two chances," Feuval announced, ignoring the imp. "Thou mayst break the carillon's hold if thou canst last one week without playing a single note on thy instrument. Ah! Thou smilest! Think'st thou it will be easy?"

I've gone years without having any instrument to play, I wrote. *I'm used to it.*

Feuval shook his head. "Thou wilt find much hath changed for thee since then. The second chance, if thou fail'st at the first, which I warn thee thou wilt, is to find someone willing to join with the carillon in thy place." He slapped his palm against the window-ledge. "Thou'lt come again in one week. Think over what I have told thee."

The curtain dropped. The shimmer dwindled around the wagon but still hovered and twined around me.

***

From a short distance I saw the pale yellow glow of a lantern and just beyond it the shadow of a slim man in a long-coat, standing near the door of our new lodgings. Cedelair was waiting for me. Pierpon cast a sly wink at me. "Do you know, I think he rather likes you, he does."

I grinned at him and rumpled his hair with my thumb. Through the long trudge back he'd shared a fresh round of memories of his home and his old companions as if nothing had gone wrong, without half a whisper of a told-you-so. I loved him more than ever.

As I hurried toward Cedelair he raised his lantern for a better look at me. He paled. "What has happened to you?"

"The kho-laeth," I explained. "It's trying to claim me."

"That ghost-man's been tricking her all this time," snarled Pierpon, a savage spark in his eye. "'Oh, moon-tree, thou hast done me goood!' I'd like to give him 'good'!" He aimed a blow at the air, nearly toppling from his perch.

For an instant I caught myself thinking the look of worried sympathy that came over Cedelair's face might be worth the ordeal.

Nightmare Lullaby

He rested his hand on mine with a steadying touch. "Tell me the full story."

In simple words I described what had befallen me. With the thought of Feuval's deception tearing at me, I needed to finish the tale quickly before I started to weep. Pierpon's expressions and gestures served as ample embellishment.

"She was splendid, she was!" the jickety crowed when I'd finished. He sailed down the length of my right arm, coming to rest in the cup of my palm. "I was all set to burst out and give Master Goldmask what-for, never mind whether he could see me or not, but she didn't need me! Wouldn't give the man an inch. 'I have me,' she says, 'my body and my soul, and they aren't yours to take!' You would have been proud of her."

"Proud of me," I echoed, bitterness swelling in my throat, "when my own stupidity got me into this."

"You thought you had a friend, and you tried to help that friend," Cedelair returned. "That's your offense. Now we must think what to do about it. You say you can break the hold if you go for a week without playing the bell-board."

I nodded. "Feuval sounded sure I wouldn't manage it."

"The first thing to do, then, would be to put it down."

With a dazed blink I regarded the instrument, still nestled in the crook of my left arm. I gritted my teeth and made myself lay it on the ground. My freed arm tingled with a sense of wrongness that strengthened as I drew upright.

"How do you feel?" asked Cedelair, business-like.

"Like I should pick it up again," I admitted.

"I feared so," grumbled Cedelair. "The best thing for you, Mistress Meliroc, would be to fill your mind as full as you can with other things."

I breathed in, to feed my heart-fire. Other things, like the way Cedelair had formalized my name again, when a few hours ago he'd talked to me as a friend. What did he think of my newly luminescent complexion? Might he find me just a little bit pretty?

"For example, you know our town is plagued with nightmares. The potions I brew to ward off sleep are only a temporary fix."

"Of course, sir."

Cedelair opened the door and ushered me inside. "If we're to stop the plague," he told me, "we have to get at its cause. For that, I must ask your leave to look in on your dream again."

I winced at a tug at my spine, whether at the door closing between me and my bell-board or at the memory of Cedelair's eviscerating glower of the night before I couldn't be sure. "How could my dream help that?"

He coughed hard. "Because the curse originates with you."

Another pull, its pain shooting into my chest. "You mean I'm a plague bearer?"

Cedelair answered with a grim nod.

Faces flooded my view, all the people in that town in the grip of a fear that had marked their eyes. The shy, trembling child at the glass shop. Bookseller Mennieve, with her motherly smile. My friend Valeraine, who had never in her life been frightened by a nightmare before those knife-wielding gold-caps had set upon her. I had set them upon her. "This is what you saw in my dream last night, then. The thing that made you hate me."

"I don't hate you, Mistress Meliroc," Cedelair returned with a sad shake of his head.

"Last night you did."

"I didn't understand. I know better now. You are not to blame."

"Absolutely right," agreed Pierpon. "Not your fault at all."

"You are ill," Cedelair explained. "If we can get a better look at your dreams we'll have a better idea how to cure you. And once you're cured the curse will be lifted."

I choked. "We?"

"Valeraine and I," he clarified. "Your friends. On your side."

I made a desperate grasp for hope. Yet a gulf of misery opened under my feet, its drifts snatching at my ankles to pull me down. "What if there is no cure?"

"You mustn't think that. You have to trust me."

I arched my neck in a struggle for dignity. "Why couldn't you tell me this before?"

"If you stood where I'm standing and saw your face as I see it now, you wouldn't have to ask." He gripped both my hands. "You look as if you half despise yourself. Don't. Someone is doing this to you. It isn't shame you should feel. It's anger."

"Too right," affirmed Pierpon. "Get angry."

With a breath through my teeth I remembered Valeraine's question that day of our first walk to town. "Where did your must come from, Meliroc? Who set it on you?" I had told her I didn't know what she meant, when in truth my throat had closed tight at the very thought of telling her about the Bitter Chord. Of course that cruelest of sorcerers had set it on me. She had vanished but left it behind to fill the void.

"You can fight her," Cedelair asserted. "With our help, you can win."

Fight her. Bright yellow eyes gleamed from the shadow of their cowl. A voice whispered in tones to chill the soul, "You are a big, ugly, worthless shell. Inside you are naught but dust and air." *Fight her.* My hate surged. My heart-fire leaped higher, higher, until I could taste it in my throat. *Fight her.* My hands reached out to grasp the cape. It crumbled to ash. The eyes glowed brighter, mad with fear and pain. Then the lights were gone. Thin wisps of smoke trailed where they had once been.

Cedelair jerked his hands away with a backward step. "Too hot, my good giant."

My arms fell limp at my sides. I drew long breaths to cool myself.

"Now, will you trust me?" he urged. "Will you open your dreams to me again?"

"Of course, sir."

"Then come. Valeraine's waiting for us."

I walked down the corridor beside him in silence, holding tight to the string of hope. Still the question echoed through the hollow of the gulf. What if there is no cure?

The answer rose into view – the carillon-wagon, its walls gleaming in welcome.

16. The Exploits and Adventures of Valeraine the Victorious, Part One, Continued: The Monster in Its Lair

Valeraine the Vociferous fought not to think too hard about the task ahead of her. She had planned it out in her mind as far as she was able, but now she could do naught but wait, and what was worse than waiting? Heroes were not meant to sit still.

She had her favorite distraction, at least. All the wisdom of her old mentor might have crumbled to ash in the fire, but now she had a new mentor, given into her hands by the generous Mennieve – Valdarte the Valiant. How like her own name that sounded! Better still, her new comrade had recommended this mentor, and tomorrow she could talk with him about her. Was he a comrade, this Master Bonfert, or perhaps her true predestined sweetheart?

She sat on the edge of Master Cedelair's bed. Two phials of freshly brewed sleeping draught rested on the night-stand across from her. She stretched and struggled for breath. She was Victorious Valeraine. She was up to the task.

The door opened. Cedelair strode in, and a pace behind him came Meliroc, looking as if she had been caught in a shower of stardust. A startled gasp caught in Valeraine's throat. She laid her book on the night-stand and indulged in one last thought of her new comrade before she squared her jaw and met her master's gaze with a purposeful nod.

Cedelair touched her shoulder. "Are you ready?"

"Past ready, sir," she declared.

Nightmare Lullaby

Her master picked up the phials and turned to hand one of them to Meliroc. "Are you ready?"

Meliroc nodded. She looked more like a spirit than ever with that silver glow.

"Why are you shining, Meliroc?" Valeraine asked.

"I came upon a pool of light," the giant replied with one of her strange faint smiles. "I leaned over too far and fell in."

Cedelair coughed. "One trouble at a time," he said. "You can tell Valeraine the whole story tomorrow."

"Just so, sir." Meliroc plucked out the stopper then took a quick sip. Her eyelids drooped almost the instant she swallowed. She trudged to the opposite side of the bed, where she lay down on her side, head bent and legs folded. In the next second, her eyes sealed shut.

Valeraine's temple smarted. "Is she all right, sir?"

"I fear she must contend with more than one geas. But as I said, Raine, one trouble at a time. If we can't get rid of the *leyshak*, nothing else we might do for Meliroc will matter in the slightest." She could hear his fight to keep passion from his voice. "You remember your part in this?"

"It's simple enough, sir. I follow you and Meliroc into your separate dreams."

"And then what?"

"I watch and wait until the *leyshak* screams. If I see a chance to strike, I strike. If I don't, I pull out."

She gnawed at the tip of her tongue. Books on sorcery said so little about dreams, as if their authors had decided by common consent that dreams were one area of life even the most minor magics shouldn't touch. In obliterating all memory of the *leyshak*, the jicketies had done humankind no service. Now no book or lesson could offer a clue how to destroy one.

Yet one book gave a hint. One of her grimmest escapades had taken Brave Bennelise into the dream of a mad king where, through imagination and force of will, she had forged a sword to strike off the head of the phantom dragon that had been plaguing his nights. Was not the *leyshak* a little like this ghost-dragon? Brave Bennelise, for all her excellence, was no magician, yet she had conjured a blade from thin air. Valeraine the Venturesome, her pupil and admirer, was equipped with magic. In this instance, the pupil might best her mentor!

Raising the phial as in a toast, Cedelair took a gulp. Valeraine sat beside him on the bed's edge, and as his eyelids sank closed, she rested her open palm on his shoulder and concentrated.

***

A murmured phrase from the *Seventh Tongue* opened two light-flooded pathways before her. Her mind and body split apart. While her body sat glassy-eyed on the bed, her mind formed itself into a simulacrum she saw as through a fogged mirror. A shock of cold wind whipped across her heart. The simulacrum could lose its way, disappear into the light of the mind it entered. If this should happen, could Cedelair restore her to herself? Which dream would swallow her, Cedelair's or Meliroc's?

You are Valeraine the Victorious. You will not yield. Straining to see beyond the glare, she divided again. Her vision cleared as it stretched wide to take in two dream-scapes. One part of her sailed, a will o' the wisp on the wind, into Meliroc's wild riot of color and song. The other part tumbled headlong into the heart of a garden full of massive, fat-stalked plants with wide spreading leaves.

Cedelair stood among the hole'vaiths, his shoulders bent as if a stone sat on his neck. As she neared him his thoughts and feelings wove into her own. His sore heart sagged under the weight of every wrinkle. Ordinary aging would have been a gradual wearing away, not an abrupt diminishment with lines and crags forced on one like chains. He'd looked everywhere, read til his eyes had bled, and prayed til his throat had burned for a counter-spell that could free him, yet he'd found nothing. He was twenty-two. He would spend the prime of his life as an old man.

Twenty-two, noted Valeraine, his age just after the battle, five years ago. Here, then, was the mysterious and tragic past she had always wondered about, not a roiling black storm but a drizzle of dreary gray.

The plants shaded and sheltered him. He willed their stalks to grow strong. He did not want to be found. He had no use for pitying stares or whispers like wasp-stings. "Such a shame." "Such a handsome young man, too." "Well, magic is risky." "How do you suppose Roselise is taking it?"

Nightmare Lullaby

A laugh tinkled like the shatter of icicles. He clutched his shivering arms. "Who in his right mind would think I'd marry you now?"

His heart wrenched in such pain that he cried out. A crushing silence followed on the heels of that horrible laugh. The years plodded on, bearing down hard, grinding his spirit down to the nub.

Meanwhile, Meliroc was dancing bodiless at the heart of her whirling rainbow as a sweet and terrible song rushed through her spirit, a green song for a green man.

Cedelair heard a rustle in the stems and leaves around him. For an instant he imagined Roselise bursting through the verdant wall to cling to his neck, tearful, contrite. He hardened. Even if she begged his forgiveness he wanted none of her now. Couldn't they all leave him alone?

"Cedelair." A voice called his name. A pearlescent woman rose before him, her uncannily tall, sleek figure draped in a gauzy silver robe. Her white hair floated over her shoulders and down her back, almost reaching her knees. Hovering an inch from the ground, she stretched out her arms to him.

"W-what do you want?" he stammered.

"To hold you," the towering phantom replied, "to kiss you, and to give you back your youth. Suffer no more, my love."

She caressed his shoulders. As the warmth of her touch moved through him he knew her. Her name sang in his mind. He wrapped his arms about her waist and pressed himself against her. Her hair fell cool and soft over his face. His heart swelled til it ached, yet he reveled in that pain. He lived. He lived.

Valeraine breathed a tense sigh. Very soon the *leyshak's* scream would burn this moment from his memory. Wrong. "*Ei'lorzha*," she breathed. Remember. "*Ei'lorzha*." She sent the spell running through the dream.

He tightened his arms about the woman, breathing deep. She was so soft. Hair like down, smoothing away his wrinkles, making him young again. Desire quickened in him, mingling with that burst of love. "I love thee," he whispered, trembling. The old-fashioned address suited her, majestic divinity that she was. "I love thee," he repeated, his hands caressing the small of her back. "I love thee, I love thee."

"Say my name," she said, winding gentle fingers through his hair.

"Meliroc," he breathed through a giddy smile.

"Keep saying it and hold me close. Then it can't come."

"Meliroc." He almost sang the name. "Meliroc. My Meliroc, my beautiful, wonderful Meli-meli-roc-roc."

"Meli-meli-roc-roc?" *Lifelord save me, even I didn't think he was that far gone!*

She threw her head back with an ecstatic grin, wrapping her arms around his shoulders to lift him until his face hovered before her own. She leaned towards him. Heat pulsed through him. He pressed his mouth to hers, and with a shiver she responded. An azure fire wrapped about them, locking them together in that kiss.

You've never been free. You never will be. The whip flashed and stung. Color and air blinked out, and the white figure materialized under the whip, crouching, hating the lash, hating the voice even more. *You think he cares at all what becomes of you? You think he could? You, a beast, a fiend, a thing?*

Meliroc strained to lift her head. She would meet those cruel yellow eyes. She would talk back to that pitiless whisper. *Why do you hate me so? What wrong have I done you?* Her heart burned wild with rage as she waited for an answer.

Yet a rain of blows was the only reply the Bitter Chord would give. The pain broke her, as it always had – as it always would – no escape – no hope – Valeraine clenched as Meliroc's sorrow knifed through her. Her vision went black. The will o' the wisp that was Valeraine whooshed back through the tunnel, evicted.

A shriek shook the air, rending Cedelair to the bone. Even as Valeraine shared his pain, she felt a tiny thread of relief. This dream hadn't thrown her out. She hadn't lost her chance.

The queenly phantom's arms quaked and lost their hold. He fell hard upon the ground. She stiffened with terror, her gaze searching the sky. The scream sounded again. Cedelair's head burst with it. His beloved began spinning in mid-air, flinching as if something were striking her. An anguished cry broke from her. "My love, help me!"

He reached up to catch her ankles, to pull her down and hold her, but his grasp slipped and he tumbled back to the ground. He struggled to his feet and tried again to clasp her, but the force of her spin knocked him down once more. The whirl obliterated her features.

Is this what he fears most? Valeraine shuddered.

Nightmare Lullaby

A last plea for help died in the air. Only a cloud of smoke remained where the towering girl had hovered. The weight of his wrinkles crashed down upon him tenfold.

A woman's voice whispered out of the smoke like the hiss of a snake. In that voice Cedelair could hear a smallness of soul, the antithesis of his beloved giant. He knew that should she appear she would be wearing a cape with the hood pulled low over her face, and two yellow beams of light would glint from the hood's shadow.

"You can't have her. She belongs to me."

The alien scream ripped through the air. Cedelair felt the pounding of the heavy wings that circled above him. "What more can you do to me?" he shouted. The muddy soil was swallowing his calves, inching toward his knees.

His anger scorched Valeraine. She swallowed it, willing it to fire her spirit to action. Now was her moment. She fixed all her energy on the beating wings, the furious shriek. As she drew a breath all the way from her toes, she envisioned that energy as a pulsing streak of lightning. She called on the *First Tongue, the Tongue of Making. Ihari ne biadanu vei.* The lightning bolt flashed in her palm. She folded her fingers around it and let its force shoot through her. She pictured the fury, with its whirlwind legs and feathered face and smoke-spouting pitch black mouth.

Raising her eyes to the sky, she fired a command. *Show yourself.*

Cedelair, unaware of her, sank lower still into the soil. His skin had taken on a greenish tinge, as if he were slowly transforming into one of his plants. Yet he didn't care. For a sweet moment he had loved and hoped as never before, his youthful infatuation nothing beside it. Yet she was lost to him. His wrinkles were spreading, his sags deepening. He was growing ancient.

Valeraine's fury mounted. *Show yourself!* her mind cried again. She reared back the arm that held the lightning bolt, her blood hot with the spirits of her mentors.

The wingbeats roared. The monster had heard her and was coming. The same voice that had taunted Cedelair breathed in her ear. "Soon you will wish the gold-caps had you."

The sky split apart to reveal a being so vast that her vision could scarcely stretch to contain it all. Its mouth gaped in a grotesque parody of a smile, and its dagger-teeth gleamed through the smoke. "You wished to see me, little trespasser. Here I am."

"Where is Meliroc?" she shouted.

"Meliroc has ceased to be. And so shall Valeraine."

It raised its talon-tipped fingers and dove toward her, mouth agape to emit the shriek. Waves of matchless grief smothered the crouching Valeraine. Meliroc must lie hidden in all this sorrow, trapped, forced to behave in ways she could neither understand nor control. In every dream her suffering raged and the *leyshak* turned it into a weapon.

The ebony talons gleamed brighter with each second. Valeraine imagined they dripped with her blood. Her gown was stained red as if they had already torn her. Her fingers fumbled, then tightened around the lightning bolt. She must strike now! *Brave Bennelise, Valdarte the Valiant, be with me and be in me. I am Valeraine of Nisslaire, Valeraine the Victorious.*

The wind under the massive wings beat down with all its force. The ruby eyes blazed in rage. She noticed, for the first time, two vertical slits at the center, the mark of a poisonous serpent. Venom seared through her blood to burn and shake her. The bolt slipped from her grasp and fell with a crackle at her feet. Fire sprang up around her, catching the hem of her skirt. She raced in terror back to her waiting body and slammed into it. It jolted and gasped.

She blinked awake, sweat-soaked, teeth chattering. She had failed. She had confronted the *leyshak*, had met its eyes with weapon in hand, and had failed. Her image of Valeraine the Victorious shriveled into ash and blew away with a puff of breath. She swallowed tears.

Cedelair groaned as he rolled over, waking. He, too, shook furiously, death-pale. Sitting upright, he looked into Valeraine's face. She strove to tell him with her eyes that she cared what he suffered and would help him if she could. She clasped his hand.

"You said – ahem! – you said you remembered only the scream," he mentioned.

"Yes, sir. That's the way the *leyshak* works."

"And yet I recall every detail of what I just went through."

The tears dried behind her eyes as she stiffened her spine. "Because I sent a remembering spell through your dream," she blurted out. "You needed to remember, sir. Isn't that where more than half our trouble comes from? Not remembering?" Her face grew hot as she waited for his rebuke.

"You did well," he choked.

She shook her head. "Not well enough."

"You drew it out. Now we know it can be done. Just how did you get hold of a weapon? A bolt of lightning, of all things?"

"*Brave Bennelise and the Sky-Brigands* gave me the idea," she replied, the momentary blush of satisfaction squelched by the memory of her retreat. "But in the end I couldn't use it." She sniffed. "I'm not a hero."

"Perhaps not yet." He patted her hand. "Those women in armor you're so fond of reading about, do you think they were born slaying monsters? I'm sure they tried and missed a few times, even if your books don't say as much. You did more just now than I could have done. You'll be a great sorcerer, Valeraine. Great, and much loved."

Resting against him, she let her tears fall. She had always admired her master, yet at this moment she loved him.

"Just as well you didn't strike it down," he added. "I fear we'd have lost Meliroc, as well."

She remembered herself flying out of Meliroc's dream at the instant her friend would have transformed. The cold whisper shook her mind's ear. "It spoke in that hooded woman's voice."

"She's like a parasite," he growled with a black scowl. "She latches onto Meliroc, forces her to change shape, then hangs on for the ride. We might say she is the *leyshak*. If we're to strike her down without hurting Meliroc we've got to split them apart."

"Which we've no idea how to do." Valeraine sighed.

The giant slumbered on, her features twisted in pain. The parasite would ride her until its night's work was done. Valeraine's stomach churned. She had never felt sorrier for someone in her life. *I can't be the hero of this tale, Meliroc. You have to be.*

Cedelair knelt beside Meliroc. His hand hovered over her tear-stained face, the light in his eyes soft with the longing Valeraine had seen and felt in his dream. "It was supposed to be over and done," he grumbled, shaking his head. "But she loves me still." She heard a rattle in his throat, a breath catching there. He lifted his finger and gently traced the line of the sleeping giant's cheek.

"You damned troublemaker," he said.

17. Cedelair prays and plants

How did the fire start?

The question crept down the side-paths like a winding trail of smoke. It slipped through the keyholes of shop doors and seeped up from the cobbles under the wheels of vendor-carts. It swirled in the dust mites on the glassworks' hardwood floor. A single iteration sufficed to fix it in the mind of anyone who heard it.

A few offered mundane explanations – a candle carelessly knocked from a table, a spark tumbling from the hearth onto the rug. But these answers only ran up against what everyone in Crainante knew. Cedelair and Valeraine were sorcerers. Surely they could have magicked the fire away before it spread too far. Assuming it had been an accident, of course. But if not an accident, then what? Why?

How did the fire start?

By the time Cedelair and Valeraine marched into the square with their basket of potions to sell, accompanied by their strange white pillar of a bodyguard, theories were springing up, none of them offering assurance or comfort. A new, fearful whisper trailed down the streets.

He's living in town now... our neighbor... our neighbor...

***

The feeling that had leaped up to seize Cedelair by the throat now held him in a vise. The sensations of his dream, the helpless horror and the nerve-shaking desire, hung on tight. It hurt him to look at Meliroc now, with that florescent shimmer in her face and hands, the sign of the carillon's claim.

"We should have stopped her going to that wagon," Valeraine had muttered with an acrid frown when he told her of the carillon-man's treachery. "We could have put a stop to it any time, but we did nothing."

Cedelair could not let himself imagine how heavily he stood to pay for the crime of having done nothing.

Meliroc followed him and Valeraine into the square, throwing her warm shade over them as usual. "It's as before," he told her in mind-speech. "We need you to tell us who's suffering worst, so we can distribute our potion."

"Suffering worst." She grimaced as if in pain. "That light's in your eyes now. Did you dream last night, sir?"

"My first dream in five years," he admitted.

"Part of your investigation?"

"Yes." Her hand trembled. Her emotions did not seep into him as they had the day before, and he was grateful, though he wondered why they'd stopped.

Her little smile thinned into a thoughtful line. "When our work is done, sir, could we visit the temple?"

"Why?"

"I think I'd like to pray. You did advise me to think of other things, and this morning I can't stop thinking about praying."

"What set you thinking about that?"

"This morning when I woke up with my throat sore and my eyes red as always, I saw the sunlight coming through the window, and I don't know quite why or how, but I started to wonder if something in that light might be... listening."

"Have you ever prayed before?"

"Never, sir."

"Call me 'sir' once more, Meliroc, and I'll forbid it," he warned her with a wink. The time for "sirs" and "Mistress Melirocs" was past. "Have you never wanted to pray before?"

She shook her head. "I was told the Lifelord didn't make me so he wouldn't hear my prayers."

"What a detestable thing to say," he rumbled, his fingers curling into fists.

"Yet perhaps if I pray for those he did make, he'll hear me. I will need you to show me how it's done."

He gripped both her hands. "Hear this first. Whoever told you the Lifelord didn't make you, don't believe it. I command you not to believe it."

"I don't think that will work, si – Cedelair," she told him, with a smile halfway between laughter and tears.

"Then understand this. The first lesson we're taught is that love is the true mark of the Lifelord. Do you love, Meliroc?"

He felt her tighten against a convulsive shudder. "Yes."

"There. That makes you his child. No, far more than that. You are his most splendid creation."

The burst of delight in her eyes outshone the carillon's eerie mark. "I would very much like to kiss you, Cedelair," she told him, beaming, "but someone would see."

He clenched his teeth. Meliroc had filled his eyes as she had filled his thoughts, but now he perceived the crowd that had gathered to gape, mouths hanging open in little round holes of shock, like a school of pop-eyed fish. Only now did he realize that in his heat he'd slipped into audible speech. He stiffened in defiance. He did not regret a word he'd said.

He smiled as he fixed his gaze on Meliroc once more. "We'll go to the temple together. I have a prayer of my own to offer up."

***

In the square all motion ceased as the people turned their faces toward the music of the bells – all but Cedelair, who gazed at Meliroc. While all others appeared locked in a dream of pure feeling, in her he sensed brewing, building thought.

A low hum breathed in his ear, then rounded into the tone of a singer finding her first note. Another note followed, and another, weaving and merging with the chimes. Meliroc was answering the carillon with her own melody. Her singing thought-voice grew stronger with each measure. Her lips quivered in an open-mouthed grin.

Something stirred at the corner of his view. Her fingers were drumming near her sash, at the handle of her mallet. A thread-like disquiet slipped through the music's spell as he saw she had her bell-board strapped to her side, tucked under her cloak. She was bursting with longing to play. Her voice swelled to match the bells in power. He sensed something escaping, taking flight. He closed his eyes, the better to hear the strains answering each other until at last they flowed

Nightmare Lullaby

as one. Through three songs this went on, and that sense of unity, of not knowing where the carillon ended and Meliroc began, rang stronger with every bar. He could almost believe that she wanted to join with it, or worse, that she was meant to.

The bells' last ring faded, and silence slipped on tiptoe through the crowd. Meliroc's head sagged forward.

"What possessed you to bring that thing?" he mind-spoke to her.

"What thing? Oh." She glanced down at her sash. For an instant she looked shocked to see the mallet and feel the bell-board. "I must have put it on with my clothes. I didn't realize." Her neck quivered. "I do hurt less with it near."

"Well, then, carry it. But I forbid you to play it."

She nodded, almost smiling as she accepted his command.

They went on with their work until at last they had distributed the fene'vaith potion to as many as would take it. The aura of discomfort like the crackling sting of tiny lightning bolts had diminished in the wake of the carillon's performance. Yet none of his customers met his eye for more than a second.

***

Large cities were graced with massive white polished-stone temples to the Lifelord, with glimmering spires and vaulted ceilings and bright-hued frescoes on every wall. A town Crainante's size had to be content with a humble structure of oak planking and faded brown river-rock, its only adornments a modest spire with a golden tip and a single stained-glass window with azure panes surrounding the figure of a maroon rose, the work of Xuot Nimbletouch. Cedelair always beamed in pride at the sight of this rose, finer than any flashy fresco or gold-gilt frieze.

Relieved to find the temple empty and also that Valeraine had slipped away to talk with Bonfert and left him and Meliroc alone, he moved down the aisle to the kneeling-rail before the altar. There rested the temple's most vital ornament, a pair of open hands chiseled from marble and plated pale gold, frozen in an inviting beckon. As she followed him, Meliroc stared, fascinated, at these hands.

"They're the Lifelord's hands, supposedly," he explained to her. "When we pray, we put our hands in these hands, like so." He slid his own hands into golden palms. "We beseech the Lifelord silently with closed eyes. Then we wait to feel his answer. Our more devout townsfolk claim they've felt these marble hands change to flesh."

"Have you ever felt an answer?"

His memory foundered, reaching for the last time he'd clasped the marble hands. "Sometimes I feel as if a spirit sweeps through me," he told her. "A warm breeze, a little like the warmth you can make with that coal in your heart. Then comes a strange, speaking quietness. It tells me I'm not alone, however lonely I think I am."

"Do you believe it?"

He nodded with a strange twinge. His prayer was moving in him. He squared his shoulders with a low breath then closed his eyes. *O Lifelord, hear me. Show me how to help this woman Meliroc. And help me to win her honestly.*

Brief prayers made the best prayers.

Blinking, drawing his hands from the carving, he turned to meet Meliroc's watching eyes. Wordlessly he slid aside, and she moved into his place. With a soft little sigh she took hold of the marble hands, lifting her gaze toward the ceiling. Her fingers grew taut, her touch firm, as if she hoped quite literally to seize the Lifelord's blessing. Her breath stilled, and his own breath stopped with it.

At last she relaxed, slouching as she exhaled. "I am not his enemy," she said, her thought-voice almost too soft to be heard.

"I would dearly love a few sharp words with whoever told you that," he grumbled through his teeth.

She pursed her lips in thought. "The carillon isn't wicked, you know."

"What is it, then?"

"Lonely," she answered. "When it sang for me today, I felt it reaching, trying to be... something. It sounded almost like my own heart." Her shoulders stiffened as if she were summoning courage. He noticed she had not let go of the carving. "Sir – Cedelair – I need your help."

"However I can help you, I will."

"I need to know what you saw in my dream. The particulars. That's the only way I can fight."

The twisted face of the nightmare fiend peered through a haze in Cedelair's mind. His stomach writhed at the thought of describing it for Meliroc, of trying to explain how she disappeared into it. Yet he knew she was right.

Nightmare Lullaby

"Come, then." He tilted his head toward the door. "This isn't the place to speak of such things."

"This is the very place to speak of such things," she insisted. "Here, with these hands so close, I'll be less afraid."

Again he found himself helpless to argue with her. When he reached toward her she pulled her hand away from the carving and twined her fingers with his.

Then he told her.

***

That night he dreamed again. After years of avoiding sleep he now welcomed dreaming. He would endure sinking into the soil of his garden for the chance to hold Meliroc in his arms. As before, the conscious Valeraine slipped into the dream after him.

"There is progress," she told him over the breakfast table, in mind-speech.

"Do tell," Cedelair urged her.

"I heard a change in the *leyshak's* cries. A touch of fear mixed in with all that bitterness and grief. Not our fear, but its own."

"Why should it be afraid?"

"That's the best part." She leaned forward with an open-mouthed smile. "I sensed her. A tiny string pulling against the *leyshak's* force."

Cedelair cast a quick glance at Meliroc, who was enjoying a buttered muffin. So she was fighting. She was using the knowledge he'd given her. If that tiny string grew bigger, might it pull the *leyshak* down?

A thought had been flitting around the back of his mind, that perhaps he should give the fene'vaith potion to Meliroc alone. If she kept awake, enjoying rest without sleep, the *leyshak* would not emerge, and both she and the townsfolk could have peaceful respite. Now the thought winked out. She had to dream. Only in that suffering could she gain strength enough to overcome her enemy. She needed time. But how much time did they have before the *leyshak* left a mark that could never be erased? *Never under a month, sir, forgive my unwelcome news...*

He gulped his tea to quiet his pitching stomach.

***

He sent Valeraine into town without him, instructing her to give the phials of *fene'vaith* potion to the first people who asked for it and to assure the others that she would have more tomorrow. He needed to plant a new garden, and Meliroc's magic warmth would make the work more bearable, with wintry blasts promising to bring more snow. So she must remain with him.

Pierpon saw right through his excuse. "Snow, snow, the goblin's toe!" he scoffed, poking his head up from Valeraine's basket. "You want her company, you do." He snickered as he sank beneath the cloth and Valeraine carried him over the stoop.

Mennieve had set aside a plot of ground behind the Echo House expressly for Cedelair's purpose. There he and Meliroc worked side by side, shoveling the snow to uncover the rock-hard earth, then pouring their warming spells into it, she stoking her heart-fire to its highest peak and he intoning the needed words in the *Fourth Tongue*, visualizing the spread of green over the frosty gray-brown. By the time the soil began to soften pain was battering his back and hands. He fell back against Meliroc, who wrapped her arms around his shoulders to hold him steady. He felt a tickle at his heart, impressed afresh with how strong she was, how big. He had never imagined how sweet it could be to fall in love with a giant.

His head cleared as the ache subsided. The earth was ready for planting. This work was his. Meliroc did her part, her gaze and touch cloaking him with warmth. He noted the bell-board strapped to her side and the way her hand hovered near the mallet. "Is it still hard not to play?" he asked her.

"Harder," she admitted. "I hear the carillon in my head all the time. It plays every song I think of."

"Have you tried not thinking of songs?" The question tasted bitter in his mouth.

She shook her head. "Then I wouldn't be me anymore. There would be little point in fighting."

Again he felt the smile in spite of himself, the urge to clasp her waist and press close to her. "Soundly spoken, my good Meliroc."

"You're helping me a great deal, you know," she pointed out. "Forbidding me to play, teaching me to pray, and giving me other things to think over." Her gaze rose from his hands to his face. "If you can while you're working, would you tell me a bit more about your growing up?"

"It's dull stuff, really."

"Not to me. Please tell me... let me see... about the worst walloping you ever got."

At this he had to chuckle. "What makes you think I ever got a walloping?"

"A high-spirited lad who wades barefoot in brooks? You must have gotten into trouble once or twice."

"Fair enough," he sputtered. "I'll oblige you."

When his tongue was not busy with his growing spells, he shared with her tales of youthful mischief, wading in the mud because he liked looking at his squishy footprints and then marching across the clean rug without bothering to wipe his feet, falling out of his favorite tree and cutting his temple so that his frantic mother didn't know whether to kiss him or smack him, learning ribald songs from the older boys who played in the glassworks' shadow and then singing them at top volume when his parents hosted a dinner party and told him to "make himself scarce". Meliroc lapped up these stories with a hungry smile and a flash of eye which told him she was locking each word in her memory.

As his tongue tired, a soft note hummed in his ears. Another followed, more open-toned. The notes knitted together into a phrase, and the phrase flowed into a wordless carol that went straight to the heart of the stories he'd shared, a little bit shame-faced yet full of vigor untouched by fear of time or change.

"It's even merrier than the first one," he told her after her thought-voice fell silent. "Call it 'Serenade for Cedelair in Trouble'."

"I like that," she pronounced, grinning.

"Do your songs ever have words?"

"No. They start where words leave off."

He drew his mouth tight. The smile he felt coming on would have rendered him transparent.

They worked on. At her request he helped her plant a packet of seeds, guiding her hands and casting his own growth spell through her fingers. She shuddered with excitement as she saw the green buds rise and begged to do it again. So they both planted, and finished the work faster. By sunset he had his new garden, though the plants would need another day to grow strong enough to be uprooted for potion-making.

Meliroc, rising to her feet and brushing the loose soil from her trousers, cast a smile full of wonder over the new expanse of bright green. Cedelair rose beside her, beaming with pride. "From planting to harvest in only a day," he proclaimed. "The best magic there is." He turned his grin on her. "Thank you for your aid."

"I serve..." She silenced her thought-voice with a vigorous shake of her head. "I was happy to do it," she amended.

A warm hand wrapped close around his heart. He realized that of the days he had spent with her this was the one he most wanted to keep. He cast his thoughts into the future and saw the two of them side by side in a garden, sharing songs and tales as they planted, his work becoming their work, and both of them loving it equally.

What future did she see?

Nightmare Lullaby

18. Meliroc steps over the line

    The thick skin on which I depended had worn away to onion-thin, a maelstrom of feelings roiling just beneath. I strove to hold myself in check by imagining a taut string extending from my neck to the base of my backbone, a fraction of steadiness I could draw tight. Yet inside I jumped at everything. My hands had started to shake again. Sometimes I could hear my wrist-bones rattle.

    I was being punished, not for the terrible thing I'd done, but for the terrible thing I was.

***

    If I could get through five more days without playing my bell-board, the carillon would loose its hold. I did not let myself think about Feuval, whose hope of freedom would be lost. He had never been my friend, after all.

    The day moved through its routine. Again I walked with Cedelair and Valeraine through the square in Crainante with Pierpon nestled unseen in my cloak-hood. My sorcerer-apprentice friend raised her cry of "Me-di-cines!" and cast her beckoning gaze at passers-by, but few came near us. The very ones who would have benefitted most from Cedelair's sleepless draught hung back, chins tucked into their coats and shawls. The monster, the *"leyshak"*, glared at me from their eyes. Then the carillon played. The *leyshak* drew its claws from my heart and my trembling hands calmed.

    When we'd finished work we went to the temple, where Cedelair and Valeraine watched as I petitioned the Lifelord. *Show me some way I can win free, some way I can be neither leyshak nor carillon but the me I'm only beginning to know.* I wasn't sure if I believed a divine creator had breathed life and love into the earth and would hear my plea. But the idea moved me. Like the bells' music, it quieted the shiver in my hands. With a reluctant sigh I plodded to the exit and back onto the side-path, Cedelair and Valeraine flanking me.

A cluster of townsfolk eyed the temple door with a collective look that threw a chill upon me. At first I thought they wished to pray and were vexed that I had taken so long at the altar, but they walked away, grumbling under their breaths with heads close together. How had I offended them? Yet on the walk home I realized that the full force of those glares had not been aimed at me.

***

"How dare they!" Valeraine fumed as she stormed back and forth across her chamber floor. "How dare they look at him like that, when he's doing all in his power to help them!"

"They know, they do, these nightmares come from magic, vixen," Pierpon spoke up from his nest in the crook of my arm. "Who has to do with magic but you and Cedelair?"

"I do, and it's my fault," I protested, hot-faced. "Maybe I should tell them outright that I'm the cause of the plague."

"You'll tell them nothing of the kind, Meliroc," Valeraine countered. "It is not your fault. It's that woman with the yellow eyes, wherever she is. Safe and sound and far from all the trouble she's causing."

"Besides, snow-giant, it'd do no good," the jickety pointed out. "They'd hate you more, but they'd hate him no less."

"It's enough to make me want to curse the lot of them!" the young sorcerer snarled. "After all he's done! You don't know, do you, Meliroc? Of course he wouldn't have told you. Mennieve had to tell me." She laid a firm hand on my arm. "You must never, never mention this to Cedelair. He won't thank you for it. Do you vow?"

"I vow," I answered quickly, my heartbeat already racing.

"I vow," added Pierpon.

Valeraine cleared her throat then smoothed a wrinkle from her skirt. "Five years ago a woman named Tearlac visited Crainante. A sorcerer looking for a town to serve, she called herself. She wanted Crainante and wasn't of a mind to share it with Cedelair. She kept setting up contests, and he would always win. Each time he bested her she grew angrier, until she couldn't contain it any longer. She called down lightning strikes to set fire to people's lands and houses. 'Let your magical champion save you now,' she said. Five people died and countless more were hurt, but at last Cedelair managed to expel her. He laid a spell around the town's borders so that if Tearlac ever set foot here again she would catch fire and burn to ash. But she got in one parting blow."

"The age spell."

"Cedelair has kept to himself ever since. He blames himself for not banishing Tearlac sooner. He had no idea the woman would go so far."

"He didn't know much about sorcerers, then," I returned and regretted it at once. Of course Cedelair had never imagined Tearlac would attack the town. Honorable himself, he'd expected some semblance of honor from his rival. The shame he must feel even now cut sharp through me. I yearned to dash down the corridor, burst into his chamber and fold my arms about him, and swear that if anyone scowled or snarled at him again I would smash the ingrate's head against the side-path. But I drew tight the string of my backbone. Cedelair must not guess I knew how he'd come to look aged, unless he told me himself.

Of that there seemed little likelihood. He had spoken scarcely a dozen words to me all day. I urged myself not to worry, for he had spoken almost as little to Valeraine as to me. With all the problems at his throat, he needed a bit of peace and quiet. I should do as he wished and keep a cordial distance. Yet I would have given everything up to my very soul to hear him call me out to the garden or ask my help bringing a potion to boil. Far from fading, the emotions the *imfaphia amorat* had roused were growing ever more insistent. I would have lightened every burden he bore if someone could have shown me how.

A fine chance I had of that, when I was the heaviest burden of all.

***

On the fourth afternoon of the difficult week, Cedelair sent Valeraine back to the house without him, explaining he needed to speak with me alone. I scooped Pierpon out of my cloak-hood and set him down in Valeraine's basket with utmost care. Though dozens of eyes were fixed on us, none of them could have glimpsed the pixy-man.

"Where are we going?" I asked Cedelair, trying to steady my jumping heart-fire.

"To my old place," he answered in mind-speech. "I want to see my tree again."

A small throng huddled on the side-path outside the bookshop, scowling at Cedelair. I noticed among them my least favorite townsman, a big man with wolfish features, clad in wrinkled trousers and a dust-blackened smock. He mouthed a word, surely the vilest of insults if the venom in his eyes were aught to judge by.

"What's that great dog of a man's name?" I asked as I turned back to Cedelair.

He stifled a smile at my description. "Holbart. He's the head blacksmith."

"Is he an old enemy of yours?"

"Holbart thinks the world is spoiling for a fight with him."

This put neatly into words everything I sensed in his look. But why would so many of his neighbors cluster around him to assault Cedelair with their ice-cold stares? How I wished they might shout something, however foul! Better that than a silence that felt like a fist waiting to swing.

Sunset hung on the edge of dusk by the time we reached his old property. His mouth twitched as he glanced toward the heap of ashes half blanketed with snow and the upturned earth of the old garden. He rested his open hand against the frost-crusted trunk of the grand oak and let out a strangled sigh, and with a blink he shook his head. I could do no more than rest my hands upon his sagging shoulders.

"Meliroc." He pressed the bridge of his nose as if afflicted with a headache. "I've watched you cope." He glanced up at me with a forlorn wisp of a smile. "I'm very proud of you. And very sorry that I wasn't kinder to you when you first came to us."

I remembered what I'd been then with a swell of queasy loathing. "It's I who owes apology," I told him. "I judged you and Valeraine harshly for things that were never your fault. And you've done far better by me than all those who welcomed me with open arms."

"I hope I have." He turned to face me as he dug into his coat pocket. "I have made an elixir especially for you." He pulled out his closed fist, uncurling his fingers to reveal a tiny gray phial.

"This was one of the first potions I taught myself to make," he told me. "I was heady with my new power. I made elixirs I'd never make today, to strike an enemy blind or to tie his tongue or to turn him cold so he'd never be warm again. But I would only try them out on myself, so I made this useful little antidote." He held the bottle towards me. "It's yours. To do with as you please, if you would be free."

I understood. If I drank this potion *imfaphia amorat* would be well and truly out of my system. I rolled the bottle in my palm and imagined the liquid slipping down my throat to blot away the love and all that went with it. No more rush of heat to my blood. No more thrill at the sound of his voice. No more that sense of joy deep in my core merely to be with him, to know him, to think of all he was and would be.

A thought stole upon me, a gentle brush of wings.

"How do you know I'm not free already?" I asked him. "Perhaps the love-spell did dissipate when I played my last song, just as you intended."

"But you still love me, Meliroc."

"Yes. But it isn't potion-love any longer, if it ever was."

He backed away from me. "That's hardly likely."

"Why did you keep me, when you so clearly didn't want me?" I reminded him. "Because you knew I'd suffer if you sent me away. You took me on as a burden rather than see me come to harm. That's what a good man does."

"Valeraine talked me into it."

"She could never have persuaded a lesser man." I reached for his hand. "Since then you've helped me. You've understood me. Perhaps all that potion really did was show me my own heart." I smiled down at the bottle. If I swallowed the elixir inside, it would affect me not at all. Of that I was suddenly sure.

I opened the bottle and gulped down the potion. Closing my eyes, I felt it settle on my stomach. A tingle swept through my limbs. Something broke loose and flew free inside me. I opened my eyes slowly to gaze down at Cedelair's anxious face. My heart swelled. My blood burned.

I bent forward and pressed my mouth to his. All I'd thought and felt about him since we met I poured into that kiss. My nerves sang and soared with it, bursting at their ends, filling me with a giddiness I wanted to seize fast and hold forever. I kissed him till I could no longer breathe, then pulled away, reluctant but faint with joy. If I'd had a proper voice I would have made a fool of myself and giggled like a tipsy tavern wench.

Yet even in the tingling rush I knew what would happen next. He would turn his head with a grimace or take a polite backward step with his eyes on the ground. My string of control threatened to blow loose as I waited for his rejection.

"Is it true, Meliroc?" he asked in a strangled whisper. "You could love a little man like me?"

My senses were playing tricks. The brightness in his eyes was surely a play of the light. He wanted me to love him? My head still teetering from the kiss, I let myself believe it. I tousled the hair at his temple. "You're not so very little," I told him, bending down to kiss his brow.

With a dazed chuckle he folded his arms about my waist, clasping the small of my back. "I dreamed of this," he breathed. "You're not going to go away again, are you? Start spinning and..." He choked as a tremble gripped him.

His words made no sense. I was the one dreaming. Yet I would trust as long as I could this illusion that he truly feared to lose me. The freckled face of his old love winked in my memory. How gently she had broken his heart. "I am not Roselise, Cedelair. I won't go away."

"No, you're not Roselise. You're so much bigger than she was."

"No doubt."

"Bigger in every sense," he explained. "Bigger in mind and heart and soul, so big you take my breath away. I'm in awe of you, Meliroc."

The same tremble that had shaken him now seized me. My breath escaped me.

"In awe," he repeated. "I can't wait to see how high you'll soar once you're free, my marvelous giant." His fingers danced up and down my back. "Lift me up as high as you are."

I hooked my arms around his waist and hoisted him gently into the air until his face was level with mine. He kissed me hard. The giddiness swept through me again. I would surely have fainted with it had his lips not parted from mine just in time and his head dropped upon my shoulder. With one arm I held him aloft, and with the other hand I caressed his hair.

"I couldn't say a word before. I thought you only loved me because of the potion." He nibbled at my chin, and again that silly giggle bubbled in my throat. "I love you, my large heart. Please don't doubt me. I love you."

Please don't doubt me. Now I knew I wasn't dreaming. My heart-fire exploded in such a conflagration that I half-feared my embrace would burn him.

I sank to my knees with him in my arms.

***

He lay in my embrace, his head upon my heart. His magic swept through me, fresh and vital, until I felt I could make the trees blossom with a wave of my hand. My green man. I could be a green woman, an earth-healer with fingers of life. For him. With him.

Kissing his temple, I sang to him, shaping my mind-voice into fiddle and harp and flute. He told me more of those stories I loved, of how he had grown from child to man. "I want you to know everything about me," he whispered low in my ear.

He told me about Tearlac, and the lightning strikes, and the spell that had seared a mask of age onto his face. His voice thinned into a painful monotone as he forced himself through this tale. "She came here to face me," he said. "My presence drew her here. They blame me."

I ran my fingertips over the lines around his mouth. "You do them good every day of your life," I pointed out just before I kissed him.

When I broke from him I found him beaming. "How did you know I am not old?"

I had no real answer for him, for truthfully I wasn't sure. So I tilted my head and returned his smile. "Your eyes have the impatience of youth. I should think anyone who got a good look at you would know you for a young man."

The fire of delight drove off the shadow of Tearlac. He tightened his arms about me. "I felt old inside. Then you came to me."

We settled into silence then, relishing each other's closeness. I drank in the smell of him, that scent of sweet water and clean earth and root and stem. The stars winked into view as we breathed in time with one another.

Even after we started back to Mennieve's house, Cedelair lighting our path with a pale blue flame that hovered in his palm, the warm tingle lingered. I thought of days to come at this man's side, helping him in his work and discovering my own. I would learn plant lore and use my heart-fire as he used his growth spells to nourish the seeds. I would find a new instrument to play, one that would neither break nor try to steal my soul. We would share what we loved, day in and day out. Cedelair's smile told me he was thinking along the same lines. He strode with a bounce in his step.

We moved down a wooded path. A pine limb stirred in the corner of my eye, and a clump of snow plopped to the ground. Yet even the tiny glimmer of torch-light failed to disturb our confidence that for this little while only we existed.

Something hissed, quick and sharp. Then something whipped itself around my legs, locking my knees together and sending me hurtling forward. "That's it, lads! Down she comes!" someone bellowed, but as I tried to turn toward the speaker something slammed hard against the base of my skull. I heard Cedelair shout my name, but through a burst of mind-throttling pain I could see no more than a filmy outline of his figure and a ghostly shadow of a torch fire. Panic had snuffed out the flame in his palm.

Cloudy man-forms swarmed about him, dragging him away from me. He cried out, but something choked him off. A hand gripped my hair and yanked upward, while the cord around my legs drew tighter still, pinching, biting. Sharp points pressed against my neck. My swimming vision barely perceived the working end of a pitchfork and beyond it a sneering face with rage-red eyes.

"No nonsense out of you, big one! Make a move or a noise, and I'll run you through."

Still dazed with agony, I was almost happy to hear clearly again, until I realized what I was hearing: a fury of blows, kicks, and snarls. Torch-light blazed over the shadow-men's heads as they massed in a circle, but Cedelair I could not see or hear.

"It was due to you our houses burned!" roared one of the shadows, aiming a kick at something on the ground.

"And then you set fire to your own house!" shouted another.

"You're not safe to have around, Master Sorcerer."

Kick! Kick! Kick! I writhed as I felt each blow in my own ribs. One boot came down hard on my back, another on the back of my knees. The cord around my legs threatened to cut through my trousers.

"What'll we do with him, friends?"

"Show him out of town!"

"Then he'd only be somebody else's headache."

"We need to stop his magic."

"His tongue," the largest of the shadows spoke up. In the torch's flicker I recognized the beefy blacksmith who wanted to fight the world. "That's what you said, wasn't it, Orqual?"

A sniffling voice followed. "A sorcerer works magic by speaking languages nobody else can understand."

Kick! Kick! Kick! Kick!

Anger burned thick in my throat. I couldn't have uttered a noise even if I'd wished to. I couldn't even cry out Cedelair's name, not that that would have helped him in any case. I had no proper voice. *This shall be thy voice.* Feuval's words slipped into my mind in an insinuating whisper.

My hands remained unbound. These thugs must have thought, if in their vicious stupidity they could think at all, that as long as I couldn't rise to my feet I posed no threat. I began to move the fingers of my right hand with such cautious slowness that my captors couldn't perceive it. I held my breath, my heart an aching knot in my chest.

"Get him to his feet," the blacksmith grunted. Three men reached down into the circle to hoist Cedelair upright. The blacksmith waved the torch in his face. Blood trickled from his temple, and bruises were already spreading over his eyes and jaw. A black cloth covered his mouth. His head wobbled. He was barely conscious.

The fist tightened around my hair. Pain-flashes blinded me again. Yet still my fingers inched closer to my mallet.

"We're going to take the gag off you, Master Cedelair," the blacksmith growled through his teeth. "But if you make a single sound, that's it for your precious giant."

The pain-flashes faded to a spotty haze. My fingers curled about my mallet handle. As the pitchfork's points pressed harder against my throat and the cord burned more roughly around my legs, I slid the mallet free from my sash and moved my elbow half an inch. I couldn't strike more than one plank, but that was all my bell-board needed. I cracked open my panicked mind to let the "Sorrow Song" pour into it.

A hand ripped the cloth from Cedelair's mouth and clamped across his jaw, pulling downward. The other men closed in behind him to pinion his arms as the blacksmith reached into his coat. The torch-light glinted on the edge of a blade.

They're going to cut out his tongue. Lifelord, they're going to cut out his tongue!

I struck the note. The chime burst into a blossom of silver light over the thugs' heads.

My skull threatened to shatter as I disobeyed Cedelair's prohibition. Yet even as the cord about my legs convulsed, bruising my knees and tendons, I saw the pitchfork-man step backward. Heartened, I fought through the agony to strike the plank again, and this time another note burst out, the second in the "Sorrow Song". A fresh spark leaped up from my bell-board to light the glade, revealing the shock on the thugs' faces.

"What's the matter with you, Embe?" snapped the blacksmith. "Gut her! Run her through!" The pitchfork-man could only blink.

I struck the plank a third time, and a fourth, and the Sorrow Song took shape. The carillon light wove through the trees. I fired a cold stare at the men who held Cedelair, their faces creasing in woe, their hands beginning to shake. Cedelair slumped out of their grasp.

"Kill her!" roared Holbart, his voice raw with fury. His eyes, too, glimmered with mist. I quaked to the point of nausea, as if my bones would splinter from the inside. But the bell-board's silver-white web held me together. As my pain swelled, the melody in my head grew more bittersweet. I let the ache infuse my notes, sending it into my listeners. Cedelair's shoulders heaved as he let out a sob, followed by a garbled word. "Play." As the prohibition lifted, so did the near-maddening pain.

The men shrank from me. Holbart pointed a shaking finger. "Gut... curse it... kill... why doesn't somebody stop her?" His voice cracked, no longer raging but pleading.

Cedelair lifted his teetering head. "Because it's too late," he choked, a faint smile on his bleeding lips. "She is in your souls now."

"Cut me free and I'll be quiet," I said.

Nightmare Lullaby

"Cut her free," gasped Cedelair, "and she will be quiet." He let out a thready whisper of a chuckle. "Though it won't do you much good. You'll remember that song as long as you live."

As his voice faded in the air his strength winked out. For a single eviscerating second I couldn't see him breathe, as if he'd given up his life with that last warning. A stab of grief rang through the note I played. *It's too late,* a low voice intoned, the beat of a heavy drum in the back of my brain. *Too late.*

I heard a sharp swish. I could move my legs. Grabbing my instrument under my arm, I stood. While I gritted my teeth at the yank of agony at my spine, I watched the men back away. As I glanced from them to Cedelair, fury pulsed hot through my veins. If I touched one of them I would kill him. I saw in their faces that they knew it.

"Stop her, Embe." The blacksmith could barely eke out his command, his voice was so choked in tears. I doubted Embe even heard him. No hand moved to hinder me as I strode towards Cedelair, then sank down beside him and wrapped my free arm about his shoulders. His head fell upon my chest. Tears and blood damped my tunic. Tightening my hold, I let myself believe my embrace could mend him, as it had mended my broken bell-board.

I loomed over the men with my most dangerous glower. "Go away." They couldn't hear my words, but they felt them. They trudged off with hanging heads.

Too late. The drum-beat shook me as I watched my chrysalis-light spin about Cedelair. My touch wouldn't heal him. He needed the bonesetter's care at once. I started forward with as fast a stride as I could manage, following the tracks by moonlight. I felt him breathe, felt his heart beat, and knew I had saved him. Yet now that I knew he loved me I would lose him.

Only one thought could offer any comfort. *Cedelair, my love, we still have three days more.*

19. Cedelair faces desperate measures

Pain drove him out of knowing and came with him when he opened his eyes again. The thin light of a foggy morning slipped through the curtains. Meliroc's hand clung to his.

His jaw was bandaged. Coviet the bone-setter was splinting his ribs. Daggers dug into his sides to fire darts of agony down his limbs. Through a pained haze he could see Mennieve sitting on the edge of his bed and Valeraine standing near the foot. His apprentice was talking in an angry snap. He heard just enough to know she was telling Coviet the story Meliroc must have given her, of what had been done to them.

Coviet bent down to speak in Cedelair's ear. The elder sorcerer heard him as a call at the distant end of a tunnel. "Who were the men?"

The daggers stabbed as he breathed hard. The memory of Meliroc face down on the ground, her legs bound and a pitchfork at her throat, made his stomach wrench. Oh, how he wanted to shout their names and damn them in doing so! Yet his tongue proved too weak to move.

Meliroc kissed his hand. "Later," she said, "when he's had time to rest."

Valeraine relayed the message to Coviet. "I'll come back this afternoon to check on you," the bonesetter told his patient, then quietly left the room.

Valeraine gave her master a steady look. "I can brew the medicine you need," she said. "You'll be on your feet in a little more than a day." Then she too bustled out of the room. Mennieve glanced from him to Meliroc, then followed Valeraine.

A little more than a day. That would leave him less than two days to spend with Meliroc before she disappeared into that devilish bell-box. She would never know the joy of walking free of her *geas*. The broken jaw and bruised kidneys he might have forgiven, but those men had destroyed her and would never know or care how.

Her gaze seeped into him to soothe his anger. Those eyes, he felt sure, could heal him as well as any potion. He understood now why her thoughts and feelings no longer passed into him. That had been the potion's effect, when he'd made himself the object of her love. It had ceased after she'd found her last song for Feuval. Yet her love had not. This large-hearted being had looked into a soul grown black and cold and had found something worthy of love.

He found his tongue could move. "Will you play for me, Meliroc? Too late now for me to forbid you." He coughed, wincing at the throb in his chest. "I want to hear your voice."

She kissed his hand once more and set it gently down upon the bed and took her bell-board into her lap (it was never very far from her). Soon a wave of bright music enfolded him, a surge of feeling given form in notes and measures. The song that revealed the truth of love.

The gnawing fire in his head began to subside.

***

She remained at his side, sometimes playing, sometimes mind-singing, sometimes telling him funny tales of peculiar creatures, until Valeraine called her away. He knew she was only helping his apprentice bring the healing potion to boil and would soon come back, but he felt the room's empty silence like a creaking weight. He hummed her love melody to lighten the burden.

She returned with Valeraine, who carried a small bowl of soup in her hands. He sniffed and detected the hole'vaith tincture, an elixir to speed the knitting of broken bones and the mending of torn, bruised flesh. "Now you may judge how worthy an apprentice I am," she declared as she fed it to him. After the first swallow he could feel the potion going straight to his injuries and setting in to work.

"I don't know why I should be surprised," Coviet remarked when he came two hours later to examine him, Mennieve in tow. "To say you're making a miraculous recovery sounds a bit absurd when you're in the miracle business."

"This particular miracle is not of my making," Cedelair pointed out, smiling and nodding in Valeraine's direction.

"Ah! Congratulations, young mistress," the bonesetter returned. "Keep your bandages for tonight, Cedelair. Tomorrow morning, most likely, I can take them off for you." He stiffened his neck with a formal frown. "Can you give the names of those men?"

Cedelair swallowed hard, feeling as if a bone had lodged in his throat. "Holbart," he began.

"No surprise there," Coviet grunted.

"He beat me, along with Forthier and Dumorel and Loiz and Nolfai," Cedelair told him. "Subert and Grazon brought Meliroc down, and Embe held a pitchfork to her throat to keep her still." His gaze shifted to Valeraine as he added, "Acelin was there as well. He brought his foot down on her back."

"Curse him," Valeraine growled through her teeth.

"Four others stood sentry. Thandif. Rosbert. Linbel. Orqual."

Mennieve sucked in a shocked breath. "Orqual?"

"I thought you and Orqual got along," said Coviet, a tremor in his voice.

"His nephew Feot was my friend," Cedelair pointed out. "I used to talk to Feot about the Magic Tongues. Orqual heard me often enough, I'm sure. He told them. That's how they got the idea to cut out my tongue." He clenched his fists. "I want these men punished, Coviet. They've done me a wrong greater than they imagine."

"Cedelair, dear lad, we're none of us ourselves," Mennieve spoke up, with a placating look that would have moved him any other time. Orqual the chandler had long been a friend of hers.

Cedelair scowled. "Those men hurt Meliroc."

Mennieve patted his hand. "Meliroc's right there." She nodded towards the giant, who sat on her stool close beside the bed. "She isn't hurt."

"They pulled her to the ground! They threatened to kill her!" he shouted. An instant later he winced as he remembered that he lay in Mennieve's own chamber that she'd shared with Fimbre. His injury had drawn her back inside the Echo House. The last thing she deserved was to hear him raise his voice to her.

"I need to speak with you alone," he told her.

Nightmare Lullaby

Meliroc caressed his brow, then rose from her stool and left the room. Valeraine followed quickly. Coviet lingered a little longer, glancing with concern from Cedelair to Mennieve and back again before he finally took his leave. When Mennieve moved to the stool Meliroc had vacated, Cedelair clutched her hand. His tongue trembled. "You – you – h-have to understand," he stammered. "Meliroc..." His voice faded into a gasp.

"You love her," Mennieve guessed. "You can't forgive those men for laying hands on her."

He shook his head. "It's w-worse than that. Those men took her from me. You'll believe me."

Struggling against the bone in his throat, he told Mennieve the story of the kho-laeth, and how its duplicitous master had woven a net around Meliroc with music and words of friendship. "She only wanted to help him," he spat, bitter ash in his mouth.

Mennieve paled as she heard the story to its conclusion. "That I'm improving so quickly is due to Valeraine, not to those animals," Cedelair told her. "They would have done worse than slice out my tongue if Meliroc hadn't stopped them. Now she's lost to me. So you see why I can't forgive Orqual or any of them."

Mennieve shuddered. "What exactly would happen to Meliroc if she gave herself to the carillon?"

Cedelair drew himself up, steeling himself against a fresh pang. "She would become a spirit, existing to make the carillon's music."

"That's why she looks like a phantom, then, with that odd light around her."

He nodded. "Soon nothing will be left of her but that light."

"I see." She coughed behind her hand. "Is there really nothing to be done? No way to save her?"

"The only way doesn't bear thinking about. Someone would have to go to the carillon in Meliroc's place."

"Willingly, I presume." At his nod, she continued. "I've read stories about this sort of enchantment. It wouldn't want just anyone. It would need somebody with a soul for music." She stroked his hand. "I sing, you know."

A memory of himself and Rybert huddled against Mennieve's skirts while she sang in a light, clear voice brushed against a nerve. "Why do you mention that, Mennieve?"

She flexed her jaw. "You needn't give up Meliroc for lost, dear lad. I will take her place."

"Are you mad?" he cried. "I won't hear of it! Meliroc won't hear of it!"

"Listen to me for a bit, Cedelair. I am..." She drew the corners of her mouth tight. "I won't see the spring come."

Cedelair's head pitched with a wave of pain as he absorbed her words. He hadn't imagined he could hurt worse.

"All life holds for me now is the chance to see those I love happy. It gave me joy beyond knowing to think of you in love again, lad. And if I can be the means of your winning your love, I can't think of anything I'd rather die for."

"It wouldn't be dying!" he protested. "It would be worse than dying." He envisioned the beckoning marble hands. Mennieve was a woman of faith. "You'd never join Fimbre and Rybert in the Lifelord's care."

"Everything falls under his eye, lad, even an enchanted carillon. One day I will join my loves in his care. That I know." She pressed her cheek against his hand. "I want to do this for you and Meliroc."

He winced at a stab at his temple. "I can't think – I can't"– Thoughts knocked hard against each other. Meliroc lost – Mennieve dying – disappearing into spirit – Meliroc praying – Meliroc playing – Mennieve singing – swallowed by light – "I have to talk to Meliroc."

"Of course you do," Mennieve agreed, patting his hand. "Find out what she says about it. Though truth to tell it makes no difference. I mean to do this for you, whether you like it or not." She hopped up from the stool. She leaned down to kiss Cedelair's forehead. "You've made me very happy this day," she declared. She strode from the room with a light little whistle.

Very happy. The veil of mist over his eyes thinned and faded, and he realized that she had looked happy. Her tongue had faltered, reluctant to say plainly, "I am dying," but with each word she'd spoken afterward her eyes had gleamed ever brighter with delighted resolve. A giver by nature, she'd thrilled at the thought of bestowing this last great gift on someone she loved.

Everything of the old days had disappeared on the wind with the ashes of his home. He'd thought that at least Mennieve, his fixture of comfort, would remain. Yet when the warm breezes returned she too would be gone. What had he left?

Nightmare Lullaby

Meliroc.

***

Weighed down though he was, his heartbeat still quickened when she returned to his side. She clasped his hand as before and tilted her head at him with a serious smile that made him want to laugh.

"Mennieve talked with me a while," she informed him.

"No doubt she told you about her proposal."

"She gave me instructions to talk you around."

He propped himself up on his elbow and marveled at how swiftly the pain in his ribs had dissipated. He would heap lavish praise on Valeraine when he saw her next. "And what do you think of it?"

"I think it will be terrible to lose her, one way or another." She reached out to stroke his brow. "Cedelair, my love, she thinks she'll solve all our problems. But there's still the problem she doesn't know about."

The *leyshak*. He mouthed the word but wouldn't voice it.

She nodded, her smile wilting. "It's been in my mind all day. I feel its evil, like claws tearing my insides."

He clutched her hand. Then he kissed her wrist. "It isn't you, Meliroc."

"It's here because of me. I brought that trouble on you last night."

"It was not --"

She rested her hand on his mouth. "I'm not finished. Last evening I was happier than I'd ever dared imagine being. It makes me wonder how much happier still I could be if I were part of your life from here on in, if you wanted me there."

"I want you there, large heart." His lips moved against her fingers. "Oh, how I want you there."

"But not yet. As long as I can feel that monster's claws inside me, I can't offer you myself."

"We'll get rid of it," he vowed, heartsickness creeping upon him again.

"If we can't," she said, "if it's still there when my time runs out, I go to the carillon. No one will ever again have nightmares because of me."

He nodded. Her words seared him, but he saw their sense. Two nights more? So little time to track down the one thing that would make the final difference. But he would find it. He had no choice.

He realized then that she was indeed "talking him around" to Mennieve's proposal, surely without knowing it.

"We drive the *leyshak* away," he declared, new strength in his voice. "No more must. No more yellow-eyed woman. Only my magnificent Meliroc. And then?"

"And then..." Her hand trembled in his. "The carillon would never harm so good a soul as Mennieve. It's a healer, Cedelair. It could mend her. She wants to give us a future, and Lifelord help me, even if you despise me for it, I could not refuse. I am too selfish."

A bitter laugh chafed the back of his throat. He could hardly judge her. She understood the kho-laeth far better than he did. He could believe it was a healer, when he had felt that soothing touch in the bells' music. With all his heart he wanted to believe it. He would lose Mennieve, whatever befell. But he wanted to keep Meliroc. Lifelord help him, he was too selfish.

"First we get rid of the *leyshak*," he pronounced. "Then we will face what comes next."

20. Meliroc confronts the enemy

I'd read in books of how hours creak by for soldiers awaiting a battle. Now I felt it. My sizzling nerves wouldn't cool until my fight was done. But Cedelair, on his feet by morning as he'd predicted, knew how to make a little of the time pass pleasantly. He would take me to the banks of the brook where he'd played with his friends.

We avoided the town square by slipping through the house's back door and onto a narrow path that would lead us into the countryside. Light snow danced in a soft breath of wind, and I draped my cloak about Cedelair's shoulders so that he might feel it as I did, as the brush of tiny feathers.

He'd warned me I would not see Doriot Brook at its best, with the water frozen and the bare elms rimmed with frost. I tried to imagine the scene in springtime shades of emerald, gold and azure, yet found I preferred the snowy banks and the frozen water wreathing the stones like a silver scarf. With so much of my memory smothered in black, it ill behooved me to look backward. Here and now I stood at the beginning of my past, the time I would smile to recall in years to come.

We rested upon the bank, my arms folded about him, his head lying against my breast. I kissed the top of his head, then brushed my fingers down the length of his hair.

He smiled up at me, stretching his arms and neck. "So good to be up and about." He sighed. "No more rib-splints, no more 'stay absolutely still'. No more Valeraine reading aloud from that silly book of hers."

"'Valdarte the Valiant'?" I gave him a teasing smile. "Come now, you liked it. Admit it."

"I endured it," he countered. "Never could have guessed how keen my apprentice would be to take advantage of a captive audience."

I shook my head. "Fibber. When you thought Valdarte might fall into the bottomless bog, you looked positively frantic!"

"Why should I worry about that, when the series has three more books in it?"

I tickled the back of his neck. "Now, now, Cedelair, my stick-in-the-mud, what was your favorite bit? The battle with the fog demons? The march on the Shorl-King's castle?"

He covered his mouth as he cleared his throat. "If you must know, the part where Valdarte left the golden rose on Armancour's doorstep and then ran away before he could find it. Strange how she could face down a horde of fog demons single-handed, but she couldn't manage to look a man in the eye and say 'I love you' in plain words."

"What a romantic you are." I kissed his brow, fondling the hair at his temple.

"I never was before, large heart," he returned, beaming. "You bring it out."

I wrapped my arms about his waist. "You liked the book, you liked it, you liked it," I teased in sing-song, rocking him back and forth. "Admit it, and I promise I won't tell Valeraine."

"It was... diverting," he sniffed.

"Di-vehh-ting," I mimicked in mock-disdain as he settled in my arms, chuckling under his breath. A joyful spark winked like a will o' the wisp in his eyes.

"Do you like Crainante?" he asked me suddenly.

"I don't really know it. But I know I've been happy here." My answer sounded strange, yet I felt its truth.

"But you wouldn't regret to leave it? I mean, if I left it? I've been thinking that perhaps we shouldn't rebuild in the old spot. We should start again someplace else."

I grinned so wide it hurt. At this moment "we" was the most wonderful word in any language. "If it's what you want, I'll gladly go with you," I assured him. "But if you're thinking of leaving because of what happened the other night it's a terrible idea."

"It isn't that. With Mennieve gone, there won't be much of my old life left. I'm tired of old things. I want something new."

"That's it, then. Once we've put a stop to this dream-plague, we'll set out in search of a new home." I drew him closer, bending down to tuck his head under my chin. "We fit so nicely, don't you think?"

"I'll never look any younger, you know," he pointed out, a twinkle in his eye.

"So? I'll never get any smaller."

"Smaller, you say?" He reached up to fondle my neck. "Ah, Meliroc, sweet long-legs, how could any smaller woman compare with you?"

His words dizzied me like honeyed wine, but still I felt moved to tease him. "So if I were to shrink somehow, you'd have no further use for me?"

"You'd always be my large heart," he avowed, "but since that hasn't happened yet, I beg your leave to adore each and every foot of you." He ran his fingertip down the edge of my chin. "Ah, yes," he murmured, his lips close to mine, "we fit each other superbly." He kissed me long and deep.

Lightning split my head, shaking my thoughts into place. We, we, we – that marvelous word! There it lay, the key that could vanquish both the *leyshak* and the Bitter Chord.

"Tonight, Cedelair, we must dream together," I said. "The same dream for us both."

***

Through the parlor window I watched the sun set, while Cedelair and Valeraine discussed my case in one of their magic tongues. "Meliroc something, something, something, something Meliroc." I should have objected to their talking about me in a language I couldn't understand, but the sound of Cedelair weaving my name into his peculiar lingo sent a thrill up my spine.

Valeraine touched my shoulder. "Master Cedelair has told me what you want to do, Meliroc, and it's a brilliant idea. I think we know how to make it work."

Cedelair clapped a hand on his apprentice's shoulder with a proud smile.

"To dream the same dream, you'd need a third party to control it." She pointed to herself. "I'd observe but stay out of it unless things get so nasty I have to wake you. Bear this in mind, you must never lose sight of each other. If you do, for even half a second, one of you could get lost."

A chill question crept across my mind. "What happens to people who die in dreams?"

"I don't think anyone knows," she replied. "I suppose the simple answer is that people don't die in their dreams."

"Not in normal dreams. Not in the ones Pierpon makes. But in these..." I broke off at a pounding in my head.

Cedelair rested his hand on mine. "What frightens you, Meliroc?"

"The *leyshak*. It won't go away without a fight." I slid my arm about his shoulders. "Promise me, Cedelair, you'll kill it rather than let it harm you."

"We don't know what would happen to you then."

"It doesn't matter. Promise me."

"I can't"–

"If you don't, I'll go this minute to the carillon."

He hiccoughed, his mouth twitching from frown to smile and back again. "Life with you will not be easy," he muttered. "I promise you. But it won't be necessary." He kissed my fingers.

With his look and his vow sealed fast in my memory, I slipped away to Valeraine's chamber and found Pierpon stretched out on her bed, peering over a book. At the sight of me he gave a joyful shout and leaped onto my arm. With a pang of shame at my neglect of him, I sat down on the bed to play a few rounds of our eight-note game with him. We took turns hammering out snatches of music until he started to rub at his eyes.

"You're frightened, you are," he mentioned.

I nodded in admission. "The *leyshak* is going to die tonight, one way or another."

"Hurrah for that!" the jickety crowed. "I'll expect you to tell me everything in the morning."

If I am still here. The words burrowed like a barbed arrow into my mind.

I hadn't intended to speak, but somehow Pierpon heard me. "You're no *leyshak*, mam'selle Meliroc." He hugged my wrist. "I'll see you in the morning, I will."

Nightmare Lullaby

With the familiar swell about my heart I brushed his hair with my thumb. "I love you, little man," I said, and tucked him under my chin.

"I love you back, large woman." He stretched out his arms to clasp my neck. "No *leyshak* better hurt the friend I love."

***

Notes fell upon my face like a cool mist. I breathed in delight and opened my eyes by inches. A crystal-bright waterfall rose before me, flanked by two verdant slopes. The sunlight upon the foam drew out a twinkle of myriad colors, each one holding a note. A color-choir.

With the mist seeping through my smock and skin, I rushed forward to the pond. Singing pools splashed up to my bare calves. I lifted Cedelair onto my back, and as I leaped through the fall with outspread arms we dissolved together into that riot of colors. The notes swirled, melted, and spun as we drank in this bodiless lightness. No wall of flesh or bone separated us. His joy sang with mine. From air we became mist that thickened into water. I pooled and bubbled around a river-rock, all shades of silver. Cedelair's green flowed through me, and each cast was changed.

Then I felt something slip upon the damp, slick stone. My foot. I was solid again.

Cedelair gripped my elbow while I scrambled for balance. A dusky sky hovered over our heads. A blaze of gold sprang up between us, encircling me. I closed my eyes against the glare as two long sticks took shape in my hands.

Light from a lamp overhead shone on the carillon bells that hemmed me in. Outlines of faces hovered in the dusk beyond. Valeraine. Mennieve. Coviet the bone-setter. The glass-blower and his staring child. The counting-man's servant. The bully I'd bowled down the side-path. The elderly couple at the gem-stall, and the children who'd played around all those stone sentinels in all those town squares. Everyone I'd noticed in my travels watched me with expectant eyes.

I'd read stories of dreamers appearing naked before crowds. With a cold shiver I glanced down to find myself robed in gold-trimmed scarlet velvet.

At the front of the crowd stood a figure swathed in white satin and masked in gold. "Play," he barked in command. I recognized Feuval's voice, though he had never spoken so sharply to me before.

"I – I don't know how," I stammered, the old tremble rattling my fingers.

"Thou dost know!" bellowed the carillon-man, striking the bell closest to him. As it shook out its note color-lights flickered then beamed in the hearts of its neighbors. The glow spread around the circle until a color beat inside every bell. I knew the sounds the hues made, what note would answer with each bell I struck.

Dizzy with triumph, I launched into my merry-hearted tune. A firework flared with each fall of the mallet. The music flowed faster through me, the resonant peals of the bells feeding my drive. Fresh choruses sprang up in my mind, variations on their heels. Colors hovered in an arch above my head, the rainbow ceiling of a temple.

I paused to catch my waning breath, and in that instant the crowd sent up a cheer. My mind cried out to Cedelair. "Hear what I can do!"

No call answered.

I peered past the colorful flares to seek him in the crowd. Dread gripped me, needles sinking into my skin. *You must never lose sight of each other.*

"Play!" the carillon-master commanded.

"Cedelair!" my mind screamed.

"Play!" thundered the gold-masked man.

My hands quaked, disconnected from my will. The notes inside me shook loose from all pattern. I winced at the dissonant cacophony as the mallets fell, their handles stuck fast to my palms.

"Cedelair!"

No answer.

The notes hammered my head without mercy. A shriek shot to my throat. Legions of sorrows beyond my own gathered and swelled in that shriek. Horror-twisted faces flew at me from the crowd. Whirling lights struck at me from their eyes. I reeled backward, but my hands still swung the mallets.

"You wanted to play." The carillon-man's mask pressed close to me, but the voice was a woman's. "Now you have your wish." Two yellow points of light gleamed from the mask's eye-holes. "I made this carillon especially for you, dear Roc. Don't I always give you what you need?"

Though the chill in my blood sharpened to agony, I knew what needed doing. I'd play, all right. Here at last was the "hardest heart" that needed to weep.

Nightmare Lullaby

"Play, play, play!" Her wintry-gale whisper grew fierce as the yellow lights brightened. "The music of madness, the only music you can make."

An icy noose was tightening about my throat, threatening to choke the scream loose.

"You'd like to cry out, wouldn't you? Then do."

My stomach pitched. I could reach the song. I only needed know Cedelair wasn't lost. *Cedelair, please come back, please find me...*

Silence, still and cold. I groped in the dark and found only empty air. How had I lost him? Under the waterfall we had merged into a glorious we. Then my enemy's carillon had pushed him away. Grief added its weight to the hammering chaos of notes. Grief – the root of the song I needed. Better to feel it than to feel nothing, like an empty shell with naught but dust and air inside... My wrist throbbed in protest as I forced my right mallet down hard upon the bell I wanted.

"Just what do you think you're doing?"

One by one I gripped the notes and shaped them into the melody. Grinding my teeth, I pounded out the song's first measure. The notes rang strong and clear.

The Bitter Chord sniffed. "Think you can get the better of me?"

For the first time I caught a hint of fear in my enemy's whisper. The third measure followed smoothly on the heels of the second.

Keep playing, Meliroc.

The song poured out to sweep away the chaos. My mallets' touch lightened to draw out the melody's bitter-sweetness. Joy mingled with sorrow in my tears. Cedelair had found me.

"Stop!" the Bitter Chord shouted. "This isn't the right tune!"

Another bar and you'll have her, Cedelair's voice whispered in my mind's ear.

"Stop it!" the Bitter Chord shrieked in a fury. A dart of light shot from her eyes to strike me full in the face. Pain rattled the notes in my head, but I played on until at last a veil of mist muted the yellow gleams and I knew my song-magic was striking home.

Something moved in the corner of my eye. Cedelair, in the way of dreamers, had passed through the circle of bells and now stood at my side, arrayed in a long-coat of forest green velvet, his hair finely combed and drawn into a horse-tail. A spear of silver light glimmered in the grip of his right hand. "A good thing I have an apprentice who reads adventure books," he mind-spoke with a side-long smile at the weapon.

As iron shot through my spine the Bitter Chord's eyes fired another blow. Cedelair raised his spear to deflect it. Slipping out of the circle once more, he advanced on our enemy with weapon upraised. The white-shrouded figure's shoulders began to shake. A whimper escaped her as Cedelair pressed the spear's point against her neck.

"It's hard to shoot blows from your eyes when they're filled with tears, eh?" my beloved remarked. "This is the song that can make the hardest heart weep. What grief does it call up? This moment, perhaps, knowing your time is through?"

"Only one thing can stop me from playing this song," I declared, "and that is for you to go away and never come back. Bitter Chord, dissonance, harmony-breaker, I turn you out!"

She sniffed. "You'd send me away, Roc? That's gratitude, master! I taught and trained her, put food in her belly and clothes on her back. Who else would have cared for such a beast as that? She'll turn on you, too, see if she doesn't."

Cedelair reared back. He landed a heavy blow on the Bitter Chord's jaw. The white-clad figure quaked too furiously to fight back or even rise from where the blow had felled her. "Please, please, silence that demon!" she moaned.

"Are you going to leave her in peace?" Cedelair demanded.

When the Bitter Chord hesitated, a burble in her throat, I added, "It's only going to get worse. And if you come back into my dreams, you'll hear it again."

"Yes, I'll go!" cried the Bitter Chord. "Let me up, will you?"

"In a moment." With his free hand Cedelair reached down to grasp the edge of the golden mask. "Whatever you do, Meliroc, do not stop playing."

Cedelair yanked the mask from the face it concealed. I half-closed my eyes, the better to concentrate on the music, but I could see a translucent shade, a misty suggestion of facial features. Though tears soaked the hollow cheeks, the lips were set in a cold smile.

"Cedelair," the woman croaked. "It has been a while."

21. Cedelair looks into the past, and Meliroc seeks a way out

Cedelair had recognized her voice the moment she'd raised it from whisper to shout. "This doesn't surprise me at all, really." He smoothed his face into a cool, impassive mask. "It's so in keeping with your nature."

Tearlac responded with a soft snicker. "Our natures aren't so different. Everybody wants to win. Another round to you, Cedelair. Let me up, there's a good man." How she spoke in such an airy tone while tears were drenching her face Cedelair couldn't fathom.

Tearlac. Revulsion burned in his head. Five years hadn't changed her in the slightest. Her eyes, the one beauty in that forgettable face, shone the same deep blue-green that had made Roselise jealous. Yet they glowed bright yellow when they struck at Meliroc. Obviously she'd learned certain magics he'd never bothered with. "I want to know a few things first," he said, pressing his spear-butt against her collarbone.

She smirked. "Of course. No matter the circumstances, we can never resist the lure of knowledge. But how can you concentrate with that racket going on? Be a dear, Cedelair, and tell her to stop."

"Play on, Meliroc!" he called out with a smirk of his own. "Go on, Tearlac. Enlighten me. What are you doing in Meliroc's dream?"

Taut, Tearlac swallowed. "Your defeat of me broke my spirit," she began. "I wandered far, not eating, not sleeping, thinking over the battles I'd lost, pondering all I'd done and all my rivals had done against me and why. I never have told anyone before, do you know?

Think yourself privileged. I went from village to village challenging sorcerers, because my old master saw me growing too powerful for his liking and cursed me never to win a contest. I had to prove him wrong, you see? I never managed it, and every battle I lost only made me angrier. The death-hope took me. I would have passed from the world, but a strange set of fellows took me in and nursed me. The Sleep Mages, they called themselves, the only mortals who understand the mysteries of dreams. I stayed alive to learn what they could teach me.

"These good people told me the stories of the jicketies, the nightmare-dealers. With their gift the Sleep Mages could actually talk to those creatures. From them I learned that jicketies come in two kinds, the imps of Jicket Castle and the giants of Jicket Mountain. They dwell on opposite ends of the dream-world and know nothing of each other. The imps rebuke us for petty vices. They all have names ending in –on. The giants punish great crimes, and unlike their tiny brethren, they're gifted with fire-burning coals in their hearts. All their names end in –oc."

Meliroc dropped a note. With a heavy breath she forced herself onto the next measure.

"The coal-fire is meant to keep their hearts warm and their spirits strong, for it's their job to enter the minds of the worst of humankind," Tearlac continued, "but some centuries ago, a few of the giants went mad. They decided all humans deserved to suffer, and so they turned themselves into incarnate nightmares who could enter many dreams at once. They absorbed all the sorrow from the dreamers' minds and hearts, then gave it back to them a hundred-fold to drive them all mad. The *leyshak*, they were called. The ultimate retribution. In the end the jickety-imps blasted them out of existence. But these monsters had once been jicketies themselves. If the jickety-giants had turned themselves into *leyshak* before they could do it again. The idea entered my head to take vengeance on our kind by loosing a *leyshak* on the world. But to do that I needed a giant.

"I had frightful nightmares, Cedelair, but only the imps came to me. Evidently I wasn't yet a great enough sinner to attract a giant. So I called the imps to me, just as the Sleep Mages had shown me, and I snapped their necks. It took five nights, five imps, before I got what I wanted at last. One of the big ones came for me."

Meliroc's face contorted in disgust. Cedelair guessed she was imagining Pierpon in Tearlac's clutches. The same vision turned Cedelair's own stomach, even as his blood chilled at what he knew was coming.

"I stood in the middle of a desert plain, and my throat burned with thirst. I was surrounded by people with grudges against me (you were there, Cedelair) and each one held a jug of water. When I begged for a drop, you emptied your jugs onto the ground. Then I tried to eat the wet sand, but the second I touched it it turned dry again until my skin shriveled against my bones. A truly horrible dream."

"Horrible," echoed Cedelair, glancing at his spear's point.

"In the manner my masters had taught me, I commanded the giant to reveal itself. Up she sprang from the sand. I was ready for her. I seized her and pulled her out. I woke up and there she was, on her knees beside my bed, trembling and weeping, all the color drained from her hair and skin." Tearlac's thin lips parted in a grin.

"You nauseate me, Tearlac," Cedelair growled.

"Poor dear, she had no idea what had happened to her." Tearlac laughed. "Only I could guide and protect her in this strange place. I stole away with her before the Sleep-Mages could wake. How she brayed and bawled! I had to cure that, first thing. So I wiped her memory clean, made her an empty vessel I could shape to fit my will."

Meliroc blinked, her face puckering in woe. The vision's words at Sorrow's Lake echoed bitterly in Cedelair's mind. *You are nothing more than what I say you are.*

"A jickety believes it is doing good," Tearlac continued. "Its duty presumes that even the blackest of sinners has a conscience a nightmare can wake. The ones who went mad stopped believing this. They came to hate and in the end became beings who were made of hate. So I had to teach my prize to hate. I would be kind, and then I would be cruel, so she never knew what to expect from me. I made her cringe and weep and fear." She beamed, as if relishing the taste of her words. "I shaped what she suffered and loosed it in her sleep. I watched the seed grow. Yet it was a long while before she turned. My fault, I see now. I taught her to read, believing she would suffer more if she could think. I indulged her fancy for music, so it would hurt all the worse when I tortured her. But she got it into her head there was good to be found in the world. I couldn't snuff out that coal-fire inside her. It went on burning even after I fixed the geas."

Cedelair struggled for breath and found it thick and hot in his throat. The urge to strangle this cruel, gloating woman burned like acid in his hands. Desperate, he locked gazes with Meliroc, seeking courage from the glimmer in her eyes, willing love to overmaster hate.

"Once she was properly bound," said Tearlac, "I sent her straight to the sorcerers I'd battled. I could guess how they would use her. All those stupid little men who thought themselves so mighty clasped this viper to their bosoms and made her even worse! She would stay with them a while, infect their towns with such dark dreams that the poor people couldn't even remember them. Once I knew they were sure to go mad, I'd move her on. I couldn't let her see what she'd wrought. I kept blotting its signs from her memory. That hope of finding good was still alive in her, you see. I couldn't take the chance that she might do away with herself if she knew how lost she truly was."

If my mind could strike you down... Cedelair clenched his spine, fought with all his will the urge to murder. Again he looked at Meliroc and let himself feel the pain in her heart. Whatever Tearlac had done, whatever she might still intend, Meliroc needed him now.

"And now, at last, here she is, in your precious Crainante," his enemy snickered. "You made sure I could never come back, but you couldn't have counted on her, could you? You were the unpredictable factor, I admit. I couldn't imagine how you might use her."

"Because he's good!" Meliroc burst out over her music. "In a million years you would never understand him!"

Tearlac's eyes twinkled. "So, Cedelair, my man of surprises, you made this incarnate misfortune love you! After she ruined your home you take her part!"

Bile surged into Cedelair's throat. "I take her part because none of it is her fault. That hope of good in the world? That's her! Her own soul, beyond your reach. She has thrown you off with her own power." He stood, lowering his spear. "Now go. Leave her alone."

Tearlac let out a gasp. "Thank you." With a grunt she pushed herself to her feet. She marched up to Meliroc with a jut in her chin and a cocky sneer. Cedelair tightened his grip on his spear, his watchful eye on her.

"Think you've bested me at last, your Bigness?" she jeered. "We're not finished yet, my wild Roc."

Meliroc squared her shoulders, and Cedelair readied himself to launch at his enemy. But Tearlac moved neither arm nor hand. She spat out a word like a snake's hiss, a word Cedelair could not place.

The sky paled into a flat gray like the canvas of a painting. A wisp of cloud shaped itself into the figure of a prune-faced woman with tangled gray hair, clad in a tattered maroon gown, staring ahead at nothing. The nightmare mark had swelled to wipe the color from her eyes, to render them an ever-whirling ghastly white. Red bite-marks dappled her hands. Lacerations from jagged fingernails marred her haggard face.

Meliroc glared upward, a gurgle in her throat.

"Do you recognize her, my fright?" Tearlac asked in a sing-song lilt.

Cedelair did. It was the old lady whose husband had delighted her with the gift of a bracelet with azure stones.

"This is how she looks now," declared Tearlac, "her life a nightmare that will never end. But she is only one of many. Look upon them all, dear deplorable."

Faces flooded the canvas, men and women and children, old and young, all torn, writhing, red with festering scars and sores. Some were wreathed in a mass of wild hair. Others bled at scalps that had been scratched and ripped bald. Most had the same white, swirling eyes as the old woman, but a few sockets oozed blood, the eyeballs torn out. Cedelair's head pitched as these faces threatened to overwhelm his senses. He managed a look at Meliroc and found the terrors etched on her face.

"Meliroc, don't look!" he shouted.

Meliroc drooped, her head sinking into her arms. Tearlac snickered. "Too late, Cedelair, old man. She will never forget them. But there is one thing she must see yet. You must see."

An image of Tearlac herself appeared on the canvas cloud, mouthing words he could not hear, staring up in horror as a shadow swallowed her from above. A pair of ghost-white hands taut with rage reached down to grasp her throat.

"Behold, the work of hate!"

The hands twisted, and the Tearlac on the canvas-cloud sagged in their grasp. Her head lolled to the side. The hands released their hold and she dropped lifeless to the ground. In the same instant a stormy blackness swept the vision away. The blood in Cedelair's veins and the breath in his chest froze into hard, stinging crystals.

"Do you see now what you are, my sweet abomination?" crowed Tearlac. "A murderer!" The word spun from the sorcerer's mouth, a chain of silver smoke. *Mur-der-er*. Venom glimmered in the syllables as it wrapped about Meliroc, to bind her arms fast to her sides.

"You wrung the life from me." Tearlac paced in a circle around the giant. "That let me into your head. I am your prison, Roc dear, your blood-geas!" The smoke-chain wound tighter with each word she spoke. The veins bulged in Meliroc's neck as her head lolled backward. "And you think you can chase me out with a song?"

Meliroc let out a tiny pain-wracked gurgle.

"Yes, that's it," Tearlac hissed. "You know what you have to do, what you were made to do. It's time you understood there can be no good in the world for you."

Life surged back into Cedelair. With a roar he charged headlong toward Tearlac. Bright yellow light from his enemy's eyes slammed into his chest like a massive hammer. Cedelair's weapon toppled to the ground. Without a second's hesitation Tearlac seized it and rammed its butt into Cedelair's stomach, knocking him flat, then pressing the point to his neck as he had with her.

"Would you take a murderer to wife, Cedelair?" she crooned in his ear. "Cleave to her until at last she wraps her ice-cold hands around your throat?"

The spear-point began to shimmer. His senses dimmed, draining out of him as blood from a deep wound. His muscles grew coldly flaccid, his breath thread-thin. The weapon was drawing the life from him.

"There is no way back from this dream, Ced," whispered Tearlac. "Not for me. Not for Roc. Not for you."

Remember your promise, Cedelair. Remember to kill it. He barely heard the words, could not quite put together where they came from.

A scream shattered the sky.

***

Through the darkening veil he saw something with vast wings and a contorted womanish face move behind Tearlac. Its rage sliced through the throb in his head as the scream burst out again.

The great fury sent a stream of black smoke into Tearlac's face. It wrapped about her neck, a deadly echo of her latest curse. Her eyes rolled back. Her shaking hands fumbled, loosing their hold on the spear. Cedelair grasped it and scrambled backward while the *leyshak* wrapped its arms about Tearlac and lifted her into the air.

Something shot forth lightning-swift from the whirlwind. An instant later the *leyshak's* arms opened and Tearlac plunged to the ground, blood pouring from a gaping wound in her chest. Hovering over the body, the *leyshak* reared back its head and screeched in triumph.

Cedelair sat upright. The *leyshak*, still roaring savagely over its fallen enemy, didn't appear to notice him. But any moment it would turn on him. He had promised to kill it should it try to kill him. This thing was not Meliroc.

Neither was the cold-handed murderer Tearlac had shown him. He knew Meliroc. And he knew Tearlac. The vision of her first death flashed again through his mind, just as she'd wanted Meliroc to see it – the looming shadow, the pitiless hands twisting around the throat, Tearlac's face pale and writhing with terror as she mouthed a plea for her life... a plea for her life...

No. Quite the opposite.

The *leyshak* spun about and dove towards him with outstretched arms, prepared to close a new victim in the same fatal embrace it had given Tearlac. He urged strength into his spear arm. But before he could aim his blow the fiend jerked to the right, its whirlwind whipping across the top of his head. Cedelair saw its eyes cloud in confusion.

Meliroc. She was there and fighting. She had turned the *leyshak* aside. He had to tell her what he knew, so that Tearlac could never torture her again. If she was just strong enough to understand, the blood-geas might lose the last of its power.

He stiffened his shoulders as the winged devil circled in the air. It swooped once more, fury doubled in its eyes, determined its strike would not miss this time. Yet just as it was bearing down it jerked to the left. The *leyshak* screamed again, enraged at failing again to make its kill.

He watched as it made another loop. It came for him again at triple speed. His stomach squirmed. He had a gamble left. If it failed Valeraine would touch his shoulder in the morning and find him cold and empty-eyed. Everything he loved would be forever out of reach.

He called on his mind-voice, firing into it every ounce of strength that remained to him. As he spoke he dropped the spear at his feet. The wind roared around him, battering him. The ebon smoke blinded him and flew into his open mouth to smother him. Yet still he held fast to consciousness as his mind cried out to her.

***

The monster encased me, its insides a sandpaper burning away my skin. I wanted to sink out of knowing, anything rather than hear the *leyshak* scream with my own pain, its cry full of all those wracked faces the Bitter Chord had shown me. If I could vanish to somewhere their sorrows couldn't find me! But my case was hopeless. I felt my hands around my enemy's throat, the flow of blood and strength of bone beneath. I felt her break under my stranglehold and saw her fall in a heap at my feet. Murderer. I could claw at my living *leyshak* prison until my fingers wore away. Nothing and no one would help me.

I'd killed her awake. Now I'd killed her in my sleep. The *leyshak* had me, fierce with all my built-up hatred. No way out of this dream, except to die. *Kill me, Cedelair. Save yourself.*

The *leyshak* hungered for more blood on its claws. Cedelair faced it, spear upraised, his glare steel-bright. He remembered his promise, but these claws would tear his throat before he could strike. Through all its rage, it was laughing at that toothpick of a weapon. In its mind Cedelair was already dead.

No more murder. I pushed. The *leyshak* turned, sweeping away from Cedelair. Its fury scorched me, and my head spun with pain. I felt it turning back, its bloodthirsty gaze locked on its victim. I pushed. Still it swooped at him. I pushed again. Irritation stirred in it, as if a gnat were buzzing at its eyes to throw off its sight-line. I pushed again. It veered off course. Its anger burst afresh, yet a tremor of coldness brushed against the scalding heat. Though my pain doubled with each push, I shivered with something like hope. I had cracked the wall.

Nightmare Lullaby

The thing went into its murderous dive once more, hungry to extinguish me as well as Cedelair. He stood tall in its path, arms locked at his sides, the weapon cast down at his feet. The *leyshak's* ribs shook with cruel laughter. It would not miss again.

A voice reached me, a wink of light through the swirling dark. *Meliroc, hear me. Listen to me, Cedelair who loves you. I saw her mouth moving. I know what she was doing. She was using the Seventh Tongue. She was forcing you, taking your will away from you.*

My hands around her throat – something pulling – in my mind – not me–

She committed suicide, using you as her weapon. It was her only way to turn you into what she wanted. The leyshak is Tearlac, not you. Never you.

Not I – never I–

You are no murderer, Meliroc. You are my love, my marvelous giant, my large heart. You are a thousand times stronger than that prison she made for you. Break out.

I reared to force the *leyshak* clear of him. The rim of its whirlwind knocked him back. The sense left his eyes.

I fired strength into my arms and hands and pushed at the sides of this cocoon. As it winged higher Cedelair shrank into a dot. If I escaped now my body would shatter against the ground. What happens to people who die in their dreams? That didn't matter now. One way or another, I had to get to Cedelair.

Land. I fired the command at the *leyshak.*

It shot back a flare of scorn. I reeled. It convulsed. It tried to speak to me. Before it had always spoken in the Bitter Chord's voice.

You killed her. You killed yourself.

The *leyshak* let out its paralyzing shriek. My head started to swim, and I pulled it back sharply to dry land.

She tried to make *me* out of nothing, but only nothing can come from nothing.

The creature trembled harder as its shriek began to dwindle.

You have no life. No reality.

The crack I'd made widened and deepened to a crumble. The *leyshak* was sinking.

There is no *leyshak. I am Meliroc. I am a jickety.*

The fiend floated down. Its horrible cry faded into heavy silence.

I. Meliroc. My own thing. My own... voice.

In that instant I knew I could speak. I let out a call from deep in my throat and shivered at the sound of my voice. With one last push I shouted my name. The wall shattered with the crash of crumbling bricks. Feathers shot through the air as I sprang free and settled beside Cedelair, the grass pillow-soft beneath me.

I held my breath as my gaze hovered over my hand, but not the hand I remembered. Under the translucent silver veil of the carillon's mark, my skin had turned a deep beige, almost pale brown. I raised my opposite hand before my eyes, and glanced down at my legs and found them the same shade. I took a tress of hair between my fingers. It was the same coal-black hue as Pierpon's. Jickety black.

My vision flickered as something folded about me and lifted me. My neck went limp. I lay on the floor at the foot of Cedelair's bed, and he was nestled against me, his arms about my waist. With a weary blink Valeraine peered down at us from atop the mattress.

I drew a quick breath. Then I cleared my throat. "It's gone." My voice shook so wildly I could scarcely understand the words, yet it was my voice, in my mouth and throat.

"It's gone," I repeated, flexing my vocal chords. "Gone, gone, gone, gone, gone." My voice grew stronger with each echo of the word. "It exploded. You should have seen the feathers fly!"

Cedelair slid his fingers into my hair with a throaty chuckle. "I'm an idiot," he murmured. "I never realized you could be even more beautiful." He trembled as he kissed me, his fingers cupping my chin. Delight sang in me. My breath rose to meet his kiss.

"Cedelair." I kissed his fingers. "Cedelair. Ced-e-lair." A giddy laugh bubbled up in me, and I opened my throat to let it out. "I love the way your name sounds when I say it."

22. Last

When Crainante's fever broke every citizen felt it.

Those lying awake while their bodies rested felt the brush of an airy finger upon their minds. They closed their eyes and slipped gently into slumber. Those racked by the worst nightmares of their lives saw the terrors retreat, leaving soft purple darkness behind. As one the town slept.

The sun had crested before Mennieve woke on her cot. She blinked at the light through the window and sighed. She pulled her shawl across her shoulders and trudged to the door. Drawing back the curtains over her display window, she stared out at an empty street and knew she was the first to wake. Stretching, she threw open the door.

The gentle tinkle of the carillon bells greeted her, a sound like a squeeze of the hand, or a sip of warm tea, or a little boy swinging on a wooden gate.

***

Telling Pierpon of my dream-battle in my own voice and watching his face as he listened gave me a thrill that only the memory of my first kiss from Cedelair could match. I beamed brightest at what I knew would be my pixy-man's favorite part.

"I was right!" he crowed, jig-stepping across the bureau. "I told 'em, I did! You never were a *leyshak*! You're a jickety!"

"That's right," I affirmed. "A jickety, like you."

"Well, not exactly like me. But you could be my big, big, big, big sister. My sister the snow-giant of Jicket-Mountain!"

"I'm not snow-colored anymore," I pointed out, chucking his chin with my fingertip.

"You found me in the snow and saved me from it. You're my snow-giant for always."

"Yet since we're kin, if ordinary humans can see me, they should be able to see you. You should come out in the open. Sit on my shoulder where everyone can see."

He scrunched his head down between his shoulders, a sign he was thinking over the matter. But at last he shook his head with a click of his tongue. "I'd rather not."

"Is it really more fun to hide all the time?"

"I don't want to get any closer to humans than I already am. If they could see me and talk to me, I'd be less of a jickety, I would." He let out a groaning sigh, a strange sound for my cheerful friend to make.

"But we awaken the conscience. Humankind would be lost without us."

"That is true," he returned, nodding. "But in all our history no jickety has ever liked humans. We can't be as ruthless as we need to be, if we see things from their side. Look at you, poor Jickety Meliroc. You're in love with one of them! How will it be for you when you go back home?"

"I'm not going back 'home'," I told him with conviction. The *leyshak's* killing of the Bitter Chord had not restored my memories of the life she'd taken me from. Were that life suddenly handed to me I wouldn't know what to do with it. "I think you're wrong, though. If you see things from their side, you'll know better how to touch their consciences. Why, Pierpon, when you go home you'll be the most successful jickety in history." I rumpled his hair with my thumb, my favorite gesture with him. "You should let yourself be seen."

He hoisted himself onto my wrist, where he gave my hand a hearty kiss. "Wise as you are, snow-giant," he said, "I'd rather leave it as it is, I would."

My soaring spirits wilted a little as I saw I would not convince him. I bent down to kiss the top of his head.

In my shining mood I loved them all – Pierpon, Cedelair, Valeraine, Mennieve with her warm, round face, the counting-man's kindly formal servant, the bonesetter, and the glass-blower with his garish yellow coat. Love sang in my blood and warmed my bones.

Nightmare Lullaby

Why a bittersweet pang should follow hard upon it, I did not then understand. Some as yet unformed thought was weaving through the back of my mind, waiting to make itself known.

***

I must have come close to driving my friends mad that day, because I talked and talked and talked.

I shouted, whispered, murmured, muttered, bellowed, blustered, declared, declaimed, anything that could be done with a voice. I recited my favorite love poems from ancient Farienne and read aloud from my Compendium of Otherworldly Creatures, flexing my vocal muscles. Stories I'd kept locked in my head tumbled off my busy tongue. My friends bore with me patiently. Cedelair looked as if he enjoyed listening almost as much as I enjoyed talking.

Before very long I started to wonder whether my new voice could hold a note. In my head I sounded the notes of Cedelair's lullaby. I opened my throat to try the first verse on "ah". At first I faltered, just missing the pitch, but I swallowed and tried again until at last I felt secure enough to sing the words while I looked straight at Cedelair.

"The gleams of the stars kiss your brow,
The beams of the moon touch your face.
They love you, oh, they love you,
As I love you,
My man of grace."

Cedelair sprang up from his chair to wrap his arms about my waist. "I've never heard a sweeter voice," he murmured.

I believed he would have felt so even if I'd been a tone-deaf croaker, but still I flushed with pride. "Would you teach me some more of your mother's songs?"

He grinned as if he'd hoped I would ask this very thing, and for the next hour we sat side by side on the window-bench in the parlor, singing together. He beamed all the while, but a glimmering mist in his eyes told me we were sharing a joy that ached.

My bell-board rested across my knees. I sensed it waiting to claim my attention. One of my hands clasped Cedelair's, while the other rested on my mallet. I imagined bells ringing under the notes I sang. I would have to surrender it when the carillon shifted its allegiance to Mennieve. Would the chimes in my head fall silent or linger as a hollow memory? The ache under my joy began to swell until I lost the heart to sing.

I needed to be alone. I pressed close to Cedelair and kissed him, praying he would understand.

"You've a lot to get used to," he told me. "Take a bit of time to sort things out."

After another kiss I left him, my bell-board under my arm. With my bell-board I could think. I would have to remind myself how I'd managed to think before it had come to me. I'd found songs then. Surely I could do so again, train myself to love some new instrument. All those other instruments, I now understood, had broken under the weight of the hatred the Bitter Chord had foisted on me. With her gone, a world of instruments was open to me.

Yet this bell-board had remained whole when I'd played the first note. Indeed, it had knitted back together in my clasp after I'd splintered it. Even with the monster digging into my heart my bell-board had sung for me, strong enough to oppose the Bitter Chord's hatred and the *leyshak* she'd fashioned from it. Oppose the *leyshak*...

The face of the now-mad old lady flashed into my view. So many had that same desolate look, minds broken by the *leyshak* and the woman who had called it into being. The Bitter Chord had known, as I had not, what the monster would do to these people. She had turned that knowledge into the veixal's shadow, the chill at my back, the quiver in my hands.

The bell-board had stopped that quiver, too.

I struck a jangled sequence of notes as the faces flew at me. Music could shape chaos into order, could give confusion form. Hadn't Feuval said the carillon's mission was to heal? Oppose the *leyshak*...

I played with a steady hand the first three measures of my "Sorrow Song". As the chimes reverberated I caught another melody hiding behind them, a lament for these people with haggard faces and wasted minds. I teased notes out of the gaps in the old song and slowly, carefully, wove something new.

In my imagination, a light of reason winked in the maddened eyes.

A soft knock sounded in back of the song. I called out "Come in," but I couldn't stop playing or turn to the door. The music drove

Nightmare Lullaby

me forward, moving softly from major to minor and back again, a song to quiet a howling soul. The door must have opened and closed, and the person must have come into the room to stand beside me, but I could only hear the music.

After the last note faded a hand touched my arm, and cricket-feet scurried up my spine. Even with the melody hovering over my heart, I turned to Cedelair with a beaming face. "What thoughts inspired that lovely tune?" he asked as I caressed his hand. "I believe you've found another one that could make the hardest heart weep."

He, too, had seen those twisted faces. "It's in honor of the ones who went mad," I explained.

"Tearlac is responsible for what happened to them," he reminded me with a hint of sternness. "You, sweet large heart, have nothing to be ashamed of."

"It isn't shame. I only wish I knew a way to help them." I winced as I glanced down at my bell-board, bright with the silver-white strings of light. Oppose the *leyshak*... mend the broken... *Thou wouldst hold its power in thy hands...*

"Do you want to try to find them?"

"I don't know," I answered honestly. I snapped the reins of my mind as it reached for an unwelcome thought. He wrapped a sturdy arm about my shoulders. "I'm not Roselise, Cedelair," I murmured, not knowing why I said it, frowning at the bitter taste the words left behind.

***

Happy endings came with tears.

Cedelair had learned this from experience. One couldn't triumph over an enemy without losing something vital in the process, particularly an enemy like Tearlac who could strike even when defeated. *Blood-geas.* Like a parasite, he'd once thought, and how right he'd been. The small-hearted woman he hated above all others had been living in the head of the giant he loved. His stomach quaked at the thought of it.

He watched and listened as Meliroc talked over the instruments she would play and the town they might settle in together, a place with rolling hills that turned purple at sunset, a bathhouse with a hot spring, and a three-floor bookshop. Every few minutes she would stop and kiss his brow or mouth, and he would tingle in delight. He insisted he merely imagined the strain in her smile.

Not long before sunset Mennieve and Master Bonfert came to the door. Some friends were gathering in the square for a celebration, the bookseller announced. Odilon had brought his mandolin and Coviet his pipe, and all were ready to dance and sing, but they needed Cedelair, the man who had delivered them from the shrieking dream-fury, to complete the party. He would not have refused her in any case, but Valeraine made the matter certain by leaping over the doorsill with a joyous shout. Master Bonfert offered her his arm and led her around the bookshop toward the square, telling her about a new series of adventure books.

Meliroc had vanished from the parlor at the sound of Mennieve's knock. Now she reappeared, cloaked and ready, resplendent in trousers and silver-trimmed heliotrope tunic. Cedelair noted the Pierpon-sized lump in the folds of her lowered hood.

Mennieve's eyes went wide. "Why, my dear lady Meliroc, how lovely you are!" the bookseller cried. "You're a very Queen of Araby! What happened to you?"

Meliroc met her surprise with a whimsical grin. "I dreamed of the desert sun, and it baked me."

"And you're talking now!"

"More than one curse has been lifted."

"Come, then, come! No more delays. We're all waiting for you!"

The crowd of "all" proved smaller than Cedelair had feared, a little more than a dozen people, all of whom had been civil to him since he'd lost his home. Sundiffe the counting-man was among them, and Rousel the butcher, Suizat the constable, and Vociette the weaver. He could smile at them without effort. Perhaps he would even indulge in a sip from that jug they were passing hand to hand.

Perched on the statue's base, with a look-out gaze toward the bookshop, Odilon and Coviet spotted him first and gave a hearty greeting shout. The others applauded and stamped their feet. Suizat, who held the jug at the moment, raised it toward him. Yet as he drew nearer with Meliroc they quieted and stared. They must wonder whether the dusky willow-rose could be the same creature who had set them trembling and muttering protections under their breaths. The same, yet not the same. They'd felt the unnaturalness of her bleached skin and hair, but now her true colors and true beauty were restored.

Nightmare Lullaby

Cedelair folded his arm about her waist with beaming pride. Meliroc was his girl and he wanted everyone to know.

"A song!" Odilon bellowed at last. "Cedelair's song! Let the man who delivered us choose what we hear!" The gathering stamped and whistled in approval.

Cedelair gazed up at Meliroc. "Here's your real deliverer," he proclaimed. "Let her choose the song."

The folk exchanged bewildered glances, but Odilon beamed at her. "Well, then, tell us what she'd like to hear."

Chuckling audibly, she called out, "'The Sun after the Storm'!"

Another puzzled blink, another head-scratch, and then the gathering cheered her selection. With proud step she took position at the statue's base. She unstrapped her bell-board and drew out her mallet.

"Dance with me, Cedelair!" Menneive cried, seizing her old friend's hands. He leaned forward to kiss her temple, ready to hop when the music began.

Odilon and Coviet played first, establishing the melody. At the chorus Meliroc joined in with a light counterpoint, the remnants of raindrops pattering off the leaves as the sun broke through. Astonished at how like the carillon these small bells sounded, the crowd slowed their spins and listened with fascinated gazes. Meliroc beamed at these looks, clearly thrilled at the chance to share her bell-board's music before she surrendered it. Yet her eyes glowed oddly with attention, as if she were listening for something in the distance.

Another song followed and another. Her fellow musicians included her in their company with smiles and nods and signaled when they wanted her to take the melody. She responded and complemented as if they'd rehearsed together for weeks. But still her smile looked distant. Something in her seemed to drift apart. *She's leaving.* The thought shot like a dart through Cedelair's mind.

Menneive, seeing his frown, drew him apart from the crowd. "What's wrong, dear lad?"

"I don't know." He snatched at a short breath. "Something's not right with Meliroc. It's as if she's here and not here. I can't think what's going on in her mind."

"Have you tried asking her?"

"A man should never ask a question if he's afraid of the answer."

"What's to be afraid of?" she asked with a roll of her eyes.

He coughed to drive the thickness from his throat. "I'm not sure I have words for it."

"When the next song starts ask her to dance," she advised him with a gentle chuck at his elbow. "You may find the question comes more easily."

He doubted this. Stepping in a circle with Meliroc, their movements in harmony, would only make the matter worse. All the same, he longed to dance with her. As the song wound down he pushed his way through the crowd, determined to reach her before the next tune. He held out his hand to her. "Will you dance with me, Meliroc?"

"I've never danced," she returned with a shy smile.

"You move with the flow of the music. I'll show you."

She clasped his hand and let him draw her forward, while Odilon and Coviet nodded to each other and began a soft, sweet melody. Cedelair stepped out first, and Meliroc followed his lead, watching his feet. As she wove about him with unsure step and abashed grin, she looked and felt more present, in tune with the moment. When he strengthened his hold on her hand, a shock of warmth coursed through him, the fire of her heart-coal leaping.

How could he feel this obvious sign that she was happy and still fear? If that shimmer in her eyes was the beginning of tears, surely they were tears of joy.

A pang ripped through his head. With a shudder he stumbled into Meliroc, who clutched his shoulders and swept him out of the ring of dancers. She brushed her fingertips over the furrows of his brow.

"They look happy, don't you think?" she mentioned, with a tilt of her head toward Valeraine and Bonfert. Though they spun in time with the other dancers, they were deep in conversation, doubtless about some fictional adventurous exploit. Valeraine, with her cheerful temperament, was always quick to smile, but he'd never seen her beam more brightly than now. And serious, competent Bonfert matched her light.

"She doesn't spend enough time with people her own age," he mused aloud.

Meliroc nodded, a deep shadow in her thoughtful look.

"Meliroc," he began, in a feeble quake of a voice, "do you want to leave me?"

Nightmare Lullaby

She drew him close, her arm about his shoulders. "No," she answered.

"Let me put it another way. Do you want to go with the carillon?"

She flinched. Her mouth began to quiver.

"Don't be afraid." He reached up to brush the corner of her lip. "Tell me honestly. I know you are not Roselise."

She gripped his hand as if for dear life. "I – I think I ought to," she replied in a whisper. "It mends the broken. It mended me when I first heard it. It moved me to save Pierpon. All that is good in me came to light because I stopped and saved Pierpon that day." She blinked hard, stiffening. "I could find those people, play for them, make them whole again. They need me, Cedelair."

He pressed against her, arms wrapped around her waist. "I need you, Meliroc."

"I need you, too."

He clung more tightly to her, seeking her warmth. *I need you, too,* she had said, but somehow he heard, *I need you to– .* She needed him to help her.

She needed him to let her go.

For another moment he nestled close to her, dizzy with hurt and with love for her. Then with a heavy breath he let his arms drop to his sides, stepped away from her, and turned to Mennieve.

He had only to shake his head to see perfect comprehension come into her eyes. With a solemn nod she melted back into the crowd. Her sacrifice would not be needed. But her shoulder would be badly needed when he came back tonight. He would tell her all there was to tell, of Tearlac, of the *leyshak*, of villages emptied and minds destroyed. Every word would sting, but he would speak. He would not let her or Valeraine or anyone else lay blame on Meliroc. The rancor that had eaten at him after Roselise's farewell kiss had no place here. Roselise had left him because she wasn't the woman he'd thought her. Meliroc was leaving him because she was exactly the woman he thought her, his large heart, unwilling to let a wrong lie when she had the power to right it.

I can't lose her... I won't... He snatched at breath. His dream was upon him. She was spinning out of reach while he tried in vain to hold her.

Her ears pricked up. The absent glow in her eye sharpened into an attentive glint. The veil of light hovering around her pulsed and brightened. She glanced toward Valeraine, who was still too absorbed in her talk with Bonfert to notice anything amiss. With a teary blink she blew the young sorcerer a farewell kiss. She squeezed Cedelair's hand once more, and together they started toward the call.

***

The clouds part. Confusion clears, and every sense sharpens to the point where it could cut through you. You know more in that moment than you ever wanted to know. You know what you have to do. You know as well that doing it will tear the heart from you.

Cedelair and I trudged together toward the wagon using one of his small blue flames to light our way. The wagon's walls quivered, and the bells within hummed a greeting. "Thou comest." Feuval poked his head through the window. "Thou dost understand at last." The whishk hopped onto the ledge with an indignant flap of his mouth.

I nodded, loath to share my voice with Feuval. The carillon might be a healer, but its player was still a deceiver.

"The carillon welcomest thee in gladness," the masked man went on. "It doth feel thy grief and would soothe it." I heard him sigh, though no breath stirred the white satin that covered what should have been his mouth. "I swear to thee, fair moon-tree, never did I intend thee harm."

Cedelair clenched his jaw. "If you have somewhere to go, then go," he grumbled.

A haze formed around Feuval. A sweep of wind stirred the curtain, and before I could squint the window was empty – no white satin, gold mask, or man-figure. The breeze had carried him away to Lifelord knew where.

The whishk shook himself with an irate squeal. "All your doing," he snapped, shaking his fist at me. "I loved him and he's gone. Nowhere to go but the graveyard. All big-big's fault!" With that he launched himself from the ledge and sped off into the darkness. I watched him vanish with an unwonted brush of pity.

The wagon's walls stretched themselves with a splintery groan, up and out, so that the new eight-foot occupant could move about freely in satin sheath and mask. One of the walls dropped open and

Nightmare Lullaby

fell slowly to the ground to form an entrance-way, the array of bells ranged just beyond. Bells and walls all gleamed, strong as the sun and silver as the moon. Waiting for me. Impatient. I put my arm about Cedelair, as if to shield him. You can wait a minute longer! I thought angrily at the carillon.

The bells sang, an inviting chord of unearthly beauty. My heart ran after it even as I lifted Cedelair to clasp him tight, caress the lines of his face, and enjoy once more the wonderful smell of him, plant stalks and clean earth and perfumed smoke rising from cauldrons. Could I really leave him, this man I wanted so much to hold forever, who had shown me what "we" meant and what "home" might be? Tears spilled down my face. Cedelair kissed them as they fell.

"I'll go on praying just as you taught me, Cedelair," I managed to say. "I'll pray you can forgive me one day."

"What have I to forgive you for?" he returned.

"I told you I wouldn't go away."

His hand reached out to cup my chin. "Didn't you see how those walls stretched to make room for you? That thing and I have more in common than I'd thought. My heart grew bigger to make room for you, and you will never leave it, however far you travel."

I kissed his brow, eyes, lips.

Something stirred at the back of my neck, and I swallowed in shock. I'd forgotten Pierpon! I might have marched through this opening with him still tucked in my cloak-hood! I shook myself. What could have possessed me? I could only think of when I'd been forbidden to play my bell-board, yet I'd strapped it on anyway, feeling it part of myself. Pierpon had become like that for me, like foot or hand or eye, as easily taken for granted and as agonizing to lose. It struck me hard then, as I stared at the carillon's open mouth with cold, creeping horror. I would be alone.

I lowered Cedelair to the ground, reached behind my neck to close my fingers about Pierpon, then knelt down.

"What do you think you're doing?" he piped with a sniff.

I opened my hand to deposit him upon the ground. "Setting you free."

"Oh, no, you're not." He clung to my thumb. "I'm coming with you."

My heart jumped to my throat. "What madness is this?"

"Heed what he says," Cedelair put in, very quiet.

"You can't come with me, Pierpon," I insisted.

He snorted. "Try to stop me then. I'll crawl up and down and around you like a fly, I will. Could you catch me? No, no."

"But you're going home," I reminded him. "Back to your castle, where you'll be the most illustrious jickety of all time. Your people need you."

"They kicked me out. They'll get on fine without me. You're another matter. Big as you are, you're still awfully young, and you could use some looking after."

"Heed what he says," Cedelair repeated.

"You taught me to love music, you did," Pierpon went on. "I want to help you make it. I'm coming with you and that is that." So saying, he raced up my arm and hopped onto my shoulder, gripping my sleeve with all his considerable strength. There would be no dislodging him. He was with me to stay.

Cedelair chuckled under his breath. "Bravo, Master Jickety," he declared, with a wink at Pierpon. "It soothes my heart to know she won't be alone. Keep good watch over her."

"Never fear on that score, Master Cedelair," the jickety declared. "Give my best to the vixen, will you? Tell her I always liked her, I did."

At this Cedelair nodded with a knowing wink, as if he'd suspected as much.

I looked into the little man's round face and trembled at another rush of love. I didn't deserve Pierpon. But Lifelord save me, I was glad to have him.

Cedelair caressed my hand. "I wish there were a place in that wagon for me, too. You'd best go in before I change my mind and try to stop you."

I forced myself to turn from him, to fix my eyes squarely on the wagon, on the flood of white-gold light that poured through the opening to swallow me in an embrace. I moved toward it, drawn by an illusion that beyond that blare lay home. The wall rose up to close me in, the bells pealing a cheerful greeting. The bell-board lifted itself from my side and fitted itself into its old position, while Pierpon rose from my shoulder to hover in mid-air. Cool mist sank through my skin and flesh and into my bones to wear them away. I felt a tickle of pleasure, then nothing. Gone were hunger and thirst and weariness.

Gone, in a tiny gasp, was my heart-fire. Gone was any terror or despair I might have felt at this sudden emptiness, yet somehow there remained a trembling expectation of something wonderful about to fill it.

The chrysalis-light strengthened into a swathe of ivory silk, giving me my frame once more. The mallets sprang into my newly-formed hands, and an energy shook through them, shooting memories into me. I was trapped inside the *leyshak*, burning, clawing while it screamed and drowned the world in a black smoke of misery. Then I was kneeling in the garden plot behind Mennieve's great house, with Cedelair's hands resting on mine, his green magic quickening with life the seeds I'd just planted. Death in one hand, life in the other. They coursed through me, two white-hot streaks of lightning, side by side.

A third bolt surged to fuse them together. The helix burst me wide open, and an ocean of feeling, of being, poured into me – all those griefs in the *leyshak*'s scream, sorrows and losses and loneliness, yet with them hopes, plans, prayers. Dreams joyful and sad, words cruel and kind, smiles, tears, kisses, clasps of hands, beloved voices, everything that moved the heart and mind, all roared in me at once, filling me with a frenzy of delight my flesh and bone could never have withstood. Had Feuval felt this?

Feuval was not what I sought. The words beat through the shivering bells. *There was no love in him when he entered here. He could never have made the songs thou brought'st to me. Far more wilt thou do than ever he could have done.*

The carillon itself, I realized. It could speak to me, and I to it. It must have always heard my mind-voice, though Feuval had not.

A golden mask spread across the sheath where my eyes would have been. My sight sharpened. Faces swam in that limitless ocean of dreams and griefs. Cedelair, still standing beside the wagon, watching, waiting. Valeraine, dancing hand in hand with her sturdy friend. Mennieve, standing misty-eyed on the rim of that ring of dancers. My spirit-gaze settled on this woman who had looked into my face and touched my hand that first day I'd gone into town, and who had been ready to take my place inside this wagon. She would not see spring come, she'd said. In the sweep of the ocean I could hear a soft, sad prayer. *Let me see him happy again before I die.*

My fingers tightened around the mallets. *Carillon, may I give one more song to this town?*

The bells hummed an affirmative reply.

My spirit's eye on Mennieve, I called my song for a merry heart into my mind and merged it with "Serenade for Cedelair in Trouble" to shape a new melody, bright with joy not only present but to come. So much still to look forward to. I imagined the notes flowing into Mennieve to smother that unnamed malady as light sweeps away dark. She blinked and gazed upward. Her gaping lips trembled in a smile. She knew I was playing for her.

All the while the colors of the notes blossomed and burned like fireworks inside me, while Pierpon danced in mid-air around the sparks. I remembered all those dreams now, when I'd transformed into color and spirit. Those were my dreams, before the Bitter Chord had intruded to work her will. I'd been reaching for them every time I had played my bell-board.

I had burst my chrysalis. With the bells' power in my hands, I had become absolutely and completely myself.

As the last note dwindled, my vision receded to the inside of my wagon once more. Pierpon swept the heavy black curtain from the window, then he settled on the ledge. "Take a look!" he piped.

Outside the window stood a man with a face I'd seen only in flickering shadows, with a sharp nose, an angular chin, a clear brow, and eyes that glimmered with a joy nearly as boundless as the ocean that filled me. Cedelair with the mask of age stripped away. The magic in my song for Mennieve had spilled onto him as I'd never imagined it could. I reached out to caress his smooth cheek, to tease the soft brown hair at his temples. I mind-sang for him once more, the song that revealed the truth of love.

"When they see me, I'll tell them what happened," he declared. "I will cry out with all my love and pride, 'This is the work of Meliroc of the Carillon'."

My spirit-heart raced and swelled. He had called my soul, my self by name. *Meliroc of the Carillon. I seek out parched places and rain music down upon them.* "What will you do now?" I asked him, brushing my fingers down the line of his chin.

"Let me see," he hem-hawed. "Valeraine's done very well in this business. It won't be long before she's ready to take my place here. Then I may look for some new home. In the meantime, I'll try my hand at mixing a little with those people in the square, making friends with them. You were right, sweet Meliroc." He kissed my fingers. "I can still mend my mistake."

I folded my memory around the wonder in his smile, the hope in his eyes, and the youthful smoothness in his baritone voice. A melody brushed at the top of my mind, but I shook my head as a new realization came to me. *Not now. Not yet.* Once I'd played the *leyshak's* victims back to health, my duty would be done. The carillon would bring me back to the place I wished to be. I would have my own heart's desire at last. On my way home I would make that melody.

"When you dream of my bells playing a song you've never heard before," I told him, sweeping my fingers across his brow, "you will know I'm on my way back to you."

"I'll listen for you every night." He drew a shaking breath. "Go now. Share your large heart with others who need you." His mouth twitching, as if he were swallowing a pang, he forced himself to step backward. For a moment the tide of spirit went still inside me. My hands hung at my sides, numb, desolate.

The walls shook. The curtain dropped with a jolt. Pierpon clung fast to my sheath as the bells shivered in an expectant chord. The wagon was rising from the ground to bear me away. The tide rose in me again. My head rocked, dizzy.

A part of your magic moves in me now, Cedelair. When I heal them you'll be there too. Every song will carry your name.

At the moment I lost him, I loved him most.

THE END

Gilded Dragonfly Books
Other Works by Nan Monroe

Atterwald
by
Nan Monroe

This is a tale of the hal'ryth'kei, the people of the second skin, creatures who are two beings, with two natures in one.

It begins with an enmity between two tribes, a difference beyond reconciliation...

Chapter One

"...O that our power
Could lackey or keep wing with our desires...!"
John Marston, Antonio's Revenge

Brendis had always loved to watch the owl-people parade into view at sunset, riding proud upon their deer. Lately, however, he had a special reason to stare

He laid his hoe down at his feet, licked his upper lip and frowned at the stinging salt taste of sweat. He looked up and out, toward the rim of trees on the horizon. He held his breath at the clop of deer's hooves.

"Back to work, Bren," his brother cautioned in his sniffling voice. Arne was still busy with his hoe, Brendis knew from the crunch of turning earth beside him. "You know how Mother bellows if she catches you idle."

"I don't care."

The first owls emerged from the wood – silver-haired gentlemen in top hats and black, sharply tailored frock coats, nodding with regal condescension at the mouse-people at work in the field. Why they did that, Brendis could not say, for the mouse-folk paid no heed to the parade. Only he seemed to know the owls were even there.

Nightmare Lullaby

More owl-folk appeared, all in neat frock coats, all with slim, bolt-straight figures. A tiny part of him hated them and their beauty and aristocratic mien. He loathed finding himself transfixed by them.

His stomach spun as his special reason rode into view. Unlike the others, she wore a riding-suit of pale gray, with a white kerchief about her neck and a gauzy veil streaming down her back. But even without these odd color choices, she would have stood out from the rest. Some of them might wear their honey-gold hair in ringlets. Some of them might have skin like white rose-petals while others might boast soft oval faces with clear gray eyes, but all these beautiful features combined in her alone. Even they might have added up to nothing but for her smile, so wistful and pensive that he constantly wondered what she might be thinking.

Brendis had to think of the golden maiden by some name or other, so he had invented one for her, "Verina," the Glory of Her People. This satisfied him for now. To present himself to her and learn her true name would content him for good.

But his kind did not speak to hers.

He remembered asking his mother just why this was. She had sniffed a non-answer. "Because it isn't done. All we need know about them is that they're there."

Brendis had vowed then and there never to ask his mother a serious question again. In the five years since, he'd kept that vow.

"Pick up that tool now, Bren!" Arne snapped.

Brendis reclaimed the hoe and went through the motions of pawing the earth with it, never taking his eyes from Verina. His breath stilled

The leader of the parade, the tallest and proudest-looking of the silver-haired gentlemen mounted on a six pointed stag, folded into himself. His shoulders shrank and his arms and limbs retracted, and suddenly, where a man had been, a wide-winged gray owl hovered in mid-air.

On their leader's signal the other owl-folk transformed.

Gilded Dragonfly Books

Short Stories By Nan Monroe

From Haunting Tales of Spirit Lake

SYBILLA DISANTE AND THE SEPIA WORLD

By

Nan Monroe

The night before my parents were killed in a car accident I dreamed of a huge baby buggy smashing through a window of the twentieth floor of a high rise.

I am not, nor have I ever been, a great talker. My custom has always been to observe, listen, and hold my thoughts inside. People call me "unknowable," and I can't say they're wrong. After the accident I hugged my silence more closely than ever, but in a strange moment when I felt my heart would turn inside out if I didn't speak I told Ethan Chance about my dream. Ethan was my closest friend, because among all the kids my age, seventeen, only he shared my passion for black-and-white movies. Even when I don't care to talk about my feelings or my views on society and politics, I can enjoy a good conversation about Casablanca or Metropolis.

He listened as I described the shattering window and the buggy disappearing over the ledge. Then he told me in an awed hush, "You're psychic."

I laughed him off but cringed inside. I might like to tell myself stories about ghosts and imagine that the wall separating past from present from future might be frayed in spots, but to suggest I might be psychic was to drag those gossamer daydreams into the bitter cold realm of reality. I didn't want to be psychic. If I'd somehow prophesied my parents' deaths, then the right word from me might have saved them. This I couldn't bear to think. So I changed the subject very quickly to Dr. Strangelove.

Yet in the days that followed I started to wonder whether my sweet-natured cinephile friend had cursed me, or if my Creek grandmother had been right when she told me that gifts can be born

Nightmare Lullaby

from grief. My sense of sight began to play tricks. When I walked alone on the edge of the wood that bordered Spirit Lake I would spy a ripple in the air, such as we sometimes see in the thick heat of a summer day. It looked like a curtain moving, and I thought I could glimpse a shadow-scape beyond the lush trees and glassy lake, a scene with the sepia shade of a nineteenth-century photograph. People moved through it in the garb of long ago, going through the motions of working and chatting with each other and not paying me the slightest heed.

Only imagination, I insisted to myself. I'd always daydreamed of the past, though I'd never gone so far as to wish to live there. I didn't care much for the look of the present, and I'd never really mastered its language. At times the nowaday world around me looked and sounded like an esoteric, incomprehensible foreign film with the subtitles turned off. Perhaps my heavy heart had led me to conjure a world that looked prettier – at least from a distance.

Yet when I blinked and rubbed my eyes, and tried to assure myself of the solid reality of my surroundings, the sepia world still hovered in the background. The faces of people in that world became clear, plain, commonplace faces, yet somehow each line and curve etched itself on my memory with the clarity of familiarity. Somehow, somewhere I had seen them before. If they opened their mouths to speak, I would know their voices.

From A Stone Mountain Christmas

Christmas Rose

By

Nan Monroe

    Christmas is light.
    Christmas glows, shines, glistens, shimmers, and twinkles. Only fitting, some would say, for a festival meant to celebrate the birthday of the Light of the World. But even those who never darken the door of a church may be dazzled by Christmas light – the light that blazes in a profusion of colors, a light that can pass through the grayest soul and turn it into a rainbow.
    Christmas light is the one thing I'm sentimental about. I say "thing" deliberately, because I make a point of not feeling overly warm and fuzzy about things. People are another matter. I can get very sentimental about people. Not many people, just a few. A handful. And they're all bound up somehow with Christmas light.
    This is about one of them.

***

    All the Christmases of my childhood can be boiled down to one. I was eight years old, and my dad decided the time had come to replace our artificial tree with a real one. Dad was the light master. He would string and re-string lights onto that fake tree in his quest for the perfect configuration of colors. I could barely see the tree for all the lights he draped over and around it. But at last the scraggly four-footer proved too small for his ambitions, and he came home with a lush six-foot-plus Virginia pine, a scented green canvas with sufficient breadth to suit the artist in him. My dad turned that tree into a blazing miracle.
    Every morning those three weeks before Christmas, I would pull myself out of bed before sunrise, before my parents woke up, and creep into the living room where the tree stood. I'd plug in the electric cord and hold my breath a half-second as I watched that brilliance of

color burst out to repaint the room. Light would flood every corner, so that nothing in my sight range was commonplace. I'd stand over the heat vent and stare at the tree and dream strange dreams, not about presents or about anything material and tangible, but about thoughts and feelings that existed only in that Christmas radiance. Of course an eight-year-old couldn't make sense of it. Even today I struggle to find the words for it when I remember. But I know I'd never felt anything quite like it before and have seldom felt it since.

Another little thing about that Christmas that has stuck in my memory is an angel I made of cardboard and construction paper and glitter and glue, a school crafts project. It was the sort of cheesy ornament a kid can hand to her parents with a proud, toothy grin – well, maybe, if that kid is better at drawing straight lines and circles and figuring out how to get mileage out of a pair of blunt elementary-school scissors than I was. My angel looked like a refugee from Halloween Town in The Nightmare Before Christmas. My parents did what parents of third-graders do and posted it on the fridge and called it lovely. But even my eight-year-old mind could grasp the difference between my effort and the other kids'. My teacher called it avant garde, not a very fair phrase for a third grade teacher to use. I managed to look it up, so I knew she'd been fumbling for a compliment to pay me. It didn't bother me much, for I didn't aspire to an artist's life. I was still in my wanna-be-an-astronaut phase.

I probably wouldn't think much about that angel now if I hadn't met Rose Coleman much later.

My childhood rolled on, with every Christmas much the same – the big Virginia pine, the blaze of light and color, the standing over the heat vent in the darkness before dawn to admire the way the tree glimmered when all other light was turned off, the swell of emotion I could only describe as "Christmas." Then came the year things changed, the year of "your mom and dad can't live together anymore but we both love you." I was fifteen.

I can't give details. To this day, neither of them will give me a straight answer about what happened. Whatever it was, it crept into the family picture so stealthily that I never dreamed anything was wrong until they hit me with the cliché. Dad was staying in the old house. Mom and I were moving away.

And the Christmas light went out.

Gilded Dragonfly Books
From Finding Love's Magic

Neighbor Haint
Nan Monroe

1848

Hope Caudle wore a black wool gown in mourning for herself.

She'd died when she was twelve, that dreadful year the smallpox had cast its cold, vicious shadow over Cupid's Bow. The community was too small for any death to go unremarked, particularly that of a raven-haired, dark-eyed beauty whose gift for singing and guitar-playing had brightened many a local occasion. But that year of her death, merely one of many, happened when the town had its hands so full battling the relentless disease that no one noticed her body never made it to the churchyard. Her mother and sisters laid her to rest in their back yard, a private ceremony in the dark of night. They'd mumbled solemn words over a mound of fresh-turned earth, their heads hanging and their hands crossed over their hearts, as was proper, at least for superstitious folk who half-feared that creating a false ghost might awaken true ones.

Seven years later the mound was covered with grass, with no wooden cross or symbol to mark it. No one but the mother and sisters knew the grave existed, and they never spoke of it or of Hope to any of their neighbors, as if they meant her to disappear from the townsfolks' minds as she had vanished from their midst. But one reminder lingered, wandering the house in her plain, coarse gown, putting her hand to any chore her golden lily sisters didn't care to do, which meant anything involving mop, broom, scrubbing brush, or cooking pot. Hard work was all the ghost was good for, with her face so repulsively scarred. Everyone had been so sure Hope Caudle would grow into the town's most beautiful woman.

The ghost, trapped in her solitary life-that-wasn't, sometimes stared out the window at that grass-covered rise in the earth and thought with a heavy sigh of the guitar that rested under it. She chafed by the hour that her mother had felt the need to bury that guitar. She would have given all she had to lay hands on it once more. Not that she would have played it. She understood the need to keep silent. No one must know the Caudle house was haunted. She wanted to feel the strings under her fingertips, that was all. When she took up her needle

Nightmare Lullaby

and thread to fashion quilts for her mother to sell at the dry goods store, she often fancied her fingers wept with regret.

Still, quilting was one thing her mother and sisters demanded of her that she actually enjoyed doing. The colors, shapes, and patterns of a quilt were like the beats and measures of a song, meticulous and precise. They appealed to her. She had dozens of pictures in her mind, and since her mother and sisters never wore the same gowns for more than two seasons, she had abundant material to work with.

The three things in which she still took pleasure were making quilts, reading the books her mother was just decent enough to supply her, and watching the little house across the street, the only other house on this dusty, out-of-the-way thoroughfare. Old Man Dasher lived there with his son, George.

They'd moved into it three years ago, four years after Hope Caudle had become a ghost and almost that long since her name had been mentioned outside the house she haunted. The two men had no idea she had ever existed, and somehow that sharpened her interest in them. Mr. Dasher Sr. was an elderly retired gentleman. Retired from what, Hope couldn't guess, but she liked to imagine he'd been a pirate, one of those bloodthirsty rogues who harried the shores of Savannah. Maybe he'd amassed a fortune through pillage and plunder, and now he'd settled down to a quiet life of strumming his guitar and smoking his pipe in his front porch wicker rocking-chair. A tall man, broad-shouldered and bulky, he boasted a hard, granite-hewn face and white hair as thick and abundant as a young man's. She could easily picture him striding the foredeck of a galleon in shiny black boots and a long-coat of crimson velvet. He seemed much too large to fit comfortably into that plain brown cottage across the way.

His son made a contrast some would have thought unfortunate. A slight, wiry young man more than a head shorter than his father, burdened with a withered left leg, he sometimes strode up and down the front porch with a gold-tipped cane. His father rocked and fingered his guitar strings while the young man sat still with an open book under his nose. The book alone sufficed to stir Hope's curiosity. Something new from Mr. Hawthorne or Mr. Emerson? Or a volume of verse by the English poets she loved, Coleridge, perhaps, or Keats? A certain spark of eye and the set of his angular features made her think he might favor the same books she did. She liked the point of his chin, the curve of his slender nose, the chocolate brown shade of his close-cropped curls. If only he had a good voice! Voices were of paramount importance. She felt sure he didn't talk through his nose.

Local children trudged down the narrow street and up the steps of the Dasher porch nearly every day. They would knock on the door, and George Dasher would appear with his gold-tipped cane to usher them inside, and a few moments later Hope would imagine very faint strains of piano music tapping at her window. One of her sisters had once mentioned in passing that he gave piano lessons, and Hope longed with all her might to hear those lessons clearly. Had the smallpox not cast its shadow, she might have been his pupil. She would not have made her way to his door with such lead-footed reluctance. What would he have thought of her and the simple, silly tunes she played on her guitar?

If she could just get a longer, closer look at him, she might tell the color of his eyes.

Nightmare Lullaby

From Legends of the Dragon Vol. 1

Firegale at the Festival
By
Nan Monroe

An Explanation

Only twelve of us remained in the world. We dwelled in cities far apart and concealed ourselves in underground lairs, emerging only in the forms of shadows or shrunken to a salamander's size. We might have perished of loneliness, were it not for the wizards who cared for us.

In the early years of the Thousands, I lived under Underground Atlanta.

Under cover of night I would take to the sky. I'd rise from the grate, a stream of intangible black, and shoot upward swift as an arrow toward the stars. I'd twirl around the golden dome of the Capitol and dive and loop around the shining banners of Marriott and Hilton and indulge in a wild, vain fancy of soaring in my true form, the moonlight glancing off my outspread wings, my black scales a shimmering florescent blue, a thing of beauty to delight the eyes of the lost, tired, or old in heart who might glance up from the streets below.

When I first fledged, my wizard caretaker gave me my adult name, Firegale, and told me my mission: to study what humankind says about us. That meant I had to read every word humans have written about us and watch every movie and television show and listen to every song or radio play I could find that mentioned us. I spent many an afternoon crouched in the corner of a dark movie theater, a shadow among shadows, and many an evening trailing along library shelves. My wizard helped, paying for a cable television hookup in my lair and bringing me armfuls of books and DVDs and Blu-Rays. At times it felt a bit overwhelming. But, in truth, I loved my work.

There began my passion for what humankind terms "the fantastic,", the stories that take place in great lands that never were, where people live as people never lived, yet somehow manage to tell truths missing from tales that dealt in literal realities. I learned the fantastic reaches something eternal in us, beyond trends and customs and the tides of politics. Yes, us, for the fantastic taught me how much I had in common with humankind. Lost in the fantastic, I was never lonely.

I wasn't satisfied with learning what humans said about us. I wanted to learn their stories about elves, as well, and trolls, goblins, werewolves, vampires, ghosts, mer-folk. I wanted to know of Jedi and Sith, of Romulans, Klingons, and Vulcans, of Time Lords and Companions, of superheroes and supervillains. Such tales were my food. I grew so big on them that I imagined myself bursting through the pavement that covered me.

Each year one time and place was dearer to me than all the rest. Then and there I could swim in a great sea of the fantastic, and everywhere I turned I found stories to feast upon. My wizard caretaker worked upon me the magic I couldn't work upon myself. For four short days I was, a human.

The festival was called, to my great delight, Dragon Con.

Nightmare Lullaby

About Nan Monroe

"Nan" is my mother's name and "Monroe" is my father's. To honor them I write my novels and short fiction as "Nan Monroe." My friends and family know me better as Kelley S. Ceccato, and I've written a dozen plays for the Atlanta Radio Theatre Company under this name. I'm a life-long lover of books, movies, and music. I'm married to Matt, and we have two fur children, a cat and a dog. We live in Georgia and make yearly pilgrimages to the Renaissance Festival, DragonCon, and other spots where we can immerse ourselves in all things geeky.

Gilded Dragonfly Books

Connect with Nan Monroe:

https://www.facebook.com/nanmonroe

Twitter at @nanmonroeauthor

nanmonroeauthor@gmail.com.

http://nanmonroe.com

Gilded Dragonfly Books:

www.gildeddragonflybooks.com

Follow Gilded Dragonfly Books on Twitter @GDBeditors

Gilded Dragonfly Books Blog
www.gildeddragonflybooks.wordpress.com